# NEVER BEEN WORSE

EVERGREEN PARK
BOOK 3

MORGAN ELIZABETH

*To the girls in their reputation era.*
*The best revenge is doing better, but it's okay to succeed out of spite.*

# PLAYLIST

Look What You Made Me Do - Taylor Swift
Because I Liked a Boy - Sabrina Carpenter
Call It What You Want - Taylor Swift
Won the Break Up - Maisie Peters
So long London - Taylor Swift
Grand Theft Autumn - Fall Out Boy
I Bet You Think About Me - Taylor Swift
Opposite - Sabrina Carpenter
Sunday Kind of Love - Etta James
Mad Woman - Taylor Swift
Banana Pancakes - Jack Johnson
Cold Water - Noah Kahan
Punk Rock Princess - Something Corporate
Mastermind - Taylor Swift

# A NOTE FROM MORGAN

Dear Reader,

The Evergreen Park series came to me when I needed it most. I've mentioned before that Passenger Princess was never supposed to be written, that I had a bit of a breakdown and shifted gears into this fun, silly world, and it was... It was perfect.

The truth of the matter is, like for many people, 2024 was a rough year for me. I closed out my popular revenge series and very much started to second-guess myself, my place, and my talent. I came to terms with things about my life that I was unhappy with, lost friends I thought would be by my side forever, and I cried. A lot, if I'm being honest.

I identify a lot with Harper who finds herself so deluded in a relationship that she lost sight of who she was, of what she wanted, and who *she could be*. Now, while for Harper, it was her boyfriend, I think it's a good reminder to do a regular audit of your life and the people in it and where you want to go and make sure that those things line up.

I hope you read Harper's story and remember that you can dream big and that your dreams should never be conditional on anyone else.

Anyone else's happiness or success or assistance. And even more, I hope you have a Wes and an Ava and a Harper in your corner, cheering you on while you figure things out yourself. I do, and I'm so grateful for those three people I know I can always and forever count on, both to cheer me on and, sometimes, to give me a bit of a reality check.

It's bittersweet to close out this series that reminded me how much I love *love*, how much I love romcoms, and how much I love happy endings. I hope you love it and, especially Harper and Wes' story just as much as I did. If I do say so myself, they might be my favorite yet.

Never Been Worse is inspired by my favorite album of all time, Reputation, and circles around topics of revenge on a cheating, narcissistic ex. There is a lot of explicit language and adult situations. In this story, there are two friends who are pregnant, though the main characters are not, and there is no loss in this story. Please always take care of your mental health first! Reading is supposed to be our happy place.

Love you to the moon and to Saturn,

-Morgan

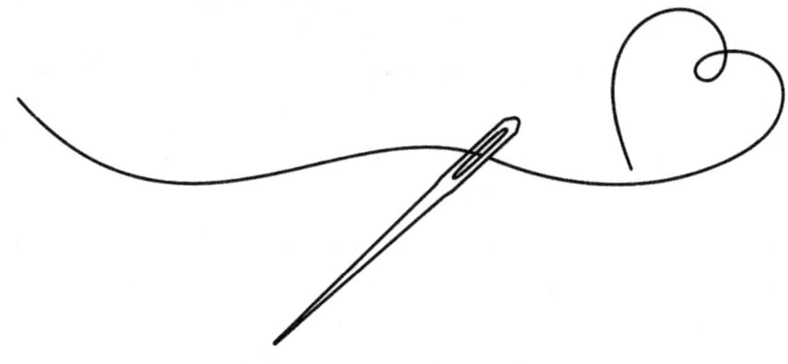

# ONE

## HARPER

"Do you think Jaime will be suspicious when I come home covered in glitter?" Ava whispers as we walk down the sidewalk on the street I lived on up until a week ago.

"You? No. You're literally always covered in glitter." When I turn to look at her, her lips are pursed, contemplating my words before she shrugs.

"That's fair," she admits. For once in her life, Ava, along with Jules and me, is wearing all black, her long blonde hair tucked up into a black beanie she said would *complete the ensemble* with a large black tote bag over her shoulder.

"Nate knows I'm here, so he won't have any questions about why it's stuck to every surface for a week or two," Jules says as our steps slow in front of a familiar house. "Not that it's much different than a normal day, considering Sophie insists every art project needs some glitter."

"Nate knows?" I ask quietly over my shoulder as I open the gate and walk to the front yard, looking around at the house I once thought would be my forever home with a surprising lack of home-sickness.

I guess it's okay to admit that this never felt like forever. Not really.

"Well, yeah. I tell him everything," Jules says with a shrug. "Plus, he'd probably check my location and see I was at your old house and have questions."

"Jaime doesn't know. I like to keep him on his toes," Ava says with a smile.

"That poor man," I murmur and wince when Ava smacks my shoulder. The girl is tiny, but *fuck* is she strong. "Sorry! I was just joking. He loves that you drive him up a wall."

"He really does," Ava says with a blissful smile before going into boss mode. "Okay, Jules, do you have the glitter?"

Jules nods, digging into the giant duffel bag she brought, starting to take out container after container of glitter. Superfine, chunky, star-shaped hearts. She keeps pulling containers out of the seemingly bottomless bag. When she shifts, and the light of the moon hits her, I see she also brought seed beads, tiny bells, and sequins.

"Oh my god," I whisper, watching her pull out a small handheld seed spreader.

"This was Nate's idea," Jules says with a wide, satisfied smile, and I fight the urge to laugh out loud, thus drawing attention to ourselves before we finish our task.

"Nate told you to bring that?" I ask incredulously, and she nods.

"He said it would be easier to evenly disperse it if we used this."

Ava wastes no time, opening and dumping containers into the plastic tub one by one. "Harp, go in my bag. There's a bottle of dish soap. Start squirting that everywhere," she says in a quiet order.

"Dish soap?" I ask wide-eyed, and Ava's face transforms, a wicked grin spreading over her lips.

"If he tries to wash the glitter away with a hose, it will all suds up."

"You're insane, you know that?" I ask with a smile, but at the same, grab the blue bottle, uncap it, and start liberally squirting it all over the grass. Ava comes behind me, turning the handle on the spreader and sending a fine mist of glitter over the yard. When it plumes out like magical smoke, I laugh out loud before covering my mouth to hide it.

"You're sure he still doesn't have cameras?" Jules asks, looking around as she starts to take a box of forks out.

"Yeah, they're banned in this HOA, thanks to Jeremy complaining that they *invade his privacy*. If you install one, you get a huge fine."

"It was probably so he could fuck his side piece without you knowing," Ava says under her breath.

My hands still as the thought tumbles through me, her words ringing with truth. But as quickly as it comes, I push the thought away. The hurt and confusion can be inspected tomorrow. Tonight is for payback.

"Ava!" Jules says in a hushed reprimand as she starts stabbing forks into my ex-boyfriend's lawn. We picked it out together, but since we weren't married and my credit is shit, I'm not on the title.

"What? It's true," Ava says with a shrug, continuing to coat the lawn in glitter.

"That doesn't mean we should just spit it out there. This is all very fresh for Harper," Jules says as if I'm not even there.

"Can we please keep it down so no one hears arguing and then decide to come check on things?" It's too dark to see Ava's eyes roll, but being her friend as long as I have been, I know they're well into the back of her head.

"Everyone in this neighborhood hates Jeremy and loves you. No one is going to say a word even if they *do* see." That's true, considering Jeremy was constantly calling the HOA on his neighbors about the most basic things, like children laughing too much or having a play sprinkler in the front yard during a heat wave.

"Remember when you told us he yelled at a little girl on Halloween for getting glitter on his walkway with her butterfly wings?" Jules asks. "Hell, if someone was a dick like that to Sophie, *I'd* glitter his lawn."

I look her way, blinking in confusion. "Uh, you're actively doing it, Jules."

"I'm in charge of the *forks*," she says, lifting a white plastic fork into the air and waving it around like I'm not picking up on the *facts* of the matter at hand. "I just *brought* the glitter and a seed spreader."

I don't remind her that this was entirely her idea a few nights ago. How we'd drank a little too much and started to make the most unhinged list of ways to get back at my no-good, dirty, cheating son-of-a-bitch ex.

Forking and glittering came after I remembered how meticulous he was with his lawn, not that he ever did the work to maintain it. He mostly just bullied the yard guy he hired until he eventually quit, and Jeremy would have to find a new one once more. I'm surprised he hasn't been blacklisted in Evergreen Park at this point.

We decided on glitter because even when he gets *most* of it out, it would be a long, long time before all of the glitter was completely gone. If he wanted to make it glitter-free quickly, he'd have to completely rip up and reseed the yard.

We make quick work of our sweet, sweet revenge, finishing with the glitter and moving on to the forks in the dark night. We're almost done and home-free when it happens.

My back is to the street, my eyes on the ground when tires crunch behind me, but that isn't what has my heart dropping into the glittering lawn.

No, it's the red, white, and blue lights reflecting merrily in the grass and the short, quick beep of a siren.

*We are so totally fucked.*

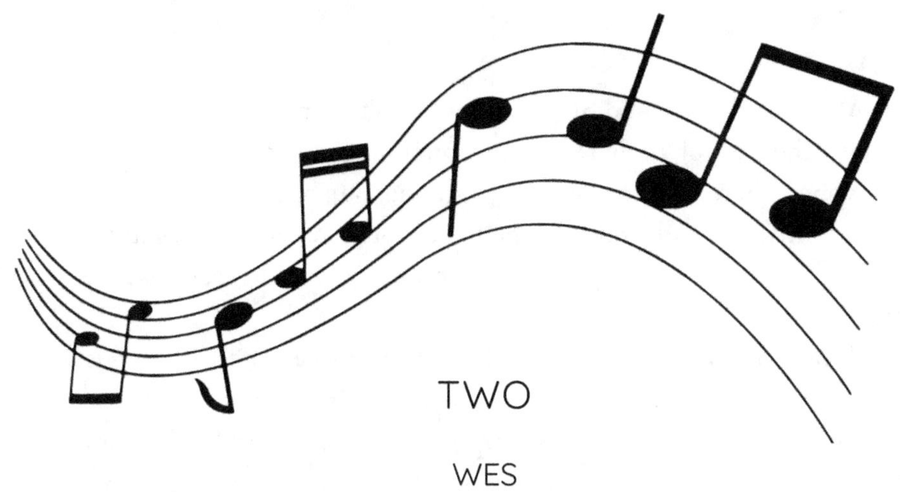

# TWO

## WES

"We've got some great news," Riggins says, his wife next to him, face aglow with happiness.

"Let me guess, you finally knocked up Stella?" Reed asks with a laugh, but when they don't laugh along, instead smiling wider, the room goes quiet, each of us looking from Stella to Riggins, to each other.

"No fucking way," Beckett says low, a wide smile spreading on his lips.

"I want to make sure I told Evie first, of course, but you guys were our—" Stella starts.

"Uncles!" Reed interrupts, moving over to Stella and kneeling before her stomach. "I'm going to be your favorite, of course—"

"Stop being a creep, Reed," I say, but I can't fight the smile as he turns and glares at me over his shoulder.

"Yeah, dude, get off my wife," Riggs says, pushing Reed in the shoulder gently, though Reed makes a show out of falling dramatically.

We all roll our eyes at him.

We're at Riggins and Stella's house in our hometown of Ashford. They called all of us here for an announcement of some kind, so everyone is here: Beckett and Reed, Jaime, our bodyguard but more importantly, a friend, and Leo, the band's publicist. I knew it must be something that would impact *everyone* when even the ever-busy Leo was here.

"She's just about twelve weeks, and her due date's in August. Which means we need to postpone the upcoming tour."

Our band, Atlas Oaks, was supposed to go on a worldwide tour to celebrate our new album that comes out in four months. Stella, who helps our lead singer and guitarist, Riggins, write songs, was planning to come with us, but with this new update, that won't be feasible. We've been a band since we were in high school, Riggins playing guitar and singing, Beckett on drums, Reed on bass, and myself on lead guitar. We've seen each other through some of the darkest days and highest highs and are more of a family than a band at this point. At the end of the day, we will always put one another above the fame.

"Of course we do," Reed says, the answer obvious to everyone in the room except, it seems, Riggins, who looks distraught as he runs a hand through his hair.

"The tour isn't a huge deal, Riggs," I say, my brow furrowed as I take him in, and I can see Stella biting her lip, a hand to her lower stomach, already protective of their baby.

A *baby*. Fuck.

It's strange to think about, considering we've been a group since before most of us even graduated high school, and now Riggs and Stella are...having *kids*. Jesus. "We can push it off a year or three for all I care. Or..." I start, my brow furrowing. "Or do you guys want to stop touring altogether once the baby arrives?"

Maybe that's the reason for the formal meeting and the panic on their faces from the moment we all stepped foot in their home. Maybe they want to stay here and focus on their family. Both can easily continue their careers as songwriters without Atlas Oaks.

My gut twists at the mere idea of not having a band to tour with, of not seeing the world and playing music with my best friends.

"God, no, we want to keep touring," Stella says with a quick shake of her head. My confusion simmers more as I try to understand why this great news is anything but.

"It's the press," Beckett says, the quiet man of our tight-knit group, making sense as always. "Right?" Stella and Riggs look at one another, and then she nods. "You don't want to tell the press you're pregnant yet."

"We want to keep it under wraps. It took us a while to get here, so just in case anything...happens, I'd like to keep things quiet. And I don't want the press on our asses. But because the last time you guys postponed..." It kicks in then, the problem we're going to face. The last time we postponed a tour was because Riggins was in rehab for alcoholism.

"I'd come out with it to avoid the drama," Stella continues, biting her lip again. "But I'm really early. And with my depression, I'm high-risk. If something happens, I don't want the entire world to know about it. I also don't want them hounding me. They finally backed down a bit, which has been so nice."

The reunion of Stella and Riggins, music's one-time power couple, was huge news, especially when Riggins told the world he was married to Stella and had been for several years, despite their long-term breakup. Add in the drama of Stella's mom and Riggins's struggle with alcohol, and they just recently stopped getting followed every time they simply went to the grocery store.

"If you announce the tour is postponed without explanation, the press will think it's like last time, and Riggins fell off the wagon," Beck fills in bluntly. Even if we told the world Riggs wasn't in rehab and that we just needed a break, the paparazzi, the forums, and social media will absolutely run with whatever version sells the most paper or gets the most likes.

"We need a different reason," I say, with Reed, Beck, and Jaime, who has seen the worst of how the press can be, nodding in agreement.

Before anyone can respond, Stella covers her mouth with her hand and stands, rushing out of the room. We look around, eyes wide with confusion and concern, except for her husband.

"Morning sickness. She's been sick a ton," Riggs says, before he runs after his wife, leaving the rest of us in the living room.

Silence hangs in the room as we take in this big change before I break it. "We need to come up with an explanation for the break. Something legitimate. We need to get the press on to one of us." Beck goes white at the mere idea of the press hounding him, and I roll my eyes. "Reed or me," I say. "Don't worry, big guy. We won't make you a viral sensation."

"I can pretend I want to try my hand at something cooler, like aerial acrobatics," Reed suggests, and I sigh in exhaustion. I love Reed like a brother, but the man is out of his mind sometimes.

"Yeah, maybe we try something a bit more...believable?"

"That actually *is* pretty believable, if you know Reed," Beck says, and I glare at him because Reed does not need encouragement.

"Yeah, I was thinking more like one of us calls up Willa and see if she needs a whirlwind romance," I say of our pop star friend who has PR relationships to create buzz around her music. Riggins "dated" her when he and Stella broke up to cover up his drinking problem, and they wrote a few songs together to legitimize it.

"I volunteer as tribute!" Reed nearly yells, throwing his hand into the air.

"I think Willa is out," Leo says with a shake of his head. "Considering she was tied with Riggins's drama." I cringe, knowing that to be true.

"We could call Evie and have her spin a story?" Beckett suggests, referencing Stella's twin sister, Everest, who works as a journalist for a major music magazine.

I nod. "We should do that either way, but she's not necessarily an unbiased source of information. It could do the opposite of what we need to accomplish, prove as evidence something's up." Leo nods.

"We've got some time," Beckett says, his hands on his knees as he leans forward. "We should sit on it, think about what we could do. Being impulsive on this isn't the right move."

"Just don't mention it to Riggs, yeah?" I say, tipping my chin to Reed, the biggest mouth of all. "He's got enough on his plate."

He rolls his eyes but nods.

"He'll just tell us not to worry and then run off with some stupid last-minute plan that makes things worse. Maybe—" Reed starts, but Jaime's phone rings, cutting him off. When he looks at the screen, his face lights up.

*Ava.*

The only person on this earth who makes Jaime look that happy is his wife, and even then, sometimes he looks like—

"What do you mean *arrested?*" he barks into the phone.

Like that.

More often than not, his wife makes him look like *that.* Red-faced and annoyed and a bit panicked because she tends to often find herself in a bit of trouble. I can't hear the person on the other end of the line, but I watch Jaime's face get increasingly red.

"Jesus Christ, Ava, vandalism and *stalking?*" My eyes go wide, and Reed is bouncing in his seat, fighting the urge to laugh out loud, something we know from experience will just turn his ire to one of us. "I don't care if you weren't actually stalking the man, Ava. If you're charged with stalking and it goes through, you're a fucking stalker forever. And you're pregnant, Ava! Jesus fuck. What were you doing there?" Another pause before his head tips up to the ceiling and he sighs deeply. "Ava Wilde, love of my life, mother of my future children, you are going to send me into an early grave." Another pause before he groans. "Yes, because you're fucking insane! Why else?" There's another pause before his face turns red, a blush burning over his cheeks. "Ava, I'm begging you, please stop. I'm in a room with the

Atlas Oaks guys, and you're in a fucking police station. This call is being *recorded.*"

"Ava Wilde is an icon," Reed says low. "She's the only woman I know who would be in a holding cell and trying to have phone sex with her husband."

Jaime's eyes snap to Reed with a threat.

"Yeah, yeah. I'll be there in..." Jaime pauses, looking at the clock on the wall before answering. "Thirty. I'm in Ashford. Yeah, yeah. Love you too, Princess." One final pause before his face goes from soft to annoyed again. "God, Ava, I'm not bringing Peach. Jesus Christ, woman. See you soon." He hangs up before taking a deep breath with closed eyes like he's trying to center himself before he stands.

"What's going on?" I ask, standing as well. Whatever is going on, I want to go with him because it's *bound* to be entertaining. Plus, there's not much else I can do here. I need some time to think of a good solution, and it sounds like Riggs and Stella might need some alone time.

"Ava, Jules, and Harper all just got arrested," he says, shrugging on his jacket as Reed snorts out a laugh.

"What? How?"

"Harper's boyfriend dumped her after cheating on her. I heard them the other day, planning this crazy shit. I didn't think to stop it because I figured it was just them venting."

"Bad call," I say low, knowing Ava, and Jaime nods.

"They glittered the man's lawn."

"What exactly does that mean?" Leo asks, also standing to leave.

"They dumped pounds of glitter on his lawn, covered it in dish soap, and, according to Ava, got caught halfway through forking it."

"Awesome," Reed says, and Jaime glares at him.

"Not awesome. Now she's being charged with vandalism, stalking, and harassment." He pauses. "And littering. I'll see you guys later."

"I'm coming," I say, the decision fully made as soon as he mentioned Harper's name.

"Why?"

"Because this will be entertaining. And you never know when a famous face can help you out."

Jaime opens his mouth to argue but looks at me, then at the clock, and shakes his head.

"Whatever. I don't have time to argue with you about this," he says, then heads out the door, me on his tail.

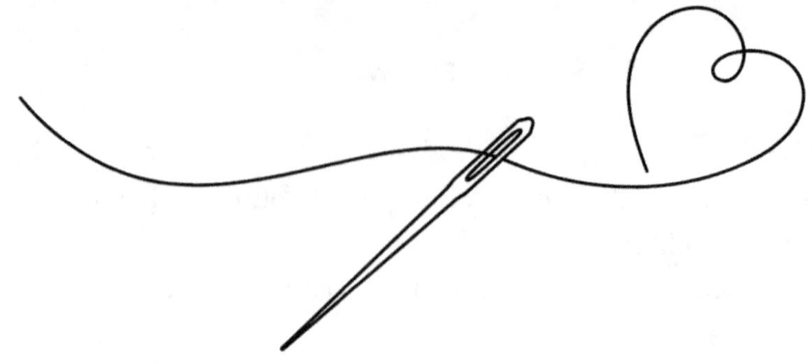

# THREE

## HARPER

*My timing has never been great, but I have to say, I think today takes the cake.*

*There was the time in middle school when I got my period for the very first time. The same day I wore the white jeans I begged my mother to buy me for months.*

*And the time I went on my first date after spending the day telling myself my tummy hurt because I was nervous, only to barf right on my date's shoes when he came to the door to pick me up.*

*But today, when I walked in an hour early after spending the day with my two best friends to find my boyfriend making out hot and heavy with his boss's daughter on our kitchen table is probably the worst.*

*"What the fuck, Jeremy?" I ask, staring at him as he moves away from the young woman with casual ease, not like a man concerned he was just caught. She, at least, has the decency to look slightly embarrassed as she sits back and straightens her shirt.*

*"You weren't supposed to be home until eight," Jeremy says, as if this is all somehow my fault. He slowly shifts and moves his hands to organize the piles of papers on the table in front of him.*

"I forgot something here," I say, no longer remembering what exactly I forgot. I think I'm in some sort of alternate reality, because I must be imagining the scene in front of me. "What is...what is going on here? How long has this been going on?"

"Oh, probably, what?" the blonde asks, losing whatever shame she had and putting on a bitchy smile. I'd only met her briefly in the past, and she seemed nice enough, but the conniving look in her eyes has me wondering if it was always a facade. "A year?"

"A year?" I ask incredulously. "How...how did this happen?" I don't actually want the details, but it's like I'm frozen here, unable to move or think or show any sign of self-preservation.

Jeremy stands, starting to stack the papers while he explains. "Clarissa came up to me because I was presenting the suggestions you helped me with—" I open my mouth to remind him those tweaks I'd given him on the pieces he showed me were presented to me as a way for him to talk to his boss about me. He'd told me my suggestions would help get my foot in the door, not something he would take credit for, but he keeps speaking. "And she told me she was having her debut this year with a legacy line. She was feeling uninspired and needed some guidance. I've been helping her, and things just...escalated."

I stand there dumbfounded, trying to say something, anything, but all that comes out is, "Why?"

"You know, when your needs aren't being met, you need to go elsewhere," Clarissa says with a snide smile I want to smack off her. Didn't she just do a press interview calling herself a girls' girl?

"What does she have that I don't?" I ask Jeremy, my voice low and careful. Even now, in this state, I know I'll regret asking that, much less in front of the woman he chose over me, but my grip on reality and common sense is quickly diminishing.

"She's an Astor, for one," he says, as if being his boss's daughter makes her the obvious better choice. "Much more of a career boost than a pageant gown designer."

That hits straight into my gut, especially considering I've confessed more times than I can count how I want to be known for more than pageant gowns, something he swore up and down for almost two years now he would help me with. All those promises of opening doors, of mentioning my name in meetings, seem pretty empty at this moment.

Was I truly this stupid, this naive all along?

Choosing the easy, solid, "safe" choice only to be completely blindsided?

"And, of course, she's got a model's physique." My eyes open as I try and think of a response or at least ask him to stop telling me all of my shortcomings, but he doesn't stop. "She's blonde."

"I could have dyed my hair," I say low and impulsively, even though I love my red hair and always have. In the morning, I'll probably be embarrassed, but right now, I'm in shock. I thought I was sticking by Jeremy, riding out the rough years when we both worked hard to build our careers so that, later, we could enjoy life together, but he was just using me as a stepping stone.

"And she's spontaneous," he continues as if I hadn't spoken, and from the corner of my eye, I see Clarissa smiling at my pain, at my humiliation.

"Spontaneous? I can be spontaneous!" I say louder than I intended to.

Jeremy gives me the kind of smile you give a small child when they say they can fly or that they believe fairies exist. "Sure you are, Harper." He might as well pat me on the head at this point. "When was the last time you were spontaneous? You plan your breakfast a month in advance."

"It's easier that way to shop!" I shout. "So I can make sure you have a solid breakfast every morning, like you asked." I think of my Sunday mornings spent meal-prepping breakfasts and lunches for us while he went out golfing or sleeping in, half of which would end up in the trash or untouched when he went out for lunch or forgot them at home.

"Honey, you should really stop now," Clarissa says, giving me a pitying look. "It's just making you look...sad."

*I blink at her, at the woman who's been knowingly fucking a taken man.*

*And what's even worse is that she pities me, like even she knows I've wasted the last few years of my life catering to this man who might not have ever cared about me, who definitely never saw a future with me if he was willing to let it go so easily.*

*The reality hits me like a train and with one look around the room, around the house I thought would be mine forever, I nod and decide it's best to get out before I do something stupid, like rip this girl's hair out.*

*"I...I'm going to leave. Go to Ava's or Jules' or...I don't know." I don't know why I'm telling him, since he surely doesn't care where I go. "I'll come back another time to get my things, we can...we can coordinate. I'm just going to grab a few things." My throat hurts with unshed tears, but I won't give them that, I won't give them that when clearly, there is no remorse here. I won't make a fool of myself again.*

*I step away, grabbing three large bags and quickly packing up my already incredibly organized things. It takes me less than five minutes before I'm walking toward the door, ready to get to my car and sob when I'm stopped.*

*"Actually, before you leave, I need something from you," Jeremy says.*

*When I turn around, he's pulling out a stack of papers and handing them to me, and once again, my world comes crumbling down.*

"Harper Abbott," the bored officer says, pulling me out of my memories.

I give a tight smile to Ava and Jules in the cell beside me and stand, raising my hand.

For the first time in four years, I acted spontaneously, and it got us arrested.

"That's me," I say.

"Come with me," she says, unlocking and opening the door, before motioning for me to step out. When I do, she locks the door behind us and guides me down a hallway.

"Where are we going?"

"The victim wants to speak with you," she says bluntly, and my jaw drops.

"The victim?" I ask. Jeremy is far from a victim in this situation. For the love of God, all we did was pour some glitter on his lawn. I would happily pay to get it resodded if that's what he needs.

"And his counsel," she adds.

"His counsel?!" I ask, aghast. "For glittering his yard?"

She shrugs, then glances down at the paper. "Says here they're looking to charge you with vandalism, criminal stalking, and harassment." My stomach plummets because those are not easy, silly charges. "Oh, and littering. Fuck, what did he do to you?" she asks, looking at me in a new light.

I sigh. "Cheated on me with his boss's daughter after stringing me along our whole relationship," I say low, her words ricocheting in my mind.

"Damn girl, I don't blame you," the officer says, pausing to take a look at me. "How long were you together?"

"Four years," I admit.

She looks at me, assessing and looking at me in a new light. "Next time, don't get caught."

I laugh at her advice, then nod as she opens the door to a secluded room. There's a small metal table inside, and my stomach churns as I see my ex for the first time since that horrible night.

"Here's how this is going to go," Jeremy says as soon as I sit down, leaning back with his arms crossed on his chest, face smug as can be. I hate this. I hate that I *gave* him this, that I let my anger and frustration win in this way.

"You're looking at a huge fine I know you probably can't afford." I open my mouth to argue, but he keeps talking, steamrolling me the way I now realize he always has. A lot of things have become awfully clear in the past week since the breakup, but mostly how the relationship I had convinced myself was idyllic was anything but. "As well as a list of charges that will go on your permanent record. I want you to know, if we don't settle this right now, I'm pushing for the most I can get."

I take in a deep breath, knowing this to be true, but then he catches me off guard again.

"This wouldn't just destroy you, either. Julianne works with children. Ava runs a business teaching women self-defense. Having a criminal stalking record won't look great for either of them." My stomach drops, my head going light as a cruel smile slides across his face.

"Jeremy, come on. It was just a dumb prank."

His lips tip up further, and he shakes his head. "It doesn't matter. In the eyes of the law, you fucked up, Harper, and you're at my mercy. Unless you want your friends to suffer."

It's then it all really hits me: he never loved me. Not even for a minute.

I'm shaking when I leave the room, leaving Jeremy. Jules and Ava meet me in the waiting room before we're released. It's a full-body shake like a freaking chihuahua, my hands barely able to sign my name as I get my things back.

"Are you okay?" Ava asks, reading me, but I put on my mask and give her a small smile.

I've always been good with a mask, hiding all of these unnecessary and incredibly pesky emotions away where they can't bother me at all. "Totally fine," I say back.

Jules gives me a hard look, opening her mouth to say something, probably to call me out on my bullshit. Fortunately, our names are called again, and I'm saved from further interrogation as we walk to the front of the police station.

"You're in so much trouble," Jaime says as soon as we're in sight, quickly walking our way and pulling Ava into his arms.

"You promise?" Ava says with a sneaky smile, and her husband looks down at her, a look of all-consuming adoration with just the barest hint of irritation written across his face for all to see before he smiles and presses his lips to hers, mumbling something I can't and probably don't want to hear.

"Sorry," Jules says as she walks to her fiancé, Nate, who pulls her into his arms. "The forking was what took the longest. Probably could have done without it." She gives him a hesitant smile, and he shakes his head, rolling his eyes at her. He's more entertained than Jaime looks, and considering the stories I've heard about him and his sisters pranking each other, it tracks.

"Told you to stick to just the glitter," he whispers low, pulling her into him.

"Yeah, yeah. Where's Sophie?" she asks, looking around for Nate's now six-year-old daughter, who is nowhere to be seen.

"With Claire. She's very excited to hear about your time in the clink."

Jules's head moves back, looking at Nate with confusion. "You told Sophie I got arrested?"

"No, Claire did. She's very interested in having a criminal in the family. Pretty sure she activated the family phone tree to spread the news."

"Dear God," Jules groans, putting her face in Nate's chest as he chuckles, the sound filling the cold and lifeless police station.

And as I stand there, watching my two best friends, the two women I would give everything in the world up for, the two women I did just give so much up to protect, in the arms of the men they love, the glaring evidence of the families they're creating in front of me, it hits me.

I have no one.

I'm an only child who rarely speaks to her divorced parents except for the requisite holiday or birthday call. I'm single after leaving my long-term relationship, and I'm quickly being left behind, at no fault to my friends.

It's at this moment that I realize why I stayed for so long. Even when Jeremy made me feel like shit or when I knew logically I would and could never have something lasting with him. If I'd been brave and ended things long before they got out of control, I wouldn't have to face this all-consuming loneliness.

My friends have found their people and are making their own families, and I'm...not. That clock I had hidden under a pillow starts ticking loudly, telling me I'm running out of time to figure out what I want out of my life and who I want to spend it with.

A familiar face walks up to me as I keep my gaze on my two best friends. His hand gently touches my elbow before pulling back like he crossed some invisible line he isn't sure he is allowed past and knocking me out of my trance.

"Hey, Wes," I say with a tight smile, giving a tiny wave to the guitarist of Atlas Oaks. Although Jaime is the bodyguard for the band, I'm not sure why he's here. Over his shoulder, I see Ava give me wide eyes and a smile, always telling me she thinks Wes is the cutest of the AO guys. I roll mine in response.

Of course I'm not oblivious that Wes is cute with his messy, longish, sun-kissed brown hair and the worn, dark brown leather jacket he always wears pulled over broad shoulders in a way that looks badass but also casual, like he's just a normal guy when he's anything but.

*And* he's tall, towering over my five foot five frame.

A deadly triple combination.

"You okay?" he asks, taking my jacket from my hands and holding it up for me, ever the gentleman. At Ava's wedding, we were paired together as bridesmaid and groomsman, so I'm used to his kindness.

I turn, too tired and burned out and hurt to even argue, and slide my still shaking hands into the sleeves.

"Yeah, I'm fine," I lie. His fingers slide gently along the skin of my neck, gathering my hair and tugging it gently out of the neck of my jacket before I turn and give him a smile. "What are you doing here?"

His boyish, crooked smile takes over his face, a stark contrast to the evil one I saw minutes ago, a dimple on his cheek catching my eye. "We were all together when Jaime got the call. As soon as I heard Ava had been arrested, I knew I had to come and see what was up. You three always have the best chaos going on."

I let out a small laugh and shake my head. "Yeah, getting arrested for littering my ex's lawn is just...wonderful."

"Kind of iconic, actually. Very rock star of you. And I would know, you know, being one," he says. I can't fight off the smile that tugs at my lips as I give him a shake of my head. "I'm serious. Jagger would be proud."

"Yes, dumping pounds of glitter onto someone's lawn is so very rock and roll of us."

He shrugs. "I don't make the rules. I just enforce them when I see them," he says, then holds my gaze for a moment longer than necessary, only stopping when Jaime speaks.

"All right, let's go," he says loud enough for everyone to hear. "Before Ava does something stupid and gets all of us locked up."

Ava shoves his shoulder, or tries to, but the man is a fucking mountain, and she is virtually a Pixie Hollow fairy.

"I'm hungry," Ava says as Jaime slides her jacket on her, similarly to how Wes just did to me.

"Ava, we ate like..." I look at my watch, realizing it was probably almost five hours ago that we ate dinner. Strangely enough, I'm not hungry at all.

"Exactly," Ava says, then puts a hand to her belly. "I'm hungry. Let's eat."

"My girl wants food, she gets food. Everyone into the SUV. You guys need to get back to Sophie?" Jaime asks Nate, who shakes his head.

"Nah, my sister's got her."

"Wes, you got anything pressing?" Wes shakes his head.

"I can always eat," he says with a grin.

No one asks me, because what do I have to go home to? Still, Wes puts a hand to my lower back, urging me to Jaime's giant boat of a car before we drive to an all-night diner.

And even though I smile as everyone laughs and jokes about the night, all I can think about is just how lost I feel.

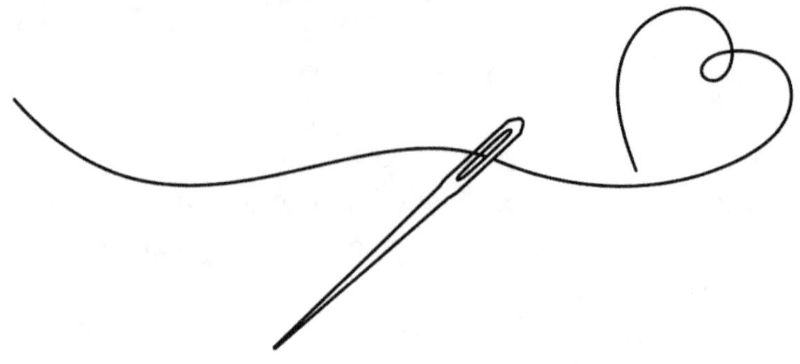

# FOUR

## HARPER

"Get up," a familiar voice says as the curtains in the small cottage I'm staying in are pulled back, letting in a flood of light that has me shielding my eyes.

"Wha—" I start, sleep still controlling my body. I wonder if this is a nightmare, another fucked-up creation of my mind.

"Get *up*," the voice says, and when I crack an eye open, Ava is standing in front of me, her hand on her hips as she glares at me like a disappointed mother. "My god, Harper, this place looks like you've been living in isolation for months, not barely a week."

"Thanks, I appreciate your concern," I say as I shift to sit up in the bed, trying to shake myself awake as I take in the inside of the small cottage behind Nate and Jules's home with skepticism. Okay, so maybe the place *is* a bit of a disaster. There are cartons of food in the garbage piled high, and every cup is dirty and piled along the small sink. At some point, I started ordering delivery when I ran out of mugs, and the white paper cups are lined up along the counter.

In one corner is a pile of laundry, and if I'm being honest, I'm not totally sure when the last time I showered was. The only pristine corner of the small studio is where I've been working on the gown that's due to my client in a few days. The nearly finished product is hanging, the beads and sequins glinting in the...midday sun?

A glance at the clock tells me it's nearly two, and considering I went to bed well after midnight, that makes sense.

"I genuinely am concerned, Harper," Ava says with a sigh, looking at me with soft eyes.

"Ava—" I start, but she shakes her head.

"And so is Jules."

That stops me because Jules hasn't said anything about being worried about me, instead giving me the space I asked for. But clearly, my friends have been talking about me, and Ava decided today she's done with my moping.

"I know the media is hard right now, but eventually, you have to step out into the world and say fuck it."

Since our arrest, Jeremy, with his ties as the head of marketing for Astor, and his new heiress girlfriend, have decided to step into society together and use my brush with the law to paint me in the absolute worst light. It seems they want to make sure I'll have no credibility if I start to run my mouth. "I appreciate it. Really, I do—" I start, but she cuts me off again.

"The media sucks," she says. "Trust me, Harper, I've seen it all."

"But you got past it and made everyone love you," I say with a grumble because even though Ava had her own run-ins with the press, they were never truly cruel and out to destroy her in the way I'm experiencing.

"And you will too, but not if you smell like Fritos and BO." I cringe at the description, and she gives me a small, apologetic look. "Sorry, sometimes being too honest is the way to go."

I hate to admit it, but she's probably right. The best way to get through to me is with absolute honesty, and looking around, I know this is *not* how I want to live my life.

Jeremy might have won this round and is in the process of

destroying my reputation, but if I live like this, he won the whole fucking game, and I don't know if I'm okay with that.

It's been two weeks since what I've been calling the *glitter incident,* and my reputation has *never* been worse.

While we were at the diner laughing and eating after Jaime bailed us out, Clarissa, Jeremy's new little girlfriend, began her smear campaign. She told any news outlet that would listen to her that I was the crazy ex ruining their lives.

The pitchforks from the public are out, demanding my downfall, and as social media tends to do, no one cares about the truth or the *other side* of it all, not when there's an attractive man with a sob story and a woman they can villainize. While I may have left the police station without a formal charge, I am being tried in the court of public opinion, and I am losing.

Bad.

So far, according to them, I'm an unstable and talentless hack who had Jeremy and Clarissa helping me with my designs all along. Let's not forget about being a jealous ex who is out to ruin *true love.* The two have been claiming they'd been together for months (probably true), and Jeremy and I have been broken up for even longer (news to me), and I simply haven't gotten over it.

The last is *decidedly* untrue. The uncomfortable truth is I'm realizing I don't know if I ever was in *love* with Jeremy or if I'd just grown comfortable in the illusion of our relationship.

I've had to turn off comments on my social media channels when all of the heiress's friends and fans started coming after me, calling me crazy and telling me to leave Jeremy alone, even though I would never even think of the man again if I didn't have to.

The only saving grace seems to be that it's not impacting my current clients or pageant work. I'm hoping, like all drama, this will fade behind me when the next new scandal comes along, and I'll be able to just coast on.

Hopefully.

I think.

"Come on," Ava says, leaning into the small bathroom and turning on the shower. "Get in there."

"Ava, this isn't—"

"It is, because we have..." She looks at the time on her phone before looking back at me with fierce eyes like she knows I'm going to argue. "Four hours to get you ready." Moving toward the kitchenette, she reaches into one of the lower cabinets and finds one garbage bag left in the pack.

"Four hours?" I ask.

Ava opens the bag and starts throwing the empty cups into them one by one. "Yup. We've got a charity auction to go to."

Instantly, I shake my head. "No. Thank you so much, but no, Ava."

"That's so crazy, I don't remember telling you you had a choice," she says, not missing a beat as she continues to gather up my trash. I should be embarrassed, but I can't seem to garner it, and after ten years of friendship, this is just what we do for one another.

"I can't go, Ava. It's.... It's too much."

"You're going because it benefits my charity and because you have something up for auction," she says, reminding me of the one custom gown I put up for auction. "You agreed to go over a month ago, and I'm not letting this asshat get in the way of that. There are going to be a lot of people there to network with."

"A lot of people to whisper about what a psycho I am too," I counter, waving my arms. "To whisper about how I'm spiraling and—"

"Or to whisper about how good you look despite it all. How you walked in there with your chin held high and didn't let those dumb people intimidate you. Shoulders back, tits out, Harper."

I sigh and roll my eyes. "That's all fun and cute, but I'm in a media firestorm, Ava."

"And you're *letting* them win by not going out there and telling the world you're totally fine. By not going out and explaining that, yeah, you were a woman scorned because your douche of an ex sold you lies of forever only to be fucking some other girl on the side. You can tell your side, Harper. You're just choosing not to."

She's right, of course. I could tell my side, or, at least, part of it. I had a lawyer look over the contract I signed at the station to make sure I didn't sign my life away. While there's a *you can't tell anyone about this* clause, there is no *you can't talk shit about me* clause. But I'm still scared.

"Ava—"

"I'm not taking no for an answer, so good luck with that," she says before emptying the garbage can into the large bag and tying it off. "I'm going into Jules's house to grab more bags, and when I get back, you'd better be in the shower. "

"Ava, I can't. I..." I start looking around. "I don't even have anything to wear!" I say suddenly, the answer so obvious. "I can't—"

"Yes, you do. You're wearing this," she says, moving to her bag and tugging out a beaded gown I made her for her tour that she never wore.

"That's for you," I say.

"And I never wore it. We're the same size; you're just a bit taller."

"So it will be too short," I say, clinging to any argument I can, even though I know the dress that was a bit too long on her for her likes will hit perfectly just above my knee.

"No, it'll be perfect," she says, hanging it next to the gown I'm working on. "Now go, Harper. I'm serious. Don't let me down."

It's a low blow to tell me that, but I know she did it on purpose. And it does its job, making me sigh because she's right: I told her I'd come to this as her date because Jaime would be busy, and I can't back down, even if I'm in crisis mode. My hands move to the clip in my hair, the grime and knots holding it nearly in place without the clip. I cringe as I reach for a brush.

Ava smiles, knowing she won.

"Perfect. Maybe double-wash your hair. And don't forget to

shave! You never know who you'll meet," she says with a wink, and before I can even argue and tell her there is no universe where I'm dating, much less fucking someone in the next *decade*, she's out the door, on a mission as always, and I'm left to hop into the shower and try to put my life back together.

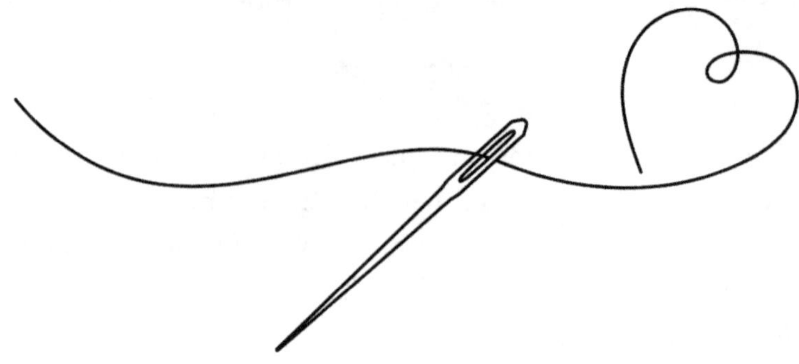

# FIVE

## HARPER

Five hours, an everything shower, a few tiny tweaks to the dress, and a thick layer of makeup to cover my dark circles later, Ava and I walk into the charity event, and even though I'm nauseous almost the entire time, which I'll never tell her, I'm glad I'm here.

When you put yourself in a bubble of your own demise, you forget that the rest of the world keeps turning and, more importantly, that not everyone is as attuned to your crumbling castle as you are. Where I expected glares and cold shoulders, I got wide smiles and *so good to see you*'s, and even a few inquiries on my dress and business card exchanges.

There have been a few awkward moments—colleagues of Jeremy's I recognize from fashion shows or the few work events he'd bring me to whisper to one another—but overall, it's been...fine.

As seems to be her way, Ava gave me exactly what I didn't realize I needed, and suddenly, I can breathe a bit again. There's a light at the end of the tunnel. Jeremy may have hurt me, may have fucked me up a little and slowed me down, but with some vitamin D and fresh hair (everyone knows nothing will ever change your outlook on life more than washing your hair and blowing it out for the first time in a while), I feel like I can tackle this disaster.

My name and reputation are tarnished, but not destroyed. I'd thank Ava for the reminder that life goes on, but then I'd have to hear a decade of *I told you so's,* so I decide against it.

"Oh, there's Jennifer," Ava says as we wander around the room, looking at the auction items. "I'm going to go say hello."

I nod, then tip my head toward the other side of the room.

"I'm going to go use the ladies' room quickly before the auction starts," I say.

Ava nods, and we go our separate ways.

It's when I'm about to leave the bathroom stall after giving myself a small pep talk, mentally planning how to move forward with my career with new vigor despite the roadblock, that I hear it. The click of heels filling the marble bathroom, followed by giggling women.

"I'm going to win the dinner with Wes Holden for Jeremy, of course," a familiar voice says, my stomach falling to the floor and the thin grasp I'd just gotten on my good mood vanishing. Shifting toward the door quietly to hear better, my heart pounds. "You know, as a thank you for helping me with my line."

Fucking Clarissa Astor is here.

"Oh, that's so cute," someone coos, clapping her hands excitedly.

"Atlas Oaks is his favorite band, and I just *know* he'd love it. We've just..." A deep sigh reaches my ears, and I roll my eyes at her fakeness. "You know, things have been so hard lately."

"You two are so strong, though. This journey is only bringing you two together. And we're all so excited about your line! It's the start of a new legacy."

I grit my teeth so hard I should be worried about the enamel.

New legacy, my ass. It was supposed to be the start of *my* legacy.

I should leave. I should slip out and—

"You know, his ex, the one that designs those little pageant dresses or whatever?" Clarissa starts, leading the conversation in a way that almost sounds casual, but I know is calculated. "I hear she's claiming the designs Jeremy and I worked on together are *hers*," she says in a fake, hushed whisper, and my blood goes cold because that hasn't happened, and even *insinuating* it could destroy my credibility.

"No *way!*" one of the girls says. "That's crazy! You designed them with Jeremy, right?"

Nausea churns in my stomach at the realization that this is her plan. Plant these tiny seeds of doubt just in case I start whispering my own facts.

Destroy my credibility before it's even an issue.

"Yeah, so I told my daddy, and well, you know how protective he is of me. He told me she's pretty much done in this industry by the end of the week."

My stomach churns as I remember the way my fabric supplier never returned my call this week and how two of my consultations were canceled.

No, no, *no!*

This can't be happening.

"I'm sooo sorry you're dealing with this, Clarissa. It sounds like his ex is insane. First, trying to tear you two apart after you've been in love for so long, then vandalizing his house, and now this?"

"It's all good," Clarissa says, bliss in her words. "It will all be cleared out soon. You know, my daddy says Jeremy asked him for permission to propose."

Squeals erupt, and I swallow down the nausea that churns with the knowledge that nothing in the past four years was real. I spent the last two waiting for Jeremy to propose, deluding myself into thinking we would be something, that every time I felt a tug in my gut that something was off, it was in my head. I let Jeremy lie and manipulate me until I was left with nothing but the husk of someone I barely even recognize anymore.

And just like that, something in me snaps, an old version of myself I've long buried stirring awake. It's then I make the decision.

A wise one? I don't know. A safe one? Absolutely not. But where has being safe gotten me?

After a life of watching my friends be spontaneous, happy, and blissfully ignorant of all of the bad outcomes of any given decision, I'm ready to be impulsive. Because fuck it. How much worse could things get?

I'm tired of being the safe, easy friend, the one who lets people walk all over her, who finds herself pinned in place by some asshole who took everything from her.

My home, my confidence, my stability.

My future.

The noise in the bathroom dies down as the women leave, and I'm doing math in my head as I walk out of the stall and wash my hands, determined to win, if only in this one, stupid way.

I march back to the table Ava and I are sitting at, grabbing a glass of expensive champagne from a tray a server is holding. I down it as I walk, grabbing a second flute before I reach our table and chugging that as well. I put both glasses on a third tray before grabbing a full one and sitting next to Ava, a wide, fake smile on my lips.

"Clarissa is here," I say under my breath, eyes on the auctioneer who is walking up to the podium to begin.

"No," she whispers with shock, and I nod. "I'm so sorry, Harper. We can leave if—"

I shake my head aggressively. "Hell no," I say. "I've got a plan." Ava looks at me, and finally, I look back at her, letting her see the pure determination and a bit of the unhinged anger that's flowing through me, and slowly, her lips tip up.

"About damn time," she says, then lifts her glass to mine, and we cheers with a wide smile.

Ava and I sit for the next thirty minutes, listening to rich people overbid on various items: a hot air balloon ride, a horrifying painting of a grinning clown, a luxurious spa trip, and a self-defense girls afternoon among them.

Finally, my attention is piqued, and I roll my shoulders back, ready to win.

"And our next item is one dinner with Wes Holden of Atlas Oaks!" the auctioneer croons.

Ava found a great person for this job; his voice and humor really keeping up the entertainment of the night, but now that he's on the one item I was interested in, I want him to shut up and get it over with.

From the corner of my eye, I see Clarissa turn to her friends with an excited smile.

*Too fucking bad, bitch.*

While I have nowhere to stay and no longer have the collection I hoped would launch my career, I have a good amount in savings that I'd been setting aside for some far-off wedding I didn't realize would never come. What better way to spend it than to get a tiny, minuscule bit of revenge on the man I can't touch without putting my friends in danger?

I down the last of another glass of champagne and smile at Ava; the look is probably a bit loopy, but what do I care? I have to focus.

"We're going to open our bid at $500. Anyone?" the auctioneer asks, and instantly Clarissa's paddle goes up.

"Five hundred," she says sweetly, and her friends clap like she's doing some grand gesture.

"Five fifty," I say confidently, lifting my paddle.

Someone behind me shouts two thousand, and Clarissa counters with $2,100.

I lift my paddle once more.

"Twenty-five hundred," I say, shoulders back, chin tipped.

"Three thousand!" a voice from the edge of the room says. This goes on, the bidding war commencing, but I stand strong.

"Seventy-five hundred," I say when it's down to just me and Clarissa. Where we're seated, I can see her, but I don't think she can see me, at least not well, as she keeps shifting to try and catch a good look at me.

"Harper!" Ava says, under her breath through gritted teeth. "Do you know what you're doing?"

"Yes. I'm winning," I whisper back, keeping that smile on my lips. "Help a girl out so I don't use all of my savings on this, will you?" I ask.

When Clarissa raises her hand up, Ava smiles, standing and moving around the room smoothly, saying hello to people as she goes along. She grabs pop star Willa Stone's hand, knowing her through Jaime, who has guarded her a few times, a few tables over, and tugs her to where my enemy is.

I watch as Ava whispers something to Willa, who nods excitedly, and then finally, they make it to Clarissa as she ups her bid to $9,750. My stomach churns at the figure, despite the tax write-off and the good cause, it's an irresponsible amount of money.

But once again, I remind myself, where has being responsible gotten me?

Ava taps on Clarissa's shoulder, and she turns around with an annoyed look before smiling sweetly when she sees Willa. Ava begins doing what she does best, schmoozing, with Willa stepping in as well, gushing over her like she's a fan, and Clarissa eats the attention up.

"Ten thousand," I say loudly.

But Clarissa is too busy being the center of attention, having pop star Willa Ford in front of her and giving her the time of day. Her friend taps her shoulder, but Clarissa glares at her, brushing her off with a bit too much force, her entire table of friends giving each other a look I take note of.

It seems her little crowd of admirers might not be as admiring of her as I thought.

"Ten thousand, going once..." The room stays quiet as I look around the room. "Going twice..." I fight the urge to smile before I win. "Sold! To the pretty girl in gold!"

Ava and Willa wave goodbye as soon as the auction ends, and I watch as Clarissa realizes she lost, her face going red with anger as she looks to the auctioneer, moving quickly to the stage to argue. I can't hear the conversation, but I see the auctioneer shake his head and shrug like there's nothing he can do while Clarissa throws a full-on tantrum.

I watch as a few attendees take pictures and post them on social media with pleasure.

Finally, I let myself smile, and after everything in the past few weeks, it feels so foreign on my lips.

"What the hell was that?" Ava asks with a laugh, a bit of concern in her eyes like she thinks I might snap.

I might, to be honest.

Actually, I'm well past snapping. I was broken in half and then crushed under Jeremy's stupid wing-tipped shoes.

"I heard her in the bathroom telling her little friends that she wanted to win that for Jeremy. And I didn't want her to have anything nice."

Ava stares at me, and I stare back.

"Harp," she starts, and I shake my head.

"No. Not now," I whisper, the lump that I've been fighting down all day building once more. "Not now."

I know she wants answers. I know she and Jules want to know how the breakup went, what happened at the police station, why I'm so devastated, and why I'm hiding away when before the arrest, I was mostly okay. They think I'm falling apart, that I'm unstable, and honestly, it's easier to let them think that.

"But soon?" she asks, reaching over and grabbing my hand, gripping it tight.

I give her a smile and lie through my teeth, never planning on telling my friends about what I gave up. "Soon. But first, I apparently now have to plan for a date with the guitarist of my ex's favorite band."

Ava claps her hands excitedly. "Oh, my god, we have to call Jules. We need to go shopping!"

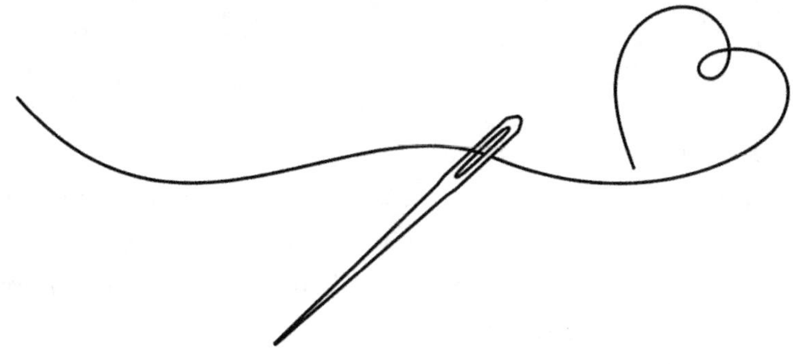

# SIX

## HARPER

The next night, I go on a ten thousand dollar date.

Ten thousand dollars I could've spent on literally anything: something for my business, part of a down payment on a house so I can move out of Jules's backyard, or an expensive attorney to see if I have any other options.

Literally *anything*.

But instead, I spent ten thousand dollars on a pity date with a friend.

Okay, maybe *friend* is being generous. A friend of a friend? An acquaintance?

And, okay, to say I spent money on a date is a bit of a lie too, considering I spent the money as a bit of petty revenge on my dumbass ex and his new girlfriend. At the time, it felt like the best option, a great idea, even. Now, with butterflies fluttering and my pulse pounding as I walk beside him in utter uncomfortable silence, it feels a bit silly.

We walk from where we parked to the Swift Building, paparazzi screaming at us, asking me about the vandalism and Wes if he knows I'm still in love with my ex.

See? I should have stayed home.

Our dinner is apparently at the top of the Swift Building, and once we're away from the paparazzi, we endure a silent elevator ride before we arrive at the top of the open-air building. Nearly an hour later, we are pushing a way-too-fancy dinner around on our plates and attempting the most uncomfortable small talk known to man.

I thought it would be an okay evening considering I've spent my fair share of time with Wes Holden over the years at parties and whatnot, but I was wrong. So fucking wrong. I'm sitting here being bombarded with the reality of what a moron I am, and Wes looks like he would rather be *anywhere* but here.

I grab my champagne glass and throw it back, the waiter, who is watching our every move, making this only more uncomfortable, running over to refill it. I shouldn't accept, considering I've eaten nothing today from the nerves, but still, I smile and lift the glass, taking another sip.

"So, how much did this date go for?" Wes asks, a hand rubbing the back of his neck awkwardly.

"Too much," I grumble, and his eyes go wide. "Fuck. Sorry, I didn't mean that, I just mean...more than I should have paid, considering I'm living in Jules's cottage for the time being, and...you know, everything else."

He stares at me for a moment, contemplating his next words, then shakes his head as if throwing caution to the wind before he speaks again. "Can I ask, why did you?"

I'm not sure how to answer this, but it can't get much worse, so I go with the truth.

"Because men are the absolute worst." He lets out a small laugh, and I smile, emboldened by his lack of offense to my statement. "It was just a petty little fuck you to my ex."

"A fuck you?" He leans forward now, intrigued, and even though I'd rather talk about anything but myself, I'm happy we're actually talking instead of just staring blankly at one another.

"My ex dumped me—" I start, but he gently cuts me off,

"The one whose lawn you glittered?"

I almost forgot he was there that night, and I give him a tight smile and nod.

"Yeah, that one. Atlas Oaks is his favorite band, and I heard his new girlfriend talking about bidding on this date because they're just *so in love* and it would be *such a good gift.*" I shrug, feeling a bit childish admitting this, but proceed all the same. "I decided I didn't want him to have anything good. They're out there ruining my reputation right now, acting like I'm some crazy ex...I don't know. Him getting to have a night with you tipped the scale. I didn't want him to have it. Or maybe I didn't want her to give it to him. Either way, I kind of snapped, and I bid too much."

"You know, I would be more than happy to repay—"

I shake my head quickly. "It's fine, the money was just sitting there anyway. It was my wedding fund," I mumble, twirling the liquid in my glass. I don't drink often, mostly because when I do, my tight grip on common sense slackens, and I make dumb decisions, like bidding ten grand on a date with a guitarist or rambling about things I should shut up about to said guitarist.

"Your wedding fund? Were you guys engaged?" His eyes move to my hand, and his body shifts unconsciously, moving away like he's trying to be respectful.

I shake my head. "No, no. The wedding I *thought* I'd be having." I let out a humorless laugh. "God, I'm an idiot."

His eyes go soft, and he shakes his head. "I highly doubt that," he says so low, I almost don't hear it over the loud wind.

"I dated the same man for four years, even though I didn't have any all-consuming, soul-crushing feelings for him. That's pretty idiotic."

Wes tips his head from left to right like he's weighing his answer. "Then why'd you stay?"

I think of my realization at the police station, how my friends are moving forward with their lives and I'm back at square one, how I think I knew that was the future I'd be facing if I broke up with

Jeremy. Still, I decide that's not something I want to share with my best friends, much less Wes, and give him a safer answer.

"Jeremy was...or, I thought he was...good enough. A safe bet to check my boxes."

"Your boxes?"

"Yeah, you know: you date, you get married, you have two point five kids. You find a career you can endure, and you do well at it, and you buy a house with a white picket fence." I take another sip of my drink and then continue, watching Wes's lips tip up, entertained by me. "Then you wait until the kids all move out, and when you're old enough to retire, you travel the world, probably on one of those seniors' cruises that go all over the world. Which is crazy because I don't even *want* kids, and I hate cruises, and I want to travel *now*, not when I'm sixty-five or whatever and have to worry about affording that *and* paying some ungrateful kid's college tuition."

He opens his mouth to add something, but I'm on a roll now, fueled by alcohol, bad decisions, and anger.

"But I thought that was what I was supposed to do, so I stayed with Jeremy because he was safe. He had a good job in the same industry as me, and we both worked hard, so he wouldn't complain about my doing it. We had the same goals, and I could *see* that future. A boring, safe future. Except he *wasn't* safe, he was an asshole who I convinced myself I liked." I'm rambling now, and I know it, but I can't stop. Something about the way Wes is looking at me makes me feel like I want—no, *need*—to get this all off my chest or I might explode. "And then he dumped me and made me look like an idiot after he cheated on me."

I take in a deep breath and sit back, waiting for the embarrassment to wash over me from my little outburst, but it doesn't come. Instead, I watch as his small smile spreads into a wide grin. Watch his arms cross over his chest and take note, without meaning to, how broad his shoulders are and how he has a tiny indent in his cheek when he smiles.

"Sounds like he's the idiot for fumbling you."

"Yeah, well, I'm the one who helped build his career without knowing it," I say then instantly wish I could take it back. It reveals too much of the truth I can't share.

"How'd you do that?" he says, not accusing or disbelieving, just with interest.

I quickly try to decide what to tell him, how much to reveal, but settle on saying what Ava and Jules already know.

"I helped him with designs he brought home from work. He always told me he was putting in a good word for me with his boss and he was building up my reputation, but it seems that never happened. He just handed them off to his new girlfriend so she could impress her father. Now he and his little girlfriend are going on a rampage, making me look like some crazy scorned ex in case I try and say something."

His face looks confused now, like there's some obvious answer I'm missing.

"Why not tell someone? Why not get on one of those talk shows or something to tell your side of things?".

"Because I am..." I run through my mind trying to figure out what to say, how to say I signed everything away to save my friends before I land on sticking as close to the truth as possible. "I am nothing. I am no one. I design pageant gowns, and Astor Fashion house is...every-thing. They know everyone. They're tied to everything. They could crush me. They *are* crushing me," I explain.

"Don't say that," he says with a shake of his hand, reaching over the small table and grabbing mine. It's warm and calloused and sends a jolt of electricity through me, which I force myself to bury. "Don't talk about yourself like that."

"It's not self-deprecating. It's the truth. The lawyers they have, the press pull, the clout—they are the industry, and I'm just some girl who designs pageant gowns."

"I have pull with the press. Ava does, the band does, we could—"

I shake my head, panic jolting me to pull my hand away and sit up straight. "No, no. No. That can't happen. I can't..."

"Harper—" he starts, reaching for my hand again, but I cut him off.

"You don't get it. He could shift his focus to Ava, to try and fuck with her. And Jules. And Jaime. And Nate. If he wanted to, was given the motivation to, Jeremy could easily destroy all of their reputations and all of their businesses, and I cannot have that on my conscience."

It's the closest I've come to the truth since everything happened, and it feels surprisingly good.

"Harper, really. We could—" he starts to say.

"I can do this on my own," I say, forcing a smile onto my lips and slipping back behind my safe, confident, aloof mask. "I won't let some idiot get to me. I'm just, you know, having a bit of a pity party. This?" I say, waving my hand between us. "This was enough. A good fuck you to my ex, showing him that I can and will get better than he ever was. It's good. It's great even." I'm selling it, and I know it.

I'm so good, I'm almost convincing myself, and when Wes crosses his arms on his chest, leaning back with a smile on his face, I know I've convinced him too.

# SEVEN

WES

"It's not enough," I say and watch her face screw up in confusion.

Harper is so beautiful, and she doesn't even know it, but right now, she's even prettier. Those walls she usually keeps tight cracked for the first time since I've met her, letting me see the vulnerability and nerves beneath that put-together facade.

When Leo called and asked if I'd be interested in signing up for an auction benefiting Ava's charity, I said yes, of course. I figured it would be with some woman with more money than common sense or a gift she bought someone she wants to put a ring on it.

When I was told *Harper Abbott* won the bid, I was taken back.

And delightfully so.

Now she's sitting across from me, spilling worries and insecurities I don't think even her friends know about or, at least, don't fully understand, and I am even more endeared by her.

"Yes, it is. Trust me. Those paparazzi photos will cross his path, and it will piss him off. It was a small win."

I shake my head. "Let's back it up. You need a place to stay?"

She shrugs, a finger making lines in the salt she knocked over distractedly. She pinches a bit of it before tossing it over her shoulder, then nods.

*Cute. So fucking cute.*

"Do you want to get your ex back?"

Her face blanches, and she shakes her head quickly. "God, no."

I figured, but I needed confirmation.

I've had an idea brewing in my mind to divert attention since Stella and Riggs told us their news, and it seems like the universe may have dropped the most perfect present into my lap.

"So you want to get back *at* him?"

"I...I can't. I think I already learned that lesson," she says with a small smile.

That wasn't a no.

"But...you want to?" I ask, and she stares at me for long moments before I add on, "Or, you'd *like* to. If you could guarantee he wouldn't be able to retaliate?"

She shrugs again, then gives me a small smile.

I take it as a yes and nod, understanding. Slowly, an idea is forming in my mind, one that is absolutely insane but one I like a fuck of a lot.

Too much, if I'm being honest, but that's neither here nor there.

"If I tell you a secret, you'll keep it?" I ask. Jaime trusts this girl, so I know I can trust her as well. I look over my shoulder at the waiter, knowing Leo had everyone involved with this dinner sign airtight NDAs as he always does.

She nods despite the confusion taking over her face with the seemingly sudden change of subject. "Of course."

"The band needs to go on a break." Her eyes go wide. "It's for good reasons, but your face tells me you know the band's history and what happened the last time we went on a break. You know Riggins's history?"

She cringes then nods. "Sorry, I didn't mean to assume and think the worst, I just—"

I shake my head before cutting her off. "No, it's fine. It's his history, our history, and we don't shy away from it. But that's where everyone is going to jump to." A small smile plays on my lips. "Stella's actually pregnant."

"Oh my god!" Harper says with a gush, her face lighting up and warmth filling me. I know Ava and her friends have gotten close to Stella, so they probably know she and Riggs have been trying for some time. "Oh, she's going to be the best mom. She and Ava will have babies around the same time!" Harper claps her hands excitedly.

"Yeah, but she's high-risk and wants to keep things under wraps for a while. She doesn't want to have the press hounding her about it. Things just barely settled down for them after everything that happened."

Harper nods with understanding. "So you need some kind of diversion?" she asks thoughtfully, and I nod. "Something to explain why the band would need to go on a break without the press jumping to the worst-case scenario."

"Yeah." My smile shifts into a grin, knowing what I'm about to say will sound absolutely insane but also knowing it could solve a lot of problems. "How do you feel about a quickie wedding?"

Her face slackens, and I fight back a laugh.

"A...a wedding?" she asks, confused. "Who's getting married?"

"Us, if you say yes."

"Us?" she squeaks out.

"You said you can't get back at your ex, but you bid on this date because I'm in his favorite band. From what I remember, the night you, Ava, and Jules came up into the VIP section, that was the reason, too, right?"

She nods. I remember that night perfectly and the way the gorgeous redhead in front of me walked up into the space. I couldn't take my eyes off of her the entire night.

"Why not up the ante?"

"By *marrying* you?" she asks incredulously.

"Don't make it seem like some kind of horrible jail sentence," I say with a laugh and a shake of my head. I knew suggesting this would fluster Harper, but also, the more I think about it, the more I like the idea. I've been waiting for the moment when I could try to get closer to Harper, intrigued by her since I first met her, and this is the perfect opportunity.

"I'm sorry, it's not. God, it's *definitely* not a terrible thing. I mean, just look at you." A blush burns over her cheeks, and she shakes her head frantically, copper locks shifting as she does. "You know what I mean—"

"I don't think I do. Please, feel free to elaborate," I say, sitting back with a smile and crossing my arms on my chest. The blush on her cheeks burns brighter, but she glares at me and rolls her eyes.

Right then, I think I could like this, bantering with Harper, the back and forth of it, her poking at me and me poking back. I could like it a lot.

"I just mean, it's crazy, isn't it?"

I shrug, trying to play it off. It's not the most *sane* proposition, but I won't be telling her that.

"We could benefit from each other, and it's a common-sense pairing. We have similar friends, live in the same town, the whole nine. We need a distraction, and a wedding and a whirlwind relationship would help with that. You want to make it so that ass can't touch you? I can help with that," I say, leaning forward.

I want her to say yes to this.

I can't think of something I've wanted more in a long, long time.

I've spent two years watching Harper, becoming friends with her and hating that she was with a man who didn't value the beauty, kindness, and intelligence that she has.

This is my chance, and I'm going to take it.

"Isn't that...kind of crazy?" she asks, and I shake my head.

"No. It's fun. Plus, then you can say that the ten thousand dollars you spent on this date really did go to your wedding." She smiles at that, and I think with that alone, I might be getting through to her.

"I...that's crazy, though."

"It's spontaneous, maybe, but I wouldn't call it crazy."

"*Spontaneous*," she says, then sits there, her eyes off somewhere else like the single word reminded her of... something. "I could be spontaneous." It's almost a whisper, her eyes still far off. Then something in her shifts and changes, her chin tipping up and her shoulders going back before she looks at me and smiles. "Yeah. Okay. I'll marry you," she finally says.

"Yeah?" I ask. I fully expected to have to convince her more, to push and prod until she agreed, but...

"I mean, as long as the terms make sense. Like...how long are we going to be married? And what kind of press will I need to be doing? What happens if my stuff starts to blow back and—"

"It won't," I say decidedly because I won't let that happen. Her face goes somehow both soft and disapproving.

"Wes, you can't—"

"I can. Leo is the best in the entire industry. Your ex and his new girl might have contacts, but they don't have even close to what Leo has. The man knows the deepest, darkest secrets you'd ever imagine about nearly everyone, and if he doesn't, he finds it. I don't know how he does it, but it's insane." Her face scrunches up like that's of concern to her, and I smile. "Don't worry. He only uses his powers for good. We'll figure everything out later," I say, then put a hand out to her. "But if you're in, I'm in, Harper."

She stares at my hand for long moments before eventually she sighs. "Fine. I'm in," she says, then shifts back as if she's shocking even herself by agreeing to this. Still, she reaches over and grabs my hand, shaking on our makeshift pact with a wide smile.

I return it, taking in how good her small, soft hand feels in mine.

"All right. Now that that's covered, are you ready to get some real food?" My chair scrapes back as I stand, then I use my grip on hers to pull her up. She's standing right in front of me now, close enough to feel her body heat, our hands held together between us.

"What?" she asks, adorably confused.

"I'm not going to let my soon-to-be wife starve," I say, tipping my chin to her plate filled with uneaten food. I don't know if it was the nerves or the overly fancy cuisine, but neither of us really ate our meals, and I'm starving.

"What?" she repeats, and I change my question.

"Do you like burgers?"

"I love french fries," she says low.

I let out a chuckle before I use my free hand to tug her closer, our chests touching, my arm wrapped around her lower back, her head tipped back to look at me. I lift a hand, letting my thumb graze over her jaw as she stares at me, wide-eyed and dazed.

I want to kiss her.

Badly.

I've wanted to for months.

But something tells me I'm going to have to tread carefully with Harper and do things on her terms, or else I could scare her off for good.

"Then let's get you some fries, little wife," I say, and when she smiles wide, I know I made the right choice.

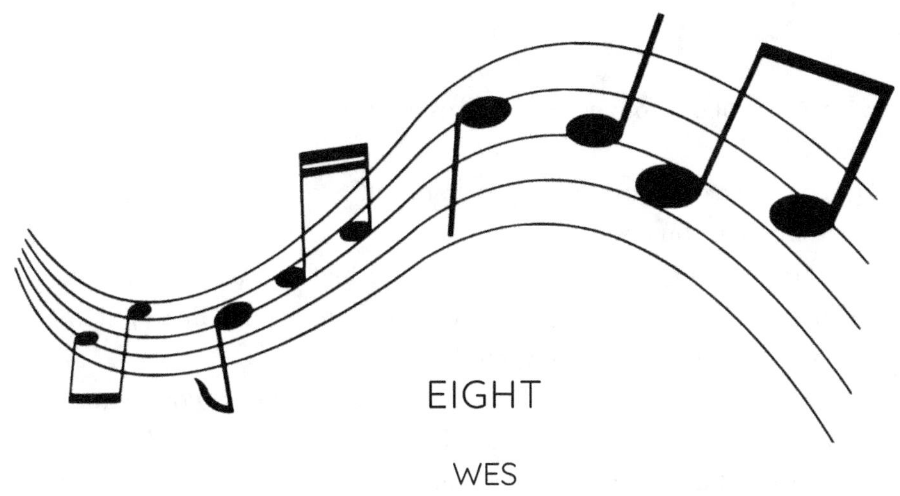

# EIGHT

## WES

*"Married?"* Leo says, his face losing all color. "What do you mean you're getting married? *How* are you getting married?"

I smile wider at his stress and panic. Leo hates anything outside of his very carefully crafted plan, and the guys and I very much enjoy stepping outside of it and watching him lose his mind a bit.

"It just kind of happened," I say with a shrug.

"That kind of thing doesn't just *happen*, Holden," he argues.

"Happened to Riggs and me," Stella says with a smile, hand on her stomach, speaking of their impulsive Vegas wedding years ago.

"You knew each other for years," Leo says with a glare.

"And I've known Harper for two years," I argue.

Our publicist sighs deeply, looking at the ceiling and trying to collect himself. I know, because we put Leo into that state pretty often. "You were supposed to go on a charity date to get good press, Wes, not to get fucking *engaged!* Jesus Christ, the papers are going to be insane." He must remember something because his eyes become saucers. "Wasn't she just arrested?"

"So was Ava," I say.

"Ava isn't about to have a fucking shotgun wedding to one of my clients, Wes!"

"Leo, it makes sense, and you know it," I say. "You needed a distraction; I got you one."

"A distraction could have been dating a high-profile celebrity. It could have been announcing some kind of home goods line or skin care or whatever the fuck you wanted."

"None of those would have explained the band going on hiatus, and you know it," I say, leaning back, because no matter what kind of fit Leo throws, I'm not changing my mind.

It's a genius idea, really, and with the way it fell into my lap, I can't help but think it was meant to be. I've wanted Harper Abbott to be mine since I first saw her in that club two years ago, but she was taken then. Now she's single, and I'd be an idiot to ignore this opportunity before me.

"But a quickie marriage?" Leo almost whines, exasperated, before sinking into a chair. "Did it have to be a quickie marriage?"

"It would explain why I want to postpone the tour."

"What's in it for her?" he asks, looking at me seriously. "She's going to have to sign a prenup and an ironclad NDA. Her friends, too."

"She knows that, and she will. It was her idea, actually," I say, thinking of our night together and how she insisted that would be something we need if we went through with this.

*"I want to make sure you're protected, no matter what happens,"* her sweet voice whispered when I walked her to her car.

"And she's got some issues with her ex, as you know," I say, trying to gloss over that, reminding him of the arrest. "And his new girlfriend is on a campaign to ruin her reputation. She needs a bit of a boost there."

Strangely enough, Leo perks up at that.

"Oh, a reputation redemption? I can work with that. I can absolutely work with that angle." He pulls his laptop closer, suddenly looking excited at the new challenge. "How do you spell her first name?"

"Jesus, Leo," Riggins says. "You've met her at least a dozen times."

Leo's face goes stern, glaring at his client. "I don't have time for names of regular people," he says, and Beck lets out a loud laugh.

"God, you sound like such an entitled prick," Beck says.

"I don't care how I sound. I care that I do my job well," Leo says, continuing with his research.

I open my mouth to say something but get distracted when my phone buzzes.

> Hey, it's Harper.

> I got your number from Ava, who got it from Stella.

> I'm not a total creep.

> I figured if we're going to get married, I should probably have your number.

> If you still want to do that, of course. If you don't, that's totally cool, it was kind of a random suggestion.

I can almost *feel* her spiraling through the phone, and I have to fight to keep a smile off my lips as Leo maniacally rambles about press opportunities and dates, not wanting to attract the attention of anyone.

> Definitely still want to do this. Currently planning it out with Leo now.

> Oh. Okay. Well, that's good. Right? Does he think it's a good idea?

I hesitate before answering, though I know I'm not giving her the real answer of *Leo is currently having a meltdown and thinks this is both a wonderful and terrible idea* because I'm not giving Harper a single reason not to go through with this.

> He thinks it's a great idea. Just working on logistics and timing.

> Cool, cool, cool. Well, you have my number now if you need anything.

> I need a picture.

> What?

> I need a picture for your contact. Everyone in my phone has one.

It's another lie to add to my list, but I can't resist the desire to keep her talking to me.

H: Oh. Okay. Please hold.

Leo is now looking at a calendar, his phone, a laptop screen, and an iPad all at once, comparing things and mumbling under his breath. It seems he's accepted this is going to happen and now is in full-on planning mode.

Unfortunately, I can't fight off the goofy smile tugging at my lips when the text comes through, even though the guys are also here and Leo is actively having a breakdown.

"What are you smiling about?" Reed asks, moving to me to look at my phone, which I quickly steal away so he can't get his greasy fingers on it. Greasy in a literal sense, because he's actively shoving french fries into his mouth like they're going to disappear soon.

"He has absolutely nothing to be smiling about, except maybe sending me into an early grave," Leo throws without looking our way.

"Nothing," I lie, moving my phone out of reach.

"Oh, that's how I know you're lying," Reed says, moving around me to try and grab my phone again.

"What the fuck, man? Leave me alone," I say, elbowing him to keep him away from me.

"No, you're all goo-goo-eyed, and I think it's over your new *fiancée*, so I want to see what she said."

"I'm not going *goo-goo-eyed*," I lie, then lean forward to grab one of his fries, which proves to be just the distraction I need.

"Hey! Leave my fries alone!" he yells, moving to his food and hovering over it as if I'm going to steal it all.

"Then stay away from my phone—hey!" I shout, looking at Stella, who is triumphantly smiling and scrolling through my phone now. "Stella, what the fuck?" I stand, moving to her, but she shifts away from me.

"Can't be mad at the pregnant chick. It's a rule," she says with a smile, then winks at Reed.

"She's right," her husband agrees with a smile, sitting back and taking in the show.

"Ha, you totally just got owned by a five-foot pregnant chick," Reed says with a laugh. "What was he smiling at?"

Stella looks at my phone, reading the texts Harper sent, then to me. "It's Harper texting him," she says.

"Is she sending nudes?" Reed asks, standing eagerly to go and look. I put my leg out, tripping him so he falls to the ground, then moving on top of him, sitting on his back, and pinning him down.

"What the fuck!?" he shouts as I hold him in place.

"You're running to look at nudes of *my* fiancée," I growl, unexpected irritation and anger running through me.

"Were there actually nudes?" he asks, a thread of mischievousness in the words.

"No, you creep," Stella says. "She sent a picture of herself for his phone contacts. But if you want to look at naked pictures of other people's fiancées, you deserve to get your face pounded into."

"I didn't *actually* think it was nudes," Reed grumbles as I get off him.

"Who is sending nudes?" Beck asks, sitting up with interest, suddenly checking back into our conversation. "Aren't you about to get married, Holden?"

"No one is sending nudes. God, all of you are terrible," Stella says with an eye roll, handing me back my phone. "Harper sent Wes a photo of herself, fully clothed, and Reed is being a creep about it."

"I didn't actually think they were nudes!" Reed shouts, and I fight a laugh. "He was just being all weird and secretive and smiling at his phone like a lovesick puppy, so I wanted to see what it was."

"Well, it seems like you already got the ball rolling," Leo says, turning his phone toward us and showing some paparazzi photos of Harper and me at the burger shop.

"Oh my god, you two look so cute!" Stella says, clapping her hands excitedly.

The article's title reads "Who is Wes Holden's New Girl?" and is accompanied by a dozen other photos I didn't notice were taken. Upon scanning the article, I realize it's mostly speculation and locations, mentioning Harper's name and Ava's charity.

"Outlets are excited about this," Leo says quietly to himself, scrolling on his ever-present phone, and I'm glad he seems more on board now. "We can definitely use this. I see the rumblings from her ex, but we can clean that up quickly." Leo is scary good at his job, so seamless and effective, he can hide almost any scandal. "We can hold an auction for exclusive rights to the wedding photos and have the proceeds go to charity." I nod, happy the money will go somewhere good. "Do you think we can swing next weekend?"

My eyes go wide with the nearness, though I knew a *quickie wedding* would be close.

"You need a real wedding, ceremony, reception, and everything, so it doesn't seem like a stunt."

"I mean...if we have enough time to make it happen, I'm fine with next weekend," I say with a shrug that is much more casual than I feel. I'm playing it cool, like this is all just some fun game or another spur-of-the-moment decision I've made, but I'm excited for this, to tie

Harper to me for a while. She's always so closed off, that I can't wait to see what happens when I get past that.

"We all agree this is crazy, right?" Beckett, the most reasonable of all of us, asks.

"In this line of work?" Leo shakes his head but then pauses, staring straight at me. "But you have to keep it in your pants the whole time, Wes, however long we agree to."

I roll my eyes. "No shit."

For what might be the first time ever, Leo sets his phone aside and leans in, his full attention narrowing on me. Everyone takes note of this once-in-a-lifetime experience as Leo stares at me intently, like he's a parent who knows his kid is about to embarrass the fuck out of him.

"I'm serious. I'll be putting an infidelity clause in the contract both of you will sign, and it will be a huge issue if you break it."

What Leo doesn't understand is that I don't *want* to hook up with anyone. I want the woman who took my breath away when I met her two years ago, the one who has been endlessly playing through my mind ever since. It's why I suggested this and pushed for it. I saw an opening, and, as unconventional as it may be, I jumped on it. Being able to help her repair the reputation that asshat has given her and having a chance to divert attention from Stella and Riggs is just a bonus at this point.

"Personally, I think it's cool!" Reed says, and Beck rolls his eyes. "Wes's having a shotgun wedding just like Stella and Riggs. Maybe we can make it a thing. An Atlas Oaks tradition. Who do you think will be next, big guy? Me or you?" Beck glares at Reed, but he just smiles wider.

"I'm not having a fucking shotgun wedding," Beck says, and then they all start arguing about who is going to be married next, but I'm busy staring at the photo Harper sent me—the photo my *fiancée* sent me—to care much.

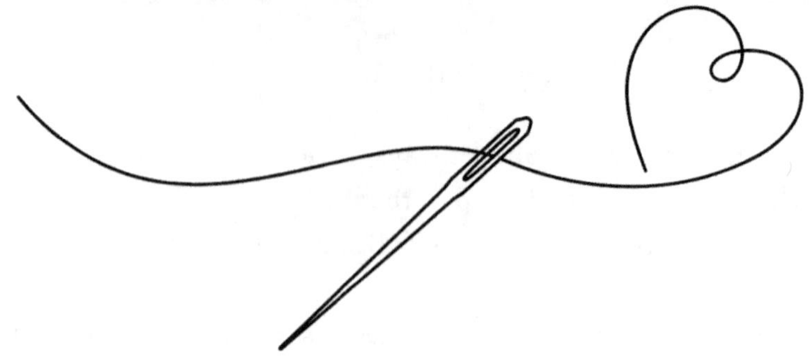

# NINE

## HARPER

"You guys look so cute here," Ava says, gasping as she scrolls on her phone while I fit the bridesmaid dress to Jules's body as she stands in Ava's living room.

Yes, a bridesmaid dress, because in less than a week, I'm having a not-quite-shotgun wedding to a rockstar to save my reputation, get some petty revenge on my ex, and help shift the focus from our friends.

The only requirement I had for this wedding was that my girls and I wear gowns made by me. With the short timeline, I went with simple, silky shift dresses for all of us with loose bows holding the nearly nonexistent back together.

It's exactly what I've always wanted. Elegant and simple. Luxurious, yet approachable.

"What?" I ask, pins between my teeth as I focus on not pricking my friend.

Ava hands her phone to Jules, who gasps much the same way Ava just did, piquing my interest even more.

"Oh my god, you do! How did they get these pictures already?" Jules asks, and I stand, putting the pins into the pillow at my wrist. I grab the phone from Ava's hands. Then I stare in shock at the photo on the tabloid website.

"Atlas Oaks Guitarist Reveals New Flame," the headline reads. Below that, there are side-by-side headshots of me and Wes, mine clearly pulled from my barebones website, his I've seen a few times in various magazines and social media posts. Beneath that is a candid shot of Wes and me at the burger place he took me to after we made our agreement, my head tipped back as I laugh in my way-too-fancy outfit, Wes lifting a fry to his mouth and looking at me with an expression I hadn't noticed before, a small smile on his lips.

The way he's gazing at me makes my belly flip and scream a million things that simply aren't true. Things that aren't something Wes Holden would think about me. But still, it sells the exact story we're trying to sell without even meaning to. He was made for this stealth fake relationship shit.

I wonder if he knew they were there taking photos, that our mission was already rolling, because I know *I* didn't think that was the case.

Quickly, my eyes move to the caption.

*Insider sources say Holden and Abbott have been dating for some time, laying to rest the rumors that she was chasing after her ex while he was having an affair with Clarissa Astor, heiress to the Astor fashion empire. Our sources also confirm Holden was at the police station when the gown designer was released two weeks ago after glittering Mr. Vaughn's lawn.*

*"The glitter was a fun joke that was taken too seriously," Leo Moretti, a representative for Holden's band, Atlas Oaks, told Fan Magazine. "That's the problem with the world these days: people are too quick to judge, too quick to look for the worst in people. Was it the most mature act? Of course not. But there are much bigger problems in our world today than whether or not someone is putting glitter on their ex's lawn."*

*The date was a part of a charity auction, where attendees told us Harper overbid on the auction item with fervency. "It was like she*

*didn't want anyone else to spend time with her man. It was so roman-*
*tic," one attendee told our team.*

*Customers and employees at the burger bar spoke to Fan Maga-*
*zine as well, telling us the couple seemed completely in love and*
*didn't seem to notice anyone around them. Reports say they were*
*laughing and holding hands the entire night, and now there are whis-*
*pers of wedding bells in the future.*

*We, for one, are happy to see Harper happy and even happier to see*
*yet another man of Atlas Oaks fall in love."*

"Wow," I whisper after reading the article. "Leo really is good at
his job." The article has everything I could ever have wished for:
putting rumors to rest, canceling out the bad press Clarissa has been
spreading by making it seem childish, planting a seed of history with
Wes and me, and, of course, making us seem like a real couple.

"Uh, Harp, I think the magazine could have just posted that
picture and nothing else, and it would have been a slam dunk," Ava
says, and I look at her with confusion.

"What?" I ask, my gaze bouncing from Ava to the phone and
then handing it back to her. She stares at the photo again, sighing
with joy. I roll my eyes when I realize what she was insinuating.
"You're insane. It's just good journalism, Ava. That's all."

"What do you think your first kiss is going to be like?" Jules asks,
and I freeze in place.

"What?"

"Well, I mean...eventually, you'll have to kiss. You're getting
married, after all."

I feel it building again, that all-consuming panic that has come in
waves since the arrest, though I can't quite pinpoint the source of it
this time.

I shake my head in disagreement. "No, we don't. Why would we
have to do any of that?"

Ava rolls her eyes, and Jules bites her lip.

"Jesus, Harp. What are you going to do when they say you can
kiss the bride? Put a hand out and shake on it? Plus, I'm sure there

will be situations over your fake marriage where you'll have to kiss him." Ava's face goes contemplative as she takes in me and my new panic. "You do know that, right?"

"I...I didn't really think about it if I'm being honest."

I grab the drink Jules made me and down the rest of it.

"Atta girl," Ava says, clapping, but I ignore her.

"I'm going to kiss him for the first time in front of fifty people." The panic builds even further with the mere idea of it.

"You should practice," Ava says, like it's some idea she *just* came up with, but I can almost guarantee she's been sitting on it for a second. The woman can't lie to save her soul.

"Practice?"

"It's actually not a bad idea," Jules says with a shrug. "That way, if and when you have to do it for a camera, it's not awkward."

"How does one practice kissing?" I ask, confused.

"Well, you see, you have two willing participants, both of whom have a set of lips," Ava starts, and I roll my eyes.

"You're so annoying," I groan.

"I think she's asking how, when her wedding is in less than a week and they don't exactly live together," Jules says.

"He's her *husband*," Ava says, throwing her hands in the air like it's obvious.

"Not for real!" I shout, suddenly feeling like I can't breathe. "And not yet! I can't kiss him for the first time in front of cameras, you guys. What if I'm terrible? What if I kiss him, and he goes, *oof, no thanks*, and calls it all off? That would be so embarrassing!" Ava lets out a snort, and Jules rolls her lips in, trying to fight a laugh. "I'm serious, you guys!"

With that, Ava stands and reaches for her keys. "Then let's go find Prince Charming."

"What?" I ask, confusion now added to my panic.

"Let's go to Wes's house, and you kiss him. Practice before the cameras."

"I can't—"

"Why not?" Jules asks, usually the voice of reason of the two. "It's better than worrying about it for an entire week." *She's right there*, I think. "Come on. Let's go," she says with a clap of her hands.

Before I even know what we're doing, we're moving out the door and into Ava's car, getting Wes's address from Jaime, and are on our way to my fiancé's house.

"Go!" Ava says, pushing me out the car door as we sit, parked in front of Wes' house. Jaime got us past the gated entrance, and now we're outside the McMansion, and I'm...panicking.

"This was a bad idea," I say, hoping it's not too late to run away. "We should—"

And then, because my life is what it is, the front light goes on.

And the front door opens up.

And my fiancé steps onto the front step.

"Harper?" he shouts across the lawn.

"Go!" Jules says. "If you run now, it'll be weird."

*You wanted to be spontaneous, Harper*, I tell myself as I move out of the car on autopilot, walking up the long path until I reach his front door.

"Harper. What are you doing here? Is everything okay?" Wes asks. He's wearing a white T-shirt that fits way too fucking well, it clinging to his chest like he just got done with a workout, with a pair of loose gray sweatpants to complete the look.

I look at him, then over at the car I just left, then step inside his house, closing the door because if this gets embarrassing, I don't want witnesses. He watches me with an amused smile as I stand in his foyer, focusing only on him before taking two steps, closing the gap between us to barely a foot.

"I think," I start, not bothering with a hello or explanation. I put my hands on my hips and try to approach this from a professional standpoint. "I think we need to kiss."

"Kiss?" he asks, a shocked expression on his face. Then there's a hint of a smile pulling at his lips, and I blush but continue on.

"Yes. If we're going to have to fake it for the cameras and whatnot, we'll have to make it seem real. I've seen those shows where they tear apart the body language of a couple, and I don't want to give anyone anything to dissect. I also very much do not want to do it for the first time on our wedding day in front of a lot of people."

"Yeah, I definitely don't want that either," he says, voice low and rumbly as he steps closer, a hand moving to the thin fabric at my waist. His wide hand burns there, but I force myself to stay focused.

"We're already trending, you know," I say. "On social media."

"Mmm, I saw that. The burger place photo of us is good." I wonder if he stumbled upon it, if he went looking, or if, like me, he has his friends sending it to him. He finishes closing the gap between us, and I'm forced to look up at him. His chin is tipped down as he smiles at me, his lips full and enticing.

*How did I never realize how tall he is?*

"So practicing kissing, huh?" Wes says, pulling me out of my reverie. "How does this work? Do I kiss you, or do you—"

I cut him off, afraid to overthink this any more than I am. I shift onto my toes, erasing the few inches needed to press my lips to his, and kiss Wes Holden, taking him completely off guard by the small gasp he lets out before his other hand goes to my jaw.

It's euphoric, his lips on mine. It's better than I could have ever imagined, and terrifyingly, it doesn't feel awkward at all. I like it all— the way his hand tightens on my lower back, the way he pulls me in against him, the way he takes over the kiss almost instantly. The way his lips part and how his tongue slides out to graze along my bottom lip.

I sigh, letting him in as his hand moves to the back of my head, using his fingers tangled in my hair to guide me where he wants me. He deepens the kiss, tasting me, nipping and sucking as he goes.

My hands move up, one looping around his neck, the other moving to his chest as he takes a step forward, pinning my back to the wall, and I groan, fingers tightening in the collar of his shirt to pull him closer.

My body is on fire, and I think the only way to put it out is to do *more*. To get more, taste more, have more. His skin on mine is the only thing that seems to soothe the ache taking over me. His hand on my waist moves down, grabbing a handful of my ass, and he groans loudly, pulling me closer to him, and I feel it then, his hard cock poking into my belly.

The man wants me, and not in a fake way at all.

It's a relief, considering how my body is pulsing with need right now, canceling out any and all common sense I should be feeling and—

My phone beeps with a new text in my pocket, my body tensing as another comes through, bringing me back down to reality.

And probably for the best, because I'm clearly too tired from a long day and out of my damn mind. Slowly, Wes breaks the kiss, leaving a few small kisses before leaning his forehead against mine, a smile playing on his lips.

"How was that for practicing?" he asks.

I step aside, moving away and wiping my hands down my dress, pulling my shoulders back and giving him a small nod.

"Good. Good. That was...that was good." I step back and put a hand out to him to shake, like this is some weird business transaction.

He stares at me for a moment before he laughs loudly, his head tilting back, and I have to fight the urge to laugh with him. Then he moves forward suddenly, his arm wrapping around my back in one move and tugging me close, looking down at me with that panty-dropping smile I worry I won't be able to resist.

"You're so into me, little wife."

"I so am not," I say, aghast. "I have to go." He just shrugs, stepping back and opening the door to let me leave, going with my insanity.

"I'll be here whenever you're ready to admit it."

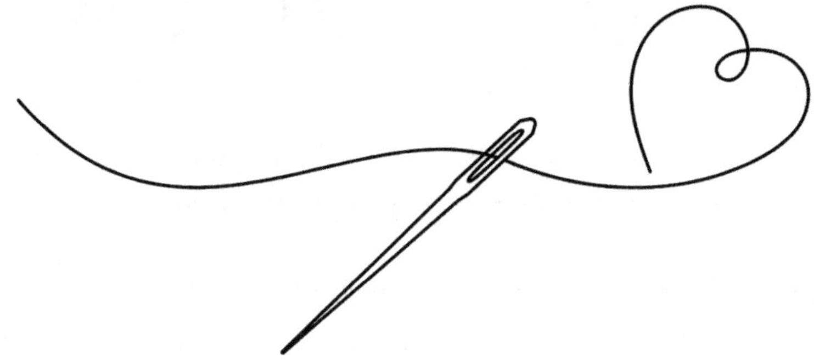

# TEN

## HARPER

Today is my wedding day.

I've had to repeat that sentence to myself over and over all day. None of it feels real, but as Ava brushes over my cheeks with blush once more, and I stare at the wedding dress hanging a few feet away, I know it's the truth.

"I can't believe you're doing this," Ava says with a chuckle, standing back to take in her handiwork, her hand resting on her very faint baby bump. Stella came in an hour ago, and they squealed together about having babies around the same time. Sophie, Nate's daughter and Jules's soon-to-be stepdaughter, smiled and giggled, asking when Jules would give her a sister, which only made her blush.

It was another vivid eye-opener. A reminder of how my friends are progressing with their lives and doing the "normal" steps, but here I am, starting over.

Or, somehow even worse, starting a completely fake relationship just to piss my ex off and save my friends from losing everything they've worked for.

*What was I thinking?* For the hundredth time today, the anxiety that's been living in my chest as of late tightens around my airways. When I said I was going to be more spontaneous, I don't know if *this* is what I meant.

"Do you think it's a bad idea?" I ask, as I look at Ava in the vanity mirror. I barely slept last night, though her master skills cover up any sign of that. This might not be a wedding for true love, but photos of it will be spread everywhere, and I don't need everyone on the earth to see me at my worst.

"No," she says quickly, applying a bit more blush onto the apples of my cheeks. "Not at all." I look to Jules, the slightly more reasonable one.

"Jules?" I ask. "Do *you* think this is a bad idea?"

She shakes her head confidently and smiles. "I think it will be good for you. I'm just bummed we won't get to see stupid fuckface Jeremy's face when he realizes you've married into rock royalty. Do you think he'll be able to listen to their music again without thinking of you?"

I think about that, knowing his entire running playlist is just Atlas Oaks and smile in bliss.

"God, that's truly amazing," Ava says with a giggle, fingers brushing over the gold W on a chain around my neck that Wes had delivered to our room this morning.

"And this is going to totally fix your media issues," Stella says gently. "I mean, Leo is a mastermind. I don't know how he does it, but he can spin absolutely everything to look good. I mean, when Riggins told everyone Willa's relationship with him was fake, he somehow spun it to make Willa *and* Riggs look good. No one even suspects it's a trend of hers, dating for PR."

"Yeah," I say with a smile. She's right, too. I've already gotten one of the clients who dropped me to reach out and apologize for believing what the media and Jeremy were spinning about me, on top of a few new inquiries.

If only I wasn't still completely artistically blocked, things would be almost perfect. Instead, every time I stare at a piece of paper to try and create something new, I hit a wall. I'm hoping once the stress of the wedding is over, my mind will clear up a bit, and I'll be back to normal.

Ava's brows furrow like she's noticing me mulling over something, and she opens her mouth to speak but is stopped when someone pops their head in.

"Are you all ready to line up?" the wedding coordinator asks, and we all look at each other and nod. We all stand while Jules grabs my bouquet and hers.

To make it seem less like a last-minute public relations setup, we are having a *real* wedding. In his planning, Leo went all out: a ceremony, the processional, professional photos, and a reception where only our closest of friends know the truth about what this marriage is. There are fifty or so people in attendance, but barely ten people know the truth. Everyone else thinks we're just so crazy in love, we don't want to wait.

"I'm nervous," I whisper as Ava grabs her own bridesmaid bouquet, and Jules hands me mine.

Ava shakes her head with a smile. "No way. You know what I say," she starts, but Jules continues the mantra Ava started years ago.

"Shoulders back."

"Tits out," I continue. and then Ava gives me a soft smile, her hand on my cheek.

"You were born for great things, Harper Abbott. Let's go start your forever."

When I agreed to go along with the ruse of marrying Wes, I didn't think much beyond the *yes* of it all. I definitely didn't consider what a wedding would look like if we were going to successfully bamboozle the press.

I didn't think I'd be in a gorgeous gown I made, the silk fabric grazing over my body, multiple strings of faux pearls draping along my back to keep it together.

I didn't expect an archway of cream roses, baby's breath, and eucalyptus to greet me as I made my way down a brick walkway littered with flowers Sophie threw down, as I walk on the arm of my father toward...

My soon-to-be *husband*.

And I sure as fuck didn't expect full-blown chills when I saw him standing at the end of the aisle in a well-fitting tux, his dark hair pushed back, a small smile on his lips as he watched me move toward him.

I *did* expect the photographer going crazy and Ava being emotional just because she's alive, a hopeless romantic, and pregnant.

But most of all, I didn't expect the way the world would fall away when Wes stepped forward, playing the part of the eager groom as he grabbed my hand once I handed off my bouquet to Jules, pulling me toward him at the altar. I definitely didn't expect the way his lips grazed my cheek in the most gentle press of a kiss or the way warmth ran through me when he whispered, *you look beautiful,* in the most sincere way.

The ceremony flew by as we recited traditional vows. Wes slid a heavy diamond-encrusted platinum wedding band onto my finger, and I returned the favor with a thick silver one.

And then it happens.

I'm staring at Wes, his hands moving to lift the lace veil over my face and behind my head, the only tradition I cared for, even if I regretted it halfway through hand sewing dozens upon dozens of tiny seed beads and gems onto the edges. His hands then move to my jaw, tipping my face up, and I take a small step closer, my body melding to his like magic.

"Spontaneous, yeah?" he whispers against my lips, and I smile as my hand lifts, resting along the back of his neck like it's the most natural thing in the world. Because, strangely enough, it feels that way: natural.

"Yeah," I whisper back, and then his warm lips are pressing to mine, a smile caught up in our first kiss like the jovial, goofy man genuinely can't keep it out, even in this moment.

His warm, soft lips move on mine, one hand slipping to my lower back to pull me in closer, touching my skin beneath the layer of pearls. His warm, calloused skin on mine soothes me, and I shift closer to him without meaning to.

I simply can't get close enough as the heat of him fills me, as my lips part, as he shifts my face with his hand just a bit to deepen the kiss. The room erupts in cheers, but I barely register it as he kisses me, long and deep and probably a bit much for an audience, but we're putting on a show, right?

The kiss finally slows, and then he breaks away before pressing his forehead to mine and smiling. That's when I feel it.

*Butterflies.*

But butterflies are dangerous.

Butterflies are big, fat liars, things that make you see possibilities when they are nowhere to be found.

I felt butterflies with Jeremy, and what that taught me was believing in butterflies gets you stuck in four-year relationships, waiting for a ship that will never sail.

I can't make any more mistakes like that in my life or my career. That's why I make a decision not based on spontaneity at all this time, but in self-protection and nothing else.

I will keep that wall up between Wes and me because even *stumbling* for my fake husband would spell total and complete disaster for everything: my friend group, my mental health, my career, my reputation, and based on those goddamned butterflies, my heart.

As we're introduced as Mr. and Mrs. Wes Holden and walk down the aisle to cheers and congratulations, I start making my plan on how to survive the next year without issues.

Step one?

Avoid my new husband at all costs.

I'm pretty successful in my mission to avoid and ignore Wes for the night whenever I can. Especially after we took what felt like thousands of photos together, his warm, calloused hands on my skin scrambling my brain each and every time.

Once we did the required entrance, I got away with the barest of pecks to my lips before I scurried off to speak to our guests.

I barely sit, spending most of the time on whatever side of the room Wes *isn't*, but my plans are foiled when the DJ gets on the microphone.

"And now, it's time for the couple's first dance as husband and wife!" he says, his voice booming through the room before guests clap and cheer, Ava's the loudest as she gives me a knowing, conniving look.

*I love my best friend, I love my best friend*, I remind myself as I glare at her, slowly making my way to the center of the dance floor where Wes is already waiting for me, a hand out like some prince ready to take me away.

Cheers get even louder when I reach Wes, taking his hand only for him to tug hard until I'm flush against his chest. The drinks I've had to calm my spiraling nerves make me a bit unsteady on my feet, and my hands shift to his shoulders to catch myself. I think for a moment we can keep this friendly, maybe middle school dance style, but Wes isn't having any of that. Instead, his arms wrap along my waist, his thumb grazing a stretch of bare skin, and I gasp at the feel of it against my will.

"Hello there, little wife," he whispers into my ear as my arms wrap around his neck awkwardly, despite our need to make this look convincing. Not just for cameras that will surely leak clips of our first dance to some tabloid. But because everyone else in this room, including my parents, who we flew out for the wedding and showed minimal surprise or even interest in my news, thinks we've been experiencing some low-key, whirlwind romance out of the eyes of the press and they're in the presence of true love.

His words send a shiver through me, my body unwittingly melting into his touch without my permission, making it all the more believable. But my pulse starts pounding as the opening strings of "At Last" by Etta James fill the room.

"You've been ignoring me all night," he whispers as he begins to sway my body easily in time with his, the cloyingly sweet tones of a song I've loved for as long as I can remember playing.

Over his shoulder, I glare at Ava, who definitely knows this is the song I wanted to one day dance to with my husband at my wedding.

"No, I haven't," I deny impulsively, even though we both know it's absolutely the truth.

"Now, now, Harper, let's not start this marriage off on a lie," he says, and I pull back to look at him, his eyes twinkling as he smiles.

"Isn't that exactly what we started this with?" I whisper.

"No," he says, then twirls me out and then back in smoothly, despite the drinks and heels that should make me clumsy. It's as if my body just instinctively knows how to work alongside his.

I hate it.

"We're both very much aware of how this is starting, so it's not a lie at all." I'm back against his chest when his hand moves up, tipping my chin to look at him. "I'd like to keep it that way."

I can't look away from him, from the earnest look in his eyes, even though a warning bell in the form of fluttering wings in my belly is going off.

"My only request is we never, ever lie to each other, Harper. That's all I ask of you. Can you agree to that?" His breath ghosts along my lips as he speaks, and it wouldn't take much at all for him to dip a bit, to press his full lips to mine again.

"Okay," I whisper without even meaning to, though the wide smile he gives me makes it worth it. It also desperately makes me want to *keep* that promise.

"So why have you been avoiding me?" he asks.

I bite my lip, and his thumb moves up, tugging it out from between my teeth before brushing over the bruised skin. The move sends bolts of desire through me, desire I should absolutely *not* be feeling.

"Because you're hot," I admit, deciding it's both the truth and the safest one to admit.

Wes's head tips back in a laugh, and it rumbles through me, forcing my own lips to tip up in response. A camera flashes somewhere, and subconsciously, I think I want a copy of that photo, of Wes's handsome face tipped back with laughter, my face most likely tipped up to look at him adoringly...

*I'm so fucked.*

"You've been avoiding me because you think I'm good-looking?" he asks, and I nod.

"You're gorgeous, and I find it annoying," I grumble under my breath, my typical filter completely annihilated from the chaotic day. Or maybe it's just Wes.

"I'm annoying because I'm hot?"

I shake my head. "No, it's annoying that you're hot. I think you're just annoying because you were born that way."

His smile widens, making him even hotter, and that confirms that he is, in fact, annoying as can be.

"Is it bad that your husband is hot?" he asks, our bodies still swaying in time to the music on the dance floor, everyone still watching us. But the way he's holding me, the way his attention is locked on me, it's almost like it's just us here, alone and bickering as we move together perfectly.

"Technically? No. I think most people tend to consider that a good thing. For me, however, very much so."

He leans forward, lips moving to my ear, his breath grazing there, sending an unwanted chill down my spine. "Why's that?" he asks. I open my mouth, but he speaks again. "Remember, no lying."

I sigh, recalculating my answer before laying it out there.

"Because this... this is *not* that," I say low, ignoring the sharp bite of disappointment in my stomach. "It can't be that."

A long beat passes, Wes swaying me to the music as he contemplates my response before he speaks. "It could be," he finally replies in almost a whisper, that hand on my bare back burning now in a different way.

His gaze meets mine, and for a moment, I consider some other universe where this is actually our first dance, the start of something beautiful.

Then a photographer takes our photo, and the flash shakes me out of my daydreams, promptly back into reality.

I am here to help sell a narrative for the band.

I am here to build my business, to get clients, and make myself slightly more bulletproof from people like Jeremy.

I am here to repair my reputation.

I am here to help make sure Stella gets the peaceful pregnancy she wants and deserves.

I am *not* here to flirt with the admittedly hot guitarist of Atlas Oaks.

I once let a man convince me we were perfect for each other while he bled me dry of creativity and destroyed my self-confidence. I have no place wrapping myself up in something like that once more.

I can't afford to lose myself more than I already have.

"It can't," I whisper, his eyes locked on mine.

With that, the song trails off, the small crowd clapping and cheering. I can pick out both Ava's loud hoot and Reed's whistle, the two basically the same person.

"We agreed to no lies," he whispers before stepping back, grabbing my hand, and bending to kiss the top of it like some gallant prince. My mind is reeling with his words, but still, I can't help but laugh at his antics, shaking my head.

He smiles back, wide and true, and in that moment, I realize my mission to keep my head and my heart completely separate over the next year might be a lot harder than I anticipated.

"We leave for our honeymoon in thirty minutes. You should probably say your goodbyes," he says, then walks off.

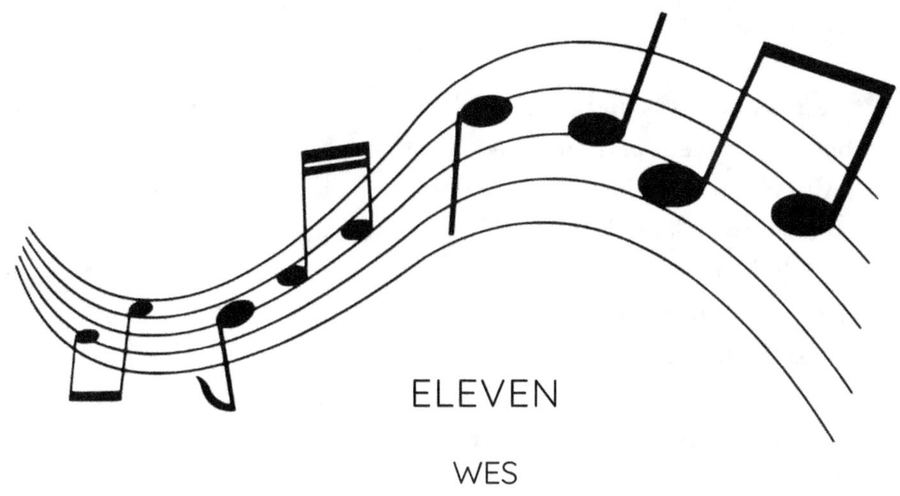

# ELEVEN

## WES

"First class," Harper says with a smile as she looks at the boarding pass I hand her. "Very fancy."

"Honestly, it's more of a safety thing. I'm not Riggins or Willa, so the recognition isn't crazy, but it happens," I say with a shrug. Although I'm grateful that I'm not as well-known of a face, because I've seen what happens when either of them goes out and does get recognized. Sometimes, it's nice to have the option to just *be*.

We move to the boarding gate in relative quiet, not uncomfortable but silent all the same. Harper is wearing in-ear headphones, and occasionally, she hums, then catches herself and stops.

"What are you listening to?" I finally ask an hour into our flight, leaning into Harper's space, unable to resist the temptation to ask. I want to be further in her space, all the way, but I'm terrified of scaring my wife off.

She doesn't lean away, but she does quickly move her phone, sliding it into her bag and avoiding my question. "Nothing."

If her frantic moves didn't give her away, the bright blush on her cheeks does, and I smile wide. "Oh, no, no, little wife, now you have to tell me," I say. "We agreed to no lies."

She rolls her eyes and sighs, and I think I'll have to push more, but then she answers, and I'm taken aback.

"'All At Once.'" She whispers the name of an Atlas Oaks song from the EP we released before we were even signed, and I sit back, unable to hide my smile.

"Oh damn, an old one."

She sighs and then reaches for her phone once more. "It's just a playlist I listen to," she explains. "When I'm anxious."

"Anxious?" I ask, suddenly worried about what is making her feel this way.

"I don't like flying," she admits. "So I distract myself to not think about the millions of ways this plane could come crashing down." She lets out a nervous laugh, and I immediately want to make her feel more at ease.

"What else is on your playlist?" I ask, hoping that maybe the conversation will divert her attention. And I'm desperate to know more about her, even if it's something as mundane as what's on the playlist she listens to when she's anxious.

"What?"

"What songs are on your playlist?" Before she can move away or change the subject, I reach for her phone, grabbing it before eagerly scrolling.

"Wes, this is kind of embarrassing—" she starts but stops when I pause my scrolling, open an app on my own phone, and hand it to her.

"This is mine."

"Yours?"

"My favorite songs. Or you can look at my other playlists. They're all labeled."

She sits there with my phone in her hands, looking from it to me and back again before giving in with a small sigh and starting to scroll. Almost instantly, she lets out a small laugh.

"Spice Girls? You have the Spice Girls on your playlist?"

"The start of girl power? Hell yeah. 'Wannabe' is amazing," I say, sitting back with a smile. The smile is mostly because I just learned my wife has *amazing* taste in music, similar to mine but with a bunch of bands and artists I've never heard of. She listens to songs from every genre, every decade, and it's fascinating to see how she pairs them into different playlists for different moods.

"Why did you give me this?" she asks, still holding my phone in her hands like it might bite her.

"Because turnabout is fair play, and I believe it's the best way to get to know someone. Their favorite songs, their taste in music. It's like a glimpse into who they are."

"I guess...I guess that makes sense," she concedes with a small smile, and I feel like I won. "I guess you can find out a lot about someone that way." Her eyes drift to the phone in her hands. "And I could use all the help I can get when it comes to you."

The irony is, if she just asked, I'd tell her everything. Anything.

I see an opening to learn more about my elusive wife and leap for it.

"Want to play a game?" I ask, reaching into the carry-on and pulling out some headphones.

Her brows furrow. "A game?"

I lift the armrest between us, and then pull her closer to me. She squeals with the movement but doesn't shift away, which I'm calling a win. Flipping open the case to my Bluetooth headphones, I slide one in one of my ears, then hand the other to her. She takes out her own headphones and puts mine in.

"Give me a topic," I say, and she looks at me confused. "We're playing musical memories."

"Musical memories?"

"Songs hold memories," I tell her, as if it's common sense, which, to me, it is. "The quickest way to get to know someone is by their memories." I half expect her to roll her eyes or shift away, but instead, she shifts closer, looking at me, then at my phone.

"Okay. How do we play?"

My blood races in my veins with the thrill of her proximity, and I smile at her eagerness to indulge me.

"One of us picks a topic—I'll go first to give you an example—and we both pick a song that reminds us of that. Then we listen to it."

"Oh...okay?" she says, still confused. It's a game Reed and I used to play all the time on the tour bus, and I'm excited to learn about my new wife in this new medium.

"Your first concert," I say and grab my phone, scrolling until I find "Good Vibrations" by the Beach Boys and pressing play.

"You saw the Beach Boys live?" she asks, incredulous.

"A bunch of times when I was a kid," I say with a nod. "My parents were big fans. I can sing most of their discography by heart."

She smiles at me, and my heart pounds a bit, like I'm a kid with my first crush.

"Very cool," she says gently.

"Your turn."

Her face screws up in an adorable look before she grabs my phone and scrolls until she hits "Bye Bye Bye" by *NSYNC. I laugh out loud.

"Your first concert was *NSYNC?" She nods. "That's kind of iconic."

She just shrugs without elaborating and eagerly says, "My turn now?"

I smile back and give her the phone, moving along with our little game.

"Okay, a song that reminds you of your childhood summers," she says, tapping on my phone a few times before the opening strains of a familiar song fill my ears. "American Pie" by Don McLean.

"That feels like a cop-out," I say with a laugh.

"I have this memory of my parents throwing a Fourth of July party when I was, I don't know, four? Five? And this song played, and we all sang it. The grown-ups were definitely a little tipsy and goofing around, and we all had sparklers. I was on my uncle's shoulders, and they were all singing loudly and…I don't know. It just reminds me of summer."

I smile at her, loving this small insight into her life.

"Are you close with your family?"

She shakes her head. "My parents got divorced soon after that summer, so it's even more bittersweet of a memory, I guess. It was probably the last time they were together. They're good parents, but I'm pretty sure I was a *save-the-marriage* baby. Once I was out of high school, I think they were relieved to be rid of the responsibility of raising me." She shrugs like it's no big deal. "It's probably why I don't want kids. I'm sure a therapist would have a field day with that."

"You don't want kids?" I ask, not judging, but because I've seen how good she is with Jules's stepdaughter.

She shakes her head. "I'd much rather travel and live my life. I love kids, don't get me wrong, but I don't want one of my own." She bites her lip before looking at me, and I force myself not to make too big of a deal, to tell her we're on the same page with this too, something I don't find often. I love kids, but I've never felt the urge to have one of my own. I'm more than fulfilled with my friends, my chosen family, and my career. More and more, Harper is proving we're a perfect match. "What about you?"

I shake my head, playing it casually. "Not for me."

She nods, accepting my answer without further question, then silence falls between us. I reach over, grabbing the phone, pulling up a song, and showing it to her.

"'We Found Love'?" she asks, confused.

"It was playing the night we met."

She smiles, her eyes wide in surprise. "Really?" I nod. "How do you remember that?"

I shrug, then lie. "Music is my job."

She takes me in, reading me, and I think she's not going to let it go before she reaches for the phone.

"My turn, give me a prompt," she says, breaking the moment, and I hand it to her, slightly relieved she didn't dig more. We continue like that, passing the phone back and forth, and slowly, I watch her melt, her discomfort and self-consciousness drift off, if only temporarily, and I make my choice.

It's not a hard one, and it's not one that I hadn't already been pondering since I met her, but that flight to our honeymoon cements it for me.

I'm going to make Harper Holden mine in a permanent way.

Now I just need to convince her of it.

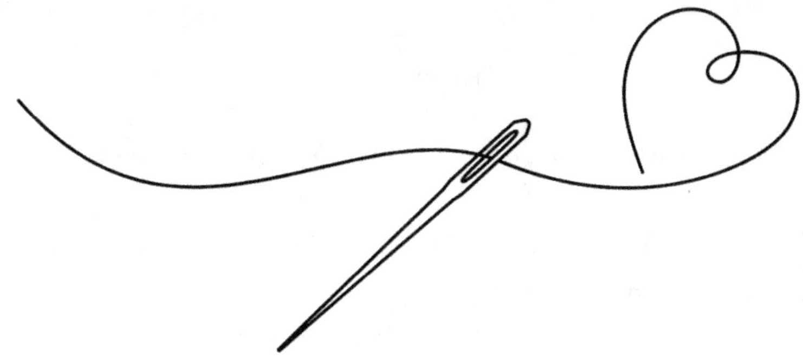

# TWELVE

## HARPER

"One bed," I say as we walk into the honeymoon suite of the exclusive hotel we're staying at. It's one of those fancy all-inclusive resorts I could only daydream about staying in on my own, and despite myself, I'm looking forward to the next few days in luxury.

Except there's only one damned bed. God, Ava would fucking love this, like a scene out of one of the books she reads.

"Our marital bed," Wes says deadpan, and my eyes go wide as I whip my head in his direction, panicking. I know we're married and all, but it's not *that* kind of married. I didn't think I'd be sharing a bed with a near stranger, much less anything...more.

"I'm joking, I'm joking, Harp. I'm staying on the couch, you're getting the bed. We just needed to book this and make it look real, just in case there are any leaks," he says with a small laugh.

His response should be reassuring, yet somehow, I hate the idea of him sleeping on the couch more than the idea of sleeping in the same bed with him.

*But do you really hate the idea of that, Harper?* that pesky voice in my head asks.

"No, no," I say. "That's not necessary. You don't have to sleep on the couch."

He shakes his head ardently. "Harper, I'm not making you share a bed. I'm sleeping on the couch."

"Then we'll make it work fairly. We can switch on and off. You take it tonight. Tomorrow, I get the couch."

"No," he says bluntly.

"Excuse me?"

"No. I'm not letting you sleep on the couch," he says like it's not up for discussion, putting his duffel bag onto a table and unzipping it.

"Wes, don't be ridiculous—"

"I have manners, Harper. I'll sleep on the couch."

"I can't in good conscience let you do that," I say, turning to him with my arms folded across my chest. "I'm fine sleeping on the couch. We can take turns, it's fair." He stops what he's doing, looking at me with tired eyes. We both took short naps on the plane ride, but considering it's officially tomorrow in the Bahamas and yesterday was possibly the world's longest day, we're both exhausted.

"My father would kill me if he found out I was making a woman sleep on the couch, fake wife or not."

"Do your parents know? About this being...?" I ask because we never actually talked about *who* would know the truth. I didn't tell my parents, but the truth is, they weren't going to ask questions, so it was easier that way.

He shakes his head. "No, I just told them it was a whim."

"They didn't question it?" I ask, wondering if his relationship with his parents is similar to mine. He shakes his head.

"Hell no. My parents married after knowing each other for a month. They don't have a single foot to stand on between the two of them."

"A month!" I say with a laugh. "Was it a shotgun wedding?"

He shakes his head with a wide smile. "No, my parents are hopeless romantics. They say it was love at first sight."

"And they're still in love?" I ask, somewhat disbelieving. He nods fervently.

"Incredibly."

"Is that what you're waiting for?" I ask, my stomach churning with a hint of guilt and something else I can't—or maybe don't want to—pinpoint. "To find your one true love and settle down?" He stares at me for long moments, which starts to make me feel uncomfortable. "You know, when you get the chance?"

Finally, he nods. "Yeah. When I get the chance." Another heavy beat passes before he claps his hands. "All right, enough talking about my parents on our honeymoon. Do you want to go down to the pool? I think Leo has tipped some people off to come take shots while we're down there, and I could use a nap by the water."

My eyes go wide at the thought, the reminder of the purpose of this "honeymoon," but I straighten my shoulders and nod.

No matter how uncomfortable it makes me, I have to remember *why* I'm here. It's not to flirt with a hot rockstar, that's for sure.

"Yeah, give me five," I say as confidently as I can before stepping back, moving to my bag to find whatever swimsuit Ava packed me.

"Are you almost ready to go down?" Wes asks from outside the bathroom twenty minutes later.

I slathered sunscreen all over, tied my copper hair up into a high ponytail, and slicked on some basic makeup in an effort to not look like a disaster for the paparazzi. Now I'm standing in front of a mirror, fiddling with the thin strings of my bridal white bikini, knowing damn well Ava picked the tiniest thing she could find.

I don't have any issues with my body, something that is a bit of an abnormality in the fashion industry, but I love it. She's got curves and dips I love and does just about everything I ask of her with minimal complaints. I've never been self-conscious about how I look or anything like that, which is why, on any other day, this tiny bikini wouldn't bother me at all.

But now *Wes* is about to see my body. Wes, who has probably spent time with some of the most gorgeous women in the world. Wes, who is now my *husband*. Wes, who is going to act blissfully in love with me *while* I wear this tiny bikini.

> You picked this out, didn't you, Ava?

I send the text into our group chat along with a photo of myself in the bikini, and Ava replies almost instantly.

> AVA
>
> Jesus, Harp, give us a warning when you send the NSFW content!

> It's a bikini.

> That I think you picked out.

> AVA
>
> But on you, it's almost indecent. I was going for hot new bride/possibly seduce your new rockstar husband.
>
> And honestly, I'd like a huge round of applause because fuck, did I nail it.

She sends me a gif of someone patting herself on the back, and I roll my eyes.

> Did you have to pick the tiniest one possible?

> AVA
>
> Yes.
>
> You're hot. Your husband is hot. Once you get your head out of your ass, you can be hot together. So yeah, it's a requirement.

I don't even know how to reply to that, something I get a pass on when Jules replies before I have to.

JULES

You look gorgeous, Harper!

How was the flight there?

Leave it to Jules to bring things down to sanity.

Good, we're going down to the pool now. I'm just wishing I had a one-piece. Or a scuba suit.

JULES

If you've got it, flaunt it, babe, and you most definitely have it. Have some fun!

AVA

LET yourself have some fun.

I won't lie about how that last text hits a little too close to my recent reality because they know better than anyone, it's not that I don't have endless opportunities to enjoy myself; it's that I'm always too worried about consequences and image and how people will take things to *let* myself have fun.

*But where has that gotten you?* That pesky fucking voice whispers again.

I'm putting on a cover-up.

I reach for the still pretty skimpy cover-up, glad that even though it dips to display my ample cleavage, it covers my ass for the most part. I look at myself in the mirror and sigh at the coverage, ready to head out. Or at least, as ready as I'm going to be.

AVA

You're a party pooper.

I roll my eyes at my friends, slipping my phone into my bag and taking a deep breath before I step out into the hotel.

"Are you going to wear that all day?" Wes asks an hour later, tipping his chin to the cover-up I'm still wearing. If I'm being honest, I'm absolutely sweating in this, the sun as strong as can be, but it could also just be Wes's presence. Wes, who did not hesitate for a second to take off his baggy tank when we got to the pool. Wes, who I've been using extraordinary strength not to stare at ever since.

But other than that, it's been relatively fine.

We found a spot with an umbrella, laying out our towels and setting my bag to the side before I grabbed some book Ava's been begging me to read and getting lost. Wes put on a pair of headphones, his hands making twitching movements every so often, confusingly switching from what I think is air guitar to drums on occasion. Not that I've been watching, of course.

"I feel like everyone is watching us," I say quietly, looking around the pool. Occasionally, I'll catch someone lifting a phone in our direction or see someone who is *clearly* a paparazzi dressed as a lounger take a photo with a professional camera.

"Then at least look comfortable," he says, sitting up and turning toward me before grabbing my wrist and tugging.

I follow his lead, putting my back to who I'm *sure* is a photographer, and lowering my voice. "What?"

"Harper, baby, you're sweating," he says with a gentle smile. "It's obvious to everyone around."

*Harper, baby.* The words wrap around me, making me shiver and feel safe all the same.

"Really?"

"Yes. Take it off. Take it off, and we'll take a dip, then you can

take your nap and put a towel over your face so you can ignore them."
It...it makes sense. "One photo op and they'll kind of disappear."

"Really?" I ask again, feeling like a parrot.

He nods, and I sigh because the towel material of my cover-up is actually making me feel like I might sweat out every ounce of fluid in my body. Slowly and nervously, I cross my arms to my waist, pulling the fabric until it's up and over my head, putting the clothing into my bag.

Wes gives me a wide smile, his eyes never faltering from mine, which, oddly, feels comforting, before his hand reaches out, twining his fingers with mine. He stands, and I follow, his fingers squeezing around mine as we move to the sloping entrance of the pool. We move through the water slowly until we're against the side of the pool, the water up to Wes's waist and my ribs.

I can't fight the urge to look around, feeling as if eyes are still on me. The feeling is confirmed when more than one camera is lifted to snap at us. From what I understand, this wouldn't be happening under normal circumstances, but since Wes's team are the ones who dropped the tip, we're letting them get whatever shots they want.

That's the whole point, after all.

"Ignore them," he says low.

"What?"

"The paparazzi. The cameras. Just ignore them."

I give him a deadpan glare.

"Uh, I'm in the tiniest bikini known to man, thanks to my best friend, and people are taking photos of me that will probably be in grocery store tabloids in a week. I can't ignore them. This is all very...new to me."

"It gets easier, but whenever you need me to, I'll hide you," he says, his face and his words earnest before he surprises me by showing me. His arm moves out, wrapping around my waist and tugging me into him, my front pressed to his bare chest, his warmth on my skin. His hand moves to brush through my hair like this is normal, and slowly, I let myself relax and ignore the rest of the world, if only for a moment.

"Next week, mark my words, there will be a 'Who's the New It Girl' article published in *Fans Weekly* about you. I'll make sure Leo lets the press know where to find your designs. People will be clamoring for whatever you're willing to share with them," Wes says a few minutes later, still in the same, shockingly comfortable position. "Whatever bullshit Jeremy is spinning will be forgotten. The press cycle works like that. But," he says, so low, I almost feel it more than hear it. "Most of all, I'm excited for everyone to know you're off the market."

My breathing falters, and for a moment, I genuinely forget about the paparazzi and the cameras and the eyes for a moment.

"That blush of yours is so fucking pretty." The words come out so quietly, as if they're for my ears only. His hand moves, cupping my chin and jaw, a rough thumb grazing over my bottom lip as I stare at him wide-eyed. "And you're so fucking mine."

"Wes, we're not—" I start, but he cuts me off quickly.

"Don't say it," he whispers. "Not here, not now." His arm around my waist tightens, pulling me closer until his face is just inches from mine, and a rush of understanding comes over me.

The cameras.

He's doing this to give them their pound of flesh so we can move on with the rest of our day in relative peace.

Still, I can't help but feel giddy at this man, this utter rockstar, giving me this kind of attention. I smile before giving him a small nod. He returns it before pressing his lips to my forehead, and we spend just a few more minutes in the pool before moving back to our chairs, where, as suggested, I put a towel over my face.

But I don't sleep, despite how much I need it.

No, all I can think about is how confusingly delicious it felt to be in Wes Holden's arms and for him to call me *his*.

We head back from the pool at four, and Wes gives me plenty of alone time in the bedroom to get ready, which I'm wildly grateful for. Too much time with this man feels dangerous, like something I can't afford to not keep my guard up with.

I'm also grateful that this honeymoon suite is huge, with a kitchen and living area set away from the bedroom, so I'm free to start over-thinking again as I get ready for dinner together.

Dinner is more paparazzi photos, which Wes promises me isn't actually usually this intrusive or obvious, but Leo wants to make sure they get good photos and lots of them to share with all of the tabloids.

By the time we make it up the stairs, I hide away in the bathroom to take my makeup off and put on my pajamas, preparing myself for what I have to do next.

The reality is, I cannot in good conscience let Wes, the man who is doing me what feels like the biggest favor known to man, sleep on a fucking couch at a luxury resort. It's simple manners, nothing more.

With one last look in the mirror, I nod to myself, take a deep breath, and open the door, stepping into the main room. Wes is already sitting up on his couch bed, and I roll my eyes before walking over to him and grabbing his pillow.

"Harper—" he starts, but I shake my head, tossing the pillow back on the gigantic bed, and turn to him.

"I can't in good conscience let you sleep on a couch, Wes."

"I'm not sleeping in that bed with you," he says, arms crossing on his chest.

I mimic the move and give him a glare. "Then sleep on it without me."

"I'm not doing that either. I'm not letting my *wife* sleep on a *couch.*"

"And I'm not letting my *husband* sleep on a couch," I counter, trying to show him what an idiot he's being. "If you sleep on the couch, I'll sleep on the floor. And I really, really don't want to sleep on a hotel floor, no matter how nice of a hotel it is."

He glares at me like I won't do it, so once more, I roll my eyes, grab a pillow off the bed, and place it on the floor.

With a grumble, Wes bends down, grabbing the pillow and tossing it on the bed again. "You're so stubborn," he says, but I just roll my eyes again.

"Are you surprised?" I'm best friends with Ava fucking Wilde. He should have known what he was getting into with me. "Come on. Get in the bed, Wes," I say with a sigh, because suddenly, the chaos of the weekend is getting to me, and I'm hit with the exhaustion of the day.

"No."

"Jesus, are *you* always this stubborn?" I ask with a glare.

"With pretty people pleasers? Yes."

I think about arguing about not being a people pleaser, but we all know that's of no use.

"What about with your wife?" I wiggle my ring finger adorned with my huge, sparkly wedding and engagement ring, and he smiles.

"Also yes. Even if I should probably play it safe so I can get past her walls without scaring her off."

"I don't have walls up," I say.

Wes lets out a deep laugh that makes me crack a smile, and he shakes his head. "Even you know that's not true, Harper." He steps closer, getting into my space, not close enough that we're touching, but close enough that my body feels that pull to his that I absolutely need to ignore.

Kissing Wes is something else. All-consuming and amazing and breathtaking and brain scrambling, which is exactly why it absolutely cannot happen again.

If I want to make it out of this marriage in one piece, my dignity, my heart, and my reputation intact, I need to play this smart. I may have jumped into this on a whim, but I can't continue that way.

That's how I fucked up with Jeremy, focusing on my wants and *could-bes* instead of the clear-as-day evidence in front of me. And the evidence here is that this is a marriage of convenience that will end in a year.

Nothing more, nothing less.

I step back, sitting on the edge of the bed and sighing. "Wes, please. If you don't sleep in the bed, I'll sleep on the floor to prove a point, and we'll both be miserable. I'll put a pillow barrier between us, but I promise, I'm going to stay on my side. I can't even *touch* another person while I'm sleeping, or I wake up," I say.

He looks at me, confused. "Really?"

"Really. So you can sleep tight knowing that I won't make it awkward or anything."

He stares at me for long moments, assessing the truth in my statement before finally nodding. "Okay," he says, then takes a step toward the bathroom. "But if you're uncomfortable at all, tell me, and I'm on the couch. No hard feelings."

"Deal," I say, plugging my phone in and moving to the side of the massive bed I've deemed as mine due to its closer proximity to the bathroom.

By the time Wes gets back and turns out the one remaining light, I'm pretending I'm already fast asleep, not eager to chat in the dark while we're lying in bed together.

But lo and behold, when I wake incredibly rested, the sound of waves crashing and the bright Caribbean sun leaking in through the blinds, I'm lying on Wes Holden's bare chest, his arm wrapped around my waist.

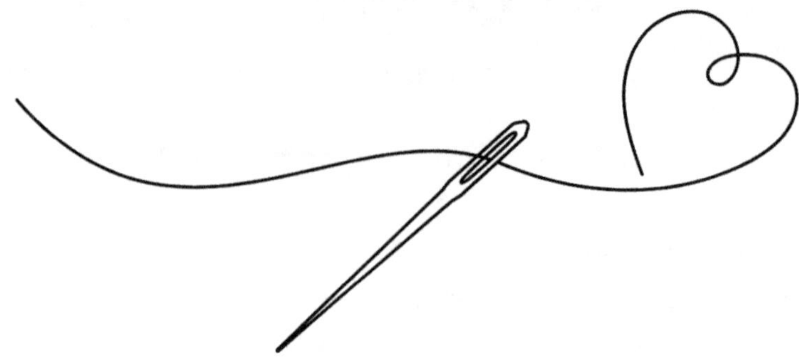

# THIRTEEN

## HARPER

The first two nights of our makeshift honeymoon, I sleep wonderfully, despite having Wes in bed with me, despite waking up wrapped around him each morning. I'm grateful that I seem to wake before him and am able to untangle myself before he notices, because I would be absolutely *mortified* if he realized I clung to him while we slept. It's strange, since for as long as I can remember, I couldn't even start to fall asleep if someone was in bed with me. It's why Jeremy and I slept in separate beds when we lived together. I tried for a week to sleep in his bed, but I became so sleep deprived, I couldn't trust myself to drive a car.

But two nights with Wes, and I've gotten the best sleep I ever have.

I am so totally fucked.

Wes has made it clear he would be just fine if we made things a little more *realistic* during our time together, but I know that would be a recipe for disaster, something I can't even let my mind wander to.

So I've done my best to stay clear of him, to hide away in my room when I can, and only talk to him when completely necessary.

Unfortunately, when I shuffled from the bedroom where I woke alone, to get a cup of coffee, I forgot about this plan, resulting in me standing next to the coffee maker waiting for my cup when Wes walks out of the bathroom in a pair of shorts, sneakers, and no shirt.

"Good morning, little wife," he says with a wide smile.

I simply stare at him. At his toned and tanned bare chest, at his messy hair, at his dimple that's begging for my fingers to graze it.

"Harper?" he asks, brows furrowed just a bit, but that smile is still playing on his lips all the same.

"I, uh...coffee," I say, stuttering like an idiot and gesturing at the machine now pouring dark liquid into a mug.

His grin spreads wider as he takes a step closer to me, reaching for a bottle of water on the counter and taking a sip.

"God, you're fucking cute in the morning before you've had coffee," he says, and then, like it's an impulse he can't avoid, he pulls me into him, pressing his lips to my forehead quick and hard. He holds it there for a moment, and I let my body relax into him, into his hold and the warmth of him, before he breaks it, stepping back. "I'm going for my run. Do you wanna go to the pool later?" I stare open-mouthed as I try and put pieces together to make words out of what he just said. "Got it. We'll play it by ear. Later, baby."

Then he's stepping back and moving toward the door, leaving me frozen.

When I hear the door click, it knocks me out of my stupor, and without even stopping to get the coffee I came out for, I move for the stairs and my bedroom, tapping my phone screen as I go.

I need reinforcements, stat.

"Hey, babe, how's married life?" Ava asks as she answers her FaceTime call.

"I'm spiraling, where's Jules?" I say as I reach the landing and move toward the bedroom.

"What?"

"I need Jules to get on the call so we can chat because I'm spiraling and I don't want to repeat myself."

"Who's spiraling?" Jules asks, motherly concern on her face as she takes us in, instantly pinning the panic on me. "Harp, what happened? I haven't seen anything crazy in the tabloids. Did something leak?"

"No. Nothing happened that I know of. I'm just having a meltdown," I say, closing the bedroom door and flopping on my bed.

"Mm, so if you're spiraling with nothing happening, I think that's a medical problem," Ava says.

"Anxiety is totally normal," Jules adds. "You've been going through a lot."

"I don't have anxiety," I say, then roll my eyes when my friends give me a *be serious* look. "I mean, not some unnamed, undisclosed anxiety. I'm just spiraling because Wes was shirtless this morning and he kissed me on the forehead like it was *normal* and..." I pause, taking a deep breath that is very much needed before finishing. "You guys, I think my husband really likes me," I say with the utmost seriousness, and Ava snorts out a laugh.

"I'm sorry?" she asks.

"I thought that was like, a prerequisite?" Jules asks. Her phone is set up somewhere in the kitchen, and distantly I can hear Nate's daughter singing some song she made up to herself.

"Yeah, I mean, if you got married because you dated and did the whole rigmarole of a relationship. Less so if you got married because he's in your ex's favorite band and it sounded like a good idea at the time."

"Hey, Harp, I hate to tell you this because you seem a bit frazzled as is, but I think your husband has liked you for, like, a long time," Jules says, carefully.

"We've *been* saying that," Ava says.

"What do you mean?" I ask, confused.

"I'm not having this conversation again. He's doing me a *favor*, you guys. That's all."

"Ah, yes, I always give the quick favor of *matrimony* to my acquaintances," Ava says.

I shake my head, not wanting to get into this. "I just need to...stop thinking about him in any way other than platonic." Silence takes over the call before Ava sighs and sits back.

"You should fuck him," Ava says, and I jolt back at the suggestion.

"*What?*"

"Oh, you totally should," Jules says, her voice going low with Sophie somewhere in the vicinity. "*You know.*"

"I just said I need to only think about him platonically. Why on Earth would I fuck him?"

"Get him out of your system and all," Ava explains with a shrug as if it's common sense.

I think about it for a moment, seeing the value in it, but then quickly shake my head before she can get any grand ideas. "No. No! You're insane. That would just... complicate things."

"Then simplify it," Jules says. "Have you thought about him while you..." The words trail off, and she blushes, but I don't understand what she's trying to say.

"While I what?"

"While you fuck yourself. Vibrator, fingers, whatever. Have you used him as your spank bank material?" Ava asks bluntly.

"I truly wonder how on earth you were crowned Miss Americana," I ask, aghast.

"I was a personality win," she boasts with a smile. "So, have you?"

"No! Of course, I haven't! We're staying in a hotel room together!"

"He's not there right now, obviously, with you screaming about being in love with him and whatnot," she says. My eyes widen, and I open my mouth to argue, but she keeps talking. "Maybe you should try. Maybe that will reset something in your brain. We packed you a vibrator."

"You what?"

"It's in the side pocket on the inside, left side," Jules says. "We thought it would be good for an emergency."

"And this is definitely an emergency," Ava says.

"You guys are insane. Why would I—" A loud beep comes from Ava's side of the call, and she curses.

"Fuck, I gotta go. I think I just burned cookies. Again. Love you, Harp. Go finger yourself and think about that hot rockstar!" she says, then hits end before I can argue.

"I hate to say this, but I have to go, too. I gotta take Sophie to the dentist," Jules says.

"And then to the toy store!" Sophie shouts from the background.

"I don't think so, miss, not with that room looking the way it does."

"But—" Sophie starts to argue, but Jules gives her *mom eyes,* and she stops. I hear her feet pound on the floor before Jules smiles and looks back at me.

"Okay, I really do have to go. But you know, Ava might be right. Just...give it a try. Or, better yet, give *him* a try. You know, if this was a movie—"

"Yeah, yeah, yeah. Go take your kid to the dentist," I grumble, but then smile when I watch her face light up the way it always does when anyone calls Sophie *hers.*

"Love you, Harper."

"Love you, Jules," I say, then she ends the call, leaving me alone with my thoughts. I toss my phone and flop back on the big bed with a sigh. Nonetheless, my mind travels to all of the gentle touches and heated looks he's given me.

*Fuck it.*

Maybe there's some truth to working him out of my system, to *scratching the itch.* Maybe I'm just wildly sexually frustrated. It's been an eternity since I had sex last, and I can't even remember the last time I made myself come. Plus, Wes usually takes about an hour on his run, and it's barely been fifteen minutes since he left. I sigh, dig in my bag, and find the purple vibrator right where Jules said it would be, then climb back in the bed.

This is so stupid.

Why do I feel nervous? I'm just going to...make myself come really quick and then move on with my life. Right? Right. And it has absolutely *nothing* to do with my new husband. None at all.

With that, I shift my pajama pants off, letting them and my underwear ball up at the foot of the bed before slowly, I part my legs. My hand shifts down my belly gently, and I force my mind to envision *generic* hands, not tattooed and calloused ones scraping along my soft skin. When I reach my center, I sigh, my legs widening further as I close my eyes and circle my clit gently.

*God, that feels good.* It's been far too long.

Yes, this is *exactly* what I need. I'm just sexually frustrated, is all. My finger slides down to my entrance, gathering wetness that's already there and sliding it up over my sensitive bundle of nerves once more, my hips bucking as I tease myself. I bet that's what Wes would do. He loves messing with me, teasing me, and I don't think that would be any different in bed.

*But this is not about Wes,* I remind myself. This is a fictional, fake man.

I sigh, sliding down again and slipping a finger into myself, pressing up to graze my G-spot, a small mewl leaving my lips as I slide out and add another. My free hand moves up and under my shirt, pushing the thin sleep bra aside and pinching my nipple, my breath catching as my mind replaces my fingers with Wes's calloused ones, my tight grip on restraint already demolished.

A groan leaves my lips, pleasure blooming quickly at the mere *idea* of his touch, of his hands on my body as my fingers roam back to my clit, my pussy already wet from the mere idea of this fantasy.

He would touch me like this, I know. Slow and teasing, taunting and absolutely soul-shaking. I picture it as I slide from my center to my clit again, tweaking it before deciding I need more, reaching over and grabbing the thick vibrator and turning it on.

I slide it along my slit, wetting the thick head and wondering what Wes would feel like between my legs. He's so fucking tall, so broad, his hands big and spanning. I know to my bones he'd be big, that he would stretch and fill me. I slide the vibrator up, moaning loudly now as it touches my clit, the sensation too much as I begin to pant, my hips moving up.

I could come just like this, a gentle touch on my clit and the mere *idea* of Wes Holden, but I want more.

I want to get him out of my system, to come hard and ease the ache in my belly and in my chest.

I move down until the head of the vibrator notches at my opening, a small moan escaping my lips at the stretch as I start to slide it in. Pleasure bubbles as I slide it out and then in again, each time moving another inch deeper, the vibrations and the stretch almost too much to handle as I picture my husband hovering over me, hands on the bed at either side of my head, his messy hair falling forward. I bet he would kiss me as he slides in, taking my breath away in more than one way, and I moan again, this time louder ,as I slide it all the way, the thick silicone stretching me.

I haven't made myself come in some time, not because I was getting it good or regularly from Jeremy, but because I just...didn't feel the need. I have never been a sexual person, thinking of sex and orgasms as just another check mark on my life task list rather than something one does strictly for pleasure.

But after spending so much time with Wes, the man whose every smile, every graze of his fingers on mine makes my entire body ignite, I feel like if I don't sate this need, I'll do something really freaking stupid.

Like open my heart for him when I just need to get off. And honestly, I don't have room in my life for *another* impulsive decision.

Instead, I scratch the itch on my own, sliding the vibrator in and out, my other hand moving to make gentle circles around my sensitive clit, reminding myself I'm doing this for *me*. Not for anyone else.

But as I pick up speed, the vibrator hitting spots inside me that have gone untouched for some time, I find my hips bucking, a low word falling from my lips with a single breath.

*Wes.*

My mind takes on a life of its own, picturing him slamming between my legs, stretching my hips wide to give himself room. His hands holding my knees open with a pinch of pain that adds to the pleasure, hovering over me, sweat glistening on his face as he fucks me hard.

I don't think he would be soft and gentle, but all-consuming and life-changing.

My mind pictures the way his hair would fall into his face, the way his eyes would lock on mine, capturing every moan, every blissful moment that crossed my face and categorizing it for future use the way he seems to do.

My hand moves up as I fuck myself, pinching and rolling my nipple hard the way I'd want Wes to, pulling it and wishing his calloused fingers were there instead of my soft ones. The pleasure builds in my belly as my breaths become heavy, as my whimpers become straight-up moans, and my mind is completely lost to reality.

*"God, look at my little wife taking my cock so well,"* he'd say, *sliding in deep.*

"Oh god," I groan, the vibrator not enough, not filling me the way I know he would.

*"That's it, Harper. God, be loud for me, yeah? A fucking sight you are, writhing on my bed for me, for my cock. Do you want me to come inside of you?"* I never let Jeremy do that, always insisting on a condom despite my being on birth control when we had our once-a-month fuck.

"God, yes. Fuck." I'd want him to fill me, to have him leaking out of me long after, a reminder of whose I am.

*"Fuck, I'm going to fill you, Harper. Come around my cock and take me with you,"* he'd groan, and I'd obey, unable to do anything but.

"Wes!" I moan in my fantasy and in reality, my hips bucking as I come undone with a low groan, sliding the vibrator between my legs once, twice, three times more as the aftershocks die down.

Laying there, my hand between my legs, sliding the vibrator out of me, and I mewl as I do, over-sensitized and still on edge as I turn it off.

"Fuck," I grumble to myself, hating that despite my best efforts, I imagined Wes, and I still feel that burning desire in me.

I am so fucked.

So *totally* fucked.

The only option for a modicum of sanity is to avoid him from here on out. To keep things so professional, it hurts, because anything more could be catastrophic in more ways than one.

Placing the vibrator on the side table to clean it after I get dressed, I shift off the bed and grab a pair of sweatpants, sliding them up my legs. I'll put on real clothes in a bit, but I think I'll go get my coffee finally and maybe take a shower before—

"Harper?" a deep voice calls through the door, and my entire body goes still. "Are you okay?"

"Uh," I start, but the doorknob twists, and I look around the room frantically, seeing the vibrator on the nightstand, grabbing it, and tossing it into my bag and burying it under a shirt just as the door opens and Wes steps in. "Hey, I thought you were, uh, going for a run?"

His eyes are dark and heated, and I know.

I *know* I fucked up big time.

*Fucking spontaneity!*

I should have at least waited until we got home like a *normal fucking person.*

"I was. Now I'm back," he says, then steps toward me. I step back, the look in his eyes hungry and all-consuming, stoking that fire in my belly again already.

He follows me step for step until my back is against the wall.

"I heard you," he whispers, his body just inches from mine, the heat of him and the masculine smell of sweat and desire rolling off him in waves.

"Heard?" I say, but I already know what he heard. Me, moaning his name as I came harder than I ever have while picturing him fucking me senseless.

His hand trails down my arm, featherlight and gentle, until he grips my wrist. "Were these in you?" he whispers, lifting my hand up until they're between us. "Were these inside your pussy? Were you touching yourself, making yourself come while you moan my name?"

"Wes, I didn't—"

"You can lie to yourself all you want, little wife. You can keep that wall up for as long as you need. It'll just make it that much sweeter when it finally crumbles, and you let me in." Then I watch in utter fascination as he brings my fingers to his mouth, trailing his tongue over them, and a moan fills the room as he does.

When he smiles, I realize it isn't him moaning at all, but me doing so at the feel of his tongue cleaning me off.

"Fucking perfect," he says, then steps closer, closing the gap between us.

My hand moves up to his neck, gripping the damp hair there as all common sense leaves my mind and all I can think about is getting Wes. Getting *more*. My head tips up, and his tips down, and then we wait there, lips almost brushing.

"I won't take anything I'm not freely given, Harper, so if you want to taste yourself on my lips, you're going to have to take it," he whispers.

And because I'm fucking *out of my mind*, I do just that. I lift to my tiptoes, pressing my lips hard to his. He groans deep, the sound vibrating through my thin shirt, against my nipples, as my mouth opens and his tongue slides against mine. I taste it there, the mix of him and me, and it's *everything*, so damned perfect.

I want more.

I want *everything* with him.

His lips trail to my neck, groaning as he tastes me, licking and nipping and sucking, and I move to try and get more from him.

Fuck it. What could it hurt to fuck my husband?

"We could..." I whisper, then clear my throat, my breathing

coming hard despite my taking the edge off just minutes ago. "We could...you know, take the edge off. Scratch the itch."

"Scratch the itch?" he asks, his body stilling.

"Friends with benefits," I say, moving my body against his, suddenly needing him more than I've ever needed anything. "A year is a long time."

Yes, yes, this makes sense. We could tamp out this burning desire between us, keep the marriage sham going, but also sate our needs in the process. Everything is so much simpler, so much clearer when it's just the two of us, when my mind doesn't get in the way.

"We could do more. Be more," I whisper.

His lips leave my neck, and he stares at me for long moments. I think he's going to give in, to agree to this and give me everything I somehow know he could give *so fucking well*, but then he shakes his head.

"I don't want you the way a man wants a friend, Harper Holden. I could never be just friends with benefits with you." His hand moves up, brushing my hair behind my shoulders. I can barely focus on anything but how much I like him saying my name like that. Like I'm *his*.

I bite my lip, knowing that is exactly why we can't be anything more than friends with benefits. Why, in reality, we shouldn't even be *that*, but I'm a weak woman. I tip my chin up, looking at him, my pulse pounding, my eyes pleading, but my voice calm and even.

"That's what I can offer, Wes," I tell him. "I can't make any promises for something more, but I can give you that."

Wrong words, obviously. His lips tip up at the edges, his fingers moving to my chin, gripping it in between two fingers and forcing my eyes to meet his. His endless depths of green eyes consume me, making me wish I could ignore reality, that I could jump and pretend the fall wouldn't crush me.

"Then, when you're ready for more, I'll be here. I get it, Harper. You were fucked over, and he messed with your head. You need time,

and you need space. But I'm not letting this get fucked and complicated just because we have wild chemistry. So I'll wait for you.

"Friends with benefits is all I'll ever be able to do," I warn, hoping
he'll change his mind. I just came, but it barely took the edge off, and
even that isn't much with his body too close and confusing.

His smile widens, making my stomach flip.

"I'm a patient man, Harper."

I groan aloud, his stubbornness turning into something irritating.

"This is silly, Wes. There's nothing to be patient for. I'm not
doing a relationship again. Why do you even want that? Why won't
you just accept what I'm able to give you while we're in this agreement? There's no need for both of us to be miserable this whole year."

His entire demeanor changes, and he shakes his head, stepping
back. "I'm not going to let this be some itch you scratch, Harper,
because this? You and me? It's something special." He steps back,
leaving me feeling cold and empty, in desperate need of his touch in
more ways than one.

"Wes—" I start, and he shakes his head, a small smile on his lips
hiding something more. Hurt? Disappointment?

"When you're ready to admit this could be something more,
Harper, you let me know. I'll be waiting."

And when he leaves, I know two things for sure:

One, my husband most *definitely* likes me.

And two, I am so *totally* into my husband, even if it's a terrible
idea.

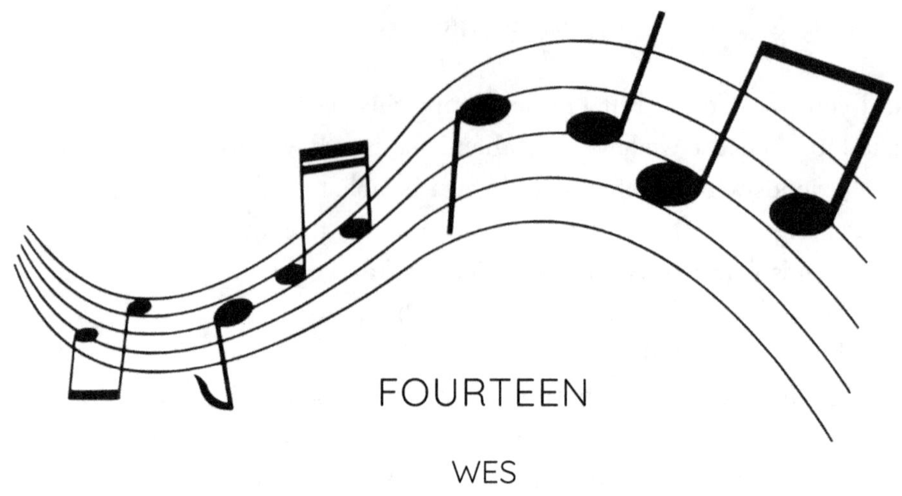

# FOURTEEN

## WES

"They work fast," Harper whispers as we move through the airport, her steps slowing as we walk past a rack of magazines. She moves closer to it, grabbing the gossip rag and flipping through.

There's a photo of the two of us inside, Harper in that tempting bikini, in my arms. My thumb is grazing along her bottom lip, her eyes locked on mine. She looks like she's fucking enraptured by me. I do, too, but I would fully expect to see that.

"Who's Wes Holden's New Girl?" the headline reads, and I smile to myself, realizing in a week or two, it will be Who is Wes Holden's New Wife? Leo has yet to spill that bit of juicy gossip, and considering Harper was only wearing her engagement ring at the resort to fuel rumors and everyone at the wedding was on tight NDA lockdown, it hasn't leaked yet. Leo loves the drama of controlling a secret and dropping it when *he* wants to.

"We look good," I say, tipping my head to the article, moving my body closer to hers, and looking over her shoulder.

A deep blush runs over Harper's cheeks and down her chest.

"I look nearly pornographic in that bathing suit," she replies, flipping the page.

There are a few more photos of us holding hands at the resort or going to dinner, but mostly from the first day there. The second day, I asked Leo not to tip anyone off and to discourage tabloids and paparazzi from taking photos, wanting Harper to have one relaxing day before we jump into the chaos of this new-to-her life. I don't know if she caught on, but if she did, she didn't mention it.

Still, the photos they managed to get are all perfect, both in making our relationship seem more *real* than before, and because they're just great shots—I make a mental reminder to have Leo reach out and get some copies because if things go the way I'm planning, we'll want them one day.

Harper must be reading the actual article instead of taking in the photos like I am because she groans aloud. You *have* to be kidding me," she mumbles before pointing to a paragraph that I quickly read.

*We reached out to who our sources have told us is Miss Abbott's most recent ex-boyfriend, Jeremy Vaughn, head of marketing for Astor Fashion House, but he declined to comment. His current girlfriend, socialite Clarissa Astor, however, was willing to give a statement to us. "She's absolutely insane," Miss Astor told Fans Weekly. "It was an amicable breakup after my sweet Jeremy learned she was only with him for his ties in the fashion industry. Clearly, her work isn't that remarkable since she's gotten nowhere but designing ugly pageant gowns in the years dating him, but she's still holding on. Just a few weeks ago, she was caught vandalizing his home because she's so obsessed with him."*

I don't expect the anger burning in my chest at the lies spread about her, but when I see the look of hurt tinged with Harper's own anger, I need clarification.

"That's his new girlfriend? The one he was cheating on you with?"

She sneers before nodding. "She's the one that's been making a full-time job of talking shit about me and ruining my reputation. Jeremy might be doing the behind-the-scenes work, but she's telling every tabloid she can about their fairy-tale romance and how I'm essentially just the evil stepsister in her story."

"Does it bother you?" I ask, and she looks at me, clearly confused.

"Her talking shit about me? Absolutely. People are buying what she's selling, and it's messing with my name and reputation."

"No, him moving on so quickly? Though, I guess, the bad press, too. All of it, really." She shifts, looking over her shoulder and reading me as if trying to understand the motivation for my questions.

She lets out a small, self-conscious laugh and shakes her head, closing the magazine and putting it back on the rack. "Well, to your first question, no. Not really. I thought I would when it first happened. Thought I'd be heartbroken to lose him and see him moving on. Let's just say, it's been... a very eye-opening month or so."

"How so?"

She takes a deep breath and begins moving in the direction we were headed. I think she's going to write me off, but then she starts to speak.

"You know, my friends are falling in love, getting married, having babies, and I'm seeing what *being in love*—and being *loved*—really looks like. It's a strange and uncomfortable feeling, knowing I spent so long with this man, convinced myself that we were going to spend forever together, and realize I never had that. I never *felt* that. I sacrificed so much for the bare minimum, and I was okay with that."

I look at her profile as we walk, her face stern as she stares straight ahead, avoiding looking at me as she shrugs. "So it's kind of...embarrassing, maybe? To see someone you'd convinced yourself you'd spend forever with moving on and not even feel a pang of hurt over losing him. I'm hurt about." She pauses, as if she's trying to choose her words carefully, then shakes her head. "Everything else."

"The bad press?"

She tips her head from left to right, weighing her response before answering.

"Yes and no. Public opinion, I don't care about, not really. It will all die down eventually, and something new and exciting will cast a shadow on it. It's a bit inconvenient and frustrating, but in a month or two, no one will remember it. Plus, we have a plan in place to combat that." Finally, she looks at me and gives me a small smile.

"That we do."

We keep walking, both of us in our own heads, before she speaks again.

"It's...the behind-the-scenes stuff."

"How so?" I'm hesitant to ask too many questions, seeming to constantly straddle the line between encouraging her to talk and avoiding her closing me out. It appears like that was the right question, though, when she explains.

"Jeremy, despite not having a creative bone in his body, has ties in the industry. As Head of Marketing, he does a lot of the talking to the press and has a *lot* of connections. He knows I want to move beyond custom pageant gowns, and I'll need to have connections to do that. I'm worried he's whispering about me and ruining those opportunities before they even have the chance to come to fruition. For example, he gave me a contact for fabric months ago, and I've been going back and forth with them a lot since. They're usually super responsive, but I called them last week, and they never returned my call. I know in my gut Jeremy has something to do with that." She shrugs, then plays it off. "But there are a million suppliers around, so that's not a huge problem. Still, it's a small industry, so it weighs on me."

"Well," I start, not wanting to belittle her worries but also wanting to help fix them. "When we get back, we can talk to Leo about it and see what he says. He has contacts for pretty much everything under the sun."

Harper shakes her head, her hair in that high ponytail swaying a bit. "That's not necessary, I don't need anyone to go out of their way for me and my drama." She pauses, then adds, "Or, more than they already are."

"You're my wife, Harper," I say. "It's not going out of my way to help you." She stops walking then, stares at me, and opens her mouth to argue, but as she does, an announcement that our flight is boarding comes overhead. "Come on, Mrs. Holden. Let's go home."

"Mr. Holden, welcome to Friendly Skies Airlines. We're so happy to have you flying with us," the flight attendant says, standing a bit too close for comfort. I give her a tight smile. "My name is Leah. I'm a huge fan, and I'll be personally attending to you for our entire flight. We're set to take off in a few, but is there anything at all I can do for you before that?"

I shake my head.

"No, but my wife would like"—I turn to Harper—"a Coke Zero, no ice?" She looks at me, slightly confused for a moment, before nodding, and I turn to the flight attendant once more. "That will be all."

Her smile falters a hint before she nods and steps away.

"Lucky guess," Harper says under her breath, pulling out a book and her headphones.

"I'm sorry?" I ask with a laugh.

"With the drink. Lucky guess. It's what I order."

Slowly, I shake my head because clearly, she still doesn't get it, how into her I am, how much I've been watching her for the past two years.

"That wasn't luck. When we go out as a group, you always ask what kind of soda they have. If it's Pepsi, you'll get water. If they have Coke, you'll ask for Coke Zero. If they don't have that and it's fountain, you get a Diet Coke with ice. If it's bottled, you'll get water." She stares at me, and I smile at the shock on her face. "I pay attention, little wife."

She stares at me for a moment, taking me in and trying to decide how to respond, but the flight attendant is returning with a familiar red can and handing it and a cocktail napkin to me.

"Here you go, Mr. Holden," she says with a purr before walking away with a wink.

When I hand the can over to Harper, I notice the cocktail napkin has a number and *Leah* written on it with a bright pink lipstick kiss on it. Rolling my eyes, I crumble it up and set it aside for the trash.

"Does that happen often?" Harper asks, cracking open the can. I shrug.

"It's not uncommon."

"Do you take them up on their offers?" I don't miss the hint of jealousy she attempts to keep out of her words unsuccessfully.

"I'm not going to step out on you with a flight attendant if that's what you're worried about," I say.

"Trust me, I know. There's a very hefty prenuptial agreement in place," she says, and I laugh. "I'm just...curious. I realized this weekend that I don't know very much about you. Outside a good chunk of your musical memories, now, of course."

I smile at the reminder of the flight here and reach out for her hand on impulse, grabbing it before shrugging. "I used to. When I was young and horny and didn't want something more." She bites her lip like she doesn't want to ask, but I stare at her, eyebrow lifted, challenging her to do it.

"But now?" she finally asks.

"Well, now I'm married," I say with a smile. She rolls her eyes and shakes her head, elbowing me but not letting go of my hand. She told me she's a nervous flyer, and I can feel the truth of it in the small shake of her hands.

"You know what I mean. Before me. Before you were tied to this."

I think about how to answer that, how to approach this without terrifying her. Harper Abbott, now Holden, I'm learning, is much more scared than she lets on.

"It gets old, you know. Being some check mark, some grand trophy. You start to crave something real. You start to wonder if people like you for you, or if it's because you're *the* Wes Holden. If it's because you're in a band or if it's because they like *you*."

"So you don't do friends with benefits?" she asks, and if I'm not mistaken, it feels like a leading question, something I'm intrigued by more than I probably should be. But I've already made my mind up on Harper and what I want us to be. Friends with benefits would just give my little wife too much room to deny whatever is building between us, even if her offer was tempting.

"I'm too old for that," I whisper, my hand reaching out and tucking a strand of her hair behind her ear. "I'm ready for more." We're veering off hypotheticals now, and she knows it.

"I'm not looking for more." Her tongue comes out to wet her lips nervously. "I don't think I'll ever want more again. I wasted too long banking on *more,* and all that did was make me ignore all the glaring red flags."

"I think you just need to learn to trust yourself more," I say. "I think you knew for some time things weren't going to work out with you two. You were afraid of what it might say about you if you walked away from it all after investing all of that time into the relationship."

Her brows furrow as she takes in my words, and I watch her, reading her the way I'm learning to love to do. It's the best way to get to know her since she is so hesitant to share. But then my eyes catch on a gold chain tucked beneath her sweatshirt, and I can't help it. My fingers reach out, grazing her skin and snaking underneath, tugging it from her shirt. Her breath hitches as I touch her, and I don't bother to fight the smirk on my lips as I settle the necklace over top of her sweatshirt.

"You're still wearing it," I whisper, running my thumb over the W charm.

"I kind of like it." A small, shy smile spreads over her lips. "It's growing on me, just like my husband."

God, I fucking love her saying that, *my husband.*

I use the grip on the chain to tug her in closer to me until our faces are just a few inches apart. "My initial looks mighty fine around your neck, little wife," I say, fingers grazing her skin as I play with the necklace between us, so close, her nervous breaths graze my lips.

"I think I like having it there," she whispers back.

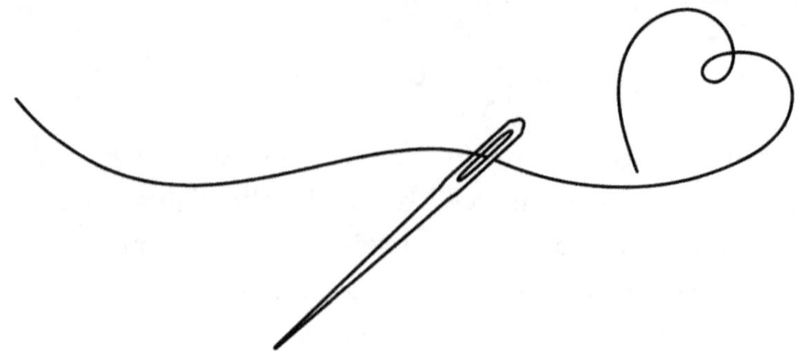

# FIFTEEN

## HARPER

"Here we are," Wes says as he opens the door to his house—my new house in Evergreen Park. I sort of remember him buying it a year or so ago and Ava talking about it, but I hadn't actually seen much less been to it before the time I came here to kiss him.

The reminder of that sends a shiver down my spine that I force myself to forget.

I step in, looking around with wide eyes as he closes the door behind us, setting our bags next to the entryway. "Jesus, this place is huge. It's just you here?" The last time I was here, it was dark, and my nerves were going haywire, so I didn't take much of an opportunity to take the giant home in, but it's just that: huge. This entryway alone could probably fit half of Jeremy's house into it.

"My assistant, Laurel, has an office here, but it's just me living here. And now you," Wes says, nodding. "You've got your own room, so you don't have to worry about bunking with me."

I turn to him, smiling. "Two rooms, huh?" I let out a small laugh. "Just when I was getting used to sleeping with you." It has to be the jetlag scrambling my brain, making me much more honest than I should be, but I can't deny that the two nights I spent sleeping with Wes Holden were the best I ever had.

His hand moves to my lower back, a boyish smile on his lips as he pulls me into him, his chest flush to mine. We haven't been this close since the absolute catastrophe in the hotel room after I made myself come, after he turned me down, and that has been intentional on my part. Because when I'm this close to Wes, common sense seems to abandon ship.

"If you want the real married experience, Harper, I'm more than willing to give it to you. You just have to say so," he whispers against my lips.

My pulse pounds as I lick my lips, trying to calm my breaths. "The full experience?"

"Mm-hmm," he murmurs against my lips. It vibrates against me, and the frequency of it must scramble my brain even further, because slowly, I lift my hand, wrapping it around his neck without the approval of common sense. That common sense has clearly fled the scene as I let my fingers twine into the hair at the back of his head.

"We already practiced this, Wes," I whisper, referencing that first kiss in this foyer. My pulse is pounding, my breaths quickening at our mere proximity.

"Oh, this wouldn't be practice, little wife," he whispers just as quietly, then slowly starts to drop his head to my lips, as if he's giving me the freedom to back away if I want to. I don't, not in the least. Instead, I eagerly await his lips on mine.

But then the sound of heels on tile fills the room, and his body goes tight as a blonde walks into the house, a wide smile on her lips.

"Wes, I'm so glad you're—home," she finishes, her smile falling just a hair when she takes me in.

"Laurel, hey, how are you?" Wes asks, then steps away from me, a rush of cold making it feel like a loss as he steps to the woman and pulls her into a hug. It lasts for a moment before he steps back, leaving an arm around her shoulders, his smile wide as he looks at me.

"Harper, this is my assistant, Laurel. Laurel, this is Harper. My wife."

She gives me a tight smile before putting a hand out, and the shake she gives me is much too strong to be casual.

I do not like her, and I have no real reason not to, other than she's looking at me like I'm competition, and suddenly I'm wondering if maybe I *am* competition. Is there something here I don't know about? I'd never heard of this woman before in my life, and he surely didn't mention her the entire time we were away.

"Your fake wife," she corrects, looking up at him with a smile like she's in on some joke I'm left out of.

I stand there with an awkward, tight smile, feeling like I want to run, though I'm somewhat appeased when his look goes from happy to assessing, like he's attempting to read her before correcting her.

"My *wife*," he says. "For all intents and purposes, Harper is my wife. Harp, if you need anything at all, Laurel is your girl. She handles everything around here—shopping, cleaning, my schedule. The whole nine."

I give another tight smile and nod.

"I'll try not to make your life too complicated," I say, expecting her to wave it off and tell me it's no big deal, but instead, she nods, turning away from me to Wes, whose arm has dropped from her frame when he stepped away, not that I was taking note.

*Laurel* clearly doesn't miss that move, her face pulling into a sour look for just a moment before relaxing back into a serene smile.

"I made sure that all of her things were put into her room. Jaime was kind enough to come and help bring her things over." Wes nods approvingly before she turns to me, that friendly look gone. It's actually impressive how quickly she can change her face. "Mr. Wilde is the bodyguard for Atlas Oaks," she says as if she's filling me in on some information I'm unaware of.

My brows furrow, and I fight my jaw going tight. "Yes, I know," I say tightly. "I was in his wedding. His wife is my best friend."

Wes's assistant cocks her head to the side and gives me the fakest smile known to man. "She is? What a small world. Wes, we have a few things to go over that you missed, and—"

"We can handle that tomorrow or next week, I'm sure," Wes says, stepping toward me and putting a hand to my lower back. The simple touch sends a shiver through me, and I fight the urge to let my lips tip up with a triumphant smile.

I shouldn't like this, his touch, and I *surely* shouldn't be feeling possessive over Wes, especially not with what just happened a few moments ago, but here we are.

"I mean, I suppose. But a few are pressing and—" she says.

"Later. I'm jet-lagged, and I want to make sure Harper gets settled." She goes to speak up once more, but he shakes his head. "Thanks for everything, Laurel. I think you can head out."

Her eyes send daggers to me, and in my mind, it's confirmation: Laurel wants Wes and sees me as some inhibitor to that mission.

It makes me furious.

"Really, I—" she starts, but I step closer to Wes, putting a hand to his shoulder, the warmth of him burning to my hand. His eyes move to mine, a bit shocked at the initiated touch, but a smile on his lips all the same.

"Do you mind showing me around our house?" I ask, eyes wide, and I don't know what kind of phantom has taken over me, making me much more bold and brave than I've ever been, but I like her. "I'm so tired from our trip." I give him a smile, then share it with Laurel. "You know how those long flights can be."

"Absolutely," Wes says, then moves, opening the door for his assistant. She glares at me before saying her goodbyes, Wes closing and locking the door behind her. By now, common sense has reen-tered my veins, and I'm standing a few feet away, feeling awkward and, if I'm being honest, just a bit childish.

"Harper Abbott, are you jealous?" he asks when he turns back to me, reaching for my hand and grabbing it, his rough, calloused fingers twining with mine.

"No, but I don't like the way she was looking at you when I was right there." His smile goes wide, and I roll my eyes, trying to tug my hand out from his, but his grip is tight. "It's common courtesy. We're *married*, you know."

"Oh, trust me, I know." His hand moves to brush some of my hair back behind my shoulder. "Come on, let's get you to your room," he says before leading me up the stairs of the too-large house and toward my room for the next year.

I can't sleep.

I can't sleep, and I know, despite every bone in my body wanting to deny it, it's because Wes Holden isn't in bed with me. I toss and turn in the giant, luxurious bed, frustrated and angry that I've let my *fake husband* get so far under my skin, until finally, I get out of bed and head to the kitchen for a snack.

Everyone knows a sweet treat can fix almost any ailment.

Fearful of bothering my new roommate, I tiptoe around, trying to find the kitchen for a few minutes before landing in the spacious room, equipped with professional appliances and neat as a pin.

I'm peering into the fridge, wishing I had thought to ask Ava to grab me some snacks for my late-night dessert habit, when a throat clears, and I jump, panicked, before realizing it's just Wes. He's leaning in the doorway, handsome as ever, his hair tousled, muscled arms crossed on his chest, and a small smile on his lips.

"Sorry, I didn't mean to scare you."

I shake my head, moving my hand to my racing heart. "You didn't," I lie, and he glares at me. I give him a small, embarrassed smile and shrug. "Okay, maybe a little. But it wasn't your fault. I was just looking through your offerings."

He steps closer, looking over my shoulder from behind me before he shifts back, leaning against the kitchen island. "Pretty empty, huh?"

"I mean, you're a rock star bachelor who hasn't been home for a week, so—"

"Not a bachelor," he says instantly, and my head cocks back.

"What?"

"I'm not a bachelor anymore." The smile on his lips is near criminal, too handsome for his own good, especially when he's just a few inches from me. This entire arrangement—living with him, pretending we're a couple, *marrying him*—may have just been the worst idea I've ever agreed to. He's far too everything, and I am much too attracted to him to make it through the next year unscathed.

"What do you normally eat for a snack?"

"A cookie. I keep cookie dough on hand to make them whenever I want some at home. I'll have to stock up," I say with a shrug. "I'll make it through one night."

"Hmm," he says with a nod, then moves to a cabinet. "I don't have fresh cookies, but I *do* have..." He reaches to the very top shelf, grabs a familiar blue, crinkly package, and smiles like he knows he just got an A on a test from me. "Oreos."

I smile wide in return because he's cute, and I'm hyped for the impending sugar rush.

"Do you have milk?" I ask the most important question when it comes to the black and white cookies.

"Do you have an allergy like Ava?" I shake my head and smile that he knows something so pedestrian about my best friend. I *don't* remind myself Jeremy never remembered Ava had an allergy, always suggesting the worst restaurant options when I ever convinced him to go out with us.

"No, I gratefully can and do eat everything without an issue."

He smiles. "Then yes. I do." He reaches into the fridge next, pulling out a fresh gallon, then grabs two tall glasses before pouring each of us a glass.

"Plates?" I ask as he peels back the plastic covering the package, and he shakes his head.

"Oreos taste better when you make crumbs."

"I don't think that's how it works," I say with a laugh, dipping my cookie in my milk as he stares at me taking my first bite with a smile. I sigh in relief at the processed sugar. My sweet tooth might not be great for me, but there are *much* worse vices in this world.

"It definitely is," he says before dipping his own cookie and eating.

"A real wild Saturday night," I say with a laugh, leaning at the counter.

"Do you normally partake in wild Saturday nights?" he asks, not judging, mostly just curious, like he's genuinely interested in learning more about me.

I shake my head. "No, no. They're not really my thing." I smile at him and, for some reason, continue. "I like Sundays best of all. A good Sunday reset, preparing yourself for the upcoming week? Way better than a party. And you can't do a Sunday reset when you're hungover." Wes chews, watching me thoughtfully, and under his careful scrutiny, I keep speaking. I could tell myself it's the jet lag or the exhaustion, but I know it's just Wes, and this strange pull I have to him. "I think the last wild Saturday night I had got me arrested, so..."

"Ah, the glitter," he says with a laugh, and I nod. "What made you land on glitter?"

"We had a long list of revenge options, but that seemed the most...impactful."

"A whole list?" he asks with a laugh, and I nod. "Do you still have it?"

I reach for my phone. "I think so, it was in my notes app," I say, then smile when I find a note titled *Ways to Destroy Shithead*. I hand it over.

"God, he should be happy you stuck with glitter. Ruin his car?"

I shrug. "He has the ugliest classic car that isn't even cool, and he brags about it all the time. I'd love to key it or something." I sigh, grabbing another cookie and dipping it. "Unfortunately, I learned my lesson, so I will no longer be fucking with him."

"A shame."

"I don't know, I think marrying into his favorite band and being temporarily more famous than him is more than enough payback. He always used to brag about how much more clout he had than me."

Wes shakes his head before handing my phone back to me. "He's a tool."

"You're telling me." And then, again, because I'm exhausted and I think my brain forgets I'm not with my best friends and venting, I blurt out, "He couldn't even make me come."

Wes snorts out a laugh, coughing and choking as I feel my cheeks get hot.

"Well, it seems like you did a pretty good job of that yourself," he says, and at the reminder of what happened in the hotel room, the burn deepens, my blush spreading to my chest.

"Look, Wes, I know I haven't said it yet, but I'm really sorry about that. I put you in a really uncomfortable position and—"

He shifts in front of me, stepping forward and pinning me to the kitchen counter before moving his hands so he's holding my face.

"Harper, baby, look at me," he says, and when I do, he keeps talking. "Never—and I mean *never*—apologize for there being this attraction between us, or for you acting on it."

My cheeks feel like they might alight, but he keeps going, shifting his body closer to mine.

"Harper, I have jacked off twice as many times since yesterday at the mere memory of you moaning my name through a goddamn door." Heat floods me, and my mind stupidly tries to figure out *when* he would have done that. "And each of those heavily featured what was once a far-off fantasy of you offering yourself to me."

"But you turned me down," I say without meaning to. "You didn't want to—"

Quickly, he shakes his head. "Oh, no. No, no, no, Harper. That's not what happened, and if that's what you think, let me set you straight." He moves, his hands going to my hips and lifting me to the counter so we're eye to eye. "I want you more than you could ever imagine, but I am not going to let you belittle this thing between us by calling it *friends with benefits*. I am your friend, and I want *benefits*, but that's not all I want. I know you don't think that's a good idea, which is why I said I'd be patient. Because I *know* we'll be the best idea when it happens. And yes, I said *when*," he says with a smile.

"You're not ready for that, and that's fine. You were fucked over, and we threw ourselves into this. I want you to know I'm ready when you are, but take all the time you need. I'll be here until then. Waiting." He gently presses his lips to mine, and my body goes slack with the simple kiss, the traitor.

It's short, but it says everything I know he means before he grabs another cookie and moves on like nothing happened like, he didn't just shift my entire world on its axis.

Not long after, a yawn leaves my lips, and Wes lets out a deep laugh.

"I should get you to bed. You're exhausted."

I shrug, too tired to watch my words. "I don't think I'll be able to sleep in that bed. I kept tossing and turning. I think I got too used to sleeping with you," I say low, a blush burning over my cheeks.

Wes crosses his arms over his chest, smirking at me. "Is that right, little wife?" I nod, eyes locked on him. "I had the same issue. It's why I came down here."

His eyes fire with heat, and a million wisecracks float through my mind, sassy or spicy things I could say to tempt and tease him. I yawn amidst my internal turmoil, and his eyes go soft, his hand moving to fully cup my cheek, his thumb brushing against my cheekbone as he stares at me.

"You're exhausted," he says to himself. "You really couldn't sleep?" I shake my head, too tired to keep the lies in place. He seems to ponder that before answering. "All right." His hand stays on my chin, keeping my eyes locked on him. "My bed or yours?"

"What?"

"You need to sleep. Maybe a warm body would help. That's probably your issue." It's almost self-deprecating, the look he gives me, removing himself from the equation of why I slept well. "You'd been in a relationship for a long time, you probably got used to it."

"Wes, Jeremy and I—" I start, suddenly needing to explain, but he shakes his head, a guard going up.

"No, not before you're about to sleep with me. Don't bring him here," he whispers. "Yours or mine?"

My mind weighs my options, already accepting and, admittedly, excited to sleep with Wes. But when I think of lying in sheets and blankets that smell like him, of burying myself in them, cocooning in the smell of him, the answer is obvious.

"Yours," I say, and he smiles gently before nodding.

"Get what you need from your room, then meet me there, okay?" And without another word or confirmation, he's walking off, leaving me more confused than ever, a feat I didn't know could be mastered.

Ten minutes later, in my most conservative yet cute pajamas, face washed and teeth brushed, I'm standing awkwardly in his doorway. Wes is lying in his bed, no shirt but a pair of loose pajama pants low on his hips, lying on top of the blankets and scrolling on his phone. When he notices me, he smiles, setting his phone down and tipping his head to the bed.

"Come on, baby. Let's get you some sleep."

I do as he asks, settling into the giant bed next to him and taking in as much of the room as I can while he gets up and turns the lights out. When the room is dark, we lay next to each other, an awkward gap between us before he lets out a laugh, shifting and tugging me until my head is on his pec, my hand on his chest, his arm wrapped around my back and holding me close.

It settles instantly, the blanket of calm I felt the morning I woke up like this, a calm I've never experienced before in my life. It's unsettling and beautiful at the same time. Moments pass in silence as Wes's breathing evens, and sleep quickly and unexpectedly starts to fall over me.

But before I slip completely, I need to tell him.

"Hey, Wes?" I ask softly.

"Mmm," he hums back.

"I know you said you don't want him here, but I need you to know. I didn't sleep with him." His body goes tighter, a barely noticeable shift, but I track it all the same, and silence takes over the room once more.

I scramble to explain, words falling from my lips, my filter already in dreamland.

"I've never been able to sleep with anyone. I'm a light sleeper as it is, I have a hard time falling asleep and...we had separate beds. I couldn't sleep with him at all."

A beat passes before Wes's sleepy rumble fills the room, his hand pushing my hair back, a sigh leaving my lips at the feeling.

"But you can sleep with me," he says, not a question but a statement.

"But I can sleep with you," I confirm. With that off my chest, exhaustion creeps up faster, swallowing me whole.

I wake without Wes, and although I'm well-rested, there's a pit of disappointment in my stomach that I don't want to admit I feel.

Eventually, I roll out of bed, shuffling down to the kitchen to try and figure out coffee. There's a note on the fridge in messy boy writing telling me Wes is at the studio today and won't be home until late. I knew they'd be doing a bunch of recording after we got back, finishing up the upcoming album, so I'm not surprised, but the hint of disappointment I'm forced to ignore is a bit concerning.

But most concerning is the way my heart flips when I look in the fridge. There's a stack of premade cookie dough, a green Post-it on the side.

*Some late-night snack options.*

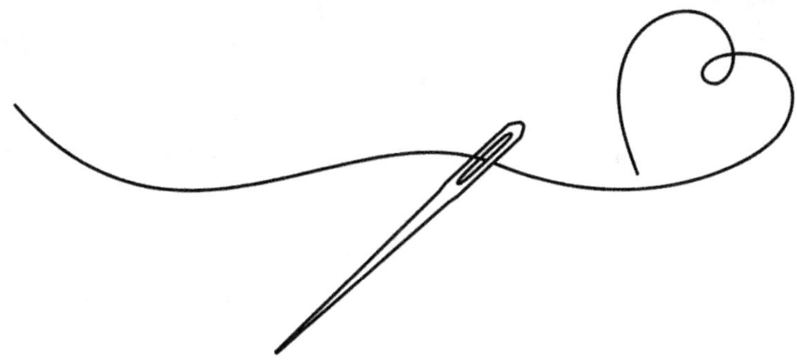

# SIXTEEN

## HARPER

The day after we arrive home from our honeymoon, Leo announces our marriage to the public and tells us we'll have to do a few press rounds. The morning of the television interviews, I walk downstairs in an emerald green shift dress I designed and a pair of black over-the-knee boots, and Wes just stares at me.

He looks handsome as ever in a gray sweater and jeans that scream hot casual and yet still says rock star somehow, something I think only he could pull off.

Things have been good between us in the week since I moved in with him, though there's been a definitive tension between us. We've both been busy, Wes going to Riggs's often for recording or practice and me having girls' night to fill in Ava and Jules and being on deadline for a few pageant gowns.

But each night, he's home by dinner and we eat together, talking a bit and continuing to learn about one another. I've learned that Wes was Billie Joe Armstrong from Green Day for Halloween three years in a row, something he says *should have been a sign*, that his favorite food is tacos, and he loves the color green. It's strange getting to know the little details about someone *after* you move in with them, but it's been nice and easy all the same.

And even though we've been sleeping together every night in Wes's bed, we haven't done anything more, not even the most basic of kisses.

But the way he stares at me now without speaking, without moving, has panic filling me.

"What?" I ask. "Is this too much? I know it's a little short, but I—"

He cuts me off with a smile. "Did you make it?" he asks, stepping forward to me, and I nod. "Then it's perfect."

His hand reaches out, fingers grazing the chain of the necklace I continue to put on every morning despite barely leaving the house. It just feels...right to wear. His fingers tuck under the higher neckline of my dress, trailing along the chain and tugging it out from where it settled under my dress and letting it lay on the fabric. He fiddles with the charm, his fingers grazing along the skin of my neck once more before he steps back.

I'm dazed for a moment, and he smiles wide like he knows.

"Do we have time to stop somewhere for coffee on the way to the studio?" I ask when I come back to myself.

"Of course, but if you want, we can make something here. I've got this giant-ass espresso machine I barely know how to work, but I can Google it."

I shake my head and laugh. "No, I know how to work it. I could make you something if you want. I just don't have my creamer, and it's the only way I like it at home."

Wes's brows furrow in confusion. "Just tell Laurel to get it. Whatever you need. I told you that when you moved it."

I bite my lip, not wanting to get her in trouble, but I can't lie, not with him looking at me in that way that sees through every fib I tell.

"I, uh, I did. I added it to the list, but she didn't get it."

"You did?" he asks.

"I don't think Laurel likes me."

He shakes his head, disagreeing with me. "She likes you just fine. That's just how she is. She's the same with Stella, a little standoffish. It's not personal, she prefers male friendships to female."

"Red flag," I say under my breath, reaching for my bag.

"What?" he asks with a laugh, and I sigh, turning to him to explain.

"It's a red flag. Any woman who says they prefer the company of men to women? I don't trust them."

He lets out a small chuckle, crossing his arms over his chest and smiling at me.

"Do you like my company?" I roll my eyes.

"Yes, of course. But my girls will always be my number one. Women...we can read people differently than men can. If a woman doesn't like the company of other women, I assume it's because she's afraid of them reading her in a way she doesn't like, which makes me wonder what she's hiding."

He shrugs on his jacket, moving for the front door and opening it for me.

"I guess that makes sense," he says as I walk out in front of him, before he locks the door behind us. "But Laurel isn't like that. You two will get used to each other, it just takes a bit."

I shrug my shoulders, not really wanting to explain to him that his assistant wants in his pants and hates me because, in her eyes, I got there first, and because of that, we will never be used to each other.

"Maybe," I say with a smile as I slide into the seat. His eyes take me in, a small smile on his lips like he finds me endlessly entertaining before he grabs the seatbelt, leans forward, buckling me in.

"Gotta keep my little wife safe," he says, then presses his lips to my forehead before slamming the door and jogging around the car. I'm dazed by the small movement as he starts the car and pulls out of the drive, taking me to my favorite coffee shop.

"Were you always an Atlas Oaks fan?" the female interviewer at the first studio asks me, making my stomach turn.

I bite my lip and give her a tight smile."Honest answer?" I ask awkwardly. Wes laughs out loud, but I continue. "Not really. I'm kind of an I'll listen to everything kind of person, but we had mutual friends, so that's really how my interest was piqued." I bite my lip once more, and look at Wes, who is still smiling and decide to drop a bit more truth.

*"Truth will make you likable,"* Leo told us when he called us this morning. He's in California with Willa, so he couldn't be here to coach us today, but he made sure to call us and give us—okay, me—a pep talk. *"The public can sniff out a lie from a mile away, so only do it when you have to."*

So I tell the truth. "I actually started listening to their music a lot more after I met Wes," I explain, leaving out that I used to not listen to the band just because Jeremy was a fan. God, how many signs could there have been that things between us were never going to work? "We were at a bar celebrating my friend's pageant win—"

"Ava Wilde, right?" the interviewer asks. It still sounds so crazy to me for people to call Ava by Jaime's last name, but still, my smile widens, and I nod.

"Yeah. And Ava saw the band in a VIP section. She went to school with Stella and wanted to say hi."

"Was it love at first sight?" she asks with starry eyes, and I shake my head, smiling, opening my mouth to speak, to explain we were friends before dating as planned, but Wes beats me to it.

"For me, definitely. At the time, Harper was taken. But we saw each other a lot because of mutual friends, so I kept on falling for her from afar."

The woman lets out an awww, but my mind can't focus on anything but the way Wes is looking at me, heart eyes and everything.

Who knew he was such a great actor?

"So, as soon as she was single, I swooped in. I saw my chance, and I took it." He winks at me, and I can't help but smile and shake my head. "Got her to go on a few dates with me, dated for a bit, and then we decided it was stupid to waste time," he says.

"That's quite literally the sweetest story ever," the interviewer says. "So you were patiently waiting for her to be ready for you?"

Wes meets my eyes, his hand reaching out to grab mine, and suddenly, it's like this isn't an interview but a private moment just for the two of us.

"No one has ever tested my patience the way Harper has, and I mean that in the best way possible. They say good things come to those who wait, and I'd wait forever if it meant I'd get her at the end of it all."

My heart skyrockets at his words, at the hidden meaning in them and the way he looks at me, and I'm pretty sure the interviewer lets out another loud aww, but I'm lost to reality.

"Your necklace is beautiful," the interviewer says. "Can we assume it's a W for Wes?"

My hand moves to the heart necklace, and I smile gently, looking at my husband. "It is. Wes gave it to me on our wedding day."

"It's kind of a tradition Riggins and Stella started," Wes says with a smile, eyes on the necklace.

"Oh?" the interviewer asks, leaning in like she's excited to get some new piece of information no one else has yet.

"Well, when Riggins and Stella got married, they got each other's initials tattooed in a heart on their wrist. Their hearts on the other's sleeve, so to speak."

I remember reading about Stella and Riggins' tattoos in an article after they were reunited, and I've seen it in person now more times than I can count. My pulse goes erratic as he turns to me and smiles, something in his eyes like he knows he's about to send me spiraling, and he can't wait.

His fingers move out to the necklace, grabbing the heart with the letter W on it and tugging a bit so I move closer to him, my eyes locked on his.

"My wife doesn't have any tattoos, so I got her this necklace," he says, and my pulse pounds.

Last night, I asked him about all of the tattoos I could see with one shirt sleeve pushed up, but I didn't bother to ask about the other arm since it was blank on our honeymoon.

But what if...

"And you?" the interviewer asks, nearly chomping at the juicy story before her. "Do you have Harper's heart on your sleeve?"

I let out an involuntary choked laugh, starting to shake my head, but he doesn't stop looking into my eyes when he nods.

"Of course," he says, his hand moving to the arm of his sweater, the one with no tattoo sleeve, and shows the interviewer—and me—a small cursive H in a heart on the inside of his wrist.

"Oh my god," I whisper, unable to guard my expression as my heart pounds even faster.

That's permanent. A tattoo. On his skin forever.

"I take it that was a bit of a surprise to you?" the interviewer asks, and I let out another coughed laugh.

"Uh, yeah. You can say that." I shake my head to try and remind myself to keep it together before clearing my throat. "I know he got a new tattoo, of course. I saw the tape, but I didn't know..."

"I was waiting for a grand reveal," Wes says, then he grabs onto that necklace once more, using it to pull me to him and bring his lips to mine. "Happy wedding, little wife," he whispers against my lips, slightly open with awe and shock, before he leans in gently, pressing his there. It's a soft, quick kiss before he pulls back, then repeats the same move on my forehead.

Finally, he sits back, looking at the interviewer, who has a hint of dumbstruck awe expression on her face.

"Wow. Well. That was...you two really are the real thing," she says with a chuckle. "And I think that's a great place to stop, as we're running out of time." She turns to the camera and starts spewing facts on where to find Atlas Oaks and me online before handing it off to the news anchor. She turns to us, her entire composure different than when the camera was on, an easy smile taking over her face.

"Wow, you two really are something. When they brought this story to me, I was sure it was some kind of press relationship. We get a lot of those, you know. But you two. God." She looks from me to Wes. "You're one lucky girl."

"No," Wes says with a shake of his head, standing and offering his hand to me, tugging me up and pulling me into his side. "I'm the lucky one."

There is barely any time between our first interview and the second one as we move across town. I spend the short drive while Wes is on the phone with Leo, trying to organize my thoughts so I don't freak out on him. It's not until we're alone in the greenroom at the next studio, changing, that I find words to say, sort of.

Sort of, because it just kind of blurts out when he catches me staring at his bare chest as he changes sweaters.

"When did you get that?" I ask, my eye moving toward his wrist.

"Get what?" he asks, a cocky smile on his lips I kind of want to smack off. Thankfully, he tugs on a new sweater, this one burgundy, hiding his wildly distracting chest so I can think.

"You know what I mean, Wes, don't play stupid. It's not cute on you." I expect him to banter with me, but instead, he answers honestly.

"After we got back. I was going to do it before, but you aren't supposed to go in pools after."

I stare at him in disbelief. "But...but," I start, then finally speak coherently. "But that's permanent, Wes."

His head tips a bit as he smiles at me. "Yeah, and?"

"And...and...and this isn't!" I say, my hands moving in the air with the panic that I feel.

"You're already under my skin, Harper Holden. Might as well

put you there myself." I can feel my eyes going wider, and Wes laughs at that before adding, "This might not be permanent, Harper, but I don't plan on having another wife after you. Why not commemorate it?"

I open my mouth over and over like a fish out of water, trying to decide what to say and how to respond, but there's a knock on the door.

"Two minutes!" the production assistant yells.

Wes steps closer, tugging me against him, my chest meeting his as we stand toe to toe. "Believe I care about you yet?" he asks low.

"A tattoo doesn't prove you care about someone, Wes. It just proves you're impulsive," I whisper, though I'm not sure if I even believe myself.

"Got it. Not yet," he says, his smile widening before he steps back. "Go. You've got two minutes to finish changing."

The second interview is mostly the same as the first, but this time, there is a male and female interviewer. It's a well-known gossip show starring Marty Man and Kelsey Smith, where the two leads bicker and argue often, something viewers love. But being on this side of things, with Marty taking the lead, I am much more uncomfortable than in our first interview.

Especially since it seems he is already not fond of me.

"It really is something," he starts after we get through the niceties. "You know, many were confused by the announcement of your nuptials."

My stomach churns at the twinkle in his eyes. It's much different than the way the first interviewer spoke to us, more like he's preparing for some *gotcha* moment.

Still, Wes smiles at me, my hand in his, his thumb brushing over my skin like a calming metronome as I try and keep my serene look on my lips.

"How long have you been together?"

"Four months," I say quickly. It's the planned answer to line up with the timeline for our relationship Jeremy and Clarissa have made. According to them, Jeremy and I broke up months ago, hence why he and Clarissa are already so close. "We kept things quiet for a bit since we had mutual friends and wanted to make sure it wasn't something that would blow up in our faces. But then we decided to just go for it."

"You mentioned on social media last year that you were planning to announce a fashion line but haven't spoken of it since. What happened there?" Marty asks with a smug smile, and my body stills because I did not anticipate them asking about me and my life.

We'd been given a list of questions to expect, all pre-approved by Leo, as I've been told is the norm. Nothing about my business was on that list or something I anticipated. Still, there's no going back, so I keep it simple.

"I just wasn't inspired, you know?" I say tightly. "There's been a lot going on, and I just..." I hesitate, smiling at Wes. "I decided I wanted more time to perfect things and to devote my energy to my current clients."

"There's some speculation your business is struggling," he says, a sneaky smile spreading on his lips that I do not like. "You spent some time dating the head of marketing at Astor Fashion, and he recently told the press he was often giving you tips on how to change your designs to improve them. Do you have any commentary on that?"

My blood goes cold, both from the question and the all-consuming *rage* flowing through me at the idea that this is the bullshit Jeremy is spreading. This is the shit he is brewing up in his campaign against me.

All of this and for *what*? Daring to live my life after him? Not letting my business and my name crumble to the ground just because his little bitch of a new girlfriend decided she doesn't like me?

The interviewer stares at me with some kind of *gotcha* face, his co-host looking at him with a hint of confusion and irritation, like she didn't see this coming either, before he continues on.

"He then went on this morning to say you were doing all of this as some publicity stunt to save your drowning business. Let me read the statement he gave after your first interview this morning." His attention goes to some teleprompter behind me as he begins reading.

"Ms. Abbott is clearly continuing in her quest of gold-digging, looking for the next best thing after detonating her relationship with me. I wish Mr. Holden all the best and hope he has a really good prenup in place—and cameras on his lawn in case Ms. Holden decides to vandalize his home when he ends things."

Marty looks absolutely jovial as he reads this statement, and I want to *hit* him. I get it, really, I do. His job is to get some kind of juicy sound bite he can twist and manipulate to get views and money, but right now, I hate him.

I give a tight, uncomfortable smile, trying to figure out how to dismantle this without making things worse, but it turns out, I don't have to.

"We're done here," Wes says, standing before I can even think of something to say.

"What?" Marty asks, shock on his face as Wes puts his hand out to me.

"I said, we're done here," Wes repeats in a deep voice that moves through me like fire, warming all of the cold spots my panic created. From my peripheral, I see a few cameras, both studio and cell phone, raised and pointed in our direction, but all I can do is focus on Wes's hand in mine, his angry face pointed at the D-list celebrity before us.

"I still have a few questions, Wes. We—" Marty tries, but Wes shakes his head as I grab his hand. Wes grips mine tight before he pulls me up and into his arms, wrapping one around me as if to protect me from whatever threat might come.

"And you lost the privilege to speak to my wife and me the second you started to spew that bullshit. I won't sit by and have anyone speak to her like that, to question her motives so blatantly, much less in front of me. I love this woman more than life itself, and it might be untraditional, but when has Atlas Oaks ever been traditional? *You've had* what, four divorces, Marty? Maybe you work on your own issues instead of creating them for others."

And then we're moving, Wes walking us off stage as he rips off his mic and throws it on the ground. We're almost off the stage, those cameras still following our every move like this is some *Jerry Springer* episode and they're going to follow us backstage.

Wes stops us before we're fully off the sound stage, pulling me in close. His skin brushes against mine as he moves into the back of my dress to remove my own mic. It follows his to the ground with a clatter before he's tugging me once more toward the greenroom I changed in when we got here.

# SEVENTEEN

## WES

I don't know what I was thinking, storming off like that, but I know Leo is going to want to beat my ass when he finds out I just left Marty Man's show in a rage.

I'd do it again, too, especially with the look of panic and sadness that was written all over Harper's face when the asshole read the *bigger* asshole's statement on live television. I wanted to punch Marty when he first brought up her dating someone else recently, but I also knew there was a distinct possibility this would happen despite the network having sent over their questions previously and Leo approving them.

After Stella and Riggs brought all of their dirty laundry to light when they got back together, the press has been more interested in our band than ever, digging into everyone's history to try and find some kind of misdeed, something that doesn't match or line up with whatever story we're selling.

But I stupidly didn't expect the cannon to be aimed at my wife.

"Wes—" Harper starts, then stumbles as I move quickly to the greenroom. I catch her, wrapping an arm around her waist to keep her steady, my fingers digging into her side protectively as we continue to move on a mission.

I need to get out of the eyes of everyone around us.

I need to get Harper alone.

"Not here," I growl.

"What?"

"We're not talking here," I say through gritted teeth before swinging open the door to the greenroom where Harper's things are and slamming it closed behind us. She turns to look at me as I lock the door, her hands on her hips with irritation. I'd find it cute if I wasn't so fired up.

"Wes, what was that?"

"What was what?" I move through the room, grabbing the few things she used to touch up her makeup and tossing them into her bag before zipping it shut and moving to her clothes neatly folded on a chair, tossing those into the larger tote she brought.

"Wes, stop. I'm talking to you. You're freaking me out."

My entire body stills with her request, my shoulders lifting and falling as I take in a deep breath to try and calm myself and find some kind of inner peace despite my blood boiling.

How dare anyone speak to Harper like that? How dare anyone put that look on her face?

"I'm not going to let anyone talk about my wife like that," I say slowly, my back still to her. "He crossed a line, and that means we were done there."

"Wes, I'm not—" she starts, but before she can finish her sentence, I turn, dropping her bag to the floor before I take two wide strides toward her, backing her into the wall with my body. It might not be my best move, considering I'm purposely moving at a fucking snail's pace with her, but any pretense of control I've been putting up is long demolished.

"Don't finish that fucking sentence, Harper," I say, then put a hand to the bare skin on her neck, feeling the need to have my skin on hers in whatever small way I can.

Today was too much. *Too fucking much.* Two interviews, the necklace, the tattoo. What was I thinking? I'm going to scare her off before I can even start to convince her to give this—give *me*—a real chance.

But I can't control myself around Harper, not anymore, not when the excuse of her having someone else on her arm is long gone. Not when she's living in my house and wearing my ring, and sure as fuck not when she's moaning my name as she makes herself come.

Not when I've tasted her, kissed her, held her.

"Wes—" she says, the word a whispered plea, not unlike the way it sounded through her bedroom door.

"You're mine," I growl, my body loosely holding her in place. She could easily escape and she's choosing not to, choosing to stay and lift one of her own hands to my cheek like she somehow knows it might calm me.

It does.

I lean into her hand, my eyes closing for just a moment as I take a deep breath to try and center myself and continue. "You're mine, Harper, so let me be the first to tell you. When you're mine, I take care of you. That means no one talks to you like that, and no one questions you. It means I protect you. I know that's a lot, Harper. I know you're so stuck in the cage you created to keep yourself safe, but you need to know that's who I am, and you need to know that's who you are to me. That?" I move a hand, pointing it to the door and toward the mess we just left. "That will never happen again, not on my watch. And if it does, I'll act the same way. I will always remove you from any situation where you feel uncomfortable, where you are made to feel less than. Do you understand?"

A long beat passes, the hand on her neck loosening so she can leave, her hand on my cheek never leaving at all. Her soft thumb shifts, grazing over the stubble that's grown since last night when I shaved so I wouldn't have to in the morning, like somehow, she's finally understanding she can ground me, that she can center me with just a single touch.

"Yeah, Wes. I understand," she says. "I understand, but it's okay. I'm okay, Wes."

I sigh with relief, the feeling all-consuming, before I take a small step closer, closing the barely existent gap between us until our bodies are pressed together.

"I want to kiss you," I confess in a whisper, my lips brushing hers because I told her that I'd leave the choice in her hands. Something tells me *when* we cross the line of me kissing her whenever I want, I'll never want to stop.

"Then do it, Wes," she replies, and with those words, I throw all common sense away, and I kiss my wife.

It starts slow, a press of my lips to hers, tentative and careful, but she deepens it almost instantly, her hand going to the back of my head, twining in my hair and tugging me close, groaning as my lips open to hers.

Her tongue slides out to meet mine, tasting and tangling as the kiss deepens, my hand moving to her waist to pull her closer still. My other hand moves up to fist in her hair. She moans as I pull on it, tugging her to where I want her and taking control of the kiss. My knees bend, and I put my hand on the back of her thigh to lift her, pressing her against the wall and groaning into her mouth as my hardening cock presses into her center. Her hips start to move in time with the kiss, and soon she's moaning, grinding against me.

My hand is moving up the back of her thigh, toward her ass, while my other hand is buried deep in the back of her hair, guiding her to move her lips along mine as I devour her.

Suddenly, there's a knock on the door, before a gentle voice speaks.

"Mr. and. Mrs Holden, I'm Lauren, the show manager, and I would just like to offer my sincerest apologies—" She starts rambling on about Marty's behavior, but personally, I need her to apologize for interrupting me *really* kissing my wife for the first time and getting close to finally touching that ass I've been dreaming about for longer than I'd like to admit.

I groan as she breaks the kiss, but thankfully she doesn't back away. I rest my head against hers, and she starts giggling quietly, the sweetest, most adorable sound I've ever heard.

"We should probably let her out of her misery," Harper whispers with a smile as the woman continues to speak through the door.

"I'd rather stay here," I admit. The hand on my neck tightens, and I look up at her again, a small smile on her lips.

"Maybe..." She bites her lip and takes a deep breath. "Maybe we can do this again later."

"Do this?" I ask, smiling.

"Is making out off the table?"

A light blush burns on her cheeks, and my heart skips a beat like this is my first girlfriend instead of a woman I'm married to, but I smile wide.

"Definitely not," I whisper, pressing my lips to hers once more before stepping back and straightening her dress. Then we gather the rest of her things and head out the door hand in hand.

My phone won't stop buzzing, and, from the corner of my eye, I catch Harper continuing to hit ignore on her phone as we drive in silence.

"I'm not going to apologize," I say under my breath, eyes on the road.

"What?"

"I'm not going to apologize. For leaving the set, for yelling at Marty. I'd do it again. Leo's going to tell me I should make a formal apology, release a statement, blah blah blah." I look to her quickly before looking back at the road. "I'm not doing it." A moment passes in silence, and I expect her to argue, to tell me I have to, but, as tends to be her way, Harper surprises me.

"You shouldn't."

"I shouldn't?"

"No. It's good, you know, for the image. It seems more...real."

I groan at her words and the fact that this still isn't penetrating her shell, that she still thinks this is nothing but some kind of arrangement, that—

"Even if it's becoming something more," she adds.

I smile then, looking at her, and see she's looking at me, a shy smile on her lips, a pink blush to her cheeks.

"Good to hear, baby," I say. My phone buzzes again, and I hit ignore before a text pops up on the car's screen.

LEO: ANSWER ME NOW, ASSHOLE.

I sigh. "But I am going to have to go to Leo's office and talk him off a ledge," I say, reaching over and squeezing her knee. Her small, soft hand covers mine, and she gives me a reassuring squeeze back. "I'm going to drop you off at home and head over there."

"That's fine," she says, "The girls are going to want a full update anyway."

I smile at that, at Harper giving Jules and Ava a full rundown of the chaos of our morning, and I'm beyond grateful that Jaime told me Ava is fully on team *Harper and Wes.*

"Stay home until I have an idea of how we should handle this from Leo," I tell her a few minutes later as I unlock the front door and walk her inside. Even though my phone keeps buzzing and Leo is probably having a heart attack at this point, I need to make sure Harper is okay and gets inside safely. "I don't want you in an uncomfortable position with paparazzi hounding you."

There's no one around, the scavengers stuck behind the gate, but this is all new for Harper. I don't want her getting overwhelmed by the press and thinking this is too much for her before I fully get past her walls.

"Wes?" she asks once I close the door behind us and turn to her, staring for a few moments before she breaks the silence.

"Yeah, baby?" I step into her space gently, a hand moving to her jaw and my thumb stroking along her cheek.

"I, uh. I'm starting to get it. Me being yours." She licks her lips and closes the gap between us, putting a hand to my neck. "And you being mine," she says low.

"Yeah? Does that mean you're going to stop giving me such a hard time?" She smiles, the look teasing and devious at the same time.

"Probably not." I let out a small laugh and wrap an arm around her waist.

"Wouldn't want it any other way." Her fingers play with the hair at the nape of my neck.

"You should probably go, before Leo shows up at the house on a rampage." She smiles wide, and I like this, this joking between us, the freeness. "But kiss me before you go."

That last sentence is said in a whisper, that blush on her cheeks deepening, and I grin before doing just that, my hand on her jaw, tipping her face up to me and pressing my lips to hers gently, holding it there for not nearly long enough before breaking the kiss and stepping back before I get lost in it.

I can't do that right now, not when I have shit to do, not when there is the temptation of no one watching and a dozen beds nearby. Instead, I use the hand on her cheek to push her hair over her shoulders and center the W necklace around her neck, stealing time I don't really have but desperately want before stepping back.

"Lock this behind me," I order as I open the door, looking at my wife standing exactly where I left her, still dazed and dreamy-eyed.

"Okay, honey," she whispers, and then I give her one last smile before I close the door, knowing if I don't leave now, I never will. And even though I know I'm going to Leo's office to get my ass reamed, I smile the whole way there because my wife is finally willing to give this a chance.

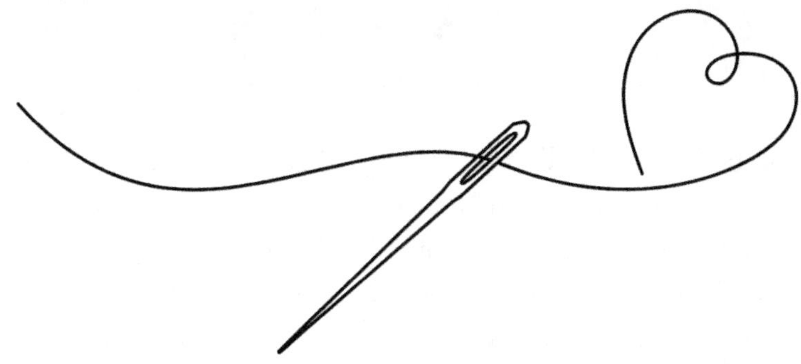

# EIGHTEEN

## HARPER

Life has started to settle, or as much as life *can* settle when everything is so up in the air. I've been busy, working on client commissions and trying—and miserably failing—to sketch something new. Instead of making any progress for a new line, I keep hitting the same damn roadblock every single time.

Wes has been gone for the past four days with the guys doing some preliminary press tours to promote the upcoming release. Unfortunately, or maybe fortunately, depending on how you look at it, we have not had any time for more than a few hot kisses since the Marty show incident, with Wes leaving barely a day later.

Instead, it's as if we're in the woo-ing dating phase, if this was a real relationship. Every morning Wes sends me a good morning text, then we message back and forth throughout the day, whether it's him telling me something stupid Reed did or playing musical memories through texts.

Wes was right: you really can learn so much about someone playing that game.

I've shared that I lost my virginity listening to "Best I Ever Had" by Drake (a *horrific* choice, especially since he very much proved to *not* be the best I ever had) and learned "Sugar, We're Going Down" was playing on the radio when Atlas Oaks got their first record deal.

Each day, Wes has also sent some kind of small gift to the house for me. The first was a gorgeous bouquet of flowers Laurel essentially *threw* at me, now sitting in my bedroom, where I mostly just work, choosing to sleep in Wes's bed even when he's not there. The next was a dozen cookies. That night, Wes called me to tell me he had some delivered to his hotel room, and we were having a virtual *cookie* date.

Yesterday he sent me the goofiest candle with his face on it that he got on some fan site and was supposed to smell like him. It completely missed the mark, but it made me smile all the same.

Now I'm in my room that I don't use for sleeping anymore, attempting to sketch and pondering what he'll send today, when there's a knock on the door. Looking up, Wes is leaning in the doorway, hair tousled and a wide smile on his face.

Without even thinking, I stand quickly, setting my sketchbook aside. "Hey," I say with a smile. "You're home." I rush to him, happy to see him and burying down what that all might mean as he pulls me into him and presses a deep kiss to my lips.

"I am. Happy to see me?"

"Yes." What does it matter anymore, being coy? I *like* Wes Holden, and I want to know where that could take us. "But I feel like I'm missing out on my fourth gift." I joke.

"You want a gift?" he asks, his arms around my waist. I shake my head and open my mouth to tell him I'm only teasing when he steps back, tipping his head to the side and grabbing my hand. "Come on, I want to show you something."

"I was just kidding," I say as he leads me down the hall.

"I know, but I still have something for you. It wasn't ready when we got home from the honeymoon, and I think it still needs some things, but I'm sure you'll have thoughts on them, so maybe it's best you see it now."

"Wha—" I start to ask, but the word dies on my lips as he opens a door that's been closed since I got here, light pouring into the hall as he guides me inside.

Large windows facing the wooded backyard line the far side of the room, letting in more natural light than I've seen in any other room in this house, with a small padded bench along the windows. On one side of the room is a large art desk currently set at an incline, and along the wall are dozens of cups with different mediums in them: lead pencils, pens, colored pencils, markers, and watercolors.

There are clear acrylic drawers holding what looks like tiny rhinestones and papers, but I'm too flustered taking in everything else to look. On the opposite side of the room is an L-shaped desk with a cozy-looking chair, three different seemingly brand-new sewing machines, and various fabrics in the organizers along the wall. When I open a cabinet, there are sewing notions in drawers: buttons and zippers and lace, quilting squares and rulers and cutting mats.

Everything and anything one might need to...create.

"What is this?" I ask, looking around, stepping toward the fabrics, and running my fingers over them reverently.

"This is...yours," he says with a small smile when I look over my shoulder at him, my heart pounding with a mix of nerves and excitement.

"Mine?"

He runs a hand through his hair nervously before stepping further into the room.

"It's a wedding gift." He shrugs and then smiles again. "The marriage was a bit last minute, as you know, so it wasn't ready when it was supposed to be."

I turn to face him, crossing my arms on my chest as my heart races. It's strange and overwhelming, this mix of excitement and gratitude and confusion.

"This isn't a wedding gift, Wes. This necklace," I say, fingers grazing the *W* at my neck, which I have only taken off to shower, "is a wedding gift. This is...way too much."

"Maybe it will inspire you," he says simply. "Come, look." He grabs my hand, moving me along the sides of the room. "This is for fabrics, though I don't know if I got any of the right kind. I figured you'd have opinions on those, so I didn't want to get too much. Most of the stuff in here is based on what Ava and Jules knew you liked, but we can swap out anything."

"Ava and Jules know about this?"

"Well, yeah, I couldn't do it all myself. But they were sworn to secrecy," he tells me.

"Hm," I add, looking around, wondering how on earth my friends didn't spill this secret to me, not even the tiniest *hint*.

"This is a desk, obviously. You can sketch here. Markers, pens, the whole nine. Ava says these are the markers you like?" He looks at me nervously, questioning it before I nod.

"Yeah, they are," I whisper before he continues to show me things. Sewing machines, thread, pins, and behind one of the cabinets, a dress form—everything I would ever need is here, as he shows me with a mix of excitement and anxiety.

"This all feels very...the Beast showing Belle the library," I say with a giggle I can't fight, suddenly giddy and brimming with new ideas.

"Does that make me a beast?"

"No, it makes you a handsome prince."

"I thought he was a beast?" he asks, confused.

I stop my perusing and stare at him aghast. "Have you never seen *Beauty and the Beast*?"

"I have no sisters, and I've been in a rock band since I was fifteen. No, I have not seen *Beauty and the Beast*," he says bluntly.

"I think that's a crime," I say under my breath but continue moving through the room, opening and closing random drawers and checking out what he's gifted me.

He laughs then moves to the art desk. "I figured this could be your inspiration center." He points to a giant cork board on the wall. "You can pin pictures and stuff here—the articles I read say that's very important, having your inspiration front and center."

The thought of Wes Holden reading articles about designers finding inspirations fills me with unexpected warmth as I inspect what he's set up. On the brown speckled cork, a few photos are pinned: one of Ava, Jules, and me from the wedding, a few photos of gowns I've designed in the past, and a shot of a beach that looks suspiciously like the one we went to on our honeymoon.

"There's something missing," I say, turning to look at him.

"I don't..." he starts, his brows coming together.

"You're not on the board, Wes."

He shrugs, gaze drifting to his hand and picking at a nail instead of looking at me.

"I didn't want to insert myself into your space," he says, as a faint blush blooms across his cheeks. "I didn't want to be presumptive. I wanted you to have a place that was all yours. Real."

I lick my lips and take a single step closer to him, feeling my heart pounding in my chest.

I've come to realize that even though I'm scared, even though he might just be caught up in the excitement of this, I made a vow to myself to be more *spontaneous*. And right now, I want to be spontaneous with Wes.

"What if I want you to be in my space?" I whisper, moving to him and putting a hand to his heated cheek.

This is more than anyone has ever done for me, and it's not about the money, though it's clear he spent a lot of it to get all of this done. It's about the thought. The way he pointed to every aspect of this room and explained why he put it there, why he thought I'd like it, the research he put into this project, this gift, as if he knew *me* before I even deigned to *give* him me.

He pulls me in close, pushing hair behind my shoulders the way he seems to love doing. "You want me in your space, little wife?" I don't hesitate to answer for once in my life.

"I think I do." It seems like we've switched positions, answering quickly and with my gut rather than my head and Wes overthinking each question, hesitating before he asks his next one.

"What is this, Harper?"

"I don't know, but I want more of it," I admit in a whisper.

"What does that mean to you?"

"It means...I don't know," I shrug, then elaborate. "It means I like being with you. I like when you kiss me, and I like having your hands on me, and I want more of that. I want to see where that can go." I'm not so deluded not to know there is something, a spark of some kind between Wes and me, but it terrifies me. It came on so quick, so fierce, and only because we were thrown into this thing.

Because of that, I'm so very hesitant to trust it.

Things with Jeremy went quickly as well. We met, we fucked, he told me he loved me in the first few weeks of us being together, showered me with gifts and attention and everything in between until I was in so deep, I couldn't see the red flags. And that red-hot mix of lust and *new*ness disappeared quickly, but I survived on the warmth of it for so long until one day, I woke up alone, shivering and unsure of how I got there.

"But I know I'd really like to, uh," I start, a blush burning on my cheeks, but I know if I want Wes to do anything, I need to speak it aloud. "Do stuff? Sleep together?"

He smiles and shakes his head gently, thumb brushing along the skin of my neck and sending a shiver through me.

"I'm not fucking you, Harper," he says, and without permission of my head, I pout.

"Why not? We're married."

He lets out a laugh then before smiling softly like he finds me adorable. "Because I don't want you to have a single doubt in your mind the first time you let me slide into you." The mere *thought* of that has a wave of heat running through me, and he pulls me inexplicably closer to him, his voice going lower. "That first time I fuck you, you're going to know down to your soul I'm absolutely wild for you, not because we're married or because you're convenient or because you're with me all the time. But because you're mine, and I've been obsessed with you since that first night I met you."

Somehow, he knows all of my arguments, all of my hang-ups, without me even speaking them aloud. It should be terrifying. But something about him knowing me this well is exhilarating; it solidifies something inside of me that I haven't been willing to look at too closely yet.

"We can do other things," I suggest in a whisper. He groans, then opens his mouth to protest, but I'm already moving to my tiptoes, closing the gap between us and pressing my lips to his.

Like every other time I've kissed Wes, the world melts away, and my senses come to high alert. Instantly, I'm hyper aware of the feeling of his hand on my lower back, of the scruff of his cheek under my hand, of the warmth of his body.

Just as quickly as I started it, he takes over the kiss, pressing my body into his and slipping his tongue into my mouth, tasting me and groaning. My heart skips at the sound, as if the mere taste of me turns him on.

He takes a step, forcing me to do the same until my back is to the wall, pinned there by his hard body, though I'm not complaining. My breaths become pants as his lips trail down my neck, as my head tips to the side to give him more room.

His hand moves, one thick, rough finger moving into the waist of the loose sweatpants I'm wearing and running along the stretchy band, teasing me.

"Yes," I whisper, my hips moving toward him involuntarily and feeling his hard cock against my stomach. I tighten my hand on his nape, pulling myself closer and grinding against him. "Please." I've never wanted—no, *needed*—someone the way I need Wes, but I can't find it in me to feel anything but excited.

"We should stop," he says, putting his forehead to mine, my back to the wall, our breathing labored.

My hand moves up his chest, hooking behind his head and tugging him close to me. "I want you to touch me," I whisper. "I want you inside of me. I want *you*, Wes."

"Am I just an itch to scratch?" he asks in a strained whisper, voice husky and breath hot along my neck.

"You know you're not," I confess, the words slipping from my lips, but it seems to be the right thing to say when he groans loudly.

"Fuck it," he says, then dips his hand below the waistband of my sweats, over my belly, past my underwear, sliding to cup me. I moan loudly at the feel of his warm hand on me, in that intimate, needy place.

*Finally.*

It feels so fucking right.

His lips are on mine, and his hand is down the front of my panties, playing along the wet seam of my pussy as he devours my lips. His thumb moves, brushing over my already swollen clit, and I sigh into the kiss, shifting my hips to get more of whatever he'll give me. He groans out a curse before his finger moves down, a single thick digit sliding into my opening and pulling a moan from me.

"I'm going to make you come, Harper, but that's it. And I need you to know I'm making you come as your husband, as a man wholly consumed by you, not as some fake relationship itch that needs to be scratched." His finger hovers halfway inside me as my hips try to move to get more. "I need you to know this is more to me, and whether you're willing to admit it yet, it's more to you, too. It always has been." He slides in a bit more. "That's why you said yes. That's why you didn't even hesitate when I asked you to marry me." He sinks in deeper, and my eyes flutter shut.

"No, no. Eyes on me, beautiful. Keep those pretty eyes open while I finger you," he says, and I groan, opening my eyes and looking at him, his eyes burning. When I lock my eyes on him, he slides his finger in deep, then pulls out before repeating the motion.

"Wes," I moan. "I need...oh, God, I need..."

"I know, baby. I know. I'll give you what you need." His finger slides out, rubbing over my clit and forcing another groan from me. His lips tip up, still parted with heavy breaths, before he slides two fingers inside me this time, stretching me. "God, you're so fucking tight, Harper. So wet for your husband, aren't you?"

I nod, unable to say anything, to *do* anything other than focus on the pleasure building in my belly. He starts moving faster, fucking me quickly the way I want, the way I need, and it tightens in my belly, and my pussy tightens around his fingers.

"Fuck, Wes," I breathe out. "I'm right there."

"That's it, baby. Fall for me, come for your husband," he groans, his forehead to mine.

With his permission, I fall, spiraling as lights flash behind my eyes, though I keep them open and locked on Wes. He groans loudly, like my pleasure brings him pleasure, his fingers sinking in deep and his palm grinding on my clit, and aftershocks race through me. A year might pass as I come back down to earth, but Wes holds me the entire time patiently.

"Oh, my god," I say. His smile widens at my words, and he opens his mouth to speak, but we're interrupted.

"Hey, Wes," a familiar and irritated voice says, and almost instantly, I shift away from Wes, his fingers sliding out of me as I rearrange my sweatpants nervously. Wes's eyes never leave me, that smile playing on his lips. "Oh, don't worry, I walk into this kind of thing all the time, doesn't faze me at all," Laurel says with a smug look.

A blush burns across my cheeks.

"Laurel," Wes says in warning, and she rolls her eyes.

"I'm just saying, it's not the first time I've walked in on you making out with someone. It's just what happens when you're someone's right hand."

I picture myself tearing out her hair and bitch-slapping her.

"Did you call that person I asked you to contact?" Wes asks, clearly annoyed. With his words, her face goes a bit cold.

"They didn't have any availability," she tells him, the conversation unclear to me, but with the way she twirls her hair around her finger, I get the unsettling feeling she's lying to Wes.

"Did you try the one in Hudson City?"

"You didn't ask me to try the one in Hudson City," she says, and I'm half surprised she doesn't pout.

Wes's jaw goes tight before he sighs deeply, running a hand through his hair and mussing it more than I did just moments before. "I'll do it myself."

He reaches in his pocket for his phone, but before he moves, he turns to me.

"I have to go on a bit of a press junket tomorrow," he says, and I scrunch my nose up. "It'll be another four days, but when I get back, we have a press thing. Willa Stone's last tour stop is on Saturday, and we're in the VIP box," he says. His hand moves to my cheek, making me forget all about the nuisance in the room.

"Oh. Okay," I whisper.

"I also have to take my wife out on a real date soon, wine and dine her." I giggle—actually *giggle* at his words, and his eyes twinkle with the sound. "When are you free?"

"Hmm?"

"When are you free, Harper? For dinner. Or lunch?"

"Oh, I, uh..." I try and think, but he's so close to me, blurring my mind, and I can't piece words together, much less make myself sound more interesting than I am. "I have no life." He smiles wider. "Except you," I add like an idiot, and his smile goes to a straight-up grin. "Shit, I didn't mean, I just..."

"Got it. You're at my mercy."

I shrug. "Yeah, I guess."

"I really like the sound of that, little wife."

"Me too, Wes."

He stares for a long moment, then leans forward, pressing another, softer kiss to my lips. "I look forward to finishing this later," he says. "Now go make something beautiful, baby."

Then he's walking off, stupid Laurel scurrying behind and leaving me in my new design room, body buzzing and, for once, my mind not even a little bit confused.

Because surprise, surprise, I like my husband.

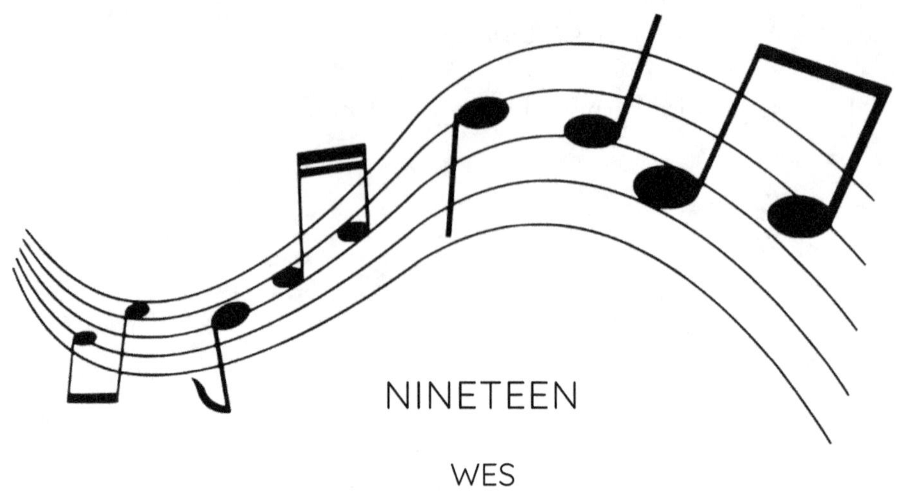



"Have you seen—" I start, staring at my phone as I walk into the ensuite bathroom in my room—our room—but the words die on my lips when I catch sight of my wife. She's in a short dress, the darker green, which makes her hair and her fair skin stand out beautifully, makeup full out, all dark and sexy with something that makes the freckles across the bridge of her nose more prominent. Her hair is long and loose, with soft curls at the ends, and she's wearing a pair of heels high enough to bring her to my chin. The only jewelry she wears is her wedding rings and the W necklace, making me feel the sudden urge to buy her more, to see her dripping in things I bought for her.

She looks breathtaking. *A fucking wet dream.*

"Jesus, Harper," I murmur, stepping closer and reaching for her, whatever I walked in here to show her long forgotten.

She laughs and steps back with a shake of her head, putting a hand between us. "No, no. I worked too long on this, and I'm not having you fuck it up."

*Fuck it up* because we've been in the position to fuck up her makeup quite a bit as of late.

After giving her the design room and making her come, kisses have been far from off the table. I kiss her good morning and good night, and we usually get to some form of second base at least once a day, making out and feeling each other up like teenagers, but we haven't gone further than that except for yesterday in my music room.

It's killing me, the wait, but it's also been well worth it. We've talked more in the past week than we have the entire time I've known her, and she hasn't avoided me *once*. Gone is her hesitation in tiptoeing toward *more* with me, and even though every day she makes it her mission to test my restraint, I refuse to go any further with her until she's sure she's ready to be mine.

"Look at you," I whisper, grabbing her hand and lifting it above her head as she twirls in a circle for me, her lilting giggles filling the bathroom and echoing around in the most gorgeous melody known to man. "You made this?"

She gives me a devious grin and nods. "I made it so you'd want to take it off."

"Mission fucking accomplished," I murmur, taking in how it clings to her curves perfectly. "You know, if we didn't have somewhere to go..."

"Don't you tease me, Wes Holden, because I'll strip down right now if you actually make good on that promise," she says, glaring at me with hands on her hips.

I close my eyes, groaning at the mere idea of that. "Harper..."

"No, don't you *Harper* me. You're the one who stops things every time they get hot and heavy."

I open my eyes, forcing myself not to smile at her angry face because she would *hate* that. Instead, I pull her in close. "If things go my way very soon, I'll have all the time in the world to fuck you exactly the way you want, little wife."

"Tonight?" she asks, hopefully.

I smile at her, lifting a hand, pushing her soft silk hair behind her shoulder. "We'll see."

She glares at my non-answer. "Maybe tonight after the concert, I'll take care of myself if you won't."

I stare at her and smile. She thinks that's a threat, but it would actually be a prize.

"Harper, baby, you want to play with your pretty pussy while I watch, I'm more than happy to be an observer." She scrunches up her nose, her blush growing deep as she rolls her eyes. But I see it there: intrigue.

Maybe tonight *will* be a fun night after all.

"What did you want to show me?" she asks, turning back to the mirror and using a finger to swipe at the corner of her perfect, full pink lips, trying to find some imperfection that isn't there. Tonight, we're going to Willa Stone's concert and then a wrap party afterward, both because it's a great press opportunity and because I want to show my wife off to all of the industry friends I've made over the years.

"Oh, yeah. Have you seen this yet?" I ask, bringing my phone over to her, the video queued up already.

"Seen what?"

I don't answer, instead hitting play once my front is to her back, my phone before both of us. I watch over her shoulder, though I've seen it countless times already: it's *that* entertaining.

It's a social media post, taken by an intern at Astor Fashion. Jeremy is smiling as he rips an envelope open, a silly cat with the word *Congratulations!* big and bold on the front. When he opens the card, it instantly starts moaning, some mechanism inside triggered to let out loud, aggressive sex noises. The room goes quiet in the video, and Jeremy's face goes beet red as he closes the card.

Unfortunately for him, the card I found doesn't stop, instead it just gets louder. Jeremy frantically opens and closes the card, trying to figure out how to stop it, and sniggers around him in the office start up. Angry that it won't stop and clearly embarrassed, he tries to rip it in half to stop the noise. Unfortunately for him, it triggers the glitter bomb inside that explodes all over his face.

The video ends, and I step back to take in Harper, who is in near tears, laughing so hard, waving her hands at her face so as not to mess up her makeup.

"I think this covers number three," I say, and Harper looks at me confused as she catches her breath. "On your *Destroy Jeremy* list. Convince his coworkers he's the worst? I don't know if it makes them think he's *bad*, but it definitely doesn't put him in a good light."

Her jaw drops with shock. When she showed me that list the first night in this house, I read over it, taking notes of which I might be able to quietly take over for her. She might not be willing to get back at her ex after last time, but I'm more than willing and capable of not leaving a trace.

"Did you do that?" she asks, a bit incredulous. I shrug.

"Just another little fuck you. It's the least he deserves."

A small smile plays on her lips as I slip my phone in my back pocket.

"You're absolutely diabolical. Can you send that to me? I need to send it to Jules and Ava," she says, and I nod, tugging my phone out again. Unfortunately, it pulls my wallet out with it, and I watch as it tumbles to the ground, a worn piece of paper falling out as it does.

Harper leans down at the same time I do to grab it, me in panic, her just to be the sweet woman she is, and we knock heads as we do. "Fuck," I grumble, ignoring my own discomfort, and my hands move to her face to inspect as we stand. "Sorry, are you okay?" My thumb runs over the spot feeling for a bump, but there isn't one, thankfully.

"Yeah, it was barely anything," she says.

There's a faint mark on her forehead, but nothing crazy. Still, because she's close and I can't pass up the opportunity, I press my lips to the spot where we met.

"All better," I whisper. Her eyes go hazy the way they seem to do when I kiss her before they go confused, her brows furrowing. "What?"

"What is that?" she asks, leaning down, this time ducking to avoid my head. It's then I remember why I knelt to grab my wallet so quickly: because something fell out. Before I can stop her, her fingers are holding onto a photo, lifting and inspecting it, the worn edges and the spots where my wallet has worn the image almost to the backing paper.

"Is this...?" she starts but doesn't finish.

I don't answer because it's obvious.

It's a photo from over two years ago in a night club in South Jersey, all the guys and Stella in the shot, plus Ava and Jules.

And, of course, Harper right next to me, a shit-eating grin on her lips, red hair lit with the nightclub lights. It's folded so Harper and I are on one side, the rest of the group on the other.

I told myself I printed it because it was the first shot we had with the whole band and Stella since we were kids, but even I knew that was a lie. We have photos from Stella and Riggs's wedding, all of us dressed up, the setting more idyllic, and the lighting perfect.

But those didn't have Harper in them.

"Why do you have this?" she asks, looking up at me.

"Ava sent it to Stella, Stella sent it to all of us." She looks at me, a look of *don't be an idiot* on her face. I sigh, then give her another lie, biting my lip. "It was the first picture I had of the whole band and Stella in a long time."

"I'm not a moron, Wes," she says.

I stare at her, trying to decide what to do, what to say next, before finally, I give in with a sigh.

"No, you're not."

"So you kept this photo..."

"I've had that photo in my wallet since Stella printed it out for me." She stares at me, and I hope she'll drop it there, but this is my Harper, my Harper, who, even though she thinks she's predictable and a pushover, the only thing predictable about her is how stubborn she is.

"Which was?"

I roll my lips into my mouth, biting down before confessing.

"I don't know, a year ago? It was a joke because I kept asking about the pretty redhead she was friends with, the bridesmaid at Jamie's wedding." Her breathing goes short and quick, and I feel the need to continue and explain. "It wasn't weird, I swear."

It feels like a lie because obviously, having a photo of a relative stranger in your wallet is a bit weird, even if you did end up marrying her. "It was a joke. She gave it to me for Christmas and said it was for my wallet, so I slid it in there."

Harper plays with the worn corners, then looks at me again.

"But..."

"But...but then I left it here. I like it. I like everyone in it, figured...figured it was a good photo." God, why am I so embarrassed by this? I try to be cool for Harper, to keep things easy and not overwhelm her, and this is *absolutely* going to overwhelm her.

"So you've had a photo of me in your wallet for over a year?"

I shrug, suddenly feeling stupid and weird, then move to step back. I'm surprised when she doesn't let me, when an arm goes around my neck, holding me close, the photo between us lost. For a moment, I want to argue, to tell her the photo is precious and I don't want it to get hurt, but then she smiles, and I can't think of anything but the woman in my arms.

I can't focus on anything but the all-consuming need to kiss her.

So I do.

Eventually, the kiss breaks, and her eyes ease open, head tipping back as she looks at me with a wide smile.

"Oh, my god. You like me," she whispers, awe in the word, and I pull her in close again.

"I thought I made that clear when I put a ring on your finger," I say with a smile.

"No, like you *like me*, Wes. Outside of being friends and conveniently married."

"I thought I made *that* clear when I fingered you in your design room." Harper's face scrunches up in the most adorable way, and I press a kiss to the tip of her scrunched-up nose.

"You haven't done it since," she says begrudgingly.

"That's because I've been into you for a long time, Harper. I've just been waiting for you to pull your head out of the sand and realize you want someone who is completely and utterly obsessed with you, and I don't want sex to complicate that."

"Oh," she whispers.

"So, are you ready to admit there's something between us?" I ask with a smile.

"I thought I made that clear when I married you," she echoes, and I give her a look, moving us until her ass is pressed against the counter of the bathroom.

"You've made a lot of things clear since then, Harper, but one of them has not been that you're ready to make this something more."

"I thought I made *that* clear when I came on your fingers in my design room," she whispers, white teeth biting into her plump, pink-painted bottom lip, and I groan, pressing my growing erection into her stomach.

"I must have been distracted," I whisper, dropping my face to hers, ready to throw everything to the wind and finally consummate this marriage the way I've been dying to for a month.

For years, if we're being honest.

"Tell me, Harper. Tell me you're ready to be more," I say, my lips brushing hers as I speak there. "Not as friends, not as friends with benefits. As my wife. As *mine*. As something that's going to last a fuck of a lot longer than twelve months."

I pray to whoever will listen that she's ready.

I'll wait.

I'll wait a month, a year, a lifetime if it means I get Harper Holden in a real way, if it means she did it on her terms, if it means she came to me willing and open.

But I'd much rather spend that lifetime loving her.

"Yeah, Wes," she says, looking up at me, nothing between us. "I'm ready."

"Fuck," I groan, dropping my mouth to hers and devouring her. I expect her to argue about messing up her lipstick or her hair, but instead, her arms loop around my neck, pulling me closer like she, too, can't resist having anything between us.

Her phone buzzes with an alarm, something I've learned she sets to keep herself on track and not lose time. I groan, leaning my forehead to hers.

"We gotta go," she whispers.

"Why?" Her lips tip up with a smile.

"Because we have to be seen at Willa's show."

"Why?" I whisper again, because I'm ready to ditch this whole plan and run.

She looks at me like there's a genuine battle in her face before she answers truthfully.

"Because I want to go out with you. I want to be seen out with my husband. And I made this pretty dress." Her lips tip up. "And because you've been torturing me for the past month. I figure it's time I repay the favor."

I groan again but press my lips to hers gently, casually, careful not to take it any further, before I step back and grab her hand.

"What my wife wants, my wife gets."

And then we're off. But I leave content knowing everything has changed for Harper and me.

# TWENTY

## WES

The concert is torture.

Pure, unadulterated torture.

We spend the evening in a VIP box, the rest of the band, Leo, and a few other people I know to be friends of Willa's also in attendance for the final show of her sold-out stadium tour, but spending the night with a mix of friends and acquaintances isn't what's torture.

It's not the concert, which, as always, is impeccable and wildly entertaining, and it's not having to spend the entire show with the band elbowing me and quietly ribbing me about falling for my fake wife when she's not paying attention. It's also not the way there are cameras on us the entire time.

The painful part of the night is watching Harper dance the entire two and a half hours, hips swaying seductively, arms over her head, enjoying herself. She's the sexiest woman I've ever seen, and she isn't even trying, simply just *enjoying* herself, and it's absolute torture. It doesn't help that there is no doubt in my mind that when we get home tonight, I'm going to fuck my wife for the first time.

I would have skipped this entire night and spent it eating her out and making her moan my name the way she did in the hotel room and again in her design room, but she really wanted to come tonight. I could see the warring on her when the alarm went off, the way she was battling with both desires. I have made a promise to give her everything she wants from here on out, and I won't break that vow just to please myself.

Not even when she pulls me in close during one of the more sultry songs and grinds her ass against me, the VIP box a chorus of hoots and hollers as she smiles over her shoulder at me. But that's when I turn her, pull in close, and kiss her, using my hand on her lower back to press her into me.

"Stop, or I'm taking you out of here over my shoulder," I warn.

She leans in, moving to her tiptoes and putting her lips to my ear. "Promise?"

I quietly groan, closing my eyes to attempt to center myself, knowing she would want to watch the rest of the concert. "Be good, Harper, and you'll get rewarded."

She stares at me, a hand moving through the hair at the back of my neck before she smiles. The song changes to a more upbeat, exciting one then, and she smiles.

"Fine, you party pooper," she says, then bounces off to go dance with Stella.

"That one's a handful," Beck says, walking over to me and handing me a fresh beer. I watch as my wife smiles and jumps, holding hands with Stella and singing at the top of her lungs.

"Don't I know it," I say, but I say it with a wide smile.

Finally, the concert is over, and I reach for Harper's hand, gripping it tight before pulling her close to me, about to whisper in her ear that we're going to sneak out now while everyone is distracted. Unfortunately, a hand on my shoulder stops me. I close my eyes, breathing in deep through my nose before Leo even speaks in my ear.

"Don't even fucking think about it," he says in a low tone. "You have to go to this after-party. A million cameras are going to be there."

"Leo," I say in warning, and Harper looks over her shoulder at me, a look of amusement on her lips.

She is *thoroughly* entertained by this.

"No." He shakes his head, and I open my mouth to argue more, but he speaks instead. "There are going to be people there she needs to talk to. Designers and fashion magazines. Willa's stylist is specifically very interested in talking to her."

I close my eyes and take a deep breath, knowing with that new information alone, I know we *have* to go. I'll do anything to help Harper reclaim her career after the damage her ex has done to it.

"An hour, tops," I say, giving him a glare.

He looks from me to my smiling wife, who hasn't heard the conversation over the noise, but I'm sure she has pieced it together.

"An hour," he agrees before walking off.

"We can't get out of the after-party," I tell Harper, pulling her in close. In her thin, skin-tight dress, I can feel every curve of her as my hand moves to rest on her lower back. *This* dress has been the biggest source of my pain and suffering tonight.

"And why would you want to get out of such a fun evening?" she asks, her smile widening, her head tipping up to look at me. She gently grazes her lips along the underside of my jaw, and I groan, something she probably feels more than hears.

I lower my hand to her ass, pressing her close to me. "Because I'm ready to fuck my wife."

Her eyes go wide, feeling my hardening cock against her. The tables have clearly turned, with her playing cool and my absolutely desperate need for her, and it's clear she's greatly enjoying this.

"Oh," she mouths, and I smile back.

"Come on. Let's get this over with."

Harper is giddy at the after-party, eyes wide as she looks around the room filled with celebrities and musicians. I forgot this, a bit jaded to it, how exciting it can be to see your idols all together in the same room, acting like normal people.

"You good?" I ask, leaning into her.

"I, uh," she starts, looking around, her eyes going wide when she catches her eye on boy band singer Mickey Kline. "Yeah. It's just a lot. I've never been to something like this, been around so many celebrities."

I'm sure her ex had the opportunity to go to star-studded events, but from what it seems like, he wouldn't have taken her if he did. I hate that she was treated so poorly, but I'm secretly grateful I'm the one who gets to give her these experiences, the one who gets to see her eyes get wide and excited.

"You want a drink?" I ask, tipping my head toward the bar in the corner. "Relax a bit?"

She shakes her head quickly, not hesitating at all, like she's already considered and vetoed this option.

"You sure?"

"I have a soda. I want..." She bites her lip, looking around, then at me, eyes landing on my lips. "I want to remember tonight fully. Nothing twisting up my mind."

My heart races, and I pull her in close, my lips going to the spot beneath her ear and pressing there as I whisper. "I have a feeling I could be absolutely hammered tonight, and every moment from the second we get home will still be imprinted on my brain for eternity."

Her body shivers beneath my hands, and I smile.

"Yeah, but I don't want to give you even the slightest excuse not to consummate this marriage tonight, Mr. Holden," she whispers, and even though the room is loud, I hear every single word, feeling it in my gut.

"Leo's not looking," I say. "We could sneak out." Her arms on my neck tighten, and her lips roll in, hiding a smile as she looks at something over my shoulder. I sigh, knowing exactly what—or rather, *who* —it is.

"The fuck I'm not," Leo says from behind me, a hand going to my shoulder. I groan, then turn to him, a shit-eating grin on his lips like he loves my misery. "Now come. Willa wants to say hi to your wife." I lean back, looking at Harper, whose eyes have gone wide with panic. "She wants to talk to you about your designs. She's already working on the aesthetic for the next album."

Harper's almost pale when I shift her, moving to guide her in the direction of our host. "Come on, little wife, time to make your move."

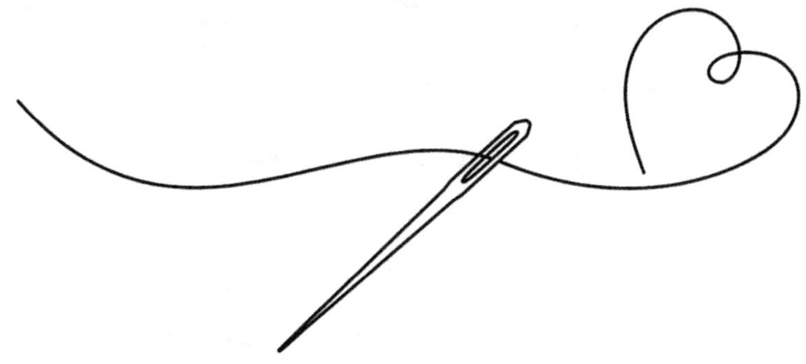

# TWENTY-ONE

## HARPER

Wes's hand goes to my thigh once we're in the car, and it burns there for the first five minutes of the too-long twenty-minute drive back to his house. I've never wanted to take him up on any of the offers of various luxuries, but tonight, I wish we'd have taken a town car or something where we could roll up the divider.

I'd be on my knees before him, his cock in my mouth, finally knowing what he feels like, what he tastes like. Or maybe I'd have just shifted my panties to the side and straddled him, letting him slide in deep.

My body shifts at the idea, uncomfortable and turned on and needing...something.

*Anything.*

"Are you okay, little wife?" Wes asks. "You seem a little fidgety."

"I'd be a lot better if we'd gotten a hotel room," I mumble under my breath, boldness fueled by nothing but lust and desire. I didn't drink at Willa's after-party, wanting to be completely present and not give Wes even the smallest excuse to put off tonight.

Now I'm regretting it, wondering if a drink would have taken the edge off. His hand moves, sliding inward but not up, gripping and gently pulling so my legs are forced to open a bit. My breath hitches, my breathing racing a bit more.

"And why is that?" he asks.

"Because then you could be inside me by now." A low groan leaves his lips, making me lick mine. Despite the dark of the car, I'm able to see the planes of his face, the look of near pain as he drives.

"Would I now? That's quite the assumption," he says, but as he does, his finger slides up gently. He moves so slowly, if I weren't so in tune with every twitch, I might not notice it. I widen my legs to give him room in response.

"Call it female intuition," I say, then sigh as his pinky finger grazes along the front of my underwear. "Wes."

"Hmm?"

"How far are we from home?" I ask, even though it's displayed on the navigation of the car. We still have at least fifteen minutes left.

"Too long," he says, finally dropping a bit of the facade. His fingers glide up along the line of my hip before tucking under and moving along the lacy seam of my panties. "Too fucking long," he repeats as his fingers move down closer to where I need him most, want him most.

Something takes over me then, all common sense and restraint fly out the window, and I lean back and further widen my legs. "I want you, Wes," I whisper, and those words pull a deep groan from my husband's lips. It's a relief knowing he's as keyed up as I am, knowing he's aching like me.

"What do you want, baby?" The *baby* shoots through me, pushing my need higher. I might even like it better than *little wife*.

"I want you to touch me," I whisper, any shred of shyness or propriety long gone.

"Where?"

"My clit. My pussy. I don't care, Wes. I just need your hands on me," I moan, hips shifting to try and get more, to get him closer, to get *anything*. Instead, his fingers continue to graze the seam of my pussy over my underwear, quickly dampening with my need.

"Show me," he says low and sultry.

"Show you?" I ask, confused.

"Guide me. Let me feel what you want." My breathing goes heavy at the idea of that, as my mind creates a movie from his suggestion, but he must take my silence as not understanding. "Take my hand and show me what you want, Harper. Now."

I groan aloud at his demand and the firmness of his words. It turns out I might like Wes Holden bossing me around.

A lot.

I do as he asks, moving my hand to hover over his, so much bigger than mine, then shifting the very tips of our fingers upward before dipping beneath the line of my panties. His middle finger grazes over my sensitive clit, and my hips shift up. The finger hovering over his presses down to get more pressure where I desperately need it, and a low, long moan leaves my lips.

"That's it, baby. Take what you need," he says in a strained voice.

I use my hand to guide the rough pad of his thumb to circle my clit, and heat explodes through me, my head tipping against the back of the seat as I moan, the feelings unbearably good, but I need more.

I need so much more, and tonight is the night I take it, moving my finger with his down to my entrance, helping him tease me, circling my opening, gathering wetness there.

"Jesus, Harper, you're fucking soaked." I moan at the reverence in his words, my mind so disconnected from reality as I slowly slide his finger into me, stretching and filling me much more than only my finger would.

"Holy fuck," he groans, and my body slackens as his finger takes over, sliding out and then in. Soon both of us are working together to slowly fuck me in the passenger seat of his car.

It's the hottest experience I've ever had; finger fucking myself with a man, the palm of his hand cupping my pussy and grinding right against my clit as I move my hips.

"That's it, baby. Ride those for me." The car is quiet except for my light moans, Wes's labored breathing, and the wet sound of our fingers between my legs. I shift to take my hand away, to let him take over since he clearly knows what he's doing, but he growls loudly, hand stopping me altogether and forcing me to freeze at the very real threat that he'll stop.

"No, you keep your hand there," he groans. "Finger fuck yourself *with* me. I want you to remember just how good we work together, Harper, so later, when you try and second-guess things, if you ever try to make yourself feel good again, you remember just how good of a team we make."

I moan at his words, and even though the meaning of them should probably spike fear in me, brewing on that ever-constant worry that something will go bad, it doesn't. Instead, I moan, my hips rocking, my hand over his, pushing deeper, tilting my hips to get where I need him most, to show him exactly what I like.

He's a quick learner, alternating fucking me hard then fast, pressing his finger up along my G-spot, his palm scraping along my swollen clit and sending bolts of pleasure through me. It starts to build, tightening in my stomach and my lower back as I moan, legs wide, not a shred of embarrassment left in my system.

No, like this, with Wes groaning and finger fucking me, with my hand above his guiding him as he speeds home to finally fuck me for real. I feel perfect. Wanton and desired and like I could do no wrong.

We stay locked like that for what feels like a heartbeat and an eternity simultaneously when it starts to build, when my pussy tightens around both of our fingers, when my hips start to move more fervently, trying to tip the scale and come when suddenly, something changes.

Wes's hand goes still, the car goes quiet, and I realize we're home. He must have broken a dozen speeding laws, cutting the twenty-minute drive by at least ten.

"Wes," I moan, my hand moving and then a whimper leaving my lips as he slides his hand out of me, taking mine with him. "No."

"We're home," he whispers, then steps out of the car.

My body is on fire as I watch him slowly round the hood to the passenger side, smiling at me all the way. Fuck that. My hand moves, slipping beneath my wet underwear alone this time and beginning to rub my clit quickly to get myself over the edge. Finally, he opens the door to find me shifting in the seat, moaning gently. I hate to admit it, but he was right: it's not nearly as good without his hand beneath mine.

"What do we have here?" he asks, eyes twinkling with laughter as I sit in the passenger seat, spread wide, rubbing myself. I *need* to come. It's an all-consuming thing now, especially with Wes's eyes on me, heated and just as needy as I feel.

"I need to come," I moan.

"Couldn't wait, could you?" he asks. He leans forward, and I expect him to grab me, pull me into the house, and fuck me until neither of us can move, but he doesn't do that. Instead, with the trees lining his property and the dark of night nearly cloaking him, he grabs my hips, shifting me, pulling me until my ass is on the edge of the seat and tugging my panties down. It's naughty, it's revealing, and it makes my heart pound.

"This isn't yours," he says low, swatting my hand away and running a thick finger through my wetness. "This is all mine now, Harper. And look how fucking pretty it is."

"Please," I moan, not even bothering to argue with that. I can be a feminist and still want my husband to own my pussy.

"Please what?"

"Please make me come, Wes," I plead, eyes on his. He smiles, then gives me what I want, no, *need.* Two thick fingers slide into me, hooking up and he starts to fuck me, hard and fast, his thumb brushing over my clit as he does. "Wes!" I shout, my head tipping back with the pleasure of it, but his free hand moves quickly to the nape of my neck, pushing my head forward until my forehead touches his.

"No, Harper. You're going to look into my eyes and know your husband is the one giving you this."

I breathe heavily and nod, and then it happens. I come, tumbling into a ravine of all-consuming pleasure that racks through my body violently. It seems to go on forever, his fingers slowing in me as the orgasm fades out, leaving me panting.

"We're home now, wife. Now I can do everything I've been dreaming about for fucking years. First though." He moves, grabbing my hand and moving so my hand is once more stacked under his, the opposite of how we spent the car ride. This time his hand is guiding mine toward my lips. "Clean these, baby."

And then his middle finger and mine are in my mouth, his eyes locked on mine. I run my tongue over our fingers, moaning at the combined taste of me and him and the fucking *promise* in his eyes.

"Good girl," he says with a smile before helping me out of the car, tugging my dress down, my panties long gone, and leading me toward the house.

# TWENTY-TWO

## WES

"Go upstairs," I say as we step inside, kicking my shoes off into a corner as I turn my back to her to lock the door behind us. "Our bed. Naked." It's a command, one I expect her to obey.

The drive was the most blissful kind of torture I've ever endured, the kind I'll revisit in my mind many, many times from now until the day I die. Though, if things go my way, I won't have to relive the moment on my own.

But as tends to be Harper's way, when I turn toward the stairs, I'm surprised to find her undoing the back of her sinful dress, letting it fall in a puddle around her until she's completely naked in the foyer, save for those heels, her wedding rings, and the W necklace. When I gave her the jewelry, I never anticipated what a fucking sight it would be for her to wear nothing but them.

Okay, that's a bit of a lie. I've pictured exactly that *many times*. I've lost count of the number of times I've jacked off to the idea of what Harper would look like in nothing but that necklace. Ever since she wore that tiny bathing suit that was the temptation to end all temptations and hid little to nothing from my imagination.

But the reality proves to be much, much greater than my imagination.

"Harper." I take in her body, all lush curves and miles of freckled skin, her copper hair falling in waves over one shoulder as she smiles before taking a step toward me. "Harper," I repeat, warning in the word because the look on her face is absolutely devious. Still, she continues to move closer until she's right in front of me, head tilting up to look at me. Instinctively, my hands move to cup her jaw, and I press my lips to hers.

I can't get enough of her. I briefly wonder if I ever will as my tongue swipes along the seam of her lips, as they open to me, as her tongue swipes against mine.

Probably not.

My hand slides down her naked back, a shiver running through her as I finally take the opportunity to hold her bare ass in my hands, groaning as I cup it and pull her into me. Maybe I'll just fuck her right here on the floor because I'm not sure if I can make it up the stairs and to our room.

*No*, this has been such a long time coming. I think I can wait another moment.

I think she's on the same page as me when her hands move to the waist of my pants, unzipping and pushing them down, my feet stepping out and kicking them to the side.

Once more, she surprises me as she shifts, moving to her knees before me. Those high heels are all I can see besides her gorgeous red hair and her full pink lips and her wide green eyes staring up at me as she wraps her hand around my cock, slowly tugging once. I groan at the feel, at the look, and at the way her eyes go wide when she looks at my hard cock, something that makes it bob with pride.

"Take off your shirt," she whispers, and I do as she asks because I think I'd do *anything* she asks right now. I toss it to the floor, and then all conscious thoughts leave my mind when her small, pink tongue moves out, trailing from base to tip in one long swipe, her eyes locked on mine as she does. A shuddering breath leaves my lungs as she takes the head between her lips and sucks, twirling her tongue over the tip.

"I told you to go upstairs," I say, my voice low and gravelly with need.

Her mouth pops off as she looks at me. "I don't want to," she says in a pout, her hand tugging at my cock.

My jaw goes loose just a bit, my hand moving to her hair against my will, gently gathering the thick locks into a ponytail. "You've got a smart mouth, you know that, Harper?"

Her eyes twinkle like she finds this to be a fun challenge. "What are you going to do about it?" she asks low, her breath ghosting along my cock.

"Guess we'll have to see, won't we?" I lean back a bit to get a better view of her tongue licking the precum off the tip as she jacks me slowly. "Suck it, baby."

Her eyes go wide with my command before they go heated. They never leave mine as she slides me into her mouth, enclosing me in warm, wet heat, and giving me everything I've been dying to feel for months. Years.

"God, your mouth feels good," I breathe, watching her slide me back out, leaving a trail of spit before she sucks hard on the head. "Fuck!"

My hand moves on its own volition, pressing on the back of her head to guide her, excitement filling her eyes at the move.

Because *of course* it does.

There is not a doubt in my mind that Harper was made to be mine in every sense of the word. Of course her likes and dislikes would line up with mine: she's my own dream come true. Slowly, her lips reach the bottom of my cock, her jaw going slack and the head slipping down the back of her throat. That's when I twist her makeshift ponytail, wrapping it around my hand and tugging her back to the tip, then slide her to the base once more. She moans around me as I guide her, as I begin to use her mouth for my own pleasure.

A deep moan leaves my lips at the sight, Harper on her knees before me in nothing but her heels, sucking my cock, eyes glued to me, her red hair wrapped around my fist. Her hand goes up, cupping my balls and I groan, tugging a bit harder on her hair.

She moans again, telling me she likes that, and I watch with astonishment as her free hand moves between her own legs, beginning to touch herself.

*Made. For. Me.*

"Fuck, Harper, you're getting off on this as much as I am, aren't you?" Her hand starts moving faster, and I start to move her head to a similar rhythm. The noises in this foyer are fucking heaven—her mouth working me, her muffled moans, the sound of her hand between her legs, playing with her wetness.

"My little wife is a good little slut, isn't she?" I murmur, looking down at her, her cheeks hollowing around me. She moans around me, head nodding as much as she's able, and her eyes slip shut with desire. My fingers tighten in her hair, tugging it tighter as I do. "No, eyes on me while you take your husband's cock deep." Her eyes snap open, looking at me, wide and obedient as I tell her what I need her to know while I have her here.

Another one of her moans vibrates along my cock, and I feel it building, my balls tightening, and I need to get out of her mouth and up the stairs to our bed now. I tug on her hair, but she slides her mouth over my cock faster, like this is some race and she wants to win.

"Harper, I'm going to come in your mouth if you don't stop." Another muffled moan escapes her, and I groan. "Harper."

But her hands are moving to my hips, one wet with her, and she urges me forward, telling me to fuck her face. "*Fuck,*" I groan, wanting that, but also not sure. "I want to come inside you, Harper."

Finally, she unseals her mouth from me.

"And you will. But first, I want you to come down my throat, Wes." Her eyes are wide with her words before she adds, "Please." I'm helpless to her, even more so when she widens her knees, putting one hand back between them and sliding in a finger, leaning back so I can see as her other hand pumps me. A loud moan leaves her lips. "Fuck my face and come down my throat and *then* fuck me. Let me take the edge off, baby. We've got all night." She tilts her head, licking the side of my cock. "Please."

Who am I to say no when she asks so nicely?

All resistance is snapped then, and my hand tightens in her hair once more, guiding her mouth to my tip and sliding in. I hold her in place, moving my hips to fuck her face. She likes it, if the way her hand moves faster and the moans coming from her are any tell. I groan, forcing my eyes to stay open so I can commit this vision to memory.

It builds, my balls tightening up once more before I warn her. "Fuck, baby, I'm going to come," I groan. She nods around me, giving me a quiet *mm-hmm,* and that's what sends me over, coming down her throat, and thrusting until I'm spent. I'm breathing hard as she swallows around me, her tongue roving over my dick in her mouth, and realizing it's barely the edge taken off.

My grip on her hair gentles, and she slides her mouth off me, giving me a small smile before her lips go loose, a gentle sigh leaving her.

*She's still fingering herself.*

"Wes," she moans, and I stand there for a moment, watching my wife finger fuck her cunt, wet from sucking me off, before I bend down, lifting her as I move toward the stairs. She shifts her body, and I feel her wet pussy on my side, and her little pants as she shifts her hips, trying to get friction any way she can. "That was so hot," she moans in my ear as I'm three steps up, her teeth biting my earlobe when I hesitate.

I should wait.

I really should.

The next time she comes, it should be around my cock, but I'm a selfish man, and the feeling of her, wet and needy on my side, cracks my restraints. I want to taste Harper Holden's pussy more than I have ever wanted anything in this life.

I place her on the stairs, ass on the edge of one, elbows holding her up on another, her hooded eyes looking down at me like she owns me.

She does, of course.

Thankfully, I'm learning it's a mutual ownership.

"Wes," she starts, confused. "We need—"

"Open up," I growl, kneeling on a few stairs below her, hands moving to her inner thighs and pulling them apart for my eyes to see my reward. When I lock eyes on her dripping cunt, I groan. She's pink and wet and pretty, already swollen and begging for my mouth. Somehow, I gather the willpower to refrain, using one finger to slide down her center, dipping two knuckles into her and pulling a moan from her before moving out and up to circle her clit.

"Fuck, my wife is pretty," I whisper, almost to myself.

I clearly did something right in this life, because this in front of me? A fucking *prize*.

"Are you going to just stare at it, or are you going to eat it?" Harper asks, staring at me, and when I look, there's a small smile on her lips, a tease in her eyes.

This fucking woman.

A perfect match for me.

I return the grin, then shift the hand on her inner thigh to her knee and start to close her legs. "If you're going to be a little brat..." I start, and she shakes her head frantically, opening her legs wider.

"No. No, please, Wes."

"You sound so pretty begging for me, little wife." And then, because I'm a generous man, and also because I've been waiting for this for years, I bend down, wrapping my lips around her clit, and I suck.

She shouts, her back arching. Her hand instantly moves to the back of my head, twining in my hair, fingers digging into my scalp just like I've imagined so many times before. Harper moans as I devour her, as I run my tongue over her clit, as I slide my tongue inside her, letting her ride it. I moan into her, and her hips buck at the vibration.

When my mouth moves back to her clit, one of my hands moves, sliding a single, thick finger into her wet cunt, and she moans my name. It's become somewhat of a chant as her pussy tightens on my fingers, as her hips move to guide my finger at the same time her hand in my hair guides my mouth, showing me what pressure she likes, how she wants me to eat her.

"Wes, Wes," she moans. "I'm going to come. Oh, oh!" I move faster, groaning into her because *fuck yes*, I've even been dying for her to come on my face, and then it happens.

My wife falls, tightening around my fingers, a new wash of wetness hitting my tongue as she screams my name. She continues to rock against me as she comes down, as my finger continues to move in her, my tongue trailing up over her to clean up every drop. Finally, when her hips slow to a stop, I stand, leaning down and grabbing her once more. My cock is rock-hard again after the small reprieve, and I take the last few remaining steps before turning toward my room.

My lips move to the skin below her neck and suck there.

"What was that?" she asks with a giggle.

"That was me starting my mission to have you on every surface of this fucking monstrosity of a house."

"Oh," she whispers, and I smile as I enter our room, tossing her on the bed. She shifts to the center, and then she's spread, one elbow on the bed, the other hand between her legs. It's like she can't help it, as if it's been building between us for so long she can't sate it with just one or two orgasms.

I understand the feeling, my cock bobbing with need as I take her in.

"Jesus, look at you." I don't move from where I stand and watch her. My hand moves to stroke my cock, and she bites her lip.

"Like what you see?" she asks delicately, unnecessary nerves hidden beneath her bravado.

"A hell of a lot. Wider, so I can watch while I roll this on," I say, grabbing a condom from the nightstand, and she obeys. I slide it on over my cock, Harper licking her lips as I do, and I shake my head, smiling at her. "Like what *you* see?"

"A hell of a lot," she whispers as I finish my task.

Finally, I crawl up the bed, up her body, before we're face-to-face, pressing my lips to hers.

Suddenly, everything changes. My need is still fevered, but it's tinged with something beautiful, like the understanding that something big is about to happen and that we're about to change everything in the best way possible.

"I'm crazy for you," I whisper, my lips brushing her, one hand in the bed, the other resting on the side of her face.

"I'm yours," she says, somehow knowing it's what I need to hear, what I've been *dying* to hear. "For however long you want me."

I line up the head of my cock with her entrance, moaning as the heat of her wraps my tip before I press my forehead to hers.

"How's forever sound?" I shouldn't do it, talk to her like this about when we're about to fuck for the first time, but I can't help it. This feels monumental, and she knows it.

"Really fucking good," she whispers, then lifts her hips, taking me into her. We groan in unison as I push into her all the way, slowly filling and stretching her until I'm seated deep inside. It's fucking perfect.

"Fuck," I groan deep into her neck through gritted teeth.

"I'm so full," she breathes, making my cock twitch.

I laugh, as I always seem to do with Harper. "Do you want this to end quickly?" I ask, sliding out slowly and then pushing back in.

She gasps, her hand moving to my neck and gripping tight, in time with the way her pussy clamps on me. "I'm just..." She takes in a shaky breath as I slide out again, seeming to lose her train of thought. "Oh my god, Wes, it's so perfect. We're so fucking perfect." It's an admission, and she knows it.

"Yeah," I whisper into her neck. I knew it would be like this with her, all-consuming and soul-changing, but I don't think I understood the magnitude of it as I continue sliding in and out of her, filling her with each thrust. Her legs move, wrapping around my hips, tightening to urge me on before her nails dig into me.

"More. Please, more," she begs

"I don't want to—"

"Fuck me, Wes. Please, I need you." That snaps my delicate tether on reality and common sense, and I pull out before slamming in. She moans loudly with that, head snapping back, back arching with all-consuming pleasure. I shift, placing my palms beside her head, caging her in. I hold her eyes as I start fucking her hard, pounding deep, giving in to what we both need.

"I'm close," she whispers, something I knew because of the vise-like grip on my cock.

"I know," I groan, grinding into her with my thrust. "I know. Me too." I continue to fuck her, liking watching her hold off, waiting for me to let her fall. I never told her that was something I liked, having the control of her orgasm, but somehow, as seems to be her way, she just knew.

Finally, I can't hold off much longer, so I groan as I pull out. "Now, baby." Then I slam in deep, feeling her pussy spasm around me, her body going still as she comes apart, and I follow her, pushing in deeper as I come, moaning her name into her ear, knowing I'll never say another name like this again in my life.

# TWENTY-THREE

## WES

I've been up for a while. I'm a morning person, always have been, something that for most of my life was a pain in the ass. It's rough when you're in a band, going to bed at two in the morning, only for your body to wake you up at six.

But for once in my life, I'm grateful for this trait of mine. That's because I've been lying here, Harper's naked body curled up into mine, her breathing soft and easy as I rub a hand up and down her back, occasionally brushing her hair back and savoring this moment. I don't know what version of her I'm going to have when she wakes: the one who jumped or the one who's scared, but either way, I'm ready.

Because last night only cemented that I'm never letting Harper go.

Although the sex was fucking phenomenal, last night was about connecting with her on a deeper level, and the smile on her face while we cleaned up. It's about how after, we stayed up late, laying together and talking about a future where there's no pressure. It was about Harper's walls finally tumbling down, about her fear abating for just long enough for me to slip in.

About *being* with her, truly and finally.

About Harper being officially *mine*.

"Morning," her voice says, croaking with sleep as she shifts.

I look down at her and smile, shaking my head.

"Good morning, beautiful," I whisper, brushing her hair back again.

She blinks, and I think she may have fallen back asleep before her green eyes are on me once more, a smile on her lips.

"You seem serious," she says before rolling on top of me, her bare chest to mine. My hands move again, shifting her hair and running them down her back. She sighs in pleasure, her eyes drifting shut with the gentle movement. She likes that, getting her hair played with, and if she wants to make that noise and face every time, I'll do it forever.

"Just...thinking."

"What about?" she asks, resting her chin on her hands folded on my chest. Looking down at her, I feel it again, that feeling like finally, I have that...thing I've been missing. Watching Stella and Riggins fall back in love made me yearn for a story of my own, wishing for someone to be that for me.

Except now I feel like I'm living my own story, like I've been blessed to find this person, *my person*, after so many years of thinking she didn't exist. It's a relief of sorts, but there's a niggling feeling in the back of my head.

"I've spent the last few years feeling guilty," I start to explain, then move my eyes to stare at the ceiling, avoiding Harper's curious gaze.

"Guilty? How so?"

I look at her quickly, shaking my head to make sure she knows it isn't about us.

"I live a life thousands of people would *kill* to live. Living my dream, touring the world, playing music. I have more money than I could ever need and spend every day with my best friends. I go out, I party, I can have any woman I want."

"Excuse me?" Harper says cutting me off, humor in the world as she pinches my side.

"I only want you, little wife," I whisper, eyes genuine as I brush her soft hair back. "But the last few years, it's felt...routine. Boring. Like I was missing something." Her breathing hitches as if she knows what I'm getting at, but I keep talking. "The parties lost their glimmer, lost their excitement after a while. These once-in-a-lifetime events turned ordinary. It's a strange feeling, becoming numb to something another version of you would have given everything to have. But seeing you last night reminded me of how *lucky* I am."

"You worked hard, honey," she whispers, her hand reaching up to brush the backs of her fingers along my scruff.

"I know. I know, and the guys did too, and we earned this. I know that. But something... something was always missing, and it has been eating at me for a while now. I should be loving this rock star lifestyle, and instead, I felt guilty because I was missing something I couldn't explain."

She's biting her lip, taking me in, and I wrap an arm around her waist, holding her to me and brushing a thumb over her lips.

"*This* is what I've missed," I whisper.

"What, me naked in your bed? You could have had this a long time ago, bud," she jokes, and I smile, but I shake my head all the same

"No. No, and it wouldn't have been like this if we just jumped in, if we didn't build *us* before we got here. Because I was missing *this*." I pause, taking in a deep breath, fighting past the need to brush over *feelings* and instead share them with Harper. "The morning after. The calmness, the easiness. Having someone to wake up to, someone you know, someone you want to spend the whole day with. Someone you can dissect the night before with over breakfast." Her eyes go wider. "Someone to cure the hangover and clean up after the party. This?" I ask, then gesture between us. "This is what I was missing."

"Wes."

I roll us, shifting so we're on our sides, eye to eye.

"Everyone wants to be there for the party, the craziness and excitement, and the rock and roll of it all. I've never had someone there for me."

She watches me contemplatively, and something must click as she tips her head to the side and smiles. "Is that why you wanted to wait?" I shrug, but the blush on my cheeks definitely gives me away. "You know I'm not with you for the whole...rock star lifestyle."

"It wasn't just that," I say. "I didn't want to rush things with you because I knew I wanted us to be something special."

"Who knew you were such a romantic?" she says gently after a pause, running her hand through my hair, pushing it back, and reading my face.

I smile at her. "You could have if you weren't so stubborn."

She stares at me, and even though I expect her to argue with me, as is her way, she doesn't. Instead, she contemplates what I said, thinking before finally she speaks in a whisper. "I'm glad I woke up."

"What?"

"I'm glad I woke up in time to have you, that I opened my eyes and realized what was right in front of me. Before you got tired of waiting, before you got frustrated over the fact that I was being so stubborn."

I roll again, this time so she's below me and I'm hovering over the top of her, caging her in. I want her in a place where there's no escape from what I'm about to tell her.

"I see you still don't get it. I'm going to tell it to you straight, Harper, so don't freak out." Her eyes go wide with nerves, but I continue on. "I would have waited forever. If it meant we'd get here, in my bed, together with no pretense, I would have waited an eternity for you to be ready. I didn't want to rush things, for you to sit there in a few months or in a year, wondering if you made the right choice. I needed you to know you were making this decision because you *wanted* to. Because you wanted not just me, but *us*. I didn't want there to be even the smallest chance you'd look at last night and regret it."

I smile at her, at her shocked face, and brush my fingers over her cheek.

"You said you wanted to be spontaneous, but this? This was never spontaneous, Harper. Not for me, at least, and one day I think you'll see it wasn't for you either. You'll see you were so willing to jump in because you knew to your bones this was right."

She lays there beneath me, silent, taking in my words, and I watch her—watch her thoughts and feelings, and finally, fears drift over her face.

"What if...what if you change your mind?" she asks nervously, and my brows furrow, not understanding. "What if you change your mind? I'm boring, Wes. I'm type A, I'm safe, and I overthink every move I make—"

I shake my head. "Since when?" I ask because she keeps saying that, but I think she's *convinced* herself of it, that she isn't spontaneous or fun or exciting.

"What?"

"Since when do you overthink everything?"

"Uh, since I was ten, and I came back to school three days after Marcie Klein told me my shoes were ugly and I told her she was a rude girl and that she should really think about how her words impacted other people because I'd thought about it all weekend and weighed my options and decided I didn't want to be too mean and hurt her feelings but that hitting her would absolutely get me into too much trouble, so some heartfelt advice would be the best line of action."

I smile wider, shaking my head at her because that's so Harper, to come back with the most specific evidence to prove her point.

"You agreed to marry me," I tell her point-blank. "On a whim. After bidding ten thousand dollars on a date with me."

She tips her head back and forth. "Yeah, I know, and that's why I'm concerned that one day, you're going to wake up and realize this should have stayed fake because I tricked you, and I'm actually really boring and—"

"And then you *married* me within a week."

She shrugs. "Because I wanted to prove a point."

"You glittered your ex's lawn."

"And it got me arrested."

"You know what I mean, Harper. You're brave and smart and kind and funny, and whether or not you believe it, you're spontaneous, too, in your own way." She opens her mouth to speak, but I shake my head, stopping her. "And even if you weren't, even if you were the most predictable person, even if you planned your outfits and meals and fucking *bathroom breaks* a year out, I'd still be wild for you."

She stares at me and opens her mouth.

"No. We're not arguing about that. Come on," I say, then slap her ass and roll out of the bed. "We can argue about how boring you are after I feed you breakfast."

I reach for the bed, tugging on the blanket she buried herself under, and she squeals, giggling. She tries to grab the fluffy white blanket and pull it up to cover her, but I'm stronger, and soon the covers are in the corner of the floor. I pull on a pair of boxers from my drawer and walk toward her, grabbing her arm and pulling her to the side of the bed.

"Wes!"

"I need to feed my wife. You lay there looking too tempting, we're never leaving this house."

"I don't see a problem with that," she counters, and I glare at her. Then she lets out a little yawn, using her hand to cover it but failing. Looking at her and then the time, which is still earlier than she's normally up, I let go, stepping away from the bed. I pull on a pair of shorts, then move to the blanket and toss it over her.

"Change of plans. I'm going for a run while you take a nap. Then we're going to take a shower together where I'll probably fuck you because by my calculations, it's been much too long since I was last in you, and then I'm taking you to breakfast."

She blushes and bites her lip, then looks at me. "Breakfast?"

"I want to take you out. Our first outing as something more." I step closer to the bed, rolling onto it and pulling her closer until we're bare chest to bare chest. My hand sinks into her tangled hair, holding her face close to mine. "You're mine now, and I want to show you off."

"What have the last two months been?" she asks breathily.

"It's been wooing you," I say matter-of-factly, pressing my lips to hers before standing again and moving to grab a sweatshirt.

"Wooing!?" she asks with a laugh.

I shake my head and smile.

"Nap," I say, grabbing a pair of socks and heading out the door. "You'll need the energy."

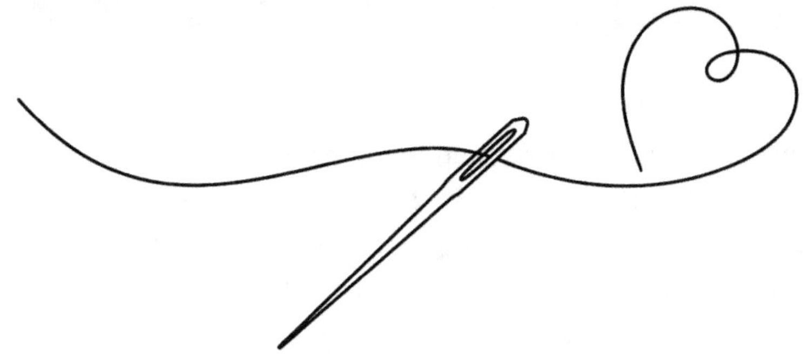

# TWENTY-FOUR

## HARPER

It's two days later when the front door rings. I look at my phone to check if I missed a call or text, thinking it might be Wes home from practice early and having locked himself out. Quickly, I make my way down the stairs, but when I open the door with a wide, expectant smile, it's not my husband standing there at all.

Instead, Ava and Jules are standing there, Jules looking concerned and Ava looking nearly self-righteous with her hands on her hips, which is *never* a good sign.

"What are you guys—" I start, but Ava pushes past me, Jules following behind her before I shut the door. "What is going on?" They stand there, Ava with her arms crossed on her chest, glaring at me, Jules a mix of worried and disappointed, already having nailed the mom look.

"What is this, Harper?" Ava asks, scrolling on her phone.

The tone in her voice creates a new panic, though, and I look at her confused. My mind runs through anything I didn't tell her, any news that paparazzi could have spread that I didn't warn them about, but I can't think of anything. I called them to fill them in on the Willa

Stone concert, the after-party, and *our* after-party, and yesterday was a normal run-of-the-mill day where I didn't even leave the house.

*Maybe Leo released something, and Wes forgot to tell me?*

"What's what?" I ask, now a bundle of nerves. She puts her phone in my face, and I squint at it, trying to see as she jostles her phone around.

"This! This dress!" she says, and finally, I grab her phone to stop this back and forth, scrolling to see whatever it is she's *actually* trying to show me. Then I freeze, my stomach falling to my feet, blood leaving my face, and I see what she's so worked up about.

*I knew* it would hurt.

I knew it would slice deep, seeing my designs with someone else's name on them, but fuck, it hurts a lot more than I anticipated.

Because there on the screen is a headline reading, "Clarissa Astor, Daughter of Fashion Icon Gerald Astor, Reveals the First Sketches of her Premier Legacy Line."

And below that is a sketch of *my* design.

A design from the line Jeremy stole while we were together, the ones he told me he'd show his boss to help get my foot in the door, the ones he gave to his new girlfriend. The ones I signed away all rights to in exchange for him not pressing charges on my best friends.

I scroll past a few more sketches, all of them more modest, slightly outdated, and, in my opinion, much less exciting versions of my original designs, and begin reading the commentary from the well-known fashion news outlet.

*New. Different. Fresh. Unique, yet timeless.*

All words to describe this line that is mine—*was* mine. Words I would have given anything to see if my name was attached to these designs as intended. I take in a deep breath and force myself to think about it from a positive perspective, to bask in the knowledge that I *am* talented and I created something special, even if no one knows it was me all along.

That should be good enough. Right?

"What *is* this, Harper?" Ava asks again, this time a bit more gently.

I remember when I first started sketching out the line, my first tiptoe out of pageant gowns, how it felt like something big was happening. I remember how, almost as soon as I had the outline for that first sketch, I showed my friends. I then continued to show them photos of different variations, updates, and additions, thoroughly excited by this new venture.

*"I think this could be something,"* I said about the idea, a couture piece for show and then more toned-down pieces for everyday wear. Ava was in awe and told me I needed to continue pursuing this because there was a market for it. She was the push I needed to create the full line.

I should have known when it was announced, they would see it and have questions. How did I ever think I would get away with this, that I could just put all of it behind me? Ava takes her phone back from me when I hand it to her, not wanting to read about it anymore.

"Those are *your* designs," Jules whispers. "Clarissa stole your designs, Harper." But then she looks at me, really taking me in the way she always has been able to, and her face tightens in confusion. "Why don't you look surprised by this?"

I sigh. I knew this day would come, though I hoped in some deluded universe that it wouldn't. "Come on. Let's sit down. I have something to tell you," I say, and then I tell my best friends the rest of the story about my breakup with Jeremy.

## TWENTY-FIVE

### WES

"What are you three doing?" I ask, walking into the kitchen after leaning in the doorway for some time, not a single one of the women noticing me as I did. I got home after a day at the studio, excited to see my wife, only to open the door to the raucous laughter of Harper and her friends.

"Jesus, Wes, you scared the shit out of me!" Ava says, putting a hand to her chest.

"I've been standing here for at least three minutes," I say with a laugh, my eyes moving to my wife, whose blush is burning a pretty, bright pink. The three of them have been sitting at the kitchen island, hovering over Harper's laptop and laughing hysterically nearly the entire time.

"We didn't see you there," Harper says, and I smile.

"I got that," I say. "What are you guys doing?"

Jules and Harper look around like they're trying to find some appropriate answer written on a wall, but Ava, as always, holds nothing back.

"Ordering a pile of elephant shit to be delivered to Jeremy's house," she announces triumphantly, continuing to type in numbers from the credit card in her hands.

I could ask what that means, but I don't think I would learn much from her answer. Instead, I go with, "And why are we doing that?"

"Because he's an asshole and deserves the shittiest karma."

I nod, trying to at least feign understanding. "Why are we planning revenge when the last time you guys glittered his yard, you got arrested?" I ask, but Ava shakes her head.

"It wasn't the glittering that fucked us," she says as if the tiny details make a difference. "It was the forking."

"It was a good idea!" Jules shouts, throwing her hands in the air. "I swear it was."

"It took forever," Ava says, glaring at Jules, who I'm assuming thought of the forking.

"It's not my fault that our intel was wrong!" Jules yells, pointing at Harper. "She told us he would be out of town, and they had no cameras!"

"He was supposed to be!" Harper shouts in return, lifting her hands in defense. "I also told you all that we were *broken up* after months of him lying to me about his whereabouts, so maybe you should have known my intel wasn't the best. I suggested we call Jaime and have him watch Jeremy for us, make sure he wouldn't be around to catch us."

"Jaime would have shot it down," Ava says.

"Then maybe you wouldn't have gotten arrested," I add, stepping further into the room, and Ava turns her ire on me.

"Yeah, and then you'd still be single and pining after Harper, so there's that."

"Ava!" Harper shouts, eyes wide with panic.

"Girl's gotta point." I make my way over to where Ava is still typing in card numbers slowly. "You can't use your credit card," I say, tugging the laptop out of her hands.

"Excuse me?" she asks, clearly annoyed and glaring at me.

"You can't use your credit card for this." Reaching in my back pocket, I slide out my wallet while opening up a new browser.

"Wes, no. Absolutely not," Harper says, taking a step toward me. "You are not paying for this."

I shake my head, continuing to open the page I'm looking for.

"This is not about paying for things, little wife. It's about discretion. If you buy anything to fuck with Jeremy with your credit card, he can track that back to you."

"*Little wife!*" Jules says in a whispered squeal, and Ava smiles at her. Harper does not.

"We're sending it as a gift," Harper says, ignoring her friend.

"Do you think he can't call up the website and ask who sent it to him *as a gift?*" She glares and then rolls her eyes. I type a few more things in, then add in my credit card.

"If *your* info comes up when he asks, it will be even worse," she says, crossing her arms on her chest like she won that battle. I smile wide, then take the code I just got back from the first website.

"And that's why I purchased a Visa gift card and am using *that* to purchase it." I look at Ava. "Are we good to submit, or do you need to add more to it?"

She smiles. "No, I think it's all pretty set. Thanks, Wes! You're one smart cookie."

I nod, not knowing if that's a compliment or not, considering it's coming from Ava.

What I *do* know is that something happened in the last twelve hours to reignite Ava and Jules's anger at Jeremy Vaughn, something that has all three of them up in arms and craving justice once more.

"Got it," I say, then finish the order and hit send. "Should be delivered next week."

"I love him for you, Harper," Ava says, with a smile.

My eyes are on my wife's when she looks at me with a soft smile.

"Yeah," she says low, and warmth runs through me at that single, seemingly insignificant word. I shift away from the laptop over to her, pulling her into my side. I expect her to go stiff or pull away, but instead, she melts into my side, her arm wrapping around my waist. Something big has changed in Harper in the last few days, and it bodes really fucking well for me. I'm not all the way past her walls, but they're cracked, and I'll take what I can get with her.

"What are you three up to next?" I ask, then press my lips to Harper's hair. Jules audibly sighs at the move while Ava smiles, like she knew this would happen all along. I'm glad *one* of us was always confident I'd make my way past Harper's walls.

"I think we earned a nice little sweet treat," Ava says, putting a hand to her stomach that's just starting to show.

"Oh, yes, please," Harper says, the words nearly erotic with want.

"Who wants ice cream?" I ask, knowing I'd do just about anything if Harper requested anything in that tone. "I know a place that has great dairy-free options for you, Ava." Her eyes go wide and I don't miss how Harper's arm tightens around my waist with appreciation for my thinking of her friend.

"I would do absolutely feral things for ice cream right now. This baby only wants sweets, but it's so hard to find anything that is actually good without milk." I almost see her eyes watering.

"Got it. Ice cream it is. I'll drive."

"YAY!" Ava shouts, then claps. "Harper, if you don't stop fucking around and tie this man down for real, I'm going to riot. He's getting us *ice cream.*"

Harper tips her head in her friend's direction, giving them a face I can't see, but when they start loudly laughing, I find myself smiling as well. Harper huffs, then moves away from me and toward the front door.

"Are we going?" she shouts when she's out of sight.

"Yeah, let's go," I say as Jules follows her out, but Ava doesn't, standing in the kitchen and taking me in.

"You're good for her, you know," she says low, like she's worried Harper will hear. "Don't stop fighting for her. She's just a little trigger shy and isn't sure if she can trust her gut these days."

"But you're saying her gut is pointing to me?" I ask, reading between the lines.

She smiles wide.

"Oh yeah. Big time, my friend," she says, then turns away toward the front door without another word.

I follow before we head out the door. Harper is quiet, letting Ava and Jules chat, but she takes the passenger seat beside me, the girls sitting in the back.

And when she reaches over to where my hand sits on the center console, gently twining her fingers with mine, I can't help but think I've somehow passed another test Harper doesn't realize she's been assigning to me.

# TWENTY-SIX

## WES

She wants to run off. It's clear in the way she's standing with her shoulders set tightly, waving out the window as Ava and Jules drive off. She's like a skittish cat I need to approach with care, but the question is tumbling out of my mouth before I can even think to phrase it differently.

"Are you still in love with him?"

"What?" she asks, turning to look at me, genuine confusion on her face.

"Are you still in love with him? Your ex. It's okay if you are, you were together a long—" My words trail off when she stops me by laughing. Full, deep, belly laughs that, if I weren't sitting on the edge of a knife, I'd be smiling along with.

"No, Wes, I am not in love with Jeremy," she says when her laughter finally settles before leaning back against the wall, arms crossed on her chest. "If I ever did love him, it hasn't been for a very long time. I think I was in love with the *idea* of him. I spent a lot of our relationship convincing myself I was in love because he was a safe choice, and I'm not a *rock-the-boat* kind of girl. Dating Jeremy was a checkmark in the column of *Harper has her life together,* you know?"

I don't, but I nod all the same. I graduated high school and started touring the country with a rock band on a whim, hoping one day it would pan out into something, but I'd never set ideals for myself, never made a list of things I needed to accomplish to feel like I had my life together the way Harper clearly does. She holds herself to such a high standard, constantly scrutinizing every step she makes. Secretly, I think even if she did check off all of those boxes, she wouldn't be content.

I wonder if that's what happened with Jeremy, if she kept waiting for each milestone in their relationship to be *more* or fix something, and because of that, she never let herself fully realize she wasn't happy and might never be.

"So you're not heartbroken over him?"

"No, I'm not heartbroken over Jeremy." Her head tips to the side as she takes me in, her smile going wider. "Is that jealousy I'm sensing, Holden?"

And then some, but I don't tell her that. Instead, I reach for her hand, grabbing it and leading her into what the realtor called a *sitting room* when I bought this place. She sits on a loveseat, and I sit on a large, comfy sofa kitty-corner to her, leaning back and crossing my arms on my chest.

"Okay, so if it's not about heartbreak...what was Ava talking about then? Why are you three inciting karma on him again?"

She screws up her face like she's trying to decide how to say something, then it shifts, and I just know she's considering lying or at least not telling the whole truth. But then some kind of acceptance floods her, and she sighs before leaning back.

"They found out something I omitted from my original story of the breakup." My heart skips a beat, but I force my body to remain calm despite my mind going through a million worst-case scenarios.

"Okay..." I say, trying to be patient.

She takes a deep breath, lets it out, and then starts.

"I had an idea for a fashion line a little while ago. A side project, something fun that was just for me, but I fell in love with it. Couture, high fashion pieces. I started working on it and decided maybe I'd show it, let it be my first tiptoe into that world. I think there's a way to tie couture lines with more accessible fashion for the everyday woman, and that's what I was trying to do with it. One high fashion piece and one or two pieces inspired by it that were more casual. I'd been working on it here and there for a long time, and Jeremy knew about it."

I nod, leaning forward and gently pushing a loose piece of hair behind her ear.

"I lied when I said the only reason I was mad at Jeremy was because he was cheating on me. There's a line his new girlfriend is premiering as her first high fashion line." I nod again, following with a rock in my stomach. "It's mine."

"Yours?" I ask, and she nods. "How?"

"I showed it to him. He works for Astor Fashion, and I hoped...I don't know."

"You hoped he'd show it to his boss, get you a meeting or something."

She nods and sighs.

"He'd been making promises like that for some time. He'd bring designs home from work that weren't working for one reason or another and show me, I'd give him some advice to fix it. He said he always told his boss I was helping, but it was a lie, obviously. He was giving the tweaks to his girlfriend so she could suggest them to her father to impress him. Anyway, he took pictures of my designs. I remember the day, and I remember being so excited. It felt like something big was about to happen."

She shrugs, then looks at me with guilt and apology in her eyes.

"A week or two after he took those pictures, I asked about what his boss thought of them. He told me he hadn't liked them, that maybe I should stick to pageant gowns." My jaw goes tight as I put the pieces together, as I understand the level of manipulation Jeremy subjected Harper to. "But it seems like he had actually shown them to Clarissa. She loved them, they tweaked them, and now they're her *legacy line.* It was announced today." Harper worries her lip between her teeth, refusing to look at me as she picks at the skin on a nail.

I reach out, grabbing her hand and holding it in mine. Finally, her eyes meet mine when she continues.

"When I walked in on them cheating, they were looking at designs. I went to leave, knowing we were done. I told him I'd be back later, but he told me to stay." She shrugs, her eyes fading off like she's caught in some shit memory, and anger pulses through me, knowing this asshole created this. Not just that look on her face but the constant battle she's now facing in believing in herself and trusting her feelings and instincts. "He told me they were taking my designs. He wanted me to sign them away to make things easy for him. I, of course, said no and walked away. I didn't hear about it again, so I thought it was behind us." A deep, deep sigh filled with regret leaves her. "And then we glittered his lawn."

It all starts to click then: why no one was charged, why Harper seemed to fall apart after that, why her reputation started to spiral.

"He didn't press charges because you gave him the designs."

She gives me a sad smile and nods. "It was the only option."

*The fuck it was.*

"Harper, there are always—"

She shakes her head, her jaw tight as she looks at me.

"He was threatening Ava and Jules. Criminal stalking and harassment charges for both of them, which could have destroyed their careers. It was my only option. There will be more designs, new dresses, and gowns, but Ava and Jules fought hard for what they have, and Ava is the reason I even have a successful business as it is. I'm not letting my bad choices be the reason theirs crumble."

I understand it, unfortunately, how it could have played out. How in that moment, faced with a *now-or-never* opportunity, my ever-selfless wife would pick her friends over her own happiness. "But they still went after you," I say, that part seeming out of place.

"Unfortunately, though I made sure that the girls would be left out of everything, I didn't think to make sure he and his bitch of a girlfriend wouldn't talk shit about me. The next day, they started their press cycle, just in case, I assume. If you remove someone's credibility after you steal their life's work, it's hard for them to come at you with their truth. If you make the world believe they're jealous and crazy and irrational, they have no leg to stand on against you. Add in that her platform is thousands of times more powerful than mine, and I was fucked."

I sit in silence for long moments, letting it all sink in, finally understanding the whole picture.

"Why didn't you say anything before, Harper? We could have—"

"He has the ability to ruin me, Wes. I didn't have a formal copyright. He could easily say I stole the designs from *him because* I'm some bitter ex. It would be the end of me and my career. I can ride out whispers and rumors, but I couldn't survive that. It was easier to let it go. Plus, I'm the idiot who believed in him. I deserve that."

"What? No." I say, gripping her hands tight and hating, knowing that's truly how she sees this, some lesson she has to learn because she trusted the man, because, in her mind, she should have known better. "You know this isn't your fault, right? He's an asshole. He's a terrible fucking person who manipulated you for years. That's not on you. Tell me you know that, Harper." She stares at me but doesn't answer, just shrugs her shoulders and gives me a small, sad smile.

"Harper," I start, but she shakes her head, not wanting to hear my condolences.

"It is what it is. I don't care, not really. It's behind me. I just want to move forward."

"That's why you said you don't want to get back at him. That auction...you said it was a whim."

"I was a little drunk," she admits with a smile. Despite the heavy topic, she seems a bit lighter, like finally confessing this has freed her in some way.

"And that's why he started speaking out about you. Because

marrying me meant you might have a bit more credibility, more of a platform if you came out against him. He wanted to make you look like you were out to get him before that happened." She nods as more pieces fall in place. "What about the elephant shit?"

She shrugs, a small smile playing on her lips.

"Ava and Jules found out about the designs. Not the threats against them, because it would destroy them to know I gave up my work to protect them. They're angry he took what's mine. Of the long list of revenge they were talking about, that seemed like the least problematic." I wonder what else was on that list and if I could make them happen with my resources.

"Wes, no," she says, clearly reading my face. "I don't want to make things worse than they are. If he thinks I'm fighting back, he'll go harder. Even if you and Leo help preserve my name publicly, he can ruin it behind closed doors. He could get me blacklisted if he wanted."

"He can't just—" I start because he can't get away with this.

"No, he can, and honestly, that's just the industry. It's fine, so long as I keep my mouth shut and let it be."

I shake my head, disagreeing ardently. "No. That's not your life anymore," I say, moving to my knees before her, reaching up and holding her face in my hands to force her to look at me. The walls are down for once, and I can see the vulnerability, her truth.

She's hurt.

She's angry.

She deserves her petty little revenge and so much more. And I'm going to make sure she gets it.

"You're my wife, Harper. If someone wrongs my wife, we're getting even."

"We've already done that. He gets to see me moving on with someone bigger and better, and that will eat at him and his ego alive." I smile because I sure as fuck like the idea of that, but I need more.

Harper *deserves* more.

"It's not enough," I tell her. "Seeing you better off without him, it's not enough."

"I don't—" she starts, but I'm standing, grabbing her hand and pulling her with me toward the kitchen.

"Come on. We have work to do." My mind is already spinning with ideas and calls I need to make in the morning. I told Harper no one gets to fuck with her, no one gets to disrespect her anymore, not now that she's mine, and that *definitely* includes her fuckwad of an ex. "What do you want? Cookies? Wine, a soda?" I ask, reaching for a beer for myself and turning toward her. "We have a long night ahead of us."

"A long night?"

"We've got plans to make."

She sighs deeply. "Wes, that isn't—" I step closer to her, abandoning my drink on the counter and backing her into the kitchen cabinets. "I don't need revenge. I want to succeed. I want to succeed without him, that would be enough for me."

I didn't want to plant this seed in her mind, something new for her to worry about, but I know she wouldn't agree to this if I didn't.

"And if he does it to someone else?" I ask softly, my hand resting on her cheek to keep her from looking away. "What then? Or if he reaches out again, wanting more of your undeniable talent?"

Her face goes blank, clearly not having thought of that. "He wouldn't."

"You don't know that. You never thought you'd be here, either, Harper. He needs to be stopped."

"Honey, I appreciate this, really, I do." Heat blossoms at her *honey*, but it cools with her hesitance. "We tried messing with him once before. It ended terribly."

"Baby, no offense, but you did it sloppily and impulsively," I say, and the glare she gives me has me smiling.

"And this time we're not?"

"No, because you're doing it with me." She rolls her eyes, but I keep going. "This time we plan it. We don't half-ass it. We're going to fuck with him, and we're going to do it strategically."

"And how do we do that?" she asks, and since it's not a full-out denial, I go with it, stepping away from her and finding the paper and pen I need in the kitchen junk drawer before leaning onto the kitchen island. She's at my side, watching me with intrigue as I write three topics and underline each one twice.

"We target the main tiers," I say. "Career, personal life, reputation." She stares at the words I wrote like she's considering it. "Come on. It doesn't even have to be anything crazy. Just inconveniencing."

*I'll handle the rest*, I think.

"It won't be anything that could get us arrested?" I shake my head.

"I'll make sure nothing can be traced back to you." She tips her head, and I roll my eyes. "Or me." Time passes, and I think I might not have gotten through to her, but then a small smile tips on her lips.

"Okay," she says, and I smile wide.

"Okay?"

"Okay. We can brainstorm revenge. Nothing crazy, and I don't know if I'll even want to act on it, but let's do it. For the catharsis." She's close to me, smiling wide, and god, she's beautiful.

She's all mine and whether she wants me to or not, I'm going to protect what's mine.

"All right, little wife. Let's start planning."

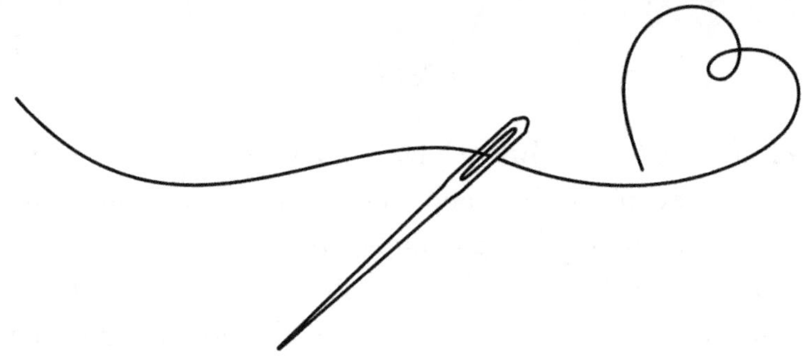

# TWENTY-SEVEN

## HARPER

"Hey, you ready to go?" Wes asks, standing in the doorway of my design room in a pair of dark jeans and a maroon-colored sweater. We're going on a lunch date in Hudson City, fully planned by Wes.

"Yeah, sorry! I had an idea," I say, sketch pad in hand, as I sit on the cushioned bench near the window. The idea came to me while I was getting ready, and I rushed through my makeup to run over here and get it down before I lost it. Ever since I told Wes, Ava, and Jules everything, my mind has been freed, that creative block gone, and I couldn't be more grateful. "I'll be done in a second."

"No need. It can wait. Everything can wait for the creative genius," he says, and I roll my eyes.

"I don't know if I'd go that far." I furrow my brows, confused by him standing in the doorway of the room still like he's a vampire who needs to be invited in. "You can come in, you know."

"This is your sanctuary, Harper. I won't come in if you don't want me to."

"That's silly," I say, waving him in. "Come in. Sit. Keep me company. I'll just be another minute, and then we can head out."

He steps in as I finish the silhouette of a gown, and from the corner of my eye, I watch him taking in the small changes I've made to the space, a few photos here and there, supplies reorganized, and a few new additions to the cork inspiration board.

"Wow," he breathes, seeing the finished design for what would have been the centerpiece of my first line, the only design Jeremy doesn't have. I finally gave in the morning after I told Wes everything and started to sketch it out, needing to just get it out of my system and hoping it would help my creative block. It worked, inspiring a brand new line, the basics of which are pinned next to that first design. It's outlined on a large piece of poster paper with *New Line* on top. Words are scribbled on it, textures and vibes, and emotions I want the wearer to feel. There are a few inspirational photos pasted there as well as a few swatches of colors.

I'm incredibly excited about it, and I'm sketching what I *think* could be the focal point of the collection. "I finally got past my creative block," I tell him proudly.

"I see that," he says, staring in awe at my work.

Warmth blooms in my chest at this incredibly talented man speaking like that about something I made, knowing in my heart he's not just saying it to be nice. I've never had that before, and even though a small part of it makes me feel uncomfortable, like I shouldn't be accepting his praise, another part realizes it's just residual conditioning from Jeremy to make me question everything he said.

I add the last line to the base of my sketch, an off-the-shoulder gown with a snake-like pattern, before I stand and walk over to him.

"Can I put this on my socials?" he asks, pointing to my board and the original design. I can feel a blush roll down my cheeks and neck to my collarbone at the mere idea he'd *want* to do that.

"You want to put that on your social media?"

Finally, he looks at me, his brows together in confusion. "Well, yeah. Harper, I want to scream about you from the mountaintops. And this? This is amazing. People should know how talented you are, Harper."

"Oh. I, uh. Okay," I say with a small smile on my lips.

He leans forward, pressing a kiss to my temple before sliding his phone out and taking a photo. "Okay, I'm done. You ready?"

I nod, letting him lead me to the car.

By the time we get to Hudson City, that post already has nearly half a million likes.

"Hey, we're going to head out as planned, okay?" Wes tells the waiter at the high-end restaurant in Hudson City he brought me to.

A couple of paparazzi talked to us as we walked the four blocks from the parking garage to the front door. The entire walk, Wes held my hand and told me jokes, clearly trying to make me forget there were people around us, and it felt...easy. When we arrived, we stopped for a few photos and answered a few questions before heading in, as Leo instructed us to. Then we were ushered into a quiet, secluded room of the dark, romantic restaurant where we had the most amazing meal and even better conversation.

After we were served dessert, Wes looked at his watch, grabbed my hand and whispered that we had to go. Now he's grabbing a few bills from his wallet and handing them over. "Remember, if anyone asks, we were here all afternoon, okay?"

She smiles wide and bites her lip. "Of course, Mr. Holden. Anything you need. The kitchen staff has been prepped, you can go out the back door. There are no cameras there."

"Perfect," he says with a smile. "We'll be back soon."

She shrugs as if it doesn't matter to her, then Wes grabs my hand and leads me through the restaurant and to the staff door of the kitchen. He waves at an employee he somehow knows by name but doesn't stop as we leave through a back entrance.

"Do you do this often?" I ask with a laugh as we walk through an alleyway behind buildings.

"Escape a restaurant when there are paparazzi? I mean, not too often, but when things were crazy with Stella and Riggs, yeah, we had to do it a bit. It's a fine balance between Leo having us make appearances and living life. That's why we live in small towns like Ashford and Evergreen Park. It makes it easy since no other big celebrities live there, so the paparazzi aren't typically there twenty-four seven."

"Got it," I say, and even though I have about a million more questions, I shut my mouth as we walk in the brisk cold, clearly on a mission.

"What are we doing here?" I ask five minutes later when we step foot into a familiar-looking parking garage.

"Number seven." He turns to me, laughing at what must be a look of utter confusion on my face before he pulls out a piece of paper. The paper we worked on a few nights ago. "Fuck with his super precious car." Suddenly, it clicks, and I look at him astonished. "This is just for fun. He'll get his real payback soon enough, but I thought you should get the chance to check some things off," he says, the words cryptic.

"What does that mean? And why are we at Jeremy's office building?"

Wes smiles wider but continues to walk further into the garage before turning to me.

"Which one is his?" he asks.

"Which what?"

"Which car is his?" The words echo slightly in the cold cement building, and suddenly, a hint of panic runs through me at the realization that Wes is being serious.

"We shouldn't be doing this. There are cameras in this parking garage," I whisper as we continue to walk through the garage. I learned my lesson the last time I tried to prank Jeremy.

"It doesn't matter. Which car is his, baby?" he says, hand squeezing mine.

"Wes, this isn't—"

He stops walking, putting his cool hands on my cheeks and forcing me to look at him. "Turns out, your ex makes enemies everywhere he goes. It didn't take much at all to convince the person in charge of the security room to accidentally turn off the cameras from twelve to one."

My mouth drops open, and his lips tip in a smile. "You're kidding me."

He shakes his head, his thumb brushing along my cheekbone reverently. "I wouldn't do anything to get either of us in trouble outright, Harper," he says, pulling me into his arms fully. "I just want you to get even. This guy is clearly an ass and, at the very least, deserves his life to get a little harder. I've got Leo working on countering the shit he was whispering behind closed doors, but in the meantime, which is his car?"

I stare for a long moment, knowing time is of the essence but wanting to soak in this moment, the moment where someone goes so far out of their way just because he thinks I deserve to enjoy this silly revenge. I smile finally, then point to Jeremy's obnoxious and, in my opinion, ugly classic car that he constantly bragged to everyone about. We move in that direction until we're next to the car, parked as far as possible without any other cars nearby in two spots, like the asshole he is.

Then Wes shifts the bag he brought with him and sets it down before removing a heavy-looking box. I stare at the industrial-sized roll of plastic wrap in his hands.

"What is that?"

"Plastic wrap," he says simply.

"And...what are we going to do with it?"

He looks at me like I'm being silly before answering. "Wrap his car, obviously," he says, but sets it aside before continuing to dig in the bag, pulling out a bag of candy. I watch as he meticulously opens the package and then unwraps one of the hard candies. He steps closer to me and holds it out.

"Lick this," he says, and my eyes go wide, moving to his crotch without even meaning to.

"Excuse me?"

He grins. "The candy, Harper. Though, another time, another place..." I grab the candy from his hand, and he laughs as a blush burns over my cheeks. "Now stick it to the glass."

"Wes, what the—"

"When he tries to pull it off, it'll shatter the glass." My eyes go wide.

"*Shatter it?*"

"It's cold as fuck in here. The glass is already brittle." He pulls something out of his bag and moves to the gas cap, fiddling to open it and succeeding before he tips a bottle of liquid sugar into it.

"Oh my god, you're insane," I whisper. "I thought we said nothing permanent!"

"I may have lied, though this isn't *permanent*. It's all fixable. It'll just be incredibly inconvenient and cost a bit."

My heart starts pounding at the mere thought. "Wes, this isn't a good—"

He steps closer to me, putting the empty bottle back into his bag and putting his hands to my cheeks, forcing me to look at him. "Would I put you in danger at all?"

I think about that, really, then answer honestly. "No," I say softly.

"Would I do this if I thought there was any chance we'd get caught?"

I shake my head again, because I saw the look of determination on his face the other night, the look that told me Jeremy would never be able to harm me again.

"He left with one of the account executives to New York for the day," he says, and I open my mouth to argue, to tell him I thought he would be out of town last time, but he speaks. "I know this for sure. I have connections. *Leo* has connections. I did the grunt work for this, Harper."

I stare at him and he smiles at me.

"Okay," I say finally, and he smiles wider.

"Get to licking, little wife." I watch as he grabs one of the candies, licks the back, and presses it to a window. It sticks easily, the cold window adhering to his warm spit. He throws one at my head, and I catch it before it hits the ground

"So this will shatter his windshield?" He nods, and I think of all the times he told me we couldn't take his car out when there was salt on the roads or when he yelled at an old man for walking too close to it.

"If he tugs on it, yeah," Wes says. "He can get them off without shattering it, of course. The biggest pain is going to be this." He lifts the giant roll of plastic wrap and begins opening it.

I press the last candy to the side window, feeling it freeze almost instantly to the window while Wes sticks one end of the plastic wrap to the hood of the car, then pulls, carefully tugging and then wrapping it around the side mirror to get it started.

"Take this," he says, handing me the roll over the hood, and I do as he asks. "Now pull and push it under the car."

I struggle a bit, pressing the wrap to the side before pushing it under. Wes grabs it and makes our first complete wrap. I stare at our handiwork and giggle a bit. Wes's smile is wide as he hands it to me, and I feel like we're some devious, childish version of Bonnie and Clyde, plastic wrapping a car in petty revenge.

We do this for a while until the roll is nearly gone and the entire car is nearly white, looking absolutely ridiculous when we hear it.

The clicking of heels echoes through the freezing parking garage, and I tip my head, the roll of plastic wrap midair as Wes passes it to me. Our eyes go wide, and I fight a laugh as he tips his head to the side exaggeratedly, ripping the plastic wrap. He grabs his bag and my hand as we make a break for it.

The sneakers I'm grateful he told me to wear don't make a noise as we move out of sight, hiding in a dark corner. Our breaths come in white clouds as I shiver, and Wes pulls me close to his body, the clacking of the heels getting louder as we stand, our bodies close, the bag at our feet. Wes's arm is around my back, his lips not far from mine when we hear it.

"Fuck, is that Jeremy Vaughn's car?" a woman's voice asks.

"Yeah, I think so. That's where he always parks," a man says. They're maybe fifty feet away, but with my back to them, I can't see them.

"Must have made someone angry," the woman says.

"Are you surprised? The guy's an ass to everyone except Mr. Astor and Clarissa."

"I heard he's cheating on her," the woman says, and I give wide eyes to Wes, who smiles at me.

"And again, I ask, are you surprised?"

"Do you think we should do something?" the woman asks as her heels click past us, walking away from the scene of our crime.

"No. He deserves it," the man says. "Come on, I'm starving."

My attention goes back to Wes as they walk off, his breath playing on my lips before his hand moves to my jaw, tipping my face up. He stares at me for moments that seem to stretch through an eternity. My heart races, waiting for him to kiss me as if this is the first time.

But that's how it feels. Every time Wes Holden kisses me, it feels like the first time, something new and exciting and fun, the world shifting just a bit. And each time, he takes a piece of my heart in a way no one ever has, in a way I don't think I'll ever get it back.

The scariest part is I don't think I *want* it back. I know Wes will keep all of the pieces I give him safe.

My hand moves up to his cheek as the echoes of heels drift into the distance, and I shift to my tiptoes, pressing my lips to his, unable to stop myself.

I want him. I need him.

His hand moves to my hip, pulling me in close, deepening the kiss and taking over it as he tends to do, as I love him to do. His lips move along mine, his tongue pressing to the seam of mine until I open for him, and then he slides it in. He tastes like green apple from one of the candies he stole from the bag, and I smile against his lips. He nips at my lip playfully, and a soft sigh leaves me, the move shooting straight to my belly and spreading warmth there.

"We should get out of here," he whispers when we break the kiss, a smile on his lips. "Cameras will be turned back on soon, and I'd like to be long gone before they are."

I nod, and Wes grabs my hand, twining his fingers with mine. We move quickly through the garage, heads down and unspeaking as we walk the few blocks back to the restaurant. We move through the back door again, then walk through the front door where paparazzi take our photos again, and I get it then: our alibi.

"Hey, Wes?" I say when we're back in his car, making our way to the house.

"Yeah, baby," he says, reaching over and grabbing my hand absentmindedly like it's normal, something casual and ordinary even though it makes my pulse pound.

"Thank you. For today. Well, for the past month. For...everything. You didn't have to do that. Any of it."

He stops at a red light and looks over at me, eyes sincere and warm. "When are you going to realize you deserve the moon, Harper?"

"I don't know about the moon, but I'm starting to believe I might deserve more than I've let myself have," I admit without realizing I'm doing it.

"I hope that *more* includes a future with me," he whispers, squeezing my hand as the light turns green and he starts driving again.

"I'm starting to think it might," I whisper.

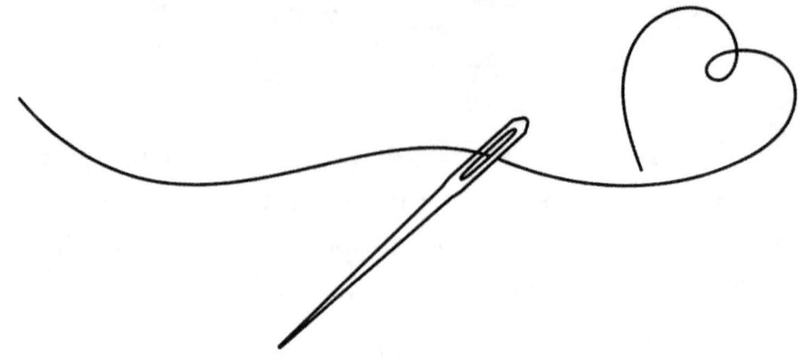

# TWENTY-EIGHT

## HARPER

It's been five days since telling everyone about the designs and two days since our little sabotage of Jeremy's car.

For a while after we got home, I worried someone would come knocking at the door to arrest one or both of us, and this whole mess would start over again. Fortunately, Wes reassured me his security contact at the garage confirmed that Jeremy thinks the culprit was some annoying local kids messing with things, and so far, we're in the clear.

Each night, I've fallen asleep with Wes, usually after he fucks me senseless, and woken up in his arms, something so foreign and yet so comfortable. The little voice in my head keeps whispering things are too easy, that this too, like almost all good things in my life, will end and blow up in my face. But for the first time in a long time, I'm forcing her to be quiet.

This morning, though, I woke without my husband. I squinted at the clock and saw it was nearly ten, then spotted the lime green Post-it, the same hue that was on the stack of cookie dough a month ago, beside it.

*Little wife,*
*Let you sleep in. I couldn't bear to wake you.*
*-Wes*

After reading that, I let out a tiny squeal, kicking my feet with the all-consuming joy of *liking* someone—*falling* for someone—before I rolled out of bed to do my morning routine. Once I was done, I went downstairs to make my coffee with the creamer Laurel begrudgingly buys now, then wandered the house to find my husband.

I think I find him when I hear the low bumping from where Wes told me his makeshift studio is, though I've never been there. I open the basement door, the beat getting louder, and I assume Wes has loud music on to play along with. Opening the door, I start to step down, and I'm quickly blown away by the setup. The walls are covered in egg carton-looking padding, creating what I assume is a sound barrier, and there are a dozen instruments along the walls.

Wes plays guitar for Atlas Oaks, but from the look of the room, he can play everything. That's confirmed when I look to the corner of the room where a shirtless Wes is wearing big, noise-cancelling headphones, sweating as he slams on the drums in front of him. It's magic to watch, his body moving smoothly and somewhat chaotically in what could be an absolute racket, but instead, sounds perfect. It's the beat of some song I somewhat recognize, despite not hearing any other part. As he ends the song, I start clapping. He must hear me, or maybe he catches a glimpse of me in his peripheral vision, because he smiles, slipping off the headphones.

"Wow," I say, leaning in the doorway as Wes wipes his forehead with a towel. He's wearing no shirt and just a pair of loose shorts, toned muscles on display, and I'm reminded just how *hot* my husband is. "That's so much more intense than I realized," I say, and his lips tip up in a smile as he reaches down, grabbing a bottle of water and taking a long drink. I definitely *don't* watch the way his throat moves with each swallow. "I didn't know you could play drums."

"I can play it all, for better or worse," he says, then tips his head, telling me to come closer.

I do as he asks, stopping a few feet from where he sits. "What do you like best?"

He shrugs. "I like them all. Drums are great when you have some pent-up..." His eyes slowly move over my body before he smiles. "Feelings."

"Oh," I say, my eyes going heated, my body doing the same. "I, uh. I can see how that would help to release those...feelings." I clear my throat, looking around the room to distract myself. "You can play that?" I ask, my eye moving to the trombone in the corner, and he nods.

"My first instrument. Started in fifth grade. Chose it because I thought I could make fart noises with it."

I let out a little laugh and move closer to him, my fingers shifting toward a wide golden symbol, a light chiming coming from them as I run my nails over the metal.

"You play anything?" he asks, and I laugh, shaking my head while forcing myself to not look at his bare chest.

"God, no. I'm about as untalented musically as one can be."

"I doubt that. Anyone can learn anything."

I give him a small shake of my head. "I tried three different instruments in middle school and sucked at all of them. In eighth grade, my music teacher, Mr. Fieldman, very kindly and very gently told me maybe I should try something else. Anything else, I think."

"Maybe you've just never had the right teacher."

"No, I unfortunately have absolutely no rhythm."

He shakes his head like he can't believe it, then tips his head toward the giant drum set. "Everyone has rhythm. Come here. I'll give you a quick lesson. Drums are a good one to start with."

I step back with a laugh. "Oh, god, no. No, I couldn't."

"Why not?"

"Because..." I pause unsure of how to answer. "That must be worth a billion dollars," I whisper, indicating his drum set.

"It's replaceable." And then he stands, grabbing my wrist in his calloused fingers and moving me until I'm standing before the massive set. He fiddles with the stool, lowering it so my feet can touch the ground, then pulls me down to sit. Next he messes with the heights of some kind of cymbal.

"Wes, you don't have to mess with your whole setup," I say.

"Every time Reed is down here, he fucks everything up. I'd much rather have my pretty wife doing it than his ugly mug." I try to protest again, but he ignores me again before grabbing a fresh pair of drumsticks from a container. He then pulls up another stool to sit behind me so my back is to his warm front. The heat of him sears through my shirt.

"We're going to do the first song I ever learned on drums." I look over my shoulder and smile.

"So, the musical memory associated with it is learning how to play drums for you?" I ask, referencing the game we played on our honeymoon.

He stares at me, long and hard, before smiling.

"Not for long." A chill runs through me before he moves, his hand covering mine to show me how to hold the drumstick. "Like this. Hold them steady, but not too tight. You want some looseness. Same with your wrists—you want control, but you also want to be able to easily move them."

"That kind of sounds dirty," I say with a laugh, and Wes is quiet before he clears his throat. "I'm sorry that was—"

"Nope, nope, just trying to distract myself. Would be weird to get a boner right now."

I snort out a laugh and shake my head. I follow his instructions, then hit the drum in front of me a few times.

"Good, you're doing great. Now you can add in the kick," he says, praising me before moving his hand down the outside of my leg and to my knee, rough fingers wrapping it and moving my leg in toward the larger drum on the floor until my foot is resting on the pedal. He shows me how to hit the kick drum, snare, and hi-hat cymbals together, and after a few minutes, the familiar sounds of "September" by Earth, Wind & Fire can be heard.

"I think I've got this. I could put Beck out of a job," I joke. He laughs, and the rumble of it along my back is distracting, making my hand lose the beat.

"Hardest thing to do as a drummer is keep time," Wes says, and I let out a small laugh.

"You don't say," I say, going back to the moves he taught me, but then he presses his lips to the spot beneath my ear. A shiver rolls through me, my hands hesitating and losing that beat again.

"Not so easy, is it?" he asks, his hand on my knee moving up just an inch, and, despite myself and all common sense, I shift ever so slightly, my legs sliding open a bit further. The skirt of my shirt dress I threw on this morning slides up my thighs, leaving little to the imagination. The groan he lets out reverberates through his chest and into my back, forcing a soft gasp from my lips.

"What are you doing to me?" he asks, his breath ghosting along my neck.

"Not sure, but I think you're doing it right back," I whisper like I'm worried that if I speak out loud enough, I'll break this moment, and I *very much* do not want to break it—not when his fingers are slowly grazing along the inside of my thigh, teasing and taunting. Until his hand is under the fabric of my shirt dress, meeting the delicate lace of the thong I'm wearing.

"You know, I saw these in the laundry and wondered just how flimsy they'd be." A finger slides under the lace as his lips leave wet kisses along my neck, sucking and nipping, my body reacting with heat and need, and again, I spread my legs just a bit, letting him have more room if he so desires.

God, I *hope* he desires.

Thankfully, he uses the invitation, sliding along the band of my underwear to my hip then down toward my aching core, then back up. He continues the circuit until I'm about to go crazy. My body melts into his, the drumstick falling to the ground with a clatter just as his fingers move further under the fabric at my hip, twisting, then tugging until a tearing sound fills the room.

"Wes!" I yelp, turning to look at him, a small smile on his lips.

"Just as I thought."

"Those were expensive," I say remembering the trip to the lingerie store with Ava before the wedding even though I told her Wes Holden was *never going to see them.*

"I'll buy you a dozen more," he murmurs, his hand tearing the other side before tugging until the flimsy fabric is away from my body, leaving me bare.

"Wes, that's—" I start to argue, looking over my shoulder at him, but then his lips are on mine and I'm forgetting what I was annoyed by, especially when his fingers start to trail up the seam of my pussy. "Oh," I whisper.

"Fuck," he groans, his lips trailing down my neck, my head tipping to give him more room. "You're so wet, aren't you?" He adds a bit of pressure, pressing until he's touching my center, then running up and over my clit before repeating the cycle.

It's amazing. It's blissful. It's erotic.

It's not enough.

"Please," I whisper needily.

"Please what?" he asks casually, like he has all the time in the world, as if he's not actively torturing me.

"Finger me. Fuck me. I don't care, just do...something," I plead, and he laughs against my neck. The man *laughs.* I turn my head again to argue, to glare at him, to yell at him—I'm not sure exactly, because before I can do any of that, he's sliding a finger into me and I'm groaning.

"I have to leave soon, so I don't have enough time to fuck you, but I'll take care of you, baby," he says, voice low as he pulls his finger back out of me, then slides it in.

I groan, my hips rocking to get more. My ass is on the very edge of the stool, but his arm is on my waist and his body on my back. It's the only thing keeping me in place, and all I can focus on is the need spiraling around me.

Need for him.

His fingers slide out, and he glides them over my clit, making me moan loud. "God, you sound pretty."

"Wes, please. Let's..." I start, but my brain malfunctions as he slides two fingers back in and starts fucking me with them, his lips at my neck.

"This is enough for now."

I want to disagree, to beg for more, to lay down on the floor and let him fuck me hard and fast, but I can't focus on anything but the heat at my lower back, the pleasure between my legs, the way his voice sounds, his breath on my neck...my hips start rocking as he finger fucks me, trying to get myself there as I climb the hill of all-consuming pleasure.

"That's it, little wife," he groans into my neck, my head lolling to the side. His thumb rolls over my clit as my hips buck and shift to a new beat, one he's creating and I'm powerless to. "Ride your husband's fingers."

"Wes," I pant, my hand moving up to his neck, looking for something, anything to hold me in place. I feel like I'm going to float away, but inexplicably, I know he'll always ground me. He breathes against my skin, as turned on by this as I am, his scruff scraping there and adding to the kaleidoscope of feelings.

My hips rock against his fingers moving inside of me. "God, it's so good. I'm so close," I moan, but then his fingers stop moving altogether, his teeth nipping at the skin of my neck as his arm holds me in place.

"Not yet, little wife. I'm enjoying myself."

I groan, loving and hating this about him, the power he holds over my body as he so gently grazes over my clit. "Wes, please," I mewl. "I need you so bad."

He groans into my neck at my admission as he starts moving his fingers inside me again.

"When I get home," he starts. His hard cock pokes at my back, and I shift toward it, trying to tease him the way he's teasing me. "When I get home, I'm going to tease you for hours. Eat this pussy, play with it, never letting you come until I say so."

I moan as the edge approaches quickly, bright, blinding pleasure coursing through me, but he slips his fingers out, moving them to just barely graze along my swollen clit.

"No!" I shout, and he chuckles.

*The man chuckles.*

I'd hate him if I didn't need him so badly.

"Don't worry, baby. I just want to make this last as long as I can. Has to tide me over until I get home." His breath plays along my neck, and my eyes close as my head falls back again. My body is out of my control as I lift a hand to pinch a nipple through my thin bra, desperate for relief. "Goddamn, you're so fucking beautiful. The next time I make you come, it's going to be on my cock."

"Yes, please," I plead. "Now. Fuck me now."

A pained laugh leaves his chest, reverberating through my back, but he shakes his head. "No, no. Not now. I like this for now."

He slides his fingers down, filling me once more, but this time, he puts his thumb to my clit, circling it and sending me spiraling, moans and cries and prayers leaving my lips as I teeter on the edge. Somehow, someway, I hold on, though, knowing I need to wait.

Wes needs to let me fall.

"God, my little wife is such a good girl, isn't she? Waiting for me to let her come," he croons from behind me.

"Wes," I whisper, unable to say any other word.

"Remember that name, baby. Scream it when you come."

And then he's fucking me fast and hard, his thumb rolling over my rolling over my clit as he does, and I'm falling, calling out his name as I do. His arm keeps me from falling to the ground as the pleasure pummels me, washing over me and leaving me what feels like a new person and basking in the aftershocks of my orgasm.

We sit there, panting for long minutes as I try and come back to my body, Wes's fingers having slid out of me, his hands lifted and rearranged me at some point so I'm on his lap, limp and content, nuzzling into his neck.

Then his phone goes off, and he groans. "I hate to do this," he says, voice low and filled with genuine regret. "But I've gotta get going to Riggs's."

"What about you?" I say, then blush because God, could I *be* less cool?

He looks at me, smiling wide and devious as he helps us stand, making sure my legs are settled before he presses his lips to mine, kissing me hard and deep.

Like a promise.

"When I come, it's going to be inside you, Harper. But we don't have time for me to do that right now, so it's going to have to wait." I pout—I actually *pout* at that—and he laughs, shifting and holding my chin in his hand, forcing his eyes to me.

"I won't be home until late." I nod, already knowing this to be the case. "Thank you," he says against my lips.

"Thank *me?*" I say, aghast. "I'm the one who came so hard I saw stars."

His smile goes wide and boyish and proud. "And I promise you, I enjoyed it more than you could ever imagine." Then he steps back and slaps my ass before grabbing my hand. "Come on. Upstairs. I gotta go."

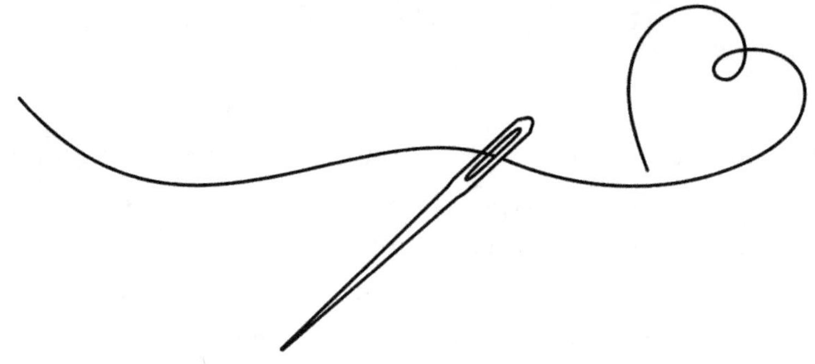

# TWENTY-NINE

## HARPER



The text comes before I've even had my first cup of coffee, before Wes has been able to convince me to roll out of our warm bed, so I see it while I'm still lying on his chest, my hand ungracefully batting at the side table to grab my phone. Then I'm squinting at the screen with half confusion, half all-consuming irritation.

It's been nearly two months since we broke up, and he's just *now* asking me to get the few things I left at his house? Most of which I've already replaced or forgotten about, so unwilling to talk to the man who fucked me over, I decided they just didn't matter enough.

"Is it from him?" Wes asks, looking at my phone over my shoulder, his voice a soothing, deep rumble against me. I've read that the purring of a cat has been proven to ease anxiety, but I think they should do a study on Wes's morning voice because some of my irritation eases just with those words. "I wasn't looking, but you got all tight and annoyed, so—" he starts to explain, but I shake my head, quickly putting him at ease.

"It's fine. I have nothing to hide from you. But yeah. It's him. He wants me to pick up my things."

"You have stuff at his house?" I shrug.

"I grabbed what I wanted most when I left and found it wasn't that much. I replaced a lot of things when I left because it wasn't worth dealing with him to get it."

Wes shrugs behind me. "Then tell him to toss it. If none of it has sentimental value and can't be replaced, tell him to go fuck himself."

Another message comes in, a photo of a beat-up brown box on the kitchen table piled high with my things, and then another text.

> Leave your key when you leave. I'll be gone until five today. If anything else is missing, I will be filing a police report.

My molars grind when another comes through.

> I don't think they'll let you off so easily a second time.

I prepare to tell him to go fuck himself as Wes suggested when something catches my eye in the box.

"*Fuck*," I say low, zooming in on the photo until my concerns are confirmed. "Shit."

"What is it?"

"It's my grandmother's book," I say, setting the phone aside and curling into Wes. Maybe if I do, the rest of this will just melt away, and I can restart the day without this nuisance.

"What kind of book?" Wes asks gently as he pushes my hair back over my shoulder. He's always a calming presence, his touch soothing.

"Her modeling book. My family isn't super close, but my mom's mother was a model before she had her. She used to show me her modeling book, the portfolio she'd bring to casting calls of her previous work. It's..." I groan, realizing I'm going to have to go over to Jeremy's house today. "It's what made me want to start designing."

I remember setting it on the bookshelf in Jeremy's office once in an effort to make things feel less *divided* in our home and forgetting about it completely. Things have been so crazy, my life so up in chaos, that I'm sure there are more things I've left behind that one day, I'll miss.

"You're going to have to go there today, aren't you?" Wes asks, and I nod and roll to my back, throwing an arm over my eyes and letting out an irritated sound.

"I really don't want to. What if he's there?" I don't know if I can handle a confrontation right now, not when things are *finally* settling in. Can't I just have *one week* where things don't go sideways?

Since Wes and I finally got together, it's been perfectly blissful. I sketch and design all day, work on dresses for clients, or even a few times, take interviews Leo set up for me to promote my work, while Wes practices or records over at Riggins's house. We're both usually home by dinnertime, and cook together before spending the evening together. It's been perfect, everything I didn't know I wanted or needed, and now it feels like Jeremy has popped that little bubble we were living in.

"If he's there, it will be fine because I'll be there too. I don't want you going alone, but only if you want me to." Despite my irritation, my chest warms with that, with Wes's desire to come with. "Or, if he's there and you don't feel comfortable going in, we call the police, and they can escort you inside. Minimal contact, and we keep everything documented. Actually, screenshot those texts and send them to me."

We've slowly been creating a file of any evidence I have of Jeremy's blackmail, any help I've given him that was used without accreditation, and, of course, the original designs I still have, post marked and unopened.

I don't plan to use any of it, but Wes suggested we accumulate it all *just in case,* and it made sense to me. I tap my screen, taking photos and sending them to Wes.

"I don't know, maybe it's not that important. Maybe—" I start, but

I'm interrupted by Wes taking my phone from my hand and putting it on the bedside table then rolling us so he's hovering over me.

"No, Harper. He does not get that. He does not get to win like that, not anymore. He doesn't control you and doesn't get to hold anything above you." I sit there in awe, a strange mix of warmth and joy and a bit of panic rushing through me as I process his words and the ferocity of which he says them. He takes in my shock with a shake of his head and a small laugh before he presses his lips to mine one more. Then he rolls off before I can argue and puts a hand out to me. "Come on. Shower, breakfast, then we head to the asshat's place."

I take the change in conversation, grabbing his hand and letting him tug me up and out of the bed until we're chest to chest.

"What, you don't want to fuck me?" I ask with a smile.

"I can certainly do that, little wife. Now come on. As you know, I'm great at multitasking." I do as he asks with a giggle, and Wes does, in fact, prove what a good multitasker he is in the shower.

"Okay, so I don't think it's much, honestly, but I want to take a look around. I don't want to ever step foot in here again if I don't have to," I say when we walk into Jeremy's house. It's nearly noon by the time we make it over here, and the brown box is sitting on the kitchen counter, untouched from when he took a photo of it.

I turn to Wes, who followed behind me as I walked up the once-familiar steps, noting with pleasure the grass is still rather glittery. But I stop in my tracks when Wes sets the bag I didn't realize he was carrying down and bends to inspect it.

"What is that?" I ask when he pulls out a giant spray bottle filled with some kind of white liquid.

"A spray bottle," he says matter-of-factly.

I nod my head and give him a tight smile. "Yeah, I got that. I, uh, what is it for? And what is in it?" I ask as he walks into the living room with the bottle in hand.

"Well, it's filled with milk."

I stop and stare, lips rolling in on themselves as I try and piece together what he's saying. "Okay...and why do we have a spray bottle with milk at my ex's house?"

"To spray things," he says, and then shows me what he means by spraying it a few times on the cream-colored couch. "Is this the one he wouldn't let you eat on?"

I stare open-mouthed as he continues to spray the fabric, leaving no visible trace of the milk he's spraying. "What are you doing?"

"Number fourteen, I think. You said he wouldn't let you eat on his white couch because you were too messy of an eater."

I blink once, twice, three times, trying to understand his words before I nod.

"Uh, yeah. That's the one." I vaguely remember telling him that the night we made our giant list, when I started to get sleep deprived and silly.

"Consider it crossed off." He then lifts the cushion and sprays the underside much more liberally than the top with the same vigor then replaces it, moving to the next cushion. I watch in utter confusion as he moves confidently, nearly completely forgetting why we even came here.

"I'm sorry, I don't...I don't quite understand."

"This is going to dry in an hour, max. That's the point of the spray bottle, it's to give a fine and even application. He won't know it happened by the time he gets home."

"Okay..." I start, still not understanding.

Finally, he finishes the underside of the cushions and stands, facing me with a wide, devious grin. "But have you ever smelled milk after it sits on something for a few days and goes rancid?"

My stomach sours and I nod, the picture he's painting starting to fill in.

"So Jeremy here is going to slowly have the most rank smell filling his house and not know where it's coming from. He can wash the blanket," he starts to spray the purely-for-decoration couch blanket I bought him for Christmas a year ago. "And change out the pillows." He sprays those too. "But the couch will still reek." Then he turns the nozzle to the carpet. "And the carpet. Next I'll do the curtains and last will be his bed."

"His bed?" I ask with a squeak, staring wide eyed at him.

"Even if he moves to try and escape it, assuming it's something in his crawl space or walls or whatever, the stank is going to follow him when he brings his furniture," he says with a sparkle in his eyes.

I understand it now, and even though it's kind of genius, it's a bit scary that he not only thought of this in the small time frame we had this morning, but followed through with it.

"I think you've been spending much too much time with Ava," I say with a laugh and a shake of my head.

He steps closer to me, pulling me in tight and pressing a hard kiss to my lips. "This is the least of what he deserves," he says, then steps back, continuing his dirty work. "Now go, check around, and make sure there's nothing else you want or need from here. I don't want to come back and have to smell this place."

I let out a laugh before doing as he asked, feeling much more light-hearted than I ever thought I would be walking these halls again. I don't see anything of mine around, so it was either tossed out or I grabbed it before I left.

I go back to the box, sifting through things to double check what he left, pausing when I see a plain envelope with *Harper* written on it in Jeremy's handwriting. I groan internally, and decide I'll handle *that* later.

When I enter the living room once more, he's finishing up on the curtains, the bottle half empty. "Good?"

I nod. "I think all of it is in the box, so we can leave whenever you're done," I say, giving him a smile.

"Got it. Just have to do the last stop, his bedroom," he says, then moves toward the room I pointed out.

It's actually kind of hot to see, this big rock star of a man committing what could go down as the most sneaky, petty revenge on a man just because he treated me poorly.

He starts with the carpet in Jeremy's room, the one I never slept in, the one he never fucked me in because he'd rather *mess up* my room than his. That should have been a sign, no? Never wanting me in his bed? Though, I suppose him never being that worried about my actually coming was also a sign I ignored. I'm thinking on that, watching Wes's toned back move beneath his Henley shirt as he moves around with the bottle, moving to the curtains when I get an idea.

It's insane, but I don't know if one could call me exactly *sane* these days.

"Wait," I say, as he lifts the spray bottle, his face looking at my questioning, but I smile and take a step closer to the bed. "What about one last revenge?"

# THIRTY

## WES

"What about one last revenge?" Harper asks, and my brow comes together in confusion as I look to her, my hand frozen as it's about to spray the milk onto his bed.

The confusion clears quickly when she steps closer to me, her hand moving to my jaw and urging me to bend and kiss her. It's hot and quick and fierce, and I groan into it, my free hand wrapping around her back.

"I never came in this bed," she whispers, and my fingers dig into her side. It's strange, the mixture of jealousy and arousal I feel. "Are you jealous, Mr. Holden?"

"Abso-fucking-lutely, Mrs. Holden," I growl against her lips.

"There's no need," she says, her voice teasing and lilting. Her hands move, drifting down my chest to the button at my pants.

"Harper," I say, but she's unzipping my fly and pushing my pants down, grabbing my cock in her hand. "*Harper.*"

"One last revenge," she whispers, and then moves to her knees. I don't stop her, completely transfixed on my wife as she brings her mouth to the head of my cock, holding my eyes as she hollows out her cheeks, sucking on the tip.

I lose any and all restraint.

She wants to fuck around her ex's house? We'll fuck around in her ex's house.

"Shirt up, hand in your pants," I demand as I wrap my fist around her hair. "Touch your pussy while I fuck your mouth, get it nice and wet for me."

She moans but does as told, lifting her shirt and bra together to reveal her pretty tits before sliding a hand under the waistband of her leggings. She moans around my cock, and I know she got to her clit.

I slide her mouth over my cock using my grip on her hair, and she moans again. "Are you wet baby? Does sucking my cock in your ex's room make my pussy wet?"

She nods around me, eyes drooping with pleasure, though staying locked on mine.

"Slide one finger inside your cunt, Harper. Finger yourself while I fuck your throat." She moans again, shifting and then mewling before rocking her hips, riding her fingers. "Such a good little wife you are."

She deep throats me as she fucks herself, moaning around me until her moans become more frantic, her body moving like she's on the edge, ready to come already. That's when I pull out, bend, and lift her to the bed.

"Pants off," I say then move to the side of the bed as she scrambles to take off her leggings.

I thank God we talked about contraception recently, so when I found out Harper was on the pill, we decided to get rid of them altogether. My hands go to her hips, and I pull her still quaking body to the edge of the bed. One leg of her leggings is still on, but I don't care. I line my cock up at her entrance and slam in deep without any pretense. She screams as I slide in, her hands going to her tits to roll her nipples between her fingers.

My woman. My wife. The most beautiful, sexy woman on this planet.

"God, it's so good," she says, and I let out a growl, fucking her hard and fast. I know we're pushing it, doing this here at all, so taking my time, teasing her, savoring this isn't an option. Once we get out of here and I get her back in *our* bed, I can.

But for now...

"I need you to get there fast, Harper," I groan, sliding in deep. Each move is both bliss and torture, the pleasure growing up my spine and tightening my balls that slap against her with each thrust. Her hand slides down her belly, starting to work her clit quickly.

"That's it, baby, *fuck*," I groan as I slam into her deep, fucking her hard with each thrust. Her tits bounce each time, and I lean forward, pinching one of her nipples hard.

"Wes," she shrieks, writhing beneath me, hips thrusting to meet mine and get me deeper. It's frantic and intense and erotic as hell, taking over every ounce of my mind and body. "Fuck!" She tightens around me, a vise around my throbbing cock.

"Come for me, baby. I'm going to fill you, and then it's going to drip out of you onto his bed."

"Oh, fuck, fuck, fuck." Her eyes roll back in her head as she tightens on me even more. Knowing what she needs, I swat her hand away and slap her clit. Her body jolts, and she screams, coming in waves beneath me and taking me with her.

I groan her name as I release spurt after spurt of cum into her, holding her tight to me as I do. I probably steal too much time, staying with her like that, but it takes some time to come back to my body.

When I do, Harper is lying there, still filled with me, a sated smile on her face. I mirror it, shaking my head before slowly sliding out of her. She shifts, attempting to move, but I shake my head, using a hand on her shoulder to urge her back down. Gently, I graze my fingers over her swollen clit, her body jerking with pleasure. She's over-sensitized, so this should be quick.

I squat down to watch, her pussy tightening as she moans gently, my fingers rubbing quickly over her clit.

"Wes," she breathes.

"Just one more," I say, my hand applying a bit more pressure. "I want to make it count."

She yells, then calls my name after I'm done with her, coming one last time for me.

As she does, I watch my cum drip out of her. Satisfied, I stand and use my hand to smear the mess we made around. When I'm done, she's staring at me, wide eyes and open mouth.

"I can't tell if that was psychotic or the hottest thing I've ever seen," she whispers, and I smile.

"I'll take either. Now get dressed and grab your box. We've gotta go." I help her stand, and my hand goes to her face to pull her in for a hard kiss. I eventually, reluctantly, force myself to stop so I can pull my pants up and finish spraying the milk.

Then I make Jeremy's bed just the way we found it.

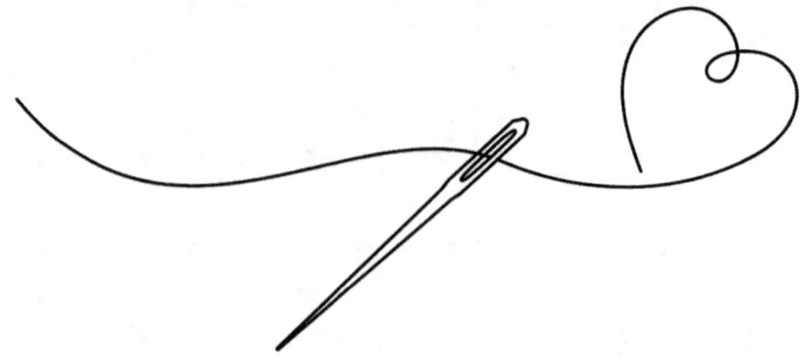

# THIRTY-ONE

## HARPER

"Hey, Laurel?" I ask, walking into the kitchen and biting my lip as I do. Wes's assistant turns around from where she's looking into a cabinet, a notepad in hand, and glares at me.

I was hoping the ice would break with Laurel and me at some point, but that has yet to happen. If anything, it's gotten worse, her glares more intense and annoyed, seemingly purposely fucking with my shit or conveniently forgetting to get things that are just for me when she goes grocery shopping.

That's why I'm here right now, though I'd rather be anywhere else. After the first time I told Wes that Laurel forgot to grab my creamer at the store, she continued to do it, no matter how many times I added it to the list. I mentioned it to her once in front of Wes, and the daggers she gave me while sweetly promising to get it next time were almost tangible. And since then, she's consistently missed every item I ask for, to the point that I don't even bother to ask anymore.

When Wes found out I was going to the store yesterday to grab the essentials Laurel "forgot" to get me, he said he would talk to Laurel about it again since, while the paparazzi are slowing down a bit, it's not uncommon to get stopped by one trying to get a juicy tidbit to sell.

But as much as I appreciate it, I don't want Wes fighting my battles, and I think she might see that as my attacking her. Because of this, I told him I'd talk to her myself. Laurel is an important part of Wes's life, whether or not I'm a big fan, and I want to cause the least amount of waves possible, especially now that we've decided we're in this for the long run.

Today seemed to be the right time, as she's in the kitchen, an iPad in her hands and surveying the fridge, seeming to make a grocery list for the week.

*Perfect. I can just ask if there's an easier way to add my stuff to her shopping list, and we can move on like adults.*

"What?" she asks with a glare at me, and I sigh with the realization she's not going to make this easier. I'm not exactly sure why the woman hates me so much, though I have my theories.

"Look, I'm not trying to make your job more difficult. I know you've been Wes's assistant for a while—" I start, but she cuts me off.

"Five years," she says, crossing her arms over her chest. "Longer than you've even *known* of him."

"That's so great, really," I say with a shake of my head, trying to steer this conversation in a more productive direction. "And he really values you and how you help out. He'd told me how you keep everything running so smoothly for him, and I've seen it too. You clearly aren't my biggest fan, and I get it. Really, I do. I'm some stranger coming in and touching everything, another person you have to keep track of, and I know that probably adds a lot to your plate—"

"I only have to take care of Wes," she says, her chin tipping up.

"Yeah, got that, but I also know Wes sometimes sends you out on errands for me, like when you had to help with my wedding gift, and, well, some of my stuff is on the shopping list. I just want to check in and see if there's an easier way for me to add things to that list. I totally get that you forget it sometimes, so I just—"

"I don't forget it," she says, clipped.

"I'm sorry?"

"I don't forget, Harper." A small smile spreads on her lips. "I just only get what Wes needs."

I roll my lips between my teeth and nod, taking a deep breath to center myself.

"Okay, well, maybe it would be easier if I took over the grocery shopping then? Because it seems silly for us both to go to the store, you know? I really don't mind taking care of it and—"

"What's silly is you being here," she says, firm and annoyed, crossing her arms on her chest and leaning a hip on the counter.

"I'm sorry?"

"I just think it's silly you're even here. It's fake, right? You're married or whatever, but it's not real. You aren't his wife, so you should stop acting like you matter to him. Instead, here you are, trying to weasel your way into his life, changing things, adding more work to *my* plate, and I don't even work for you."

Anger is starting to boil in my veins, but I fight to tamp it down. *Wes really values her, Harper. He's done so much for you, you can endure this dumb bitch.*

"I only ask because Wes asked me to."

"That's because Wes is nice. He's doing a friend a favor by dealing with you. We all know it's just to keep the attention off Riggins and Stella, but that's not even going to be necessary soon, and then what?" She smiles wide. "Then you'll be back to being a nobody, but I'll still be here. You'll be just like every other girl he's dated."

Blood drains from my face as she hits my own insecurities on the head, even if Wes has proven to me time and time again I can trust him. I think no matter what, I'll always harbor the tiniest bit of fear and worry that I won't be enough. I've worked past my fears, pushing them aside because being with Wes is well worth the risk, but you don't just *get over* something like that overnight.

Laurel clearly can see she's accomplished whatever she wanted and smiles wider. "One day, he's going to open his eyes and see I've always been here for him. Until then, I'm going to have to endure you, but that does not mean I have to cater to you."

In the corner of my eye, as she rambles on, though, I see the corner of a blue package in a cabinet. Where there used to be one packet of Oreos, there are four stacked neatly, something Wes will randomly come into my design room with—a quick cookie break, he calls it—and I'm reminded that I'm with him. He's mine.

Clearly, Laurel wants my husband, and really, I can't blame her, knowing what a catch he is, but I also know for the first time in my life that the man I'm with is *mine*, completely and totally.

I smile then.

"Don't you think if he wanted you, you'd have him?" I ask, taking a step closer to her and crossing my arms on my chest.

"What?"

"You've worked for him for five years. How many of them have you been in love with him?" She glares at me. "And not once has he even tried anything? Shown any interest?"

"He keeps things professional," she says, and I smile wider, remembering telling Wes *we* should keep things professional.

"Except when Wes and *I* tried to keep things professional since, as you pointed out, this was a fake marriage, he still couldn't keep his hands off me because he's crazy for me, same as I am for him. And babe, I'm going to warn you, eventually, he's going to catch onto your little power trip, and he *really* doesn't like people treating his wife poorly."

The color leaves her face now, and she stutters before speaking. "What are you going to do about it? Tattle on me?"

I shake my head because I won't be doing anything of the sort because the trash *always* takes itself out, and I'm happy to let her fuck herself over, but before I can, Wes's voice echoes through the kitchen.

"You're fired, Laurel," he says. Both of our heads swivel to the entrance of the kitchen, my husband prowling in with a look of total anger on his face. "Get your things and get out of *our* home."

"I—what?" she asks and even though I am a melting pot of

emotions right now, I can't fight the smile pulling at my lips as he moves closer to me, putting an arm around my waist.

"You're fired, effective immediately."

She takes us in, a united front in a way I didn't know I always wanted, then her face goes from shock to disbelief. "Wes, you're joking, right? I've been your right hand for five years, and this chick comes in and—"

"She's my wife," he says, the words coming out in a growl. Laurel must have a death wish or something, because now she rolls her eyes.

"Your wife? Wes, be real. She's only here to social climb because her little business is failing."

*Oops, definitely the wrong thing to say.*

"Out," Wes says, letting go and grabbing her bag before moving toward the front door. We both follow as he opens the door and throws the bag on the grass.

"You can't be serious, Wes," she says, walking up to him, her face transformed once again to some version of sincerity and friendship. "This is...this is all a miscommunication, a misunderstanding. I didn't—"

"You do not come into my house and disrespect *my wife.* You can come back another time to grab your things from your office. Contact Jaime, and he'll set up a time when Harper and I won't be in the house, and he will be here to walk you through. You can keep the car until then, but that is not your property, and I'll need it returned at your walk-through."

Her face goes pale, realizing how serious he is.

"Wes, we can—" Laurel starts, but he points out the door, jaw firm.

"If you don't leave right now, I'm calling the police. I'll still give you a recommendation due to our long-standing partnership, but if you don't leave cordially, that will change. You should be happy I'm doing even that, Laurel."

Her chin quivers, and she opens her mouth to speak once more, but she must see how serious Wes is being because she rolls her lips into her mouth and turns on her heel and leaves, grabbing her bag from the grass as she does before Wes slams and locks the door behind her.

The house is silent as he walks to the kitchen and picks up his phone, sending off a few texts in angry silence before finally, he sets it down and turns to me.

My stomach hurts from the anxiety of knowing *I did this.* Wes had a long-term employee he really enjoyed working with, and I ruined that. Maybe if I had just kept my mouth shut, he wouldn't look as angry and hurt as he does right now. That's the least I could have done, considering all he's done for me.

"I'm so sorry," I whisper. "Wes, you didn't have to do that. I could have—"

"Excuse me?" he asks, and I can feel his ire turn to me.

"You didn't have to fire her. You should call her, tell her you need some time, but she's not fired. I'm fine. She's been working for you for a while and—"

"And you said from the beginning she was a red flag."

I did say that.

"Maybe it was just because I thought she was into you, and I was jealous. She's a friend of yours."

"No, she's not," he says, voice low and firm. "And you're my wife." He pulls me in close, and I realize his anger and disappointment is in no way directed at me. "I told you no one talks to you that way, no matter what my relationship is to them. You do not apologize because you were right about someone. I apologize to you for not believing you the second you said it."

I bit my lip, wanting to argue, but he shakes his head before pressing his lips to mine. I bask in the sweet moment, my mind trying to recenter and catch up.

"So, we need groceries?" he asks when he pulls back, and I smile.

"I guess?"

"Then we'll do it this morning. I've never done a reset," he says, and I look at him confused.

"What?"

"It's Sunday," he whispers against my lips.

"I don't—" I start, but he keeps talking.

"So it's reset day."

My body stills at the small insight I gave him long ago and the way he remembered it now.

"Oh, we don't have to—" I start, shaking my head.

"Yeah, we do, Harper. This is the perfect opportunity. We're going to have a lazy Sunday and reset for the week." He puts a hand to the back of my head, pressing my lips to his. "It's a busy one. You have that meeting with Willa on Tuesday and two dresses due to clients, I have to go to the city with the guys on Thursday for release shit. We should start the week right." Warmth fills me, and my eyes begin to water.

"Hey, hey, none of that," he whispers. "What's going on?"

"You just...you know me so well. You remember what my week is going to be like and what I once said I like to do on Sundays, and you're making it happen."

"I remember everything you tell me, Harper, because you're important to me." He smiles wide as my lower lip wobbles again before he kisses me and moves to stand. "You'll get used to it. But before we do anything, I'm taking you out for breakfast. I have to make sure my wife is fed."

And in that moment, even if I made a million mistakes and bad decisions, I know I did at least one thing right if it means I get to have this man as mine.

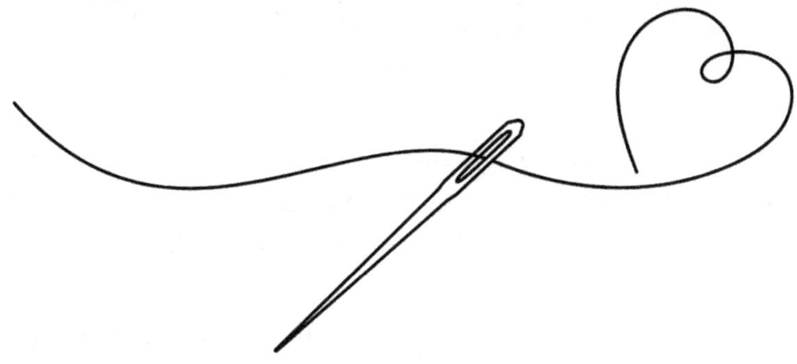

# THIRTY-TWO

## HARPER

"You can't come down yet," Wes says, and I giggle, standing at the top of the stairs.

"What?"

"I told you to relax! I'm doing something. Jesus, woman."

Wes and I spent the morning grocery shopping before we cleaned, organized, and prepped a few lunches for the upcoming week together, laughing and joking the whole time. I'd never had more fun doing basic tasks than I did today, even if the grocery store was a madhouse.

*"Maybe we swap our weekly reset to Tuesdays,"* Wes whispered while we stood at the overly long checkout line, a baseball hat pulled low over his face. *"We don't have traditional jobs, so we don't have to keep a traditional schedule."*

Warmth flooded me, realizing he didn't plan for this to be a one-time thing.

About an hour ago, Wes told me he was *ordering me* to go upstairs and relax while he set up a surprise. I inevitably argued, at which point, he carried me into the bathroom and told me to take the world's longest bath. When he said *please*, making puppy dog eyes, I couldn't help but smile and go along with it, but now I'm dying of boredom and just want to hang out with my husband.

Words I never thought I'd be saying two months ago, to be honest.

"I'm *bored*," I whine from the top of the stairs. I took a shower instead and blew my hair out so it wouldn't be wet for whatever he has planned, but after, I slid on a cute pair of pajamas, as per his instructions.

"Fine," he sighs. "It's not fully ready, but you can come down." Eagerly I make my way down the stairs, meeting Wes at the bottom. "My impatient little wife."

"I missed you," I murmur against his lips, my arms going around his neck. His smile could light up a room, it's so bright.

"Is that right?" I nod. "All right, well, come on, let me show you what I did." Then he leads me into the living room, all of the furniture pushed to the walls and a mess of blankets and pillows in the center. Candles are lit on the tables around the room, and I'm in awe that he was able to do this by himself in less than an hour.

"What is this?" I ask as he leads me around the fort-looking thing and shows me the entrance.

"We've never really had a date," he says. "Not one that wasn't planned for PR and was just for us."

The bulge in my throat grows as I look around.

On the coffee table are two glasses of milk and two plates of six cookies, which is almost hidden by a giant pillow and blanket fort he built around it with the couch cushions. He found, or maybe he bought, some twinkle lights and lined the fort he made with it, making a magical little hideaway.

"Wes," I whisper, looking and stepping closer. There's actually a *structure* to this, and I look over my shoulder at him. He's blushing now.

"I bought this kit to make forts last week because I got an ad for it and it sounded fun. We've both been so busy, I haven't had time to do a little indoor date, but today is the perfect chance. I figured you'd enjoy movies and cookies more than a fancy dinner out, though anytime you want, I'll make a reservation at Trattoria Seven, and we'll be there," he says of the famous Italian restaurant in Hudson City.

A tear trails down my face at his gesture. *This* is why I have fallen for Wes Holden. He knows me so well, constantly taking notes of what I like or don't like. It's something I've never experienced and hope I never lose.

"No, no," he says, shaking his head. "Don't cry. This is supposed to be fun," he says with a laugh, pulling me into his arms.

"It is. It's so fun, Wes. I just...no one's ever done something like this for me."

He smiles with understanding before taking my hand.

"Let me show you around. So here are a bunch of cookies, and we both have a plate. Some of them are baked from your favorite dough, and some I bought today." He tossed a few items in the cart today, and I didn't really pay attention, but now I wonder if maybe I should have. "And I found this little rating sheet, so we can decide which we like best. And inside, we have giant pillow chairs, but we can also merge them to lay together.

"Yes, that option," I whisper with a nod, and he laughs.

"All right. And I've got *Beauty and the Beast* queued up, since I've never seen it, but we can watch—"

"You want to watch *Beauty and the Beast?*"

"You said it was a classic and one of your favorites."

"It is."

"Then I want to watch it." I open my mouth, but he shakes his head. "It's as simple as that, Harper: if you want it, I want to make it happen for you."

"Wes," I whisper, emotions clogging up my throat.

"No, because if you cry, it might make your stomach hurt, and I want to eat cookies. Get in the fort, baby."

I smile at him through watery eyes. For a moment, I think about arguing, but then I say fuck it, shrug, then bend and snuggle into the pillows, ready for what might just be the most romantic date of all time.

"Okay, I see it now," he says, pausing the movie later right when the Beast shows the library to Belle.

"Right?" I ask. "This is exactly how it felt when you were showing me the design room."

He smiles then presses his lips to my hair. "You definitely had that silly, shocked look on your face," he says with a laugh.

I smack him in the arm, then resettle into his side.

"Sorry today was boring," I say quietly as Gaston falls off the side of the building in the movie.

"What?" he asks, turning to look at me, but I keep my eyes on the screen.

"Today. Reset days are monotone, but you're...you. Boring isn't really in your vocabulary. Next time, I can do it myself. Like you said, I can do it some other day when you're practicing or something, or—"

"Hey, hey. Look at me, Harper," he says, and when I do, there's nothing there, no mask, no lie, just Wes smiling at me. "This was the best Sunday I've ever had. Period, Harper. I wouldn't change it at all."

"But  " I start, because he's clearly just being nice, but he shakes his head at me.

"But nothing. Part of being with someone is doing what they like, right?"

"I...I guess?"

"Today was a good day. An *us* day. We won't always have these. Sometimes I'll be on the road, or you'll be designing late or prepping for some big fashion show." I roll my eyes, but he shakes his head, holding my chin so I can't look away. "But I'll always wish I had this, every damn night. The simplicity of just *being* with you. I told you I missed the morning after. I missed *normal*. Someone, a partner, treating me like just that: a partner. A teammate. Someone who helps with the dishes and the grocery shopping and the cooking even though I'm shit at it."

"I'm shit at it too," I whisper with a laugh.

"Then we'll learn together," he confirms, and I fucking *love* that, that he wants to learn and grow with me, that he sees this future where that's something we do. We fall into a comfortable silence, Wes brushing my hair back, the television droning on with some show I don't remember putting on before he whispers into my hair.

"Sunday kind of love." His breath tickle at the back of my neck.

"Hmm?"

"When I hear that song, this is the day I'll remember." I make a mental note to look that up, to figure out what it means, the song tickling at something in my brain. Without thinking, I give him one of my own.

"Banana Pancakes." I feel his smile against my skin, and it spreads the warmth further.

We sit in silence once more, him brushing my hair back. My head moves into his hand to try and get more, and he laughs as he scratches my head. "You're like a little puppy, wanting to get your head scratched."

"It feels good, sue me." A moment passes before I speak. "Have you ever had a dog?"

He shakes his head. "No, my mom was allergic when I was younger, and when I was out of the house, life was too crazy, on the road all the time. Riggs has Gracie, but it's hard because when we're out or on stage, you have to trust whoever is watching it." He shrugs like it's no big deal, but I hear the want in his voice. "You?"

"No, Jeremy hated pets. I always wanted one, though."

I bite my lip, nervous to speak what's in my mind, but eventually I spit it out. "Maybe we should get one," I whisper, afraid because although Wes and I have agreed this was more than some fake marriage, we've been focused on the *now*. Our conversations have never tiptoed into the future, into what happens in ten months when this arrangement is over.

He's quiet for a long minute that feels like it goes on forever, and my heart pounds, wondering if I went too far. I open my mouth to tell him I was kidding, but I don't have to when he speaks. "Would you come with us?"

"Hmm?" I'm afraid to assume what he means.

"On tour. Eventually we'll go again, all of us love it too much not to. Would you come with us?"

My heart skips a beat, and I fight the smile pulling at my lips. "If you...if you wanted me to," I say. "If you wanted me to go, I would."

"I want you to come everywhere I go, Harper," he says with ease. "I want you by my side always.

"Oh."

"To clarify, so you don't let your brain fill in gaps where I'm not explicitly clear," he says, and I smile because I love how he seems to easily have a read on me. "I want you to come on tour when we go. And I want to get a pet with you if you want it. I want it all with you."

"Oh," I say again, now just blown away by his bluntness and how lucky I am that I somehow stumbled into this, that I found this man after all of the chaos that has been my life. A man who is so deeply into me, who understands me and knows me and still wants me despite it all.

"We should do it again, you know," Wes whispers after more silence, while I think about him and what he's given me. I look at him, confused, but the confusion lifts when I see where his eyes are—a large framed photo from our wedding. I'm not sure when he put it up, but it's been there for a few weeks, at least.

"Again?"

His hand moves, pushing my hair back to look at me better. .

"The first time, we were both distracted. The reasons weren't right. I'd like to do it again someday. Me and you, getting married, but for real this time."

"I thought you said it *was* for real the first time?" I ask with a smile

"For me, it was. It was always real for me, Harper. You took a little bit of time. I'd like to see you walking down the aisle to me, knowing that it's going to be me and you forever." I roll my eyes and move to get away. "I'd also like a shit ton of guests to show you off. A gown you made exactly the way you want. Every detail, the way you dreamed of as a kid."

"Wes," I whisper, tears coming to my eyes at his thoughtfulness. He shakes his head, looking at me, then shifts us so I'm straddling his lap, his hands on either side of my face.

It hits me then, like a wave crashing over me, that I'm falling in love with my husband. It's happened so slowly, I almost missed it, but today, when we slowed things down and spent an entire day together, it hit me over the head.

This is what Ava feels for Jaime, what Jules feels when she looks at Nate. This all-consuming feeling of safety and comfort and just... knowing. No tinge of fear or doubt, just...love.

"I told you I want to give you the world, Harper. Whatever you want, I want to make sure you have it."

"I think I'm falling for you," I whisper.

"That's good," he whispers, and I try to move to look at him, glare at him even, but his hand on my chest holds me tight. "Because I've been there a long time, waiting for you."

"Wes," I whisper, but he shakes his head.

"I'd wait forever, but I'm glad I won't have to."

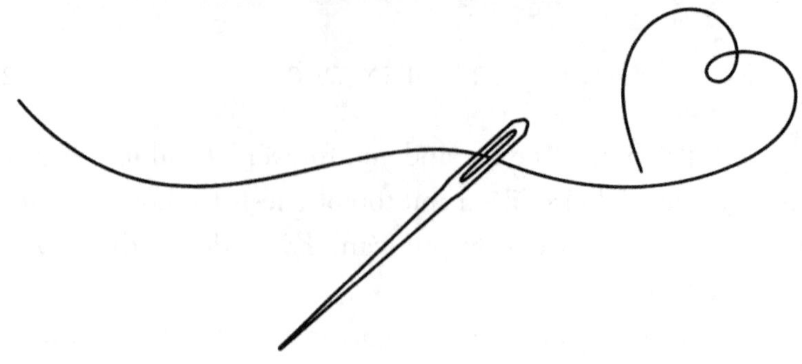

# THIRTY-THREE

## HARPER

My blissful little bubble barely lasts two more days. Two days after the most perfect Sunday known to mankind, Wes leaves our bed before the sun rises for his run, pressing a kiss to my lips. When he returns, he drags me out of bed and into the shower, eating me out before fucking me on the bench.

We get dressed together before he heads off to Ashford to meet up with the band at the studio on Riggins' property. When I finally shuffle down to the kitchen, I stare into the fridge, realizing I am, ironically, out of my creamer. Instead of running to the store, I add it to our grocery list and decide to get a little treat at my favorite coffee shop in Evergreen Park.

That was my first mistake.

My second was standing at the counter, waiting for my coffee and not running the second I heard Jeremy's voice.

"Harper," he greets, stepping beside me.

My head snaps toward him, and when I take him in, I realize how terrible he looks. Tired and worn down, his shirt wrinkled. When we were together, he never left the home without looking completely put together. I used to help him with that, making sure his things were taken to the cleaners, laying out his outfits, and ironing his shirts as needed. I doubt Clarissa makes sure he goes to bed at a reasonable hour, lines up the supplements he uses, or makes his lunches.

A bolt of satisfaction rips through me, knowing he's a mess without me, but it melts away the moment he says, "We need to talk." I'd forgotten about the letter Jeremy put into my box of things until I was putting away the few items I still cared for. Upon opening it, Jeremy's familiar writing instructed me to call him so we could talk, but I rolled my eyes at his self-importance and shoved it in a drawer, never thinking of it again.

But now I'm wondering if maybe I should have given the note my full attention.

"Jeremy, I'm not doing this. We have nothing to say to each other. I'm trying to get my coffee, go home, and get on with my day. Please, I'm begging you not to ruin what has already been a pretty great fucking day." As seems to be his way, Jeremy ignores everything I say.

"I saw the design Holden posted. The centerpiece to Clarissa's line," he starts, and my blood goes cold, the breath stalling in my lungs. "And the new one you're working on." I turn my head slowly toward him. "I want them."

"You're insane," I whisper, and he tips his head to the side.

"Am I?"

"If you think I'm going to just *give* you more designs? Yes. You're out of your mind."

"I think you'll find you're much more amenable than you think," he says. I roll my eyes at his audacity.

"We have nothing to talk about—" I start, still staring straight ahead as I do, but his next words have my blood going cold, my body turning toward him slowly.

"I know about everything. A sweet little bird told me all about your agreement with Holden. That assistant you got fired?" The breath in my lungs stutters, and I stare at him open-mouthed and watch as a small, vindictive smile spreads on his lips. "Now, if you don't agree to sit at a table with me and talk, every tabloid and newspaper in the tri-state area is going to know the real reason the band is taking a break." My blood goes still in my veins as he stares at me. "That's before it goes national, of course."

I'm trapped in a corner, once again at Jeremy's mercy, and I don't know what I did to deserve this.

"Harper?" The barista calls my name, and stiffly, I move to grab the coffee I know I probably won't be able to drink, not with the way my stomach is roiling. At the very least, I know I have to play the game, sit with him, and let him spill his bullshit.

I turn on my heel, spotting a small table in the corner, and move toward it quickly while Jeremy takes his sweet fucking time pulling out his chair and sitting.

He sits with his arms crossed on his chest, leaning back like he owns the world, before he finally speaks.

"You know, she really hates you," he says with a shit-eating grin as if the mere idea of some random woman hating me brings him joy. "So much so, she sought me out. She called me up and told me everything. How your marriage is fake, Stella's pregnancy, the worries about what the press will say." Nausea churns in my stomach, and I hold the coffee in my hands, letting the warmth sink into my cold hands to ground me. "God, she even told me that her former boss hired a private investigator to look into me."

My mind churns with this news, something Wes never told me, but I try not to show my lack of insight as he keeps rambling.

"Not sure what he'd find, of course." But for a flash, his face shows anxiety that they will find *something*. I spent so much time with Jeremy, reading into his every move and facial change, I can see there's something he doesn't want anyone to know.

I also know from that look alone he'll do almost anything to keep his secret safe, which is terrifying.

"Whatever they find, it can't be worse than trying to save your reputation by marrying some has-been rock star. Or worse, marrying some loser seamstress to hide your friend's bullshit." I let his insults roll right off my back, knowing he's looking for a reaction I refuse to give him.

He's taken enough from me, and I have a feeling he's only going to try and take more.

"What do you want, Jeremy?" I ask with a bored tone. He shifts with my words, not expecting this version of me, the one who doesn't back down, who is tired of being used.

"I want you to call off your dogs," he says quickly. "Your fake little rock star is looking into shit he shouldn't be looking into, and I want him to stop."

"What are you so afraid he's going to find?" I ask, intrigued, and watch as the mask of joviality and faux friendship melts off his face. "You have nothing to hide, right?"

"Nothing, of course," he says with a laugh. He forgets, I think, how long we were together and the way I am well-tuned to the way he laughs when he lies. "But I don't like the idea of him looking into me. What you should be afraid of is me telling the world that Riggins Greene is back on the bottle and in rehab again, which is why they really needed to delay the tour."

"That's not—" I start with a shake of my head, but he steamrolls past me.

"I wonder how the stress of that will go for Stella and her pregnancy? All the paparazzi hounding her, asking her about her husband, digging up old wounds. You know, I'm sure there's something she doesn't know from when they were apart, some bitch he fucked, some charge he paid off," he says, and my pulse starts racing. "Or you know, someone could just plant something. It doesn't really matter if it's true or not these days, as you know."

"You can't just lie, Jeremy. It impacts people. People who have nothing to do with you," I say. "Leave them out of your shit." Although I'm mad and nervous, I try to remind myself Stella and Riggins are about to announce their pregnancy anyway, and with her belly just barely showing now, they even took professional photos to share. It would discredit whatever Jeremy plans to spread.

"What about Ava and Jules?" he asks.

"What?" I ask, my words faint.

"I have a friend down at the Evergreen Police Department. He's been creating a file for me. Criminal harassment and stalking—"

I roll my eyes and shake my head. "We already handled this, Jeremy. You can't—"

"The card that went viral? And the wrapping of my car?" I close my eyes and breathe in deep, fighting the nausea that takes over. I knew we shouldn't have done that. I knew I should have left it alone, buried it, that somehow, like all the good things in my life, it would lead to disaster.

I gave him ammunition to destroy me again.

But then again, although I'd convinced myself otherwise, a small part of me had a feeling that if Jeremy knew I was designing, I don't know if he ever would have stopped his blackmailing.

Suddenly, I realize being free of him was all an illusion: he is planning to keep me under his thumb forever. As soon as he saw I had talent and also a weakness—loving my friends and being willing to do anything to protect them—I gave up any power I had.

"You can't prove it was me," I whisper, not so sure about that. "And you definitely can't prove it was them because they weren't even a part of any of that."

He shakes his head with the same smug smile still plastered to his face.

"That doesn't really matter, not when you have friends in high places the way I do, not when there is documented history. As seems to be your way, you just pissed off one too many people while rampaging through their lives, and now you're going to take them down with you."

I close my eyes and take a deep breath. "What do you want?"

The entertained look drops from his face, shifting to something mean and angry as he leans in. "Drop the investigator and give me what you're working on. I want the piece you left out the first time."

Fine. If that's what I have to do, whatever, I can make more. I can—

"And get a divorce from Holden. He knows too much, and he's digging into things he shouldn't."

My mouth drops open, and I shake my head frantically. "No," I whisper. "I won't do that."

He leans back in his chair and gives me a pitying look. "Aww, did you get a little too attached to him, Harper? You never were very good at separating business and pleasure, were you?" I bite back a response, knowing the faster I get out of here, the better. "Do it, Harper. Either you agree to my terms, or I'll alert the press today."

I shake my head again, knowing even if I *wanted* to, it wouldn't be that easy.

"He's not going to just accept my breaking up with him, Jeremy," I say, my pulse racing, my head going light with panic. "What am I supposed to say? We have an agreement in place."

Maybe the basics will convince him. If Jeremy knows about the fake marriage, he must know there's a contract in place.

"Find a way."

"Jeremy, how am I supposed to do that? You don't understand, he's not going to just..." I trail off because I don't want or need him to know just how *real* things have gotten with Wes. I don't need another person on his radar to destroy.

"That's your problem, Harper. Make something up. Tell him you're tired of him, tell him you want out, tell him you hate him. I don't know, and honestly, Harper, I don't care. I want this fucker off my ass, and I want to erase all of this bullshit." The room starts to spin as I face the reality of the mess I'm in, but some other part of me, the one who wants to somehow salvage everything, to protect the people I love, kicks in and nods.

"How long do I have?" I whisper, praying for just one more night with Wes. Just one where I can savor him and love him before it all falls apart.

A wicked smile spreads on his lips, and I know my desperate plea will go unanswered.

"I want rumors of the breakup in the tabloids by tomorrow."

"Tomorrow?" I ask, wide-eyed.

"Make it happen, Harper," he says, then stands up, grabs his jacket and the coffee I'm still cradling, and walks out.

I watch him leave, my mind reeling, before I stand up, order a new coffee, and call my best friends.

# THIRTY-FOUR

## WES

My texts to Harper have gone unanswered all day while I'm at practice, but when I pull up to the house and see Jules and Ava's cars parked out front, I'm slightly appeased, knowing she probably got caught up in an impromptu girls' day.

Except, when I step into the house, I don't hear raucous laughter in the living room like I normally do when the girls convene here. I check the kitchen and the dining room, finding nothing before I head upstairs to find my wife. Finally, I hear voices coming from Harper's design room and make my way there.

"Uh, hello?" I ask, leaning into the doorway, a mix of confusion and relief coursing through me when I see Harper and the girls there. Three heads poke up, but a voice continues on, a voice I now realize is Willa Stone's.

Set aside on a table are the remnants of a delivery lunch and multiple cups of coffee, like they're hyped up on ideas and excitement. I smile, happy that Harper's out of the creative funk Jeremy put her into.

"Oh, you're home, good. We have to talk," Harper says, looking at me, shifting the notebook in her hand to the side and crossing her arms on her chest.

"I can see that." I step further into the room and toward the cork board that looks decidedly different than I'm used to. "Hey, ladies," I say, waving to Ava and Jules.

They return the favor, but my wife continues to glare at me. I'd be a bit worried about that, but I can't seem to focus on that too long, because now that I'm closer, I can see the cork board better. Harper seems to have taken everything off of it, replacing it with lists and ideas and, more alarmingly, a printout of her ex's face, pinned to the board and seemingly used as a *dartboard*, pens sticking into the photo.

Although I'm glad to see *my* face isn't pinned to her cork board, I realize that combined with her glare, something clearly happened.

"Hey, Wes," Willa says through the phone sitting on the table.

"Hey, Willa," I say distractedly, reading the notes pinned to the board. It looks like a crime scene investigation board, and I'm surprised she hasn't put up red string connecting things.

*Find proof of Jeremy's cheating,* is pinned on, with *contact PI* underlined beneath it.

*Is blackmail illegal?* is on a note card, and a sticky note with what I think is a US legal code on it is stuck underneath.

*How do you prove blackmail?* is beneath that. Also on the board is a copy of what I recognize as the contract she signed at the police station, handing over the designs to Jeremy, with notes in the margins.

But most alarming on the cork board is the list that says *Ruin Jeremy Vaughn.*

I think it's the one she showed me on her phone that we then added to, though some of them are crossed out, and already accomplished, and the women have clearly been busy adding more to the bottom.

"Are you guys fucking with Jeremy again?" I ask with a sigh. Jules and Ava look at one another, clearly having a silent conversation, something I decide probably isn't great.

No one gives me an answer, and Harper continues to glare at me, which is an answer in and of itself. "What happened?" Suddenly, anxiety takes over as I realize they wouldn't be acting like this out of nowhere. Something happened to once again reignite their taste for vengeance.

"We have to talk," Harper repeats, standing this time, and with this new view, the words feel foreboding.

"That doesn't sound good," I say as she walks toward me.

"You're in the doghouse," Ava says with a delighted smile. It's a good thing, I suppose, that she's smiling and not planning revenge on *me*.

"Come on," Harper says, walking past me without a second glance and out of the living room. I follow her until we're in our bedroom, where she closes the door behind us before turning to face me, jaw tight and eyes burning.

Yeah, Harper is *definitely* unhappy with me.

"What's going on?" I ask. I reach for Harper, desperate to touch her, especially now that I'm on a different footing, but she shifts back, crosses her arms on her chest, and gives me a glare.

Fuck.

"I have to ask you a question, and it's important to me that you tell the truth." I open my mouth to tell her I'll always tell the truth, but she keeps talking. "The whole truth. No omissions, no nothing." Now I'm nervous because the way she says it makes it clear she believes that I've done the opposite recently.

"Of course, Harper."

She closes her eyes for a moment, taking in a deep breath to center herself before they open again, and her eyes are locked on me. "Did you have a private investigator look into Jeremy?"

That takes me back, but slowly, I nod.

"Well, yeah. I...right after you told me about what happened with your designs, I got in touch with one." I knew even then that

Jeremy definitely had skeletons in his closet, and after he fucked with Harper, I wanted to make sure we knew what we were working with, just in case. Harper didn't want to do anything to fuck with him, but at the very least, I didn't want us to get blindsided with anything. I stare at her, my brow furrowed as I try and pick through what I know so far and understand what's happening. "How did you know about that?"

"Does it matter?" she asks, attitude leaking into the words.

"Well, yes, because the point of a PI is to be *private,* and now you're looking at me like you hate me, and I don't like that at all. If part of that reason is because they told you something they found and it upset you, that's going to be a problem."

"Why were you hiding that from me?" she asks, disappointment and hurt lacing in her words, almost indistinguishable beneath the anger.

"I wasn't—" I start, then remember her request that I not lie and realize I almost just did. I sigh and run a hand through my hair. "I didn't want to get your hopes up or for you to think we'd find something to get back at him. In my defense, while I agree I should have told you, it's not like I was going to great lengths to hide it from you." I reach out to push her hair back, desperate to touch her, but she steps away from me, putting her arms across her chest. "Harper—"

"Don't touch me," she says. "I need to stay focused."

"What?" I ask, fighting the small smile dying to come out because even now, angry and clearly out for blood, she's fucking cute.

"If you touch me, it'll mess with my head, and I won't be as mad at you as I am." She pauses and glares. "And I'm really mad at you, Wes."

"You're mad at me?" I ask, though it's obvious she is, I'm just not super clear as to why or how.

"Of course, I'm mad at you! You broke my trust, Wes." My heart drops at her words, at the mere thought that I hurt Harper when I thought I was helping. "You didn't tell me about the investigator, and that put me in a shitty position when Jeremy cornered me."

The air in the room changes instantly as my gut twists and my blood starts to heat.

"You talked to him? Why would you talk to him? Why didn't you tell me you were going to talk to him? When was this?" My own anger is rising to match hers because I don't like the idea of that man breathing the same air as her, of her willingly putting herself in his presence, much less doing it behind my back.

She sighs and shakes her head before sitting down on the edge of the bed. "Not on purpose. I went out to grab coffee today, and he was there."

"Why was he there?"

She shrugs. "To talk to me, I think. It was like he *knew* I'd be there somehow."

"Is he following you?" I ask, sharp panic rushing through me at the idea of him following Harper or keeping tabs on her in any way. My mind moves through options to ensure she's safe without suffocating her, already planning a call to Jaime to get a man on her. Though, it seems she got there before me.

"I don't know. I don't think so, Jaime didn't find anything on my car, but I'm having him go through my phone in the morning to make sure there's nothing hidden on there where he could track me. If you called me and I didn't answer, that's why."

"Jaime knows about this?"

"I needed things from him, so yeah," she says nonchalantly.

I decide I can tackle her talking to *Jaime* before me later, instead focusing on the issue at hand. "So you talked to Jeremy at the coffee shop?"

"Not willingly. He forced me to sit with him because he told me he knew everything. He knows about you hiring a private investigator, about our marriage not being real." I open my mouth to argue, but she keeps speaking. "He knows about Riggins and Stella's baby. About their fears that the media would take it too far, that Stella is high risk." I can feel the blood leave my face, making my head feel light with the panic of what she's saying. Jeremy having *anything* over

Harper is bad, especially with my gut feeling that he wasn't going to just leave her alone after getting those first designs.

I can see it mirrored on her face: the panicked feeling of being backed into a corner. I can only imagine how she felt being side-swiped with this in public, where there were probably eyes on her, and she had to keep her cool. Guilt floods through me, but I force myself to push it aside to get through the rest of this conversation.

"How does he know?"

"Laurel," she says, hatred taking over her face. "She called him after she was fired."

My eyes close and I take in a deep breath. "I should have fucking listened to you about her." Harper told me she was trouble after the first time she met her, but I didn't listen. Laurel always seemed loyal, but it seems that was a facade. I'll have to call my lawyers, since she violated her NDA and a dozen other clauses in her contract, but even if I sue her to high heaven, it won't change the fact that Jeremy knows some of my—and my loved ones'— best kept secrets.

"You live and you learn. Next time, when your incredibly intelligent, beautiful, funny wife tells you someone is a red flag, you'll listen." I suppose her joking is a good sign, even if she's doing it to cover the hurt and anger she clearly feels.

"He said if you don't drop the PI and if I don't step out of the limelight, he's bringing it to the press. He wants us to get divorced because he thinks you'll stop digging if we end things."

"Absolutely not, Harper."

"He's going to say the tour is delayed because Riggins is drinking again, that Stella is leaving him, or some other bullshit that will cause mayhem."

I listen to her, trying to piece it together with what she's telling me, to understand what it means, but I don't. I shake my head at her.

"But that doesn't matter. They're telling everyone soon anyway. There's an article already being written, and photos have been taken. They're—"

"That's what I said." She takes in a deep breath, letting it out slowly before she meets my eyes again. "And then he threatened Ava and Jules again. Apparently, there's still a police report, and he's been adding to it after our most recent antics. He has some buddy on the force or something who he's been talking to, keeping it on the back burner. It wouldn't be him pressing charges but the city. If I don't do what he wants, he's going to hit everyone: you, Stella, the band. Ava and Jules and me." Suddenly, her face changes, a guard coming over it as she looks at her hands. "You were right. I think he always had this as a plan, Wes. There was nothing we could have done to stop it. He was always going to try and come for more."

My brow furrows with confusion. "More?"

"He saw your post that went viral. He wants the final design." My jaw goes tight, my teeth aching with the force, but then she finishes. "And the new ones I've been working on."

"Harper, no," I say instantly, shaking my head. Panic courses through me as I try and think of a way out of this. The PI said he has some leads, but he hasn't found anything solid yet, at least not that I'm aware of. Clearly, though, there's something there, something Jeremy is afraid we'll find, or he wouldn't be so adamant about having the investigator back off. I'm racking my mind for ideas and plans, ways to solve this for Harper, but then pause with confusion as a triumphant smile spreads on her lips.

"I'm not giving it to him, of course. We have a plan."

"We?"

"Me, the girls. Willa. I have a meeting with Leo tomorrow. I want to meet with the PI, too, if we can make that happen, though Jaime wants to make sure he wasn't compromised first and that it was Laurel who told Jeremy about everything."

"Laurel made the appointment with the investigator for me, so she definitely knows. You have a meeting with Leo? When did all this happen?"

"The Jeremy stuff was this morning, and I called the girls on my drive home. They met me here soon after. We've been working on it since." It's six now, so we're probably looking at at least seven hours since Jeremy cornered her.

"Fuck, Harper. Why didn't you call me?" I expect her to look at me with a hint of guilt or embarrassment, but instead, she tips her chin up, shoulders going back.

"I needed time."

"Time? For what? I'm your husband, Harper."

"Exactly. You're my husband, and you should have told me you hired a PI."

I throw my hands up. "So you would get annoyed that I'm digging into this when you wanted to just let it go?" Her jaw goes tight, and I know I'm digging a deeper hole, but right now I don't actually care. I shake my head. "I knew you wanted to move on, but I wasn't taking the chance that something like *this* was going to happen. And it did. Now we're ahead of things, and I have someone already digging into it."

A moment passes, and she closes her eyes, taking a deep breath before opening them again and looking at me. I'm taken aback by what I see, the anger pushed aside, the irritation and indignation gone, and all that is left is the hurt.

Fuck.

"That's not how this works, Wes," she says softly. "I was in a relationship where I trusted blindly and where I was kept in the dark on things, and I didn't like how that felt. You know that. You know how I struggled with stepping into the sun and realizing how deeply misguided I was. And you did the same thing. I needed time to come to terms with that, to gain an understanding of why, to catch my breath. Because no matter what I feel for you, I won't let that happen again, won't let someone make decisions for me, and keep secrets. It's not the relationship I want, and it's not something I'll stand for again. You can't break my trust like that, not if you want this to work long-term."

"I didn't break your trust—" I start, but when I see the flash of hurt on her face at my denial, the way her eyes water, I stop and really listen to what she's trying to tell me. I force myself to set my well-meaning but possibly self-serving intentions to the side and see things from her point of view. She is fresh out of a relationship where she was manipulated, used, and lied to, and then I turned around and moved in that same direction.

"You don't get to decide if you broke my trust or not, Wes. You don't get to decide when you cross my lines: I do. And if you can't respect that, then tell me now, because I'm not going back to being the person who accepts that treatment." She's serious, her face stern and her shoulders back. Even though I see the hurt in her eyes at the thought of stepping away from this, I know she'll do it if she has to.

I'm so fucking proud of her.

"You're right," I say, taking in a deep breath. I want to step to her, to pull her into my arms, but I need her to decide if I deserve that.

"I am?" she asks, slightly confused.

"Of course you are. You're an adult. You're strong, and I don't have to move around you with kid gloves, to manipulate the truth to do what I think is right. I should have talked to you. This is a partnership, not a dictatorship. You have a say in how these things go, and I need to respect that."

"Oh," she says, her brow furrowing, clearly confused.

"What, did you expect me to argue?"

"Well, yeah," she says with a small smile.

"You spoke your case. I listened. I don't like that you didn't call me immediately after you left that coffee shop, but trust and respect goes both ways. Next time, I'll tell you if I'm hiring a PI to look into your shithead ex, and I'd appreciate a call if you get blackmailed."

"Deal," she says with a small smile.

I sigh and shake my head. Relief runs through me when she steps forward, putting an arm around my neck and letting me pull her into my arms before I gently press my lips to hers. My body loosens just a bit at her nearness, and I come to the understanding that so long as I have this—so long as *we* have this—we can tackle anything.

Ava and Jules let out a laugh that makes its way down the hall, reminding me we're not alone in the house and she's been partaking in some kind of planning session for the better part of the day.

"So what's the plan?" I ask, reaching up and pushing a lock of copper hair that fell out of the clip at the back of her head behind her ear. When she gives me a cringe of a smile, I know instantly I am not going to like whatever it is she's about to say.

"We have to break up," she says bluntly.

"What?" I move to step back, but she holds on tighter, not letting me leave. She gives me a shrug as if that's all the explanation I'll get. "We are not breaking up, Harper."

"He knows everything and is going to come after Ava and Jules if we don't, as well as you guys."

"You try and break up with me, Harper, I'm dragging you onto a plane and hiding away with you for days, weeks, months, until you see things my way, until all of this blows over."

She smiles wide, putting a hand to my cheek and smiling wide. "You're so handsome when you get all angry and self-righteous." I open my mouth to argue, but she shakes her head. "It's happening. Not forever and not for real, just to appease Jeremy while we enact phase two of *Project Ruin Jeremy Vaughn*. Now, are you going to keep arguing with me, or can we sit down and figure this out? Together."

I let a small smile tip on my lips, knowing I'd do anything for this woman.

"Fill me in and give me my marching orders."

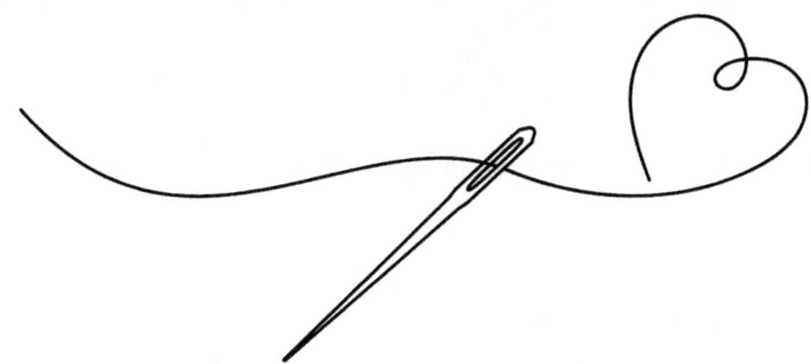

# THIRTY-FIVE

## HARPER

*Sixteen days until Project Ruin Jeremy Vaughn*



*Fourteen days until Project Ruin Jeremy Vaughn*

My phone pings with a message, and I grab it. Ava sent a screenshot to the group chat, showing a photo of me carrying a large cardboard box from the house to my car that is on the homepage of a popular gossip website, with Wes and Harper Already Over? in big, bold letters.

> JULES
>
> **The plan is in action!!!!!**

Because I'm a masochist, I search for the article, finding it quickly before skimming. It's mostly speculation and a few nuggets of information from "anonymous sources," those sources being Leo, but there isn't much actual news. Probably because there really isn't much to know, but this is all part of convincing Jeremy I'm playing nice in his threat.

But then I see it, a quote from *Holden's former assistant*, commenting on me. "She's toxic and pitted him against some of his oldest friends. It's sad, really, that he threw everything away like this."

My eyes roll, and I copy the quote, putting it into the group chat.

> **Is this chick for real? She was FIRED.**
>
> AVA
>
> **Why are you reading it? You know it's just trash.**
>
> **Because I love to torture myself. I don't know.**
>
> JULES
>
> **How are you doing?**

My friends are worried about me, that much is for sure, especially now that they know the entire story of my breakup, about how Jeremy threatened them and what I did to protect them. They were pretty angry that the real reason I gave up the designs was to save them, but in the end, they understood, knowing they'd probably do something similar for me.

> Good, knowing that it's T-minus 14 days until he gets what's coming to him.

AVA

HELL YEAH!

The day after my meeting with Jeremy, whispers of Wes and my breakup spread through the media as planned. I was anxious nearly the entire day, as I boxed up a few of my things and made a show of lugging them to the car so photos could leak, worried that Jeremy wouldn't think it was enough to quiet his threats. But by five, when I was slowly putting a few of my things away in the cottage behind Jules's house, I received a text from Jeremy.

JEREMY

Good job. When can I expect the designs?

I smiled, loving that phase one of our plan worked while simultaneously fighting the urge to throw my phone at a wall. Instead, I took a deep breath in before answering.

Two weeks

It was a simple response, and part of me expected him to argue, to tell me he wants them quicker and remind me that I'm working on his clock, not mine, or threaten me again, but he didn't. Instead, he sent a thumbs-up in what I assume I'm to interpret as an acceptance of this new deadline.

JULES

I bet you can't wait until this is over.

You have no idea.

I mean that on so many fronts, not just because I'm excited to *finally* have this bullshit with Jeremy behind me, but because not waking up in bed with Wes every morning has proven to be much more of an issue than I thought it would be.

In an effort to lean into this story of a breakup and not allow for Jeremy to suspect what we're doing, I've been staying at Jules's place, something that was a hard sell for Wes. But I wasn't risking the media whispering that maybe this was some kind of publicity stunt and it getting back to Jeremy. I'm confident in our plan and our ability to pull it off seamlessly, and I know, even if we had to enact *Project Ruin Jeremy Vaughn* tomorrow, it would work. But the creative in me who lives for a big reveal wants things to go as planned. Poetic justice in its purest form.

> **JULES**
>
> Come have breakfast with me as a distraction! Sophie is requesting it.

I smile at that text, looking at the rumpled sheets and the empty bed beside me and sighing. Then I put a pin into my dress form, stepping back to look at the progress I've made and make my way into Jules's house.

*Ten days until Project Ruin Jeremy Vaughn*

The sound of cutting shears on thick fabric fills the room in a satisfying *snip, snip, snip* when my phone lets out a beep. Quickly, I drop the scissors and check the screen, smiling at the photo Wes sent me.

My design room, the cork board still essentially an FBI crime scene, but everything else is pretty much pristine.

> **WES**
>
> She misses you

> And I miss her. Tell her I'll be back soon with lots of new projects to complete.

> I miss you.

> And I miss you more.

> I don't know why I can't just come to you at night or why you can't come home. Leo will blackball anyone who posts something he deems inappropriate.

I sigh, because this has been his line of questions since I left, but I'm determined to do things right.

> I'm not risking it.

> Nothing bad can happen.

He's right: the private investigator contacted me yesterday at the insistence of my husband to tell me what he had found and our options for what we could do with it. There were plenty, and the PI told me Wes had instructed him I was to make the final decision on how to proceed.

I decide to take a new approach.

> Just think of how hot it will be when you finally can have me.

> Or I could just have you now.

> Wes...

> I hate this.

> Ten more days.

> Love you.

> Thank you.

*Six Days until Project Ruin Jeremy Vaughn*

It's only been four days since I've last spoken to Wes, but I'm

starting to feel sorry for myself and missing Wes more than I anticipated, and I give in to my small pity party.

> Remind me this is worth it.

> Are you being serious or are you cranky?

> I can't sleep.

A call comes through, Wes's face lighting up on my screen, and I
roll over in bed, wrapped in blankets that don't smell right. I hold my
phone to my ear and don't speak.

"Harper?"

"Hey," I whisper into the dark. It's strange being alone, *sleeping*
alone, after spending so much time with Wes and living with him. I
didn't realize how much time we spent together, and without it, the
days feel immeasurably longer. I thought it would be easy since I
spent my entire relationship with Jeremy like this, living two separate
but parallel lives, but it is anything but. I miss him. I miss us. I miss
sleeping with him, and I miss talking with him, walking to his music
room, and hanging out when I hit a creative block.

I miss Wes.

I miss Wes because this time apart made me realize I'm in love with
him. Crazy, insanely, irrevocably in love with him, and I haven't told him.

"What's wrong?" he asks. "Is everything okay?"

"Yes," I whisper. "No. I don't know. I miss you."

He sighs, the sounds filling the line before he replies. "I miss you
more, little wife."

"I can't sleep without you," I say, my voice cracking a little.

"Do you want me to come over there?"

I weigh his question, then shake my head before answering. "No.
I'm a big girl."

There's a long pause before he speaks again.

"I'll stay on until you sleep," he says gently.

"What?"

"Tell me about your day, little wife." It's not the first time he's called me since I "moved out," but he's given me my space, and now I realize he's doing it to try and respect the boundaries and rules I've set.

God. He's so fucking good to me.

"My day?"

"We'll talk until you fall asleep. Then we'll only have five more days." I smile, so fucking grateful for what I've found in the chaos.

And then I tell my husband about my day, but the words I really want to tell him stay stuck on the tip of my tongue.

*Five Days Until Project Ruin Jeremy Vaughn*

I'm weighing my options on sequins when there's a knock on the door of the cottage. I stand, walk over, and open the door. Then I stand there, shocked as Stella Green walks in without a word, Jules and Ava following behind her.

"What are you doing here?"

"Wes sent us. Says you needed a pick-me-up," Ava says, walking over to one of the two dress forms and taking in my work with a wide, approving smile. I would comment, but I'm still stuck on Wes sending them.

"He did?"

Stella nods. "He also sent me with this." She digs in a bag and pulls out a crinkly blue package with a green sticky note on top.

*Some late-night snack options.*

Instantly, my throat feels achy, and I start to sniff, my eyes starting to water.

"Oh, oh, no, Harp!" Jules says, a bit of panic in her voice over my show of emotions.

I shake my head and wave at my eyes to distract myself from crying. "I'm fine, I'm fine."

"You almost cried at a package of cookies," Ava says. "That's the literal opposite of fine."

"No, really. I'm good." Three sets of judging eyes glare at me, and I sigh. "I just..I miss him. Not seeing him has been harder than I expected."

Stella's eyes go wide. "You haven't *seen* him?"

"She's being stubborn," Ava says with a roll of her eyes, sitting on the edge of my bed and kicking her shoes off as if she lives here.

"I'm being reasonable! What if someone catches him coming here!? Or me going there? Then all of this is for nothing!" Silence fills the small room that feels so much smaller, with four women now in it.

"Tell us what's really happening," Jules says in her motherly tone.

My head jerks back, and I look at her quizzically. "What?"

Ava sighs and rolls her eyes. "You're not afraid he'll get caught coming over here because you know just as well as I do Leo wouldn't let that happen. So what's really going on? Why are you punishing yourself?"

I purse my lips and shake my head to deny her, but she cuts me off.

"We're your best friends, Harper. You don't have to bend the truth for us."

For a moment, I contemplate continuing to say I'm fine, but with their discerning eyes on me, I can't.

"I think... I think I needed this time."

"Why?"

"To prove to myself I can," I admit. When Ava looks at me confused, I elaborate. "I've never been alone. At least, not in the past four years. Shouldn't I be on my own for a bit before I commit to forever? I was with Jeremy for so long, then right after I *married* Wes. I'm..."

"You're punishing yourself by trying to prove you can be single,"

Ava says, irritated by the idea and rolling her eyes. "Jesus, Harper. You're so thick-skulled sometimes."

"What? It's a valid concern. I've never...*been* alone!"

"That's a lie," Jules says.

"Excuse me?"

"You were alone almost your entire relationship with Jeremy, you just didn't want to admit it. You've been more yourself in the last two months than we've seen you be in years. You lost yourself when you started dating Jeremy, but I think every time you did something to get back at him, you stole a bit of it back. I think being loved the way you deserve had something to do with that, but it's just the cherry on top."

I sit there taking in her words and realizing the truth of them. "I love him," I whisper.

"No shit," Ava says.

"I haven't told him. I...I'm scared." I expect my friends to interrupt or ask why, but they don't, and their silence emboldens me. "I don't think I've ever been in love before. Not the way you fell with Jaime or you with Nate." Ava and Jules smile at me. "What happens if he doesn't feel it too?"

Now, Ava interrupts me with a scoff. "God, the man has been in love with you for years," she says.

"I don't—"

"Trust me, they're right," Stella says. "He's been waiting for you. When you're ready and you finally tell him, he's going to run a marathon." I laugh at the idea of that. "He's miserable, you know. Spending almost every day at my house, making *me* miserable.".

"Really?" I ask, a bit of guilt moving through me.

She nods. "Okay, now that we've covered what an idiot you're being so you can call your husband up and tell him to come fuck you into a good mood, can we *please* talk about this gorgeous dress?"

I smile, more than happy to change the subject.

"Seriously, it's so pretty," Jules says, taking Ava's hint.

"Willa's excited," Stella says, and I smile.

"Really?"

She rolls her eyes at me. "Don't play coy, Harper. It's not a good look on you. Of course, she is. She's excited to be a part of this, for one, but also because of what you're doing for her." She gives me wide eyes, and excitement takes over the leftover melancholy.

"I can't believe this is my life," I whisper. "That all of the mess led to...this." I wave my hand at the dress forms.

"You deserve it and so much more," Stella says, reaching over and holding my hand, looking into my eyes.

"Stop, you're going to make me cry," Ava says, then starts waving at her face at the same time Stella's eyes well up.

"Okay, enough of this," I say with a laugh, pulling away as my own eyes start to water at the community and support system I've built for myself. "We should go get lunch."

Lunch goes fine, with paparazzi screaming at us as we enter and leave, but ignoring them all the same. When I get home, Stella sends me a copy of the article *Fan Magazine* is publishing tomorrow to announce their pregnancy, and I cry, both with relief that they made it through this and joy that this woman I now call one of my good friends is getting her well-earned happily ever after.

I spend the rest of the day working, pinning, and sewing, completely losing track of time. It's late when the doorknob of the cottage turns, my heart jumping to my chest. I locked the door, but it seems somehow someone is getting in. Maybe a paparazzi? Some stalker? Fucking *Jeremy*? My mind skips *right* past any reasonable answers in my exhausted state and moves to the most dangerous ones, obviously.

I reach for my phone to call for help, assuming there must be some creep breaking in. I'm in the process of unlocking my screen, the fucking face recognition failing me at the worst time, when the door cracks open and a familiar face steps in, making my entire body relax.

"Jesus Christ, Wes! You scared the shit out of me!" I say, grabbing a pillow I had planned to use to defend myself and throwing it at his head.

"Hey, little wife."

Something in me snaps, then, my throat getting tight as I run the few steps to him and jump into him. He catches me, lifting me up as I wrap my legs around his hips and press my lips to his. When the kiss breaks, I press my forehead to his with a wide smile and watery eyes.

"What are you doing here?"

"I'm tired of not spending the night with my wife."

I pull back and look at him quizzically. "Did the girls call you?"

His face mirrors mine, and he shakes his head. "No? Why?"

I think of our conversation earlier and shake my head. "No reason."

He moves toward the door with me in his arms because I'm sure as hell not letting go, then closes and locks it behind him. I breathe him in, and as I do, a calm washes over me, the way it always does when my husband is near. God, I missed this. It's further confirmation that I'm well past falling and deeply in love with this man. He moves us to the bed, sitting down with me in his lap, and I lean back to take him in. He looks exactly like he did two weeks ago, but more tired, the same as I do, I'm sure.

My thumb brushes over the scruff on his cheekbone, and my heart starts to pound nervously as I decide it's time.

"Hey, Wes?" I ask gently.

One hand moves from where he's holding my waist to shift my hair back over my shoulder. "Yeah?"

"I love you," I whisper.

His hand pauses halfway before his eyes shift to stare at me. A million things run through my mind, ways to cover up or rush past what I just said, but I realize there's no point. I love Wes Holden. I have for some time, and the only thing I regret is being too scared to jump in sooner.

Then, his eyes close, a deep sigh leaving his body as his forehead moves to mine. "Thank God," he whispers. I let out a small laugh.

"What?"

"I've been waiting for this moment, Harper."

"Wes—"

"Do you know how hard it is to keep that in every day?" His hands go to my jaw as he looks into my eyes. "Do you know how hard it is not to tell you how much I love you every fucking moment of every single day?" My eyes water as he stares at me. "I told you I'd wait forever, but I'm glad I don't have to." He echoes words he told me weeks ago, a time that feels almost like another lifetime.

"I'm glad you're here," I whisper.

"Me too."

We sit for a moment like that before I realize I didn't hear a car pull up. "How did you get here?"

His smile widens. "Took a cab. I'm going to leave early and run the two miles home. No car, no evidence."

I shake my head. "You're crazy, you know that?"

"I'm going crazy without you, that's for sure."

"It's only been two weeks, Wes," I say in a breathy laugh.

"Two weeks without you in my bed, without you in my house? Might as well be a fucking eternity," he says against my skin.

"We're almost done," I whisper, trying to pull him even closer.

"Can't it be Saturday already?" he asks. I laugh and push a hand through his hair gently before leaning back and pressing my lips to his.

"We're almost there," I reassure him.

"We should have just risked it," he says, and I shake my head.

"I needed this," I confess nervously. "I think I needed this time to myself and to see this plan through."

He sighs, breath moving across my skin before moving up to look at me. "I know." His hand moves through my hair, pushing it back in a way I missed so damned much. "But it sure would have been easier if you just let me take over and destroy him," he grumbles, and I smile wide.

"Stop pouting. You're here now," I say, my hand moving up his chest and around his neck. "Let's take advantage of it while we can."

And we sure do.

*Three Days Until Project Ruin Jeremy Vaughn*

"Look what Leo sent me," Wes says, handing me his phone as he lays in the small bed in the cottage next to me.

He's been sneaking in every night since the other night, and I'm unendingly grateful, not just because I *missed* spending time with my husband but because I desperately needed sleep. It seemed my body had gotten much too used to his warm one beside me.

My brow furrows as I grab the device, a video queued up in his text exchange. I tap the screen and see a familiar restaurant, the one Wes and I went to near Jeremy's work. Except the woman he's kissing at the table is definitely *not* Clarissa.

"Are you fucking kidding me?" a voice shouts, everyone in the restaurant stilling, including Jeremy and the woman. Whoever is recording is close to where they're sitting, and you can see the color drain out of Jeremy's face. When the camera pans to the right, I see why: Clarissa is marching in, face red with anger. "You told me you were in New York today!"

"Clarissa, baby," Jeremy says, standing and leaving the woman at his side looking incredibly confused. She looks kind of familiar, maybe a reality star or a popular influencer.

"Don't you *baby* me! I've *been* her, remember? The other woman? I know how this works, how *you* work!"

I expect that to send a wash of hurt through me, knowing she's implying how her relationship with Jeremy went, but it doesn't.

Not anymore.

"It's not what it looks like—"

Clarissa reaches down, grabbing a glass of red wine and tossing it into Jeremy's face, the deep color staining his shirt instantly. "Explain that to my dad when he *fires* your ass. You thought you could fuck with *me*? You're playing out of your fucking league, Jeremy. You're *done*." And then she turns on her heel and marches out of the restaurant. I have to give it to her: the dramatics are top-tier.

When the video ends, I look up at Wes with a smile before he explains.

"The PI found he had a side piece, and a contact of Leo's spilled the beans to Clarissa. They also let her know where and when to catch him in the act."

My eyes go wide with another reminder of the breadth of Leo's reach. "You're kidding."

Wes smiles and shakes his head. "Nope. Details are being kept under wraps until Saturday to the best of Leo's ability. I thought you'd like that touch. What you have planned will wrap things up for him, but knowing he won't even have her to fall back on is truly poetic."

I stare at him with a smile, grabbing his phone and setting it to the side before climbing into his lap. I put a hand to either side of his face and press my lips to his.

"God, I love you."

"You're the mastermind, Harper. I'm just helping your vision come to life."

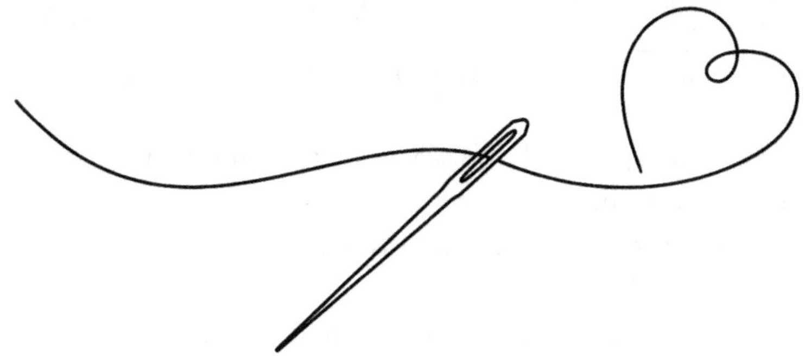

# THIRTY-SIX

## HARPER

*The day of Project Ruin Jeremy Vaughn*

I wake on my own the morning of the big day, the sun just barely creeping up in the sky. My body jolts with realization, turning to look at the body still wrapped around mine in the small bed of the cottage.

"Wes, honey," I say, pushing at his shoulder. "It's morning. You missed your alarm."

His eyes open, squinting at me before he shakes his head, shifting into my neck and pressing his lips there. "No, I didn't."

"*Yes*, you did. It's almost seven."

"Nope," he grumbles, his unshaved jaw scratching at my skin and sending a shiver down my spine. "I didn't set it."

"What do you mean you didn't set it?" I ask, suddenly panicking. He fully opens his eyes now, pulling his head back to see the anxiety written across my face. Then a smile creeps onto his lips. "Wes! Someone is going to see you sneaking out of here and know we aren't broken up!"

"So?" he asks, and I shove at his shoulder, attempting to sit up.

His firm arm on my waist holds me in place, pulling me back down until we're chest to chest.

"*So*, we can't let Jeremy know this is all bullshit yet. If he finds out, he's going to—"

Wes presses his lips to mine, quieting my argument.

"Harper, calm down," he says when he pulls back, and my nostrils flare with irritation. "Sorry, sorry, that's not what I meant. You're right and completely valid in being nervous, but we've got this handled, and we're past the point of it even mattering if we get caught lying. Even if someone got a photo of me leaving here, what would it matter? In a few hours, everything is going to be out in the world. We've got a plan."

"What if he has someone watching us? Watching me?"

Wes's jaw goes tight as it always does when I bring this up. It's not out of the realm of possibility. Especially not with the information the PI Wes hired found. If I were Jeremy, I'd do nearly anything to make sure his secret kickbacks don't reach the light of day.

"For one, we'll just add it to his file," he says, speaking of the file the lawyer Wes has hired to gather the various forms of blackmail and harassment Jeremy has exhibited. I scrunch up my nose because it still doesn't feel like a good idea, and he smiles. "And two, *it doesn't matter anymore.*"

"I just—" I start, and he shakes his head, cupping my jaw in his hands. He looks into my eyes with a soft expression that turns firm.

"Today is your day, Harper. The beginning of something amazing, something you deserve. You've barely slept in the two weeks of setting this up, finishing everything."

"I feel like you also have some responsibility for my lack of sleep, Mr. Holden," I accuse, and he smiles.

"Yeah, maybe. But am I so wrong for wanting to make sure you got the chance to sleep in just a little before your big reveal?"

I glare at him but don't argue, instead changing the topic. "Why didn't you tell me last night?" I ask.

"Because I knew it would stress you out, and I wanted you to get as much sleep as possible." I hate that he's right, that the mere idea of him not leaving in the morning would have worried me and made me unable to fall back asleep. "And I'm not sure how late you're going to come home tonight since Willa will definitely have some kind of press after-party, so I wanted a few extra hours to spend with you."

My brows furrow, not understanding. "What do you mean?"

He gives me a soft smile and then moves, rolling me to my back and hovering over my body. His hand shifts, brushing my hair back before confessing, "I'm not coming tonight."

My face drops. "What? Why not? I need you—"

He shakes his head, smiling at me. "No, you don't, baby. You don't need me there, not tonight."

"Wes—" He silences me with a deep kiss that makes me forget whatever I was about to argue before he pulls back.

"Tonight is about you. Harper Abbott, an unbelievably talented fashion designer, not Harper Holden, wife of Wes Holden. Tonight, I want everyone to ask you about your dress, about your line, about your plans. Not about our honeymoon or our alleged separation or our marriage or whatever the press is going to be dying to know. I don't want to take your shine away by being there."

"You wouldn't," I argue.

He shrugs. "Probably not, because your work is so impressive, it would distract everyone. But I want this night to be about you and only you. If I'm there, people might think that's how you got there, and I don't want that to even be an argument. You earned this all on your own."

"But I want you there," I whisper.

"And next time, I'll be there. But not tonight."

I glare at him and try a different angle. "Does this mean when Atlas Oaks is up for a big award, I have to stay home and watch from the couch?" Even though I know I'm just being a brat and that would never be the case, it stings, even the insinuation of it. I'm still healing from years of distrust and feeling like I always come in last, and sometimes that pokes its ugly head.

He shakes his head vehemently. "Harper, no. *No.* I want you by my side at every moment. Fuck, if I could, I'd have you on stage with me while we played, I want you so close every day. Just this once. Just this one time, your premiere, your first time stepping out as *you,* I want it to be just you. Every other time, I'm velcro to your side." He presses his lips to mine again. "Okay?"

Slowly, I nod, even if I don't like it. And even more, a part of me knows I'll be thankful for this one day, so I'll never be able to second guess if my success is my own or just a benefit of the man I married.

"This is the first day toward the rest of your life, Harper. The first day where you can step out of the shadow that asshole cast on you and be *you.* And the world is going to love what you made, baby."

I smile then, unable to hide my excitement. "It is really good," I whisper, pride in the words.

"It really is. Now come on. You've gotta get to Willa's, and I've got to get home. I have calls to make, and I'm sure Leo is panicking that I'm not home." He smiles and rolls out of bed, putting a hand out to me. "But first, we're showering together." I take his hand, and he tugs me up, out of bed and into his arms.

Right then I know even if this plan of ours doesn't work, even if it fails miserably and takes my career with it, at the very least, I know this entire mess brought me the best thing I could ever ask for.

The dress I'm wearing is inspired by Princess Diana's iconic revenge dress circa 1994, and I've never felt more powerful in my life. Both dresses are inspired by the princess herself, mine and Willa Stone's.

Yes, international pop star Willa Stone is heading into the *National Music Awards* wearing a dress *I* created, helping to announce my very first fashion line before she probably wins a dozen awards and announces her newest upcoming album.

The last two weeks have been an absolute whirlwind of emotions.

Just days after I attempted to break up with Wes, I was in a meeting with Willa and her entire team, telling them about my idea for mid-price pieces inspired by pieces their favorite celebrities have worn. She was all in on the idea and we started fitting her for it almost immediately. I'm also working on a full proposal for outfits for her next tour.

The day after that, Wes and I met with the private investigator he hired as well as two of the band's lawyers. The PI brought all of the information we needed about kickbacks Jeremy was receiving as well as a few instances he found of Astor Fashion designs that had been leaked to other fashion houses.

Turns out, Jeremy was the source of those leaks and was handsomely paid for his work. That information has been shared with Astor, and from what I understand, he's going to be getting some really bad news today, probably around the time I step foot onto the red carpet with Willa.

"Are you ready for this?" Willa asks, her smile wild as she turns to me.

She's stunning, as always, her blonde hair pulled away from her face and tucked behind her ears before tumbling down her back. The couture gown I made for her is glinting in the backstage lights just as I hoped, catching and reflecting every ray. I know when she steps out in front of a dozen cameras, flashes going crazy, it will look absolutely *radiant*.

It's completely bedazzled and glittering, a deep emerald green with a snakeskin pattern across her hips and stomach with a long train blooming out behind her, the tips of it red, the color associated with her most recent album.

It's like a snake shedding its skin, a rebirth, she called it, the end of her previous album's era and stepping into a new one. She always does it effortlessly and beautifully, and each time her fans eat it up.

And at this award show, she's going to do it again, this time wearing my design as a part of that announcement.

My hands shake, my fingers moving to the straps of my own dress, the off-the-shoulders sleeves and sweetheart bustline the same as on hers, but it's more low-key and is missing the train.

I don't know how we pulled it off. There were a *lot* of calls and even more talks with lawyers and professionals to make sure that doing this wouldn't result in a worst-case scenario, but I learned a lot in the past two weeks.

For example, most of the threats Jeremy was holding over me would probably never come to fruition, like his reopening the case and charging Ava and Jules. He was hoping my fear and my previous hesitance to tiptoe into something scary would stop me from acting, from speaking my truth.

But mostly, that I am strong, I am talented, and I have a killer fucking support system.

My fingers move to my neck, making sure the golden W is centered. I smile at the comfort of having a piece of Wes here with me when I need to calm myself just a bit.

I finally turn my attention to Willa and nod. "As ready as I'll ever be," I say before looking across the room to where her publicist stands.

Leo is actually my publicist now, too, since he agreed to take on me and my fashion business when I asked him, telling me it *took me long enough* to finally ask him. He winks at me, or maybe it's at Willa, as he hits post on my phone, my final part in the two-week-long strategy we've been working on since the night I broke up with Wes— or at least, tried to.

Yesterday, Leo helped me take photos of sketches and my process and even a few glimpses at finished designs for the Revenge Line, the first of many Harper Holden clothing drops.

Despite the legal battle we'll be fighting behind closed doors, I decided my plan would be to promote my brand and create a name for myself without ever mentioning Clarissa, Jeremy, or their theft of my previous designs, as per the contract I signed at the police station. But by including the focal piece that Jeremy never got, the piece that so clearly ties together the stolen collection, the piece Willa is wearing right now, I'm quietly reclaiming what is rightfully mine.

Leo hands me back my phone, which is buzzing with messages already, but it's his words that have me smiling.

"Your husband," Leo says.

I expect to see a call when I glance at my screen, but it's simply a message.

Love you. You deserve this moment.

I smile again and move to type, but then my name is called, and I'm being moved along to the spotlight, and once again, my universe tilts.

But this time, I've never felt better about where my life is headed.

# THIRTY-SEVEN

## WES

*A few months ago, my life felt like it had never been worse. I was fresh out of a relationship I thought I'd be in for forever after finding out about his infidelity. I wasn't where I hoped I would be in my career, and I was lonely, watching my best friends grow and live their lives. I was terrified that I was being left behind, that my clock was ticking.*

*I've been scared a lot over the past few years—scared to be myself, scared to open up my heart, scared to fall in love, scared to speak up for myself.*

*Most of those fears, my husband, Wes Holden, has helped me to conquer, something I'll never be able to fully thank him enough for. But I'm vanquishing the last of these demons by stepping out of my comfort zone.*

*My name is Harper Abbott, and today I'm announcing the Revenge Line. The line is meant to emulate strong women fighting back in their own ways, starting with Princess Diana's iconic revenge dress and moving through others, like Tina Turner's leather cut-out dress, to Reese Witherspoon's yellow Nina Ricci. The goal is to give its wearer the confidence she needs to take on the world and everyone who ever wronged her. I even added my own revenge dress in the line, the dress I wore to marry Wes, inspiring a modified version for a fun date night out.*

*I hope you all love it as much as I do and that when it hits stores later this year, you wear it with pride. This is for all the women who want revenge, not for those who have done them wrong, but for themselves. To reclaim what was taken from them in whatever way they feel they need to.*

*And for me, every good revenge plan starts with a killer outfit.*

*Whether you're looking for a killer revenge dress, a hit of confidence, or something to help you with day one of your happily ever after, the Revenge Line is for you.*

*I am so grateful for the life I have made and been blessed with. For a husband who has never faltered in his belief in me and who encourages me to fight for what I deserve. For friends who lift me up when I'm at my lowest. Having people on your side is more valuable than anything.*

*Thank you for coming with me on this journey. I can't wait to see where we go next together.*

I read the caption for Harper's post for the third time, pride flowing through me at the amount of bravery and patience and restraint she showed with it.

It's perfect.

It sets aside any concerns of a divorce—thank God, because she's not spending another night out of our bed—and promotes herself without *once* bringing up her past or breaking the contract she agreed to. After long talks with the lawyers we hired, we decided that it would be best to, at least for the time being, honor the contract Harper signed under duress. We don't want to give Jeremy any kind of upper hand, though I argued he would probably have bigger things to worry about by the end of the day.

I'm glad Harper isn't here to watch me wipe a tear from my eyes as I read her post again, because she would never let me live it down. Especially when that lump in my throat grows as I scroll through the photos she and Leo carefully picked for this post, all evidence of her talent, her new line, and the work she's doing with Willa. It took more effort than anticipated to explain to her that Willa's interest in her work had absolutely nothing to do with my friendship with her.

I wasn't lying.

A talent like Willa Stone can see a kindred soul from a mile away, and she saw Harper and wanted her on her team. They're already sketching and working on pieces for Willa's album cover and future tour looks, though that won't be announced for some time.

But that hesitation is also why I needed to stay behind tonight, even though I would have loved to stand by her side. She needs to know this is all her.

Turning my attention back to the television as the commercial ends, I watch the celebrity news outlet. It's one of the channels I normally skip, but today I'm watching intensely. I'm glad I am, because now a panel of celebrity fashion experts is talking about Harper's designs, critiquing Willa's outfit, the more subdued version Harper is wearing, as well as her latest social media post and announcement. They throw a few screen grabs of the behind-the-scenes photos Harper posted and seem genuinely impressed and excited about her line.

There isn't the slightest *whisper* about the lies Jeremy and

Clarissa tried to spread, just like I knew would happen. Between her post subtly telling the truth—if you read between the lines—and her new designs, no one will *care* what lies Jeremy spread.

As they move on to another celebrity, I sit back, my body able to relax just a bit, though I'm still waiting for part two to drop. Five minutes later, as I scroll the internet, looking for any and all commentary and insight on Harper's designs, I get a text telling me to turn the channel to a popular paparazzi show.

I smile as I tap the numbers, then see a clip of a man leaving a popular New York City restaurant.

"Jeremy! Jeremy!" a reporter yells, one I know to be on Leo's payroll who was assigned this very important job.

Jeremy looks at the camera a bit stunned, considering unless he's with a celebrity or his girlfriend, no one really cares about him as a person, despite his self-inflated ego. His surprise melts quickly before stepping forward to the camera as we hoped he would do. He smiles wide, his veneers too white and his look too self-important. God, I can't wait for this fucker to fall.

"Jeremy, thank you. Do you have a minute to talk?"

"Of course, I'm always happy to speak with a fan. What can I do for you?"

"Your ex, Harper Holden, was just spotted walking the red carpet," the reporter says, and Jeremy's fake smile falters just a tiny bit before bouncing back, going cruel and targeted.

"Yes, she is allegedly married to Wes Holden. She's quite the ladder climber. As you know, she started with me, but I cut her off when I realized she was only with me for my fame."

I laugh out loud and throw a piece of popcorn I popped just for the occasion.

"She's actually not with him, he and Atlas Oaks are not in attendance at the NMAs." His face screws up with confusion, but the reporter continues. "She's with Willa Stone, who she dressed. Willa just helped her announce her first fashion line called the Revenge Line. Many are reading between the lines of her recent social media post and coming to the conclusion that you may have been the inspiration for her creations. A line for women who were wronged and want to get even."

There's an uncomfortable pause as the color leaves his face, before he stutters a few times, then speaks. "I, uh, yes, well, I've spoken out a few times about the designs Harper has claimed were stolen from her. It's all a jealous tantrum my ex is throwing. She—"

The reporter shakes his head to argue, ideally to tell him that there was no mention of stolen designs and it was probably his own damn guilty consciousness speaking, but they're interrupted.

My smile widens as I realize this is actually going to work even better than we could have planned.

"Hey, are you Jeremy Vaughn?" a woman says with a wide smile.

Jeremy's irritation slips off, and a cordial smile comes to his lips as he turns to the beautiful woman. "Yes, yes, I am. And who might you be, gorgeous?"

Jesus, the man has no fucking shame. He was *just* talking about his girlfriend, and now he's flirting with a random woman?

"I'm Cindy," she lies. "Gosh, I'm such a fan. Can you sign this?"

Clearly excited about his alleged fame, he forgets the conversation he was just having and the camera still pointed at him.

"Anything for a fan." He takes the packet from her hands and goes to sign, but then the woman smiles and steps back.

"You've been served," she says and then walks off.

"Served?" he asks, then reads the front of the summons we issued overnight. The timing honestly couldn't be better, and I'm so happy I'm recording it so Harper can watch after her exciting night, though I bet by the end of the day, there are going to be a dozen angles of this on social media. "Hey! You must have the wrong person!"

The woman shakes her head and keeps walking off.

"You have got to be kidding me," Jeremy mumbles.

I know that within an hour, the social media super sleuths will have dug up and dissected the court document, revealing all of Jeremy's crimes. Even if this lawsuit goes nowhere, which I'll fight to make it go all the way if we have to, he's going to lose in the court of public opinion.

Then Jeremy's phone rings, and he looks at it, clear panic on his face when he sees the name before answering.

The hits just keep on fucking coming.

I wish we were this good, that we orchestrated this, but even Leo isn't this good. Karma is just finally getting this asshole.

"Hello? Yes, Mr. Astor, I'd—no, you don't understand, she's crazy, and I—"

"Thank you so much for your time," the reporter says and walks off, leaving Jeremy red-faced, a loud *fuck!* making its way to the camera before it's cut back to an entertainment reporter.

"Wow, so, it seems like Jeremy Vaughn isn't having a great day." The woman looks up, brows furrowing. "In fact, it looks like inside sources are telling us Astor Fashion House just released a statement that due to recent information they've collected on Mr. Vaughn, they've decided to sever ties with the current head of marketing effective immediately. My producer is informing me we'll have a full article on why on the website within an hour as well as details about the lawsuit he was just served, but it seems to be related to theft, harassment, and blackmail."

The woman next to her smiles with wide eyes. "I guess that revenge line is a bit more literal than Harper let on, isn't it?"

They laugh before I change the channel back to the red carpet, though Harper is no longer on the screen, and I sit back, content in the knowledge that he can never hurt my wife again.

# EPILOGUE

## **Wes, Ten Months Later**

"Shhh," I whisper as my wife lets out a moan as my hands drift up her thighs. My hands continue to move despite the noise, helping to hike her dress up to her waist.

She glances over her shoulder as we sit in the back of a limo, double-checking that the divider is still up.

"It's not moan-proof, Harper."

A blush burns over her cheeks, but I can't focus on that when my hand hits a patch of plastic on her thigh. "What the," I say, dipping my head down, although there isn't much room between us and even less light in the limo to see. But I don't have to look that close to see the familiar design, one that's been on my wrist for almost a year. I already know what it is, but I have no idea when it got there.

On the inside of her thigh, just below where her garter belt is, is a tattoo. A simple outline of a heart, with the letter W inside.

"Happy anniversary," she whispers.

We decided we would get married again, this time with more thought and planning, adding in everything we could ever desire, including planning a much, much more *satisfying* honeymoon one year after we got married the first time.

The date our contract expired.

Harper called it *perfectly romantic*, but I just wanted to marry her again once it was all null and void and she wasn't legally tied to me anymore. When it could be *her* choice, no outside forces encouraging her to make the jump.

We even got to have Stella and Riggs's baby boy as our ringbearer and Ava and Jaime's little girl as our flower girl. I made sure we spared no expense so Harper could have everything she ever wanted, elegant and elaborate, filled with all of our friends. Everyone in the wedding party was even dressed to the nines in designs my wife made.

The only thing we argued about was her insisting on sticking by the tradition of not spending the night before together. I thought it was stupid since we'd already been married and we stuck by that *last* time, but she insisted, and now I think I know why. I can't stop staring at it, at my initial inking her skin forever.

"Do you..." She clears her throat, then looks at me nervously, biting her lip. "Do you like it?" I brush a thumb over the wrapped mark reverently. "It's kind of permanent, so I can't really undo it, but if you want, I could cover—"

I shift, my hands shooting up to the sides of her face and pulling her to me in a bruising kiss. She whimpers into it, her hand moving back to the waist of my pants to undo them as she was doing before, but I stop her.

I'm going to fuck my wife on the way to our wedding reception, but I need her to be clear on this, first.

"If you ever talk about covering up that mark again, I'll turn you over my knee and spank you until you fucking apologize," I murmur against her lips. "That is the most beautiful thing I've ever seen."

Her smile goes wide. "You like it?"

My hand moves back under the skirt of her wedding dress, unbearably grateful it's not a giant tulle one like Jules wore when she got married to Nate or the tight one Ava wore. No, my Harper opted for a thin, silky dress, hugging her curves.

"I can't wait for it to be healed so I can kiss it and lick it and suck it." My hands move further up, smiling at the fact she isn't wearing any panties as if she anticipated this, and then I sink two fingers into her without hesitation.

"Ahh!" she moans, hips moving already to ride my fingers.

No foreplay was needed; she was already more than ready for me. Perfect, considering I haven't had my wife in forty-eight hours, and the drive to our reception won't last more than twenty minutes.

"When I eat your pussy, it'll be right next to my face. The mark that you're mine," I groan, already thinking about how fucking hot that will be. I got my tattoo almost a year ago, and another three since. I started a little *Harper Holden* shrine sleeve on my blank arm: the logo for her business and three dates: the day we met, the day I *"proposed"* to her, and the day I married her the first time.

The most important days in my life.

I have a feeling I'll be adding today's date to that stack soon.

"Ride your husband's fingers, little wife," I say, a refrain I've said many times before, but this time feels different because now we're married with nothing holding us back. Simply because we both chose this and neither of us can picture life without the other.

She feels the difference too, knows it to her bones.

Her breath hitches, looking in my eyes. "I love you, Wes," she whispers.

"I love you, Harper," I groan, then her hand moves to the waist of my tux pants, undoing them quickly and working to get my cock out. I don't stop my work on her pussy, her hips bucking and tiny, quiet mewls coming from her lips as I do.

I should probably help her, but I can't seem to make myself do anything but watch Harper and that tiny black heart on her thigh. My gaze shifts from her thigh to her face, and I smile at the look of desperation on her face.

Crooking my fingers, her hips buck when I graze against her G-spot.

"Please," she whispers.

"What do you want?"

"I want you." Her breathy pleas brush along in my ear. "I need to be full of you," she groans, then gets her hand around my cock, pumping it once.

A low moan leaves my lips, and I take my fingers out of her, wrapping my hand around hers on my cock with a weak sigh before lining myself up with her opening. Once it notches, a little mewl falls from her lips.

That's when my little wife decides to turn the table, slowly lifting and falling, fucking just the head of my cock. Our joined hands stop her from going any deeper, though she doesn't seem to be irritated by that. I take my hand away to give her room, but she keeps it up, fucking just the tip with a small teasing smile on her lips.

"If you don't sink down right now, I'm going to make you," I say through gritted teeth, and her eyes sparkle with the threat because my wife *loves* when I follow through with my threats.

Harper licks her full lips, swollen from kisses, and I shake my head as she whispers, "Make me, husband."

I grab her wrist, pinning it behind her, and with one hand on her hip, I slam her down onto me, filling her instantly. She moans loudly, head tipping back and copper hair tumbling as she sinks down to the base, and I have to bite back my response, knowing that, despite the divider, this limo is *far* from soundproof, especially when that sound is my noisy wife enjoying herself.

"Gotta be quiet, baby," I grumble into her neck, hands moving to her hips and holding her to me. Her breath is coming in little pants, and she grinds her clit on me, the walls of her pussy gripping me tight.

"You feel so good inside me," she groans into my ear, nipping my earlobe with her teeth. "So fucking perfect. I'm so full, Wes."

That does it, as it always does. She sits back, hands on my shoulders, the small smile on her lips telling me she knows she won. Both of my hands move to her hips, and I lift her, shifting our position until her thighs are on either side of me. Then I slam her down onto my cock, filling her again.

"Ah!"

"Harper, quiet," I say with a small smile that turns to a grimace as she lifts and falls again. She grinds at the base to get the friction on her clit. The moment is so hot, so filled with passion and need, I'm already getting close to the edge. From the look on her face, so is she.

"I can't," she moans, head falling back, riding my cock on a mission now, hips moving over me and fully forgetting where we are. I put a hand to her back, pulling her close until her face is buried in my neck, and her lips press there.

"Bite me if you need to," I groan, lifting my hips to get inside her deeper. "Stay fucking quiet. I don't need everyone knowing how perfect my wife sounds when she comes." She takes the opportunity I hand her, teeth biting into the side of my neck as she continues to ride me. The pain of it sends me closer to coming, my hands moving under her dress to grip her ass tightly. "Need you to come, baby."

"Mmmm," she moans into my skin, panting.

"Right fucking now," I groan, then slide a hand between us to her clit, pinching it hard. That does it, and her teeth dig into me as she comes and comes while I fill her with my cum. "Fuck, so good. So beautiful. So mine," I grunt as I come, as her body goes lax with pleasure.

We lay there like that as she catches her breath and I come back to Earth.

"So, I take it you like the tattoo?" she asks with a smile when she finally slides off me, handing me a few cocktail napkins so I can carefully clean her up.

I laugh the entire way to our reception.

Even though I tried to fight her on it, Harper had the photographer edit out the photo where she and I walked into the reception, hands held high with a wide smile on our faces. But I slip the original one—the one where you can see the perfect, red circle on my neck from the impression of my wife's teeth—into my wallet, right next to the one from three years ago.

## **Harper, six months later**

"Shhh!" I say, looking over my shoulder with wide eyes. "Did we not learn our lesson the first time?" We're walking down a slightly familiar street in a much too familiar neighborhood, and Ava can't keep her mouth shut, giggling and yapping about revenge plots and girlhood and God knows what else.

"I think this is a bit different, Harper," she says, shifting the duffel bag filled with supplies over her shoulder.

"No, it is not!" I say, shaking my head.

"Oh, it so is," Sophie says, skipping alongside me, not even attempting to quiet herself.

"Soph! This is a stealth operation!" Jules says, and Sophie smiles, tugging the sleeves of her black long-sleeve shirt down over her hands. It's a familiar scene, parking a few blocks away and tiptoeing to a house with a large duffel bag. This time, we've made sure our intel is spot on, and we've narrowed down our revenge.

Oh, and we brought a seven-year-old.

Because you have to teach them young, you know.

"When did you get so boring?" Ava asks.

"Be nice, Ava. Last time we did this, she was blackmailed for months," Jules says.

"Yeah, and she got a hot rock star husband out of it. Life could be worse," Ava counters.

I glare at my best friend, shaking my head in exasperation.

"Do you think I'll have a hot rock star husband?" Sophie asks thoughtfully, and I snort out a laugh.

"Soph, I think you have to graduate elementary school before you can even *begin* saying things like that, or you might give your father a heart attack," Jules says, pulling her adopted daughter into her side.

"I'm just trying to plan ahead. I hope it's super romantic, and we fall in love the *second* he meets me."

"I think she's watching too many of your movies, Jules," I say with a laugh.

"No such thing," she says, pressing her lips to Sophie's hair. "I'm giving her a much-needed education."

Ava opens her mouth to say something, but I shake my head, putting a finger to my lips.

"The house is *right* there." For once, everyone nods, going silent as we approach. "Who has the stuff?" I ask quietly, looking around and counting to make sure we have everyone.

Conveniently, this kid's house is in the same development as Jeremy's, though he doesn't live here anymore. Much too expensive of a neighborhood for a man who has no job and is piling up lawyer fees and lawsuits. Thankfully, the rule of no cameras allowed still stands, so we should be okay.

*Famous last words*, my mind thinks.

"Me!" Ava says, then starts handing out boxes of white plastic forks, one box for each of us. This time, Ava isn't pregnant, her sweet little Marigold home with a blissfully unaware Jaime. *"It's for the best,"* Ava said when we asked if he knew. *"He's getting old, and this kind of excitement can't be good for his heart."*

We decided against glittering the lawn, thinking it would be too obvious it was us. Thankfully, since the Revenge Line went viral after my post, people started to put my story together. In response, forking shitty people's lawns became a bit of a viral trend, so it could be *anyone* doing it.

Jules was incredibly happy about the trend being *forks* instead of glitter, in her mind reaffirming that the forks were a good idea all along.

I assign each of us a quadrant of the yard, and quickly and quietly, all four of us move around, stabbing forks into the yard. The boy who called Sophie ugly and stupid and whose parents defended him are away on vacation at Disney World, something we confirmed via social media instead of just assuming it this time.

His parents tried to give Jules the whole *he just likes her* thing, and when she argued they should have a talk with him about how to treat a woman, they called my best friend stupid and ugly. Because his parents are just as shitty as he is, I don't feel bad that this is what they'll be coming home to.

We're almost done, the entire yard satisfyingly covered in white sticks, when tires crunch behind us.

PTSD-type panic starts to roll through me, and then it happens.

"Are you guys kidding me?" a familiar voice calls, and we all freeze, forks in hand.

Slowly, I look over my shoulder to find my husband with a wide smile, leaning out of the passenger side of a giant boat of an SUV. Jaime is in the front seat, glowering through the open window, and when the rear window rolls down, a smiling but pretending-to-be-disapproving Nate appears.

"Jules, you're pregnant," he says to his wife. She shrugs. "And you're with a seven-year-old."

"So, it's a family affair then. Call it girl bonding."

"Girls' day!" Sophie shouts, then covers her mouth, remembering she isn't supposed to be loud.

"You're trying to make our children criminals?" he asks with a smile, unable to hide his laughter. "And I told you it's going to be a boy."

Jules shakes her head, convinced she's having a girl.

My gaze shifts to my husband as he catches my eye, lifting an eyebrow in question, before he shakes his head.

"This kid is a douche," I say with a shrug.

"Isn't he seven?" Jaime argues.

"And?" Ava asks. "Are you saying seven-year-olds can't be douches? Plus, his parents are just as bad."

Nate closes his eyes and breathes in because I'm sure he's heard this argument plenty of times. Our brush with revenge made Jules bloodthirsty, it seems. She's constantly suggesting crazy shit toward anyone she decides wronged any of us, from journalists who write something unflattering about Atlas Oaks to the checkout lady who looked *a little too long* at her husband.

"He deserves it, Dad," Sophie says with her hands on her hips, just as sassy as her mom and aunts. For a split second, I kind of regret encouraging this because I feel like it's only going to breed a very strong, very specific sense of justice in the girl. Then I shrug because, not my kid, not my problem.

"Get in the car before you're all arrested again," Wes says.

"You should be thankful. The last time we were arrested, you got a wife," Ava says.

"Get in the car, guys," Nate says, losing patience.

"We can't; my car is around the block," Ava says with a shrug.

"Get in the fucking car, Princess," Jaime says.

"Ex*cuse* me?" she says. "You don't—"

Nate opens his door, and when I spot a car seat next to him, I squeal, nearly knocking him aside as he steps out to fold the seat down and let Jules and Sophie climb in the back before he joins them. Begrudgingly, Ava slides in the truck but I'm not paying attention to my best friend, instead, the new best friend she made me.

"How is my girl?!" I say, putting my head into the car seat next to me. A squealing, giggling Marigold greets me, two teeth visible in the overhead light before Ava slams the door shut. My niece has a giant bow on her head I instinctively know Jaime put on her, and she claps her hands, eyes wide.

"HAHA!" Ava's daughter yells.

"Yes! It's your Auntie Harper!"

"Is everyone in?" Jaime grunts.

"Yes, but lose your attitude, you grump," his wife says.

I widen my eyes at Marigold, who giggles more.

"Ava, love of my life, mother of the biggest blessing I've ever known, I think I'm allowed to have an attitude when my wife almost gets arrested."

"I didn't almost get arrested!" she shouts, tossing her hands in the air.

I poke Marigold on her belly. "Oops, they're going at it again!" I say in a silly voice, and she giggles hysterically.

"Because we came and got you," Jaime says, putting the truck into drive and moving down the street.

"I think not," she says, and if she were outside the car, she'd probably stomp her foot.

"Please, like—" Jaime starts, and I look over my shoulder at Jules, who also knows if we don't stop this now, we're all going to have to either listen to Jaime and Ava argue for the rest of the night or have them urgently need to go home because they need to fuck. Arguing is like a weird mating ritual for them.

"I want ice cream," Jules says loudly. "Baby wants ice cream."

"Ice cream!" Sophie yells.

"I don't know if you earned ice cream, Soph," Nate says to his daughter.

"Oooh, I could go for ice cream. Wes, can you bring us to that place with the dairy-free option you know of?" Ava asks, leaning forward.

"Why are you asking Wes when I'm driving?" Jaime asks, his jealousy peaking in.

"It's all good, big guy. Let's just bask in the fact that no one got arrested tonight, yeah?" Wes asks, a hand on his bodyguard's shoulder. And because Wes has a magic touch, Jaime sighs then grumbles, but the arguing stops.

And we all get ice cream.

"How do you feel, knowing you finally got away with it?" Wes asks with a smile as we walk into our home.

I step toward him, putting my arms around the nape of his neck and smile, telling him the whole truth.

"Never been better," I whisper against his lips, and then I kiss my husband, knowing getting this—this man, this love, and a group of friends who make me laugh until I cry—is the best kind of revenge.

# ACKNOWLEDGMENTS

So we're at the acknowledgments once again and I, once again, feel... overwhelmed.

I actually never wrote them for If This Was a Movie, because, if I'm being totally honest, your girl was going through it and I panicked.

But now i feel in a much (much, much, much) better lace to do it all over again so here we go.

First and foremost, forever and always, thank you Alex. Thank you for bringing me lunch upstairs and reminding me to drink water and listening to me when I cry. Thanks for watching the kids when I have to run upstairs and add a chapter or change something and for being my sounding board. Thanks for taking on the heavy lifting of the house and family so I can live in a fictional world and chase my dreams. You are the best thing that's ever been mine, and I am forever grateful that you were at that party 14 years ago. (Oh my god, we're so fucking old.)

Next, thank you to Ryan, Owen, and Ella. You three are the greatest thing I have ever done with my life and I am so so honored to get to be your mom. But please, stop telling people at school what I do for a living because it makes my life awkward, and if you actually read this book, you are *so grounded* it's not even funny.

Thank you a million times over to Regan, who without, this and many other books, would be impossible. Thank you for being my right hand, for handling the day-to-day that I would probably panic ignore, for making sure I reply to emails, and for holding my hand when I need it. Thank you for not judging me when I disappear and for making me laugh so hard I cry multiple times a day. I don't know how I got so lucky to find a friend like you who is also willing to work with me, but I'll cry if you ever leave.

Thank you, Ashleigh, for always making me laugh, for giving me all the tea from your work, and for always being the kindest shoulder to lean on. I'm so grateful that I somehow earned your friendship because it really is a prize. I can't tell you what it means to me that you will always jump in and help out and that you travel all over just to hang out with us. I love you so much, and I can't wait to see you get married!!!!!!!

Thank you to Salma for helping to refine and perfect this beast and for holding my hand and being gentle when I need it. Thank you, Christine for helping to perfect it!

Thank you, Jay, for the gorgeous character art!

Thank you, Taj McCoy for being the best agent a girl could ask for, even if I'm literally such a mess at all times. I'm so excited to watch you flourish in the indie space!

Thank you to Valentine and the entire team at Valentine PR, I'm so grateful for your help!

Thank you to my amazing content and ARC team. Without you all hyping me up at release, this book would probably be nowhere, and I can never thank you enough for your love and support.

Finally, thank you, dear reader, most of all for reading my stories and cheering for these characters alongside me. I would be nowhere without you all and I can't tell you how much it means that you choose to take my book off of your towering TBR and give it a read. I love you so much: you all changed my life.

# ABOUT THE AUTHOR

Morgan is a born and raised Jersey girl, living there with her two sons and daughter, and mechanic husband. She's addicted to iced espresso, barbeque chips, and Starburst jellybeans. She usually has headphones on, listening to some spicy audiobook or Taylor Swift. There is rarely an in between.

Writing has been her calling for as long as she can remember. There's a framed 'page one' of a book she wrote at seven hanging in her childhood home to prove the point. Her entire life she's crafted stories in her mind, begging to be released but it wasn't until recently she finally gave them the reigns.

I'm so grateful you've agreed to take this journey with me.

Stay up to date via TikTok and Instagram

Stay up to date with future stories, get sneak peeks and bonus chapters by joining the Reader Group on Facebook!

# ALSO BY MORGAN ELIZABETH

**The Springbrook Hills Series**

The Distraction

The Protector

The Substitution

The Connection

The Playlist

**Season of Revenge Series:**

Tis the Season for Revenge

Cruel Summer

The Fall of Bradley Reed

Ick Factor

Big Nick Energy

**The Ocean View Series**

The Ex Files

Walking Red Flag

Bittersweet

**The Mastermind Duet**

Ivory Tower

Diamond Fortress

**All My Love**

www.ingramcontent.com/pod-product-compliance
Lightning Source LLC
Chambersburg PA
CBHW071536110726
47908CB00007B/1903